THE
VOYAGE HOME

THE
VOYAGE HOME

Jane Rogers

THE OVERLOOK PRESS
Woodstock & New York

First published in the United States in 2004 by
The Overlook Press, Peter Mayer Publishers, Inc.
Woodstock & New York

WOODSTOCK:
One Overlook Drive
Woodstock, NY 12498
www.overlookpress.com
[for individual orders, bulk and special sales, contact our Woodstock office]

NEW YORK:
141 Wooster Street
New York, NY 10012

∞The paper used in this book meets the requirements for paper
permanence as described in the ANSI Z39.48-1992 standard.

Cataloging-in-Publication Data is available from the Library of Congress

Book design and type formatting by Bernard Schleifer
Manufactured in the United States of America
FIRST EDITION
ISBN 1-58567-509-1
1 3 5 7 9 8 6 4 2

To Mary Black

PART I

STEPPING ONTO THE SHIP, Anne feels a wave of relief. In fact she feels—imagines she feels, because how could it be true on a ship the size of a tower block, tethered in the flat oily filth of the harbour?—imagines she feels the iron deck rise a little, like a tiny indrawn breath, to meet her falling foot. Imagines she feels the movement of the sea, after the stillness of the land. Imagines, as she imagines the sea lifts her, that it will be all right.

Her cabin is above deck, as promised, but inside it's strangely dark—a reddish gloom, light through a closed eyelid. When the steward has put down her cases and unnecessarily pointed out the shower, Anne hands him the folded 1000-naira note she's been clutching in her pocket, and shuts the door after him. Why is the room so dark? The window seems to be blocked by something; she stares out and realises it is the red side of a container, no more than twelve inches from her window. By craning her neck right back she can just glimpse a crack of sky above it. Perhaps they'll move it, maybe it's waiting to be stored below. There's an odd smell, cleaning fluid and disinfectant covering something else—something that sticks unpleasantly at the back of her throat. She runs her fingers around the window frame looking for a way to open it, but there's none.

The cabin has twin beds with matching flowery covers, big ugly round flowers like cartwheels, in turquoise and deeper blue. An anonymous room, with practical grey fleck carpet, and a framed picture of a sailing ship on an implausibly blue sea hanging over the bed she chooses, the one in the corner away from the bathroom.

Anne stows Father's case in the wardrobe, and opens up her own. There are two plastic bags of dirty washing. She felt awkward about letting the houseboy do it, and couldn't do it herself because of the houseboy. But there must be a laundry room on board.

Not yet. She sits on the bed, empty hands on her knees. Her instinct is to go straight out on deck, out of the artificially lit dimness of this cabin—but things are still being loaded, she can hear the shouts of men—the sailors, the dockers. She might be in the way on deck, they might stare at her. Better to wait here until they sail. Anne suddenly visualises the crowded rails of a passenger ship, tiny figures leaning over to shout and wave goodbye, the answering calls and waves from the shore, the blue sea widening between them. There is no one here to wave her off.

She swivels round and swings her legs up onto the bed, leaning back against the wall. The stopping, being at the end of the list of things to do, is bewildering. Since she left home— since the morning of Matthew Afigbo's phone call whenever it was, ten days ago—things that must be done have made stepping stones. She had to fly to Lagos, had to bury Father, had to clear his things; the past three days have been consumed entirely in begging and bribing her way onto this ship. To reach this empty space.

The only time she's cried has been out of sheer weariness and frustration when the big uniformed man told her the body must be sent home for burial, burial of a British tourist in Nigeria not being permitted. But he wasn't a tourist, she argued.

'He came here about a church exchange—and he worked here before, he worked here for ten years—'

The big man shook his head. 'Tourist visa. Your passport?' He stared at her photo then looked at her suspiciously. 'You were born in Nigeria? You live in UK?'

'Yes, that's what I'm saying, my father worked here years ago . . .'

Sweat glistened in the rolls of the official's neck above his khaki collar, and the little fan on his desk made slow eddies in the hot thick air. A part of her brain observed that its whirring motor was generating heat of its own which its spinning blades struggled to dispel; its functions cancelled one another out, leaving only the by-product noise. The fat man shook his head, the interview was over. When she got out of the room, hunching her shoulders and sliding her hands into her pockets, she touched the roll of notes Matthew had made her count out— the bribe she should have offered. And tears rose to her eyes.

Matthew had sorted it out; requesting an interview the following morning, wearing his dog collar and neat black suit, delicately placing the cash on the edge of the big man's desk as they sat down; nodding to Anne to hand over her father's passport, although she knew there could be no official reason on earth why she must surrender Father's passport to this pig.

She can't sit in this strangely smelling darkened room all day. It's hot everywhere—of course—but at least out there there may be a breath of wind, or a hint of coolness off the water. She takes Father's case out of the wardrobe again, and removes the faded blue cloth-bound book on which he has printed NIGE-RIA. She found it on his bedside table, among his sparse belongings in Matthew's guest room. It's old—dating from her parents' arrival in Nigeria, before she was even born. It will tell her, perhaps, what neither of them would ever tell: what happened there to smash the idyll of her early years. His elegant flowing script fills the pages, the same utterly distinctive writing he has been sending her in his fortnightly letters ever since she left home. Writing she still considers grown-up, formed, in contrast to her own rounded primary-teacher script. It is as familiar as his speaking voice. She could no more leave it unread than put the phone down on him.

Taking the old diary and Father's hat she braves the deck,

turning left to head for the rail on the side away from the dock. She threads her way between containers, expecting any moment to be turned back or forbidden, but there's no one here. Between the last container and the rail she finds a space a couple of yards wide, shaded by the container. The rumble of the crane, and dockers' shouts and cries, are all away behind her. She leans on the rail. Every kind of rubbish floats on the oily water; she stands staring down at it blankly, nostrils wrinkling at the smell, both more disgusting and more reassuringly real than that inside the cabin. She is suspended until the ship moves; it is no-time, like waiting in an airport.

Coming here hasn't helped anyone. Matthew could have buried Father more efficiently without her, could have bundled up the books and papers and air-freighted his case back to England. She could have taught the last week of term, and been there for the Christmas play. And she has taken up Matthew's time and worried him with her decision to go home by boat.

'It's a long time at sea, Anne. You'll be lonely. It would be better to get back to your routine.'

She couldn't explain to him that she needs to be lonely, she needs to be outside her routine, she needs to find out what she feels. If Father has really gone (of course he's gone, she tells herself furiously. You think he's going to ring and say it's a mistake?) then what will her life be like?

It is childish and ridiculous, of course she has a life of her own, work, friends, her house; her routine, as Matthew says, to turn to for comfort. But now there must be a space. She recognises the impulse to go by sea as somehow connected to the stubbornness Father has always filled her with. It isn't rational. The rudder is unseen, it steers down below the surface.

And it would have been impossible not to come. A man's child should be at his funeral, she thinks. But he doesn't *know* she was there, it's a fictional transaction; she must derive satisfaction from knowing that if he had been able to know she was there then he would have been pleased. From knowing she has done the right thing although nobody is there to see it. 'God sees.' Oh yeah. She still feels that hot smarting adolescent resentment at what he has instilled in her, the nasty little judging eye. Well, are You satisfied? I came to Lagos and buried him. It has been horrible. I've buried both of them now, OK?

Once the ship begins to move *her* life will begin.

'G'day.' A man has come around the container behind her; middle-aged, tall, a sheaf of papers in his hands—official. He extends a hand. 'Robbie Boyle. First mate.'

She tries to place his accent. South African? 'Hello. Anne Harrington. I'm a passenger.'

'I know.'

Of course. There are only three passengers, the retired couple and her. Every member of the crew will know. Will she be the only not-old woman, and all these men? She can feel heat spreading across her face and neck, suddenly imagines the crew going about their business, glancing up surreptitiously at the passengers coming aboard—then meeting each other's eyes and winking. They might run a sweepstake on how many of them can make it with a likely female, they might joke about her in their quarters at night . . .

Why is she thinking this? She's thirty-seven, for god's sake. The first mate stands before her with a quizzical smile, she can feel him watching her traffic-light face. She turns quickly back to the rail, but he takes a step closer. There's an awful little silence and she can't stop herself glancing round to see what he's doing behind her. Copying onto his papers a number stamped on the container. Why's it taking so long? He is standing slightly too close. This is in her imagination. He speaks as he writes.

'There's more space on the upper deck—sun loungers and stuff up there.'

The questioning inflection gives him away. Australian. 'I'm sorry, shouldn't I be—'

'No, you can stay here, no worries. You've got the run of the ship pretty much—want me to give you a tour sometime?'

'Thank you.'

'OK. When we get under way.' He gives a quick nod, then he goes.

The man was simply being polite. Probably passengers are his responsibility. He'll think she is ridiculous. Why did she have to blush?

In the evening there's a meal where the captain welcomes them. They're still in dock—waiting, he says, for a tug to take them out. He's a small squat toad-shaped German with very precise English; he introduces four other officers, including the first mate she has met, and Mr and Mrs Malone, the other passengers.

Mrs Malone is tiny, with a fluffed-up halo of thinning pinky-red hair and circles of rouge on her soft wrinkled cheeks. She darts across to sit by Anne.

'We girls had better stick together here!' and Anne is assailed by the choking fumes of her hairspray, and then more gently enveloped by her flowery sweet scent. Mr Malone, tall and hunched, sits opposite. He has a gaunt, striking face with a long purple birthmark covering half his nose and his left cheek.

Mrs Malone talks. Words bubble from her lips as Anne eats; occasionally Anne turns her head to glance at her, at her animated little monkey-face with its strange crimson lips whose colouring has run along the little lines and wrinkles that radiated out from her mouth. Mrs. Malone talks for the table as the captain stiffly nods, and her husband glares at Anne, and two of the officers conduct a subdued argument in German. First mate Robbie seems to raise his eyebrows and half smile at Anne, but she quickly looks away. Mrs Malone is talking about ships. Her husband adores ships. Cargo ships, of course, working ships, not those nasty great floating nightclubs for tourists with too much money. 'Six restaurants, gym and sauna, cinemas, why d'they go to sea at all?'

Anne nods distractedly, suddenly finding her chicken in lemon sauce inedible. They go on those big ships for anonymity, of course. How will she be able to avoid Ellie Malone? But Ellie is already turning her twinkling face to the captain.

'On a working ship they know how to look after their passengers, don't you, captain?'

He grimaces gallantly, and makes his escape when a vacant-looking youth in white begins to remove their dinner plates. Anne clutches her half-full plate for a moment then forces herself to let it go. You don't have to eat everything. You don't have to. But it is a bad omen.

'Always a treat getting to know real sailors,' Ellie confides to Anne. 'What they've not seen wouldn't fill the back of a postage stamp.'

Her cutlery gone, Anne has nothing to fiddle with, and struggles and fails to make sense of this remark or find any response at all to it. She gives Ellie a foolish smile.

'And Christmas—you'll have the best Christmas of your life on board, Anne, trust me. No cooking, no clearing up, no awkward relatives—and naval men, well, they do know how to celebrate, don't they Philip?'

Anne stares at Mr Malone who nods briefly and continues to pare slivers of cheese from the array on the board between them. These are not naval men, it's a commercial shipping line—but it doesn't matter. Christmas.

The word has conjured an image of Father in his freshly laundered surplice, standing in the pulpit at St Luke's. The vases either side of the altar are full of scarlet-berried holly and fat white chrysanthemums; all around the church the candles flicker and glow in the silence. It is the one service of his that she attends in the year. She watches the smile grow on his face as he stares at his congregation, watches his arms rise like angel's wings as if he would embrace the whole church, the whole world. 'Unto us a child is born. Let us give thanks.'

Her eyes suddenly sting and fill, but she can blink it back. A child is born. What did she think? That she would have a child before he died? Nonsense. Nonsense. It makes her furious. He was giving thanks for Baby Jesus, Anne. In his pretty little away-in-a-manger, while kindly shepherds washed their socks in the O little town of Bethlehem. There's only her now. No Father, no mother, no brother no sister. There's only her at the end of the line failing to extend it into the future.

He would have liked a grandchild, he would have baptised it and given thanks.

What sentimental tosh. He couldn't even be bothered with his *own* child at Christmas when she was little. She searches her childhood memory: there's one, can it have been their last Nigerian Christmas? Wasn't she too young then to remember? She can feel it, though, reaching out to the top of the prickly tree from the height of Father's shoulders, to balance a tiny doll up there, a doll whose frock matched hers—a doll Amoge made. After he and Mum split up she never even saw him at Christmas, not for years, and later it was only the ritual Boxing Day visit to her grandparents. Why imagine what he would have liked when it's you that wants, Anne, it's your eyes that fill up at 'unto us a child is born'. It's nothing to do with Father.

Christmas, its awful cloying power: church, Baby, family, her anger at her own inability always to reject the fraud of it and simply tell him she'd prefer to spend the week on her own. No, she would always be sucked into it, handing round mince pies to the choir, tearful in the church, smiling and raging at the false celebration and at her own lack of any other; able even less to escape once he retired, dragged back with him into the kindly cosy world of St Luke's and its bittersweet Christmas rituals.

No need now. No need now. She is on this ship to sail through Christmas like a circus dog through a paper hoop. There will be no Christmas, let Ellie twitter as much as she likes. Anne will spend Christmas staring at the sea.

There is nothing on the table she wants to eat or drink, already she knows she's a little giddy from the wine; she can haul herself to her feet, nod at Ellie Malone's smiley painted face and half raise her hand in farewell whilst turning, not looking to see if any of the officers are watching, to get herself out of the dining room. She's exhausted but it's all right; there's nothing to do, she's not accountable to anyone here. She is setting sail on her own. And there's an undertow, on which she's riding now, which is making her limbs weak and her eyes blurry, which is bearing her into oblivious sleep.

Anne wakes suddenly, to pitch darkness, head full of grinding noise. She thinks the cicadas have gone mad—turns to look through the window above Father's bed, where for the past nine nights she has lain watching the moving lights of planes coming into Lagos out of the thick dark sky—then realises she is on the ship.

The noise must be engines. She feels for the lamp switch and the room leaps into place. 01.58, says her clock. She pulls on clothes and sandals and quietly lets herself out of the cabin, making her way between the dark hulks of the containers towards the ship's rail. She can feel the vibration of the engines through her feet and has a flash again of that sudden excitement of stepping aboard. The ship is moving. And coming to the rail, suddenly the sea is open and silvered before her, covered in moonlight, with a cluster of yellow harbour lights on black falling away to the left. As her eyes adjust the misty moonlight seems brighter and brighter, shining over a sea of mercury, flooding the opaque sky with pale light. The boat seems to move very fast, charging through the water, the shore lights dropping away even as she watches. Ahead is nothing but emptiness, a flat silvery plain.

The surface of the sea is metal, a fine foil; it undulates gently but never breaks, a lid hiding whatever is beneath. She imagines the things beneath, living things that eat each other, the seabed littered with bones of fish and empty shells and pearls; old oil cans and the glint of treasure and rusting metal of wrecks. A mirror image of the world above, she thinks, full of pursuit and capture, sex and death. They have put Father's coffin in a hole in the ground. Because they arrived two hours late at the grave-yard, thanks to the road block and traffic jams, the gravedigger had gone, leaving a spade standing in the heap of earth to one side of the hole. And she and Matthew took turns to shovel earth over the coffin. It was a relief to have a good reason for sweating.

She should have brought Father on the ship, to be buried at sea. Imagine sliding him from the deck, to crash through that molten surface and disappear into another element. Instead of mundanely putting him in a hole and scraping earth on top— imagine slipping him into a world as wide and deep as the one he's lived in, imagine him floating and twirling down towards the depths, coming to rest at last amongst rocks and weeds and lurking sightless fish; imagine him rocking slightly, just a touch, with the deep swell of the sea. Instead of lying inert and weighted down by earth, to be baked by tomorrow's sun.

He's gone to his heaven, she reminds herself. It had better be true. Not in the earth, not in the sea, but in some mysterious golden space, some place of light and splendour. Irritation rises in Anne's throat. He's under that inadequate scraping of earth, why does he have to pretend otherwise? He is there like a pet hamster buried in the garden.

She takes a deep breath of the clean dark air. He's that small. As she stares at the expanse of the sea, her life shrinks to proper proportions, as the harbour lights have shrunk and dwindled to nothing behind her. Above the silver featureless horizon is the great pale reach of the moonlit sky. For a moment she can see Goya's mezzotint Colossus filling it, sitting hunched on the edge of the world, his broad back silvered by moonlight, his sad puzzled outcast face peering back and up over his gigantic shoulder, up into the heavens. The human ant dwellings that lie scattered across the black earth behind him are neither bad nor good, neither protected nor in danger; they are simply insignif-icant.

And now it is surprisingly cool; the first time in ten days she's felt cool. She turns and heads for the lit doorway leading to the little passenger lounge and stairs down (*companionways*? Why? Do you go down them in search of companions?) She is wide awake now, and reluctant to return to the confinement of her cabin; it is pitch-black at night because of the container blocking her window. It defeats the point of the cabin being on deck. In the morning she should ask them to move it. Even a few inches would be better.

She heads down the narrow metal stairs, six steps and a turn, six more to the deck below, relishing the emptiness of the ship. There are little signs in the stairwells—*Dining Room* and *Library*, B deck; *Purser's Office*, C deck. *Laundry* is on D deck. At the bottom of the last flight of stairs she pushes through the heavy door onto the corridor. It's painted grey, the bare metal floor rings under her feet. It feels as if she has strayed into a working area where passengers are not allowed. The doors on either side of the corridor are blank, not named or numbered, all painted the same dark green. It makes her think of a submarine, of hunched men in uniforms sitting watching each other, ears strained for the slightest sound . . . waiting. What is behind all these doors? Suddenly on her left, *Laundry*. She pushes the door and is immediately in the warm familiar smell of soap powder and dryers. One dryer is on, the clothes inside flying round lethargically, flopping against the glass. Three old-fashioned toploading washing machines stand with their lids up. They look like Mum's washing machine, that tall heavy slab of a thing that used to make the whole kitchen vibrate when it was spinning. She can see Mum's face, screwed up in a half-laughing grimace, trying to make herself heard over the deafening spin cycle.

The washer has gone; the kitchen has gone; Mum has gone. Anne looks at the churning dryer and realises that someone will probably return to fetch their clothes quite soon. Of course, sailors work all night, they work shifts—watches. The sense of men crawling from their bunks and dressing and hurrying to the engine room or bridge, peering into the darkness and cradling a mug of tea between their hands, glancing across lit panels of instruments and gauges, gives Anne a sudden warm feeling. They keep the ship humming on its way through the night. They make the night safe. Like parents used to.

She doesn't want to meet the man whose clothes are drying. She leaves the laundry and is puzzled for a moment over which way to turn. Left? Right? The corridor stretches away, exactly identical to either side. As she hesitates, there's a movement at the end of the corridor to her left. She doesn't want to meet anyone now. They would think it strange, her wandering the ship in the middle of the night. She turns right and hurries along the corridor, looking for the heavy swing door. The person behind her is running. She can hear his bare feet slapping against the iron floor. He's running after her. She freezes, and glances back. The man immediately slows to a walk; his right hand is half raised as if to wave to her, or beckon. As he gets closer his walk becomes more and more hesitant. She makes herself turn fully to face him, waiting.

'Please . . .' The man stops. He gestures back in the direction he has come from. 'Please?' He is the first black crew member she has seen. He's panting and sweating from his run. 'Can you help?'

'I'm a passenger,' Anne says stupidly. She can't help, whatever it is, he should find another sailor. He's standing there staring and pointing, his breath coming harshly in the stillness of the corridor—the empty silence stretches away to either side of them. Through the corner of her eye Anne realises the door to the stairs is just behind her. 'I'm sorry—I shouldn't be here, I'm just a passenger.' As she speaks she's turning, bolting, shoving her way through the door. She's running up the stairs as if he might chase after her. When she reaches the upper deck she stands still and listens, holding her breath. Nothing. He hasn't come onto the stairs.

She pushes out onto the cool of the deck. He should look

for someone else who knows about whatever it is. She wouldn't have been any use anyway. She unlocks the door of her cabin. With the lamp glowing and her books on the bedside table it looks like a haven. She quickly locks herself in and gets back into bed. It's a while before she can stop shivering.

When her hands are steadier she reaches out and picks up Father's diary. In the small sweet circle of lamplight, she folds it back at the first page.

January 20, 1962
Oji Bend, Eastern Region, Nigeria

It was dark when we arrived and since we were already late, we were taken immediately to meet Karl at his bungalow. Sad to say my anxieties about him were justified almost immediately; both Miriam and I were embarrassed by the insensitive way he speaks about the Africans. I can't imagine it will be possible to work here without challenging the more rigid of his assumptions and trying to bring a much-needed breath of fresh air to the mission. He's even older than I imagined, and rather restrained, both in speech and movement, as if he has to conserve his energy. A mass of white hair and an incredibly weather-beaten face, like a wild old sailor. His bungalow is spartan, bare breeze block with piles of books and papers but very little in the way of furniture. We spent the evening on hard chairs at his dining table, after the most bone-shaking drive I ever hope to endure.

From the beginning: we docked at Port Harcourt Tuesday evening; stayed on board for the night and caught the train early morning. Mangrove swamps at Port Harcourt, then flat rather desolate-looking cleared and semi-cleared areas, with makeshift dwellings of packing cases and corrugated tin, giving way to bush, the river Imo, views of rutted paths and tracks through the undergrowth, occasional clusters of naked children waving solemnly at the train.

On the train the humid heat was intolerable, and the stiff nap of the upholstery horribly prickly and irritating, even through a cotton shirt. We were both drenched in sweat for the entire journey (which took longer than I had calculated; it is only 140 miles to Enugu, but there was an inexplicably lengthy unscheduled halt in dense bush some miles outside Aba).

Our discomfort was increased by the fact that our water bottles, which had been filled for us on the boat, were nowhere to be found in our hand luggage. I told Miriam there was bound to be someone selling drinks on a station platform soon enough, but she raised the spectre of typhoid, and insisted we drag out the two big trunks from the luggage compartment and block the corridor with them while we looked for the wretched bottles. Eventually she found them in the grey trunk which she claims I had open last night to look for the binoculars. I didn't say anything, but in point of fact, she is just as likely as I to have slipped them into the trunk, in the last-minute tidying of our cabin. Anyway, I wasn't about to have our journey spoiled by such pettiness, so I gave her a kiss and we made up.

Enugu is a beautiful town, positioned between green rolling hills, with waving palm trees and a wide sandy river at its centre. But it was when we drew out of the town I think that the thrill of where we are really hit us both. After some distance on a surfaced road (the delightfully named Abakaliki road) we turned off onto a track. And there's nothing—just bush with clusters of palm trees, or grassy open scrubland with the odd cultivated patch of maize; women walking along the dirt road with huge piles of goods balanced on their heads, or sitting at the roadside with a few bunches of bananas or yams to sell. Bicycles wobbling off along side paths to hidden villages; other cars a rarity. We stopped to clear spatterings of squashed insects from the wind-screen, and bought orange juice from a sweet-faced girl who squeezed the oranges for us into rather grubby plastic beakers. The end-of-the-day heat lay thickly over the land, I could see the perspiration trickling down between her beautifully pointed breasts. Poor Miriam's face was a blotchy beetroot-red. She seemed perfectly happy to drink from the beaker, I noticed, despite her earlier anxieties about typhoid.

By the last stage of the journey we were exhausted; keeping the windows up against the dust and baking in our own heat. If the mission car ever had springs they were destroyed years ago—the ruts jarred through every bone in our bodies.

Karl poured us drinks then left us to deal with someone who had come to the kitchen door. We sipped, and smiled at each other, and I felt an incredible relief that we are, finally, here, after all these weeks of preparations. In the quiet we could hear strange night-time sounds from outdoors, squawks of birds and, perhaps, monkeys; the continuous whirring of cicadas. For the first time I noticed the thick moist earthy scent of the air.

During our meal, while a silent and rather frightened-looking houseboy came and went with food, I extracted something of the story of the mission from Karl. He's been in Nigeria since 1928, came over by boat from Liverpool and worked at a station on the Cross River for a while before moving up country to Umuahia and then out here—where there was nothing. Their first church was a mud hut with a palm mat roof that blew off in every storm. Miriam was curious to know how he'd got his original foothold in the villages.

'Education,' he said. 'They all want education.'

I knew she was hoping for more detail but she wouldn't press him, so I asked whether he had come here on his own.

'No, no, I brought two catechists with me from Umuahia. Jacob's still with us, you'll meet him in the morning. Mission boys, twins—you know what they used to do with twins?'

I had read this somewhere, but Miriam shook her head.

'They're supposed to be unlucky. They dump them in the bush to die. Jacob and Esau were taken in at three days old.'

I glanced up at the houseboy, embarrassed for him, but he appeared to be more concerned with dismembering the chicken than with tales of the iniquities of his people. Karl and his twins convinced two villages of the need for a school; once the boys started asking to be baptised, parental converts followed, and they built the church on the current site between the villages in 1949. The CMS wanted Karl to move on, apparently, and leave Jacob and Esau in charge. 'The numbers game,' he said. 'They wanted me to start another bush school further out, before the Catholics got there. Too many Catholics in Eastern Region. D'you know a lot of the Ibos think the Virgin Mary is a fertility goddess?'

'But wouldn't that have been good for Jacob and Esau? To be left in charge of the schools and the church?'

I hadn't meant to raise it so early, but it was the thing that had disturbed me most about Karl when we were told about our posting. He's been here at Oji Bend for twenty years (give or take a few years during the war). The only thing that makes sense in Africa today is for us to pass on skills and move out, especially since Independence. To hand responsibility back to the people. Why has he clung to it?

I don't think he sensed the criticism, because he replied easily enough that he'd wanted to get Standard 5 and 6 classes going so children could finish their primary education locally, and that the volume of medical problems he'd encountered made it imperative to establish a clinic on the station.

Miriam asked if he had medical training and he laughed grimly and said no but he'd been brought up on a farm.

'The sort of medicine I've practised has been rudimentary, Mrs Harrington, it's mainly consisted of not actively harming the patient, which is what the local custom frequently seems to demand.' He went on to describe a woman with a breech birth whom he insisted on helping after the village had left her for dead. Difficulty in labour, he told us, was regarded as punishment for sexual transgression (this is one I've not heard before). He claimed the woman's relatives were slapping her face and spitting on her, while she thrashed about screaming with the pain of her contractions.

Miriam glanced at me and raised her eyebrows. His assumptions about the barbarity of indigenous customs date him more strikingly than anything else. One of the little projects Miriam and I have in mind is collection and identification of whatever plants and herbs the Ibos use for medicinal purposes, with reports on their efficacy. Many, I'm sure, are at least as effective as western medicine, although a man of Karl's generation would probably find that hard to imagine. Miriam kindly asked him if he thought the success of the clinic had helped to create new converts.

'Obviously. It's an easy trick—cure a man's child, he'll give you his soul—even Christ stooped to miracles.'

I found his cynicism rather distasteful. He looked at me then carried on.

'Of course they convert. They want white man's power, white man's juju.'

I said jokingly that that sounded quite Victorian, but he was not in the least abashed.

'They see our wealth, medicine, weapons, power—how can they get some of what we've got? Must be the white man's god.'

Miriam cut in. 'You really think people convert to Christianity out of greed for material things?'

'That's not what I said. It's like plants growing to face the sun. They're looking where the power is. Not just material—political, cultural, spiritual. They want the god for powerful people.'

'You must find that very depressing.'

I thought she sounded rather sharp, so I laughed again and reminded him that we were both tired from our journey.

'Yes,' he said to Miriam, as if I hadn't spoken. 'Sometimes I do. And then something reminds me that He works in mysterious ways. Perhaps people always convert for the wrong reasons; but once they're in the church, fortunately some of them do seem to find the right ones.'

She put down her knife and fork. 'What would you say those are?'

'Compassion. Tolerance. The love that passeth all understanding.'

I thought then that he's a rather manipulative man; a thought which has been reinforced by subsequent dealings with him. He himself speaks Ibo fluently but when I asked him about finding a teacher for Miriam and myself he claimed there was absolutely no need.

'Fifteen years ago, yes—or even five—but everyone speaks English now. And if they don't, they need to learn.'

'But I would like to speak Ibo.'

'There are better uses for your time.'

As I said to Miriam afterwards, that is about control. If he can understand the villagers and we can't, he will remain in a stronger position. He seems to forget he's about to retire and that it's our job to actually pass Oji Bend back to the locals. When I raised the subject of the school he said we would talk about it in the morning.

'And the doctor?' I knew Miriam was disappointed not to have met him.

'Paul will be in his clinic at seven.' Karl stood up, and the servant began to clear the table. 'Don't let yourself be disturbed by his manner.'

'His manner?'

I touched Miriam's elbow to indicate to her that we should go, but she remained seated, staring at the old missionary.

'He prefers his own company. But a good doctor.'

He shook hands with us at the door but turned away and closed it before we had even gone down the steps—leaving us in such thick darkness that I couldn't see my hand in front of my face. We stood for a moment waiting for our eyes to adjust; despite the heat, there seemed to be thick cloud obscuring all the stars.

'Old pig,' whispered Miriam. I put my hand over her mouth, and we both had a fit of the giggles.

'This way, Mister David, sir.' The anxious houseboy, visible as a darker shadow behind a wavering torch, materialised to lead us through the cloying darkness to our bungalow, where a lamp glowed softly from one window.

'Luke been wait you on veranda, sir.' He melted away before I could even thank him, and as we made our way up the dim steps a figure on the veranda rose to meet us.

'Luke Okeke, sir, missus, houseboy very please meet you.'

There was nothing to do but allow him to show us into the bungalow, where our cases stood neatly in the hall; round the kitchen, dining room, bedroom, bathroom and tiny study, like the set of an old film, in the trembling glow of the tilley lamp he carried. He walked barefoot, quite silently, a tall thin young man with a huge grin on his face—he seemed personally delighted to see us. 'I bring you breakfast six o'clock, sir?'

'Yes, thank you very much, Luke. Goodnight.' I wasn't sure where he would be sleeping but he let himself out and disappeared silently down the veranda steps. We stood there with our arms around each other, feeling the soft silence of the house settling, grateful to be alone.

'You'll tell Karl when you speak to him in the morning?'

'Of course.' We'd discussed the whole issue of servants before we left England; neither of us can stand the idea.

'This is a lot nicer than Karl's house.' It is true; the walls are plastered and the whole place is newer and fresher. I wonder if it has been done because they know we are recently married. In the bedroom we knelt and prayed for His blessing on our work here, before crawling under the white swathes of mosquito netting, and cuddling together in the strange bed.

I raised the servant question with Karl first thing next day, and he looked at me rather contemptuously, I thought. 'Is Luke unsatisfactory?'

'Of course not. But we're quite capable of looking after ourselves. It seems to me to be demeaning for a black man to—'

'If Luke isn't employed by you then he must leave the mission compound.'

I didn't understand the significance of this, nor indeed see why it should be laid at my door.

'His parents are dead. He came to the mission school with his cousins but when he chose to be baptised his uncle told him he'd better stay with us. He's trying to save money to go to secondary school.'

'Surely he could find something better paid than houseboy.'

'Such as?'

How could I know, I'd been in the place less than twenty-four hours.

'We employ servants here for a number of different reasons. Firstly, most of them are very much in need of the work and accommodation; secondly, neither Paul nor I have a wife.'

'Miriam's work is not to wait on me.'

'I'm sure it's not. But I wonder if you can appreciate the quantity of domestic work there is to do in a house with no electricity—no washing machine, vacuum cleaner, electric iron, cooker . . .'

'If the Nigerians can manage I'm sure we can.'

'You know Luke has to boil and filter all your water, do you? And do your shopping, of course. We have dried and tinned goods by six-weekly order from Umuahia. The rest has to be bought at the Monday or Wednesday morning markets, both held during your and Miriam's working hours.'

'What is he paid?'

'Twelve shillings a week. And his board and lodging, the hut he shares with my boy Saul. I think you'll find it's a perfectly good arrangement.'

Miriam and I have gone over it every which way. Neither of us wants to exploit him. The wages are laughable, for full-time work. But low as they are, we can ill afford them; we've budgeted the use of our joint income down to the last penny, including savings for travel and for when we go home. On the other hand, he *does seem genuinely enthusiastic, and obviously takes a pride in what he does—he presented me with my breakfast today with a real flourish.*

'Imagine him doing the washing by hand,' Miriam whispered. 'Has he got to wash our underwear? It's disgusting.'

I can't see any way out of it. Especially not if it would cause him to lose his home in the compound. Miriam is not at all happy.

JANUARY 29, 1962

Lists of things to do; there is so much to do it comes crowding in at me like the landscape through a speeding car's windscreen, rushes at me, flies past, and I'm forgetting it already because of the new things that are here to do.

Early morning's the best time; sunrise is at six and then the light is golden and the air cool and refreshing, full of promise.

Miriam can't sleep under that mosquito net, she says she can't breathe. I'm going to rig up screens across the window and fireplace (needs doing anyway, a thousand flying ants came down the chimney last night to plaster themselves to the lamps), tell Luke to keep the bedroom door shut, and come in here before bedtime to swat any that have managed to get in. She's been crawling out from under the net at night and her wrists and ankles are a mass of bites. Sometimes she really is her own worst enemy. It is close at night but I can't say it affects my sleep, I've been up before six the past couple of days. Breakfast of bananas and pineapple, then I set off on my bicycle to explore. In the morning the dirt roads are alive with women walking to market with their produce on their heads, children setting off to school, the occasional spluttering vehicle travelling in its own cloud of dust. I've seen parrots, vultures, and yesterday morning, writhing quickly across the path, a thick brown snake.

The nearest village is less than a mile away. Karl promised to

introduce me to people but he's been unwell, so I took myself off
there on Saturday, met the Headman (excellent English) and
asked him if he could recommend one of his people to teach me
Ibo. I asked him the meaning of this word 'chi' that we hear all
the time—it is a kind of personal guardian angel, associated with
light. So the greeting we hear each day, 'I bola chi?', which Karl
brusquely explained as 'good morning', in fact means 'Have you
managed to break through darkness into light?' What a wonder-
ful Christian greeting!

The village children came flocking round; the little ones are
taught there by Jacob, one of Karl's original twin catechists. He
showed me his schoolroom and a tattered selection of ancient
reading books. I promised him I'd look into getting him some
newer ones. I asked the Headman about farming and he
launched into a diatribe about the Dutch missionaries who
apparently have various kinds of seeds to give away. He and the
elders have rejected their offers because the most important crop
is yams and the women can't see the point of 'these small trees'.
I can't make out from his description what the trees are (little
round fruits with a hard seed you can't eat?); need to arrange a
meeting with the Dutch soon. The stands of palms which soar
above other vegetation here are the vital trees, providing both oil
and wine; oil is their most precious commodity. (Note: palm oil
nuts are surprisingly small and a beautiful dark glossy red, like
big old-fashioned rose hips.)

The village itself is made up of walled compounds. Inside
each compound is a cluster of wattle and mud buildings: the
man's sleeping hut, the obi where they receive visitors, and the
rooms for wife (or wives, more than one is still not uncommon)
and children. The huts have oblong window-holes and steeply
pitched palm-thatched roofs. Many are in a seriously dilapidated
condition.

The village to the north is smaller and less prosperous. They
have no school at all, although some of their older boys do attend
the mission school. Again the Dutch, working with the

Presbyterians, were mentioned; they have visited the village to offer people lifts to a new mother and baby clinic, but it's miles away. Miriam's role really will be vital here.

The Standard 6 class is small, twenty-one of them ranging in age from twelve to twenty; at each standard more and more drop out. Which is not surprising in view of the charges to parents—£5 per pupil for Standard 6, and that's in addition to the education fund to which everyone in the villages is expected to contribute. I feel sure we could get more from the government and take less from the villagers, but I'll pursue that with Karl when I've done a bit of research.

Mark Udom, the other teacher, is a smiling round-faced chap in his late twenties. Not local, I think; his skin is even blacker than the villagers' and he has the air of an outsider. He wears a brilliantly white shirt and red silk tie to teach in, even on the hottest days. I found him reluctant to talk, which I put down to shyness until Karl told me that Mark was disappointed not to be made senior teacher himself. Personally I can't see why he wasn't. He trained at Hope Waddell in Calabar, he has two years' teaching experience—why should a white boy be brought in over him? Karl says because I have a degree—hardly relevant to primary pupils. There's the training element of course, I'll be in charge of the trainee teachers from Umuahia, I'll oversee their placements here and in the villages. But again there's no real reason why he couldn't have done that; indeed, I shall make it my business to see he shares that role and is confident about taking over as head of the school when I move on.

The food we've had so far is terrible, mostly tinned (corned beef, spam, peas, tinned tomatoes). There's no reason on earth why more fresh stuff can't be bought from the local markets, except for a lingering idea that westerners prefer their own food. I asked Miriam to explain to Luke that we're happy to try local food, but apparently he's bewildered by this and will only cook what

Miriam specifically tells him to cook—a neat little vicious circle.

There's a sad-looking vegetable plot at the back of the school. Luke tells me it's for the mission employees so I asked Karl if I could dig another plot for school students who're interested in learning about different crops. Besides the seeds I brought from England, I'm ordering a range of seeds from the Umuahia stores: maize, spinach, fluted pumpkin, okra, cassava and melon. Twelve boys from Standard 6 stayed behind this afternoon for the first gardening class. We marked out the plot and two of them scythed it while the others had a lesson on the names and uses of all the implements in the gardening shed. Their enthusiasm is delightful—the four big forks were all quickly seized by boys who wanted to have first go at digging. I offered trowels to Obi and Enuha, but they seemed less keen, although Obi did say that his sister would like to use the trowel.

'Your sister? Would she like to come to school?' I've been worrying at this problem, the disproportion of girls to boys in school. The Headman agrees that girls need schooling, and claims that most of his villagers think the same, since educated girls fetch higher bride prices. But even in the lower classes the boys outnumber the girls by two to one. When I try to speak to Karl about it he brushes the topic aside, saying that girls are more useful at home than boys, for baby minding, water carrying and firewood gathering. Clearly we will have to find ways of persuading them; so if Obi makes a start with his sister, I shall be very pleased.

FEBRUARY 2, 1962

When Miriam told me she thought she might be pregnant, my first reaction was panic—it's too soon, we're not even settled in, how will we be able to manage? But something in me has taken the news and feasted joyfully upon it, so that when she came in from the clinic last night with the result of her test I felt ready to burst with happiness. Her period was already late when we arrived here, but she put that down to the excitement and distur- bance of the move, and it was only a few days ago that she even thought of pregnancy.

It's right; it's the right time, it's the right thing to happen. We were up talking about it half the night. Everything is new now, everything is growing and changing: our lives, our work, the things we can achieve for God through our individual contributions at the school and clinic, and our joint contribution to the work of the mission—it is entirely appropriate that there should be a new baby as well. And isn't the healthy presence of her own child likely to do more to win the confidence of young mothers than months of earnest explanations about preventative medicine?

Miriam's own reaction was like mine—shock to begin with, turning swiftly to gratefulness and delight. It is as if the child is somehow His seal of approval. We knelt together this morning and thanked Him from our hearts.

Warmth and joy from everyone in the compound except Karl. Who at least had the decency to wait till he saw me on my own before mentioning tropical diseases, infant mortality, etc, and suggesting I should send her home to have it. I pointed out that African women don't have the option of whipping off to high-tech western hospitals to have their babies. To which he replied,

'Your principles may be egalitarian, but you insult both Miriam and the local women by imagining them to be the same.'

I held my tongue, but it saddens me that he feels the need to patronise me in this way.

ANNE WAKES AGAIN at the same time the following night. Two a.m. after two and a half hours' sleep. Why? She lies in the insistent blackness of her cabin, willing the outline of her window to appear; it must be a shade or two lighter than the walls, surely, even though the container is there? But when she turns on the lamp she realises the window is further along the wall than she remembered, she doesn't even have the shape of the room properly in her head.

The image of the black man is haunting her. Surely it was a dream? He stands, hand half raised to catch her attention, to gesture backwards to whatever trouble it is he needs her help for. He needs her for something serious. How could she have run away like that? How come she hasn't thought of him all day? Why didn't she tell someone or ask someone or do something to make sure he was all right? He didn't want to harm her—look how hesitant he was—how dare she pretend to have been frightened by him?

She imagines Father's disappointment. He's looking at her with that very slightly puzzled look, almost kindly; he is mystified. 'But why didn't you ask him what was wrong? Surely you could have done that?' Always so immediately able to spot the right thing to do, as if it was obvious—it *is* obvious, she tells herself furiously. I must go now and see if the man is all right.

It is not a good decision, she knows that even as she dresses. Why she has not dealt with it in daylight, with the humdrum running of the ship all around her, sailors coming and going, people to turn to—god only knows. In daylight it never even entered her head.

There's nothing to be afraid of. She will go down to the third deck, walk to the laundry room, past it if necessary, check that all is quiet and well—and then return to bed. There's nothing else to do. Of course he won't be there again. The trouble, whatever it was, will have been resolved—even to go there is silly; she dodged it yesterday and now the time is gone. She runs down the stairs quickly, nobody will see her, she'll be back in bed in no time. When it is done it can be forgotten, a small bad taste.

At the bottom of the third set of stairs she pushes through the heavy self-closing door and turns right along the corridor. This is where she stood as he spoke to her; this is where she turned to see him running after her; this is the laundry room doorway, where she first saw a movement off to her left. Everything is still and quiet. She passes green door after green door. Who are they all for? She has seen no more than half a dozen crew moving about the ship; and the other two passengers are in a cabin like hers, on deck. What is behind all these doors?

The corridor ends in stairs down. There are double doors, hooked open. She hesitates at the top, peering down, glances back over her shoulder at the silent empty corridor, then begins to descend, half crouching to see what is down there. The stairs let into a huge open area like a car deck on a ferry. The dim lighting reveals piles of sacks, and containers with black chasms of shadow between them.

As she looks, the Nigerian suddenly emerges at the bottom of the stairs. She can't prevent a little gasp, an involuntary retreat back up one step. The voice of contempt in her head; oh, how surprising. You came to look for this man and now you've found him. What a nasty shock. She forces herself to go down two steps. He's nodding at her.

'Thank you. This way.' It's as if no time has elapsed since last night. Before she has responded he turns and heads towards the shadow between containers. She forces herself down the steps and after his retreating back. As she moves into the darkness she thinks, anything could happen. No one knows I'm here. But the man is moving on quickly in front of her, along the narrow gaps between containers—already her view back to the stairs is blocked, it is too late to ask for help. She can't not follow—he is a magnet, she's dragged across the iron floor unable to resist. The light gets dimmer, there are smells; sacking, dust, the bitter tang of cocoa. He must be some kind of watchman. That's it. He must be a watchman on the cargo deck, he probably has to sleep here to guard the cargo, perhaps he's made a mistake and is afraid of getting into trouble. It will only take a moment to set him straight.

He stops and turns to her. 'Here,' he says softly, indicating the container behind him. 'In here.'

'What is it?' Anne can't imagine. Something leaking? Something spilt, maybe? Then she sees that the side of the container is missing. It has been taken off, like the back door of a lorry. The inside is lit by a candle stub on the floor, which reveals looming dark shapes and shadows—a lair, a den. What is in there?

The man steps in and picks up the candle, raising it so that it sheds more light. The bulging shapes at the back are sacks, heaped up; the ruckle on the floor is cloth, a wrinkled blanket. Suddenly Anne sees a face. A woman's face on the floor, pillowed on a folded cloth. A black woman's face, eyes closed; the light gleams for a moment on the line of her cheekbone and jaw.

'What is it?' Anne whispers again, unable to make sense. Has the watchman found her? Found a woman here, hidden? Has he brought her here, and is she now dead? Something is wrong with her surely or she would move, she would look up.

'Please.' The man gives a slight nod towards the woman. He wants Anne to go to her. Why? Sweat suddenly breaks through Anne's skin. She opens her mouth to breathe but the air has become little tiny fluttering moths, just escaping her, just escaping, flittering away before she can get a lungful. Her eyes continue to search for detail; she can see the shape of the woman's bulk beneath the blankets. As she stands frozen, utterly unable to step into the box, she sees that the picture is Rembrandt's etching, *Nativity*: the man's and woman's faces illumined, the dark shapes around them an indecipherable clutter of shadows, and the heart of the image the tiny light of the hand-held lantern; thinks simultaneously, in this moment in which no time passes, that this is an image Father would have built a sermon on, the tiny Light of the World gleaming bravely amidst so much engulfing darkness; thinks further, and still in less time than it takes to blink, of all the states Rembrandt printed off, from the first where details are discernible, filling up with darkness all along the way, to the last where nothing but the flame and a glint of Mary's face are visible, blackness having swallowed the rest; considers (equably, in no rush) the grimness of the artist's vision, the spreading swamping night—and without breaking stride in the thought, without making a pause in the interaction between herself and the barefooted man, Anne steps into the box and crouches down beside the woman.

Who is clearly ill. Her bones jut in the skin of her face, the sharpness exaggerated by the leaping candle flame. Her face is slick with sweat and her breath comes short. Her body beneath the blankets seems swollen and misshapen; Anne realises that a part of her brain at least has already registered what is going on. She turns to the man.

'Is her baby due?'

He shakes his head. 'Too soon.'

'But she's ill . . .'

'Yes. You can help her.'

'Me? But I'm not a doctor.'

He watches her quietly. What can she say?

'We must get the ship's doctor, I'll run up and find—' She is rising, but his hand is on her arm, his fingers clench tightly round her wrist.

'No.'

'She needs medical help.'

'You tell no one we are here.'

'But how can she be helped?'

'You tell no one.'

He is hurting her arm. 'OK. Is it—doesn't anyone know you're here?'

He loosens his grip. 'If they catch us they send us back.' He sets the candle on the floor again. Anne slowly straightens up. The story begins to assemble in her head. No one knows. The woman is ill. They need help. They are stowaways.

Why me? Here in the middle of the sea in the middle of the night in the dark hold of a container ship, why me? They are expecting her to do . . . what? Something heroic. 'Why have you asked me?'

'You are a woman.'

'But I don't know how to cure her.'

He shrugs.

'She could die.'

'If they send her back she could die.'

'But you must explain—tell them you're refugees . . .'

He shakes his head, turns abruptly and goes out of the box. Anne is left staring at the sick woman. The sick pregnant woman. For god's sake, what can she do? She crouches again and touches the woman's forehead. Hot. Of course, she has a temperature.

Anne stumbles out of the box. The man is leaning against the side of the neighbouring container, face averted.

'Do you have water?'

He nods. Anne stands a moment, helpless, her thoughts flickering and stuttering like a video that needs tracking. She will go back up to her cabin and think what to do.

'I must go . . .'

He turns without speaking and leads the way back through the containers to the foot of the stairs. As she starts to climb he speaks softly; 'Thank you.'

Anne does not look back.

In her cabin she gets into bed and switches off the lamp. The darkness is thick, palpable, she sees that all the air in the room is filled up with crowding atoms of darkness packed and jammed together like bodies in the rush-hour tube, slotted in like a dense three-dimensional jigsaw, solid, pressing—she reaches for the lamp switch again. Why me?

Clearly she must tell somebody. But what will happen then? It comes back to her that there's no doctor on the ship. Among the papers she signed before she came aboard was one asserting that she was in good health and in possession of any medication she might need during the voyage. There are not enough people on the ship to warrant a doctor.

Her brain is tired, flickering, catching at details of the room; is the wardrobe wood or chipboard, is her door green on the outside too, are all the ship's doors green? So if someone is ill, it must be treated as an emergency; a detour must be made to the nearest port, or they must be airlifted off. The man claims the woman will be sent back if they seek treatment. But she can't be treated on the ship. Not by Anne. Not by anyone. Could die if she stays on the ship; the same if she goes back. The two possibilities flick over heavily, repeatedly, in Anne's skull, like a revolving sign outside a garage. Open, shut. Open, shut. Only it's shut, shut. Both sides are shut.

She forces herself to concentrate, to go step by step. What are the things you can do? Make a list. 1. Tell someone. Argue that a doctor must be flown out to the ship. This is what some people could do. Father, knocking on the captain's door: 'Can I have a quick word?' His calm authority. 'Bit of a tricky situation. I'm afraid I'm going to have to ask you to keep this confidential.'

'Of course,' says the captain. And Father explains about the stowaways, the woman's sickness, the danger if they return. He tells the captain to radio for a flying doctor (a flying doctor? Her thoughts suddenly stumble. A flying doctor? That's for the bush, Africa, Australia. At sea you have a—a—helicopter doctor?

Ridiculous, there's a word for what you have, an airlift doctor, an air-sea rescue). She hauls her attention back to Father and the captain, Father is explaining that the captain should simply say a passenger is sick and must be treated aboard, that no one must know they are stowaways, and so they will remain safe. She imagines the captain readily agreeing to this. And as she waves the scene through to its satisfactory conclusion, she is swamped by the knowledge that it would be impossible for her to do this. Why should the captain agree to keep a secret? Why should the captain agree to anything other than what his job description specifies, which is almost certainly to waste no time in getting stowaways off the ship as quickly as possible? She lacks the . . . the word is hovering, just over the edge of thought, she lacks the thing which gives her father such conviction. Not charisma, not power. Moral authority. On then, dragging the dead weight of her attention to number 2. Help the woman secretly. Give her medicine. (What medicine? Anne has twelve paracetamol and a bottle of iodine in her sponge bag.) Wash her. Get her out of that box . . . Anne is staring at the twin bed in her room. She gets up and goes to it, lifts the flowery bedspread. There is a clean pillow and the same stiff white sheets as on her own. Put her to bed here. Keep the steward out. Cure her.

What if she dies here?

Keep going. Don't stop. Keep going. Number 3, Anne realises with relief, is just do nothing. If she had never gone down to the laundry room, she wouldn't have seen the man. If she hadn't seen the man, she wouldn't have gone back. If she hadn't gone back, she wouldn't have to do any of this; she could simply have the voyage she intended, the quiet period of mourning and contemplation, of staring at the sea and letting go. That dream voyage is now so unattainably sweet that just to think of it sends warm waves of grief flooding through her. Surely it has all been a mistake? It's nothing, an invention, a dream, there is only her and Father's diary and the cabin and the voyage, there is nothing else that has to be done, no emergency, no test, this is a figment of an overwrought imagination, the cure for which nineteenth-century ailment must be rest in a darkened room. Rest. Peace.

Anne is asleep. She is walking down the corridor of the ship. There are green doors on either side, endless green doors, one after another, behind them people lie awake, listening in case she passes. She must move silently, quite silently, concentrating on lifting each foot and pushing it forward through the air then setting it down again carefully, first heel then toe on the bare metal floor, so that it does not click or clang, so that she can keep going down the corridor. But it is endless, there is no end to the corridor, and sooner or later someone is bound to open one of these doors. Of course they will, the longer she stays here the more exposed she is. It dawns on her that what she must do is hide *behind* one of the doors. Find a door where no one's waiting and slip through it to safety. She stops, staring at the door on her left. It is exactly the same featureless green as all the others. But she feels it is different. She moves closer to it, listening. She hears nothing beyond the churning of the engines. She presses down gently on the heavy handle and it turns without a sound, swings open a crack. She sees the grey of sky; the bare twigs of a winter tree. This is the one. She goes through.

She is in a park, grey sky, the afternoon drawing in. Tarmacked paths run across a grassy expanse; to her right a cluster of tall, smooth-barked trees, beech she thinks, and in front of her a small group of people who have been passing through the park, dressed in their winter coats and hats. They are gathered randomly, arrested in their tracks, interrupted in their business of walking their children home from school, or carrying shopping, or exercising the dog. They are all still, watching. Only one strange man is rushing about. Anne moves from behind a tall woman, to get a better view. Some kind of performance? The man is making little runs at the crowd, rushing at them then veering away. He seems to be shouting but Anne can't hear. He is holding up his arm and something red is moving. Blood. Blood is spurting from a wound in his arm. Anne watches with interest. It is spurting, much, she supposes, as a whale spurts. There—it jets out, then falls back—jets out in an arc, falls back.

There is something rather beautiful about it, streaming like a red ribbon; the whole scene, the green park, the dogs, the streaming red ribbon. Chagall, Anne thinks, tilting her head, imagining the man floating off into the sky; it is a painting by Chagall.

The man waves his arm angrily at the crowd. He should lie down, thinks Anne, if it really is blood. He should lie down and hold it up in the air, a tourniquet should be applied. Or pressure. As if reading her mind a woman at the front of the crowd steps forward to the man, reaching for his injured arm. But the man shrieks and wheels away, spraying blood across the faces of the people at the front, who step back angrily, wiping and spitting. A man next to Anne is on the phone.

'Yes, in the park. Yes, an ambulance. I wouldn't call it an emergency, no, it's not that serious. But an ambulance.'

It is serious, Anne counters inwardly, spurting is an artery, an artery is serious. Someone should take the situation in hand. The man is lurching about, he staggers closer to the crowd. People step back from him, bumping into those behind; a few break away and move off quickly towards the trees, as if annoyed at the interruption to their homeward journey. The man suddenly falls over, lying on his back with his knees in the air.

'Is that it?' someone asks loudly. A woman with two blue and white plastic shopping bags—Anne stares at them carefully and is pleased to find that although the light is fading she can still read the shop name, Tesco, on them—steps forward and nudges the prone man with her foot. Not satisfied, she bends a little closer over his still figure, then straightens up.

'Yes, he's dead.' A moment, then the crowd breaks up—individually, or in twos and threes, people move off across the park in different directions, away into the darkness of the evening.

Soon there is no one left but the man lying on the ground, and Anne.

Anne knows she is asleep. A performance artist, she tells herself, trying to cancel the dream. A mime act, common in city parks. She is looking for the place to throw coins. Her hand is on the handle of the green ship's door.

She is looking at the darkness of her room. Can she make out a hint of lightening at the square of the window? She turns on the light and goes to the bathroom; the stream of hot urine spurting out of her makes her shamefaced at her own aliveness, its insistent warmth and functionality. A body is a machine for staying alive. She has remembered something that might help.

She drags Father's suitcase from the wardrobe and slides the clasps sideways to click it open. Rummages under the layer of books and papers, to the rigid green plastic box she remembers packing. Here. His first-aid box. She had considered leaving it for the houseboy and then been afraid that the medicines (whatever they were—she hadn't even bothered to look) might be misused, or the instructions not properly followed, that she might be creating a problem.

She takes the green box with its white cross to the bed, and opens it on her knees. Water-purifying tablets, calamine lotion, malaria tablets, vacuum-packed syringes, mosquito repellent, a packet of bullet-shaped antibiotics. Could the woman take these? She checks the date, OK, and begins to read the accompanying leaflet.

For a few moments everything seems settled. She takes off yesterday's clothes and stands under the hot shower. She brushes her teeth and puts on clean clothes. Then she sits down. What is she planning to do? Give Father's old antibiotics to a heavily pregnant woman with an undisclosed sickness? What if there's something wrong with the pregnancy? What if the foetus is in distress? The antibiotics could be dangerous, deadly even. What could be worse than pretending to be helpful, doing more harm than good?

Someone knocks gently on the door and she realises it must be the steward—breakfast time. It is impossible to move. Every ounce of energy and strength in her body has ebbed away as surely as the sea at low tide, leaving nothing but a dull expanse of wet sand, the odd flattened mound of seaweed, a landscape featureless, pointless, unable. He does not knock again, she supposes he has gone away. If she can sit here weakly then all the time she's doing that, she is not making anything happen. Time passes. She remembers, time passes, even if you do nothing. The woman will be getting worse or better. It is not Anne's fault.

It *is* her fault, she should be helping the woman. But if she is incapable of moving it is not her fault. If she is physically incapable.

This is just a ploy to save herself from having to do anything. If she brought the woman up to her cabin and the steward discovered her, it would not be Anne's fault, and the woman could be properly helped. But because Anne *knows* the danger of discovery, it would be up to her to make sure the woman was not discovered in her cabin. That isn't fair. It is so obviously unfair. With slow sleepwalker steps Anne goes back into the bathroom to comb her hair. The mirror is still misted up from her shower. She moves to wipe it clear then sees her hand before her, flat against the misty glass—snatches it away and watches as the handprint, spread fingers and thumb, the curve of palm, gathers drips and dribbles down the mirror, distorting before her eyes.

The car windows were frosted with patterns of trees and branches. Everything was still and frozen and perfect and silent and she was twisting at the key until it started to bend and she was afraid it might snap. The lock was fast as iron.

Tim came out of the house with a kettle of water, he must have been watching her through the window. 'You don't have to go now, you know. You really don't.'

'I have to be gone by tonight so I might as well go now.'

'Look, I never said—'

'I know.'

He poured hot water from the kettle over the door handle, she thought something would crack but nothing happened. He took the key from her and unlocked the car. 'Shall I come with you?'

Anne glanced at him, she thought her face was closed but he must have seen a glimmer of hope or some such foolishness because he quickly added,

'For the day I mean. We could go for a brisk walk and lunch in a pub with a fire somewhere—'

'And I could deliver you back in time for you to change the sheets before your wife comes home.'

'Yes.'

'No.' She got in the car. It filled with her steaming breath which froze instantly on the insides of the windows. He poured more warm water on the windscreen and it thawed the white frosted patterns then refroze in a clear swirl. She turned on the engine, it caught on the third go. He opened the door and leant in.

'Nothing has changed. I don't know what's the matter with you. Nothing has changed.'

She was crying. Her tears were making molten stripes down her crusted face like the kettle water on the windscreen. Her belly was hollow as a gourd. She shut the door and locked it and turned on the heater which blew icy air, and she sat in the blind throbbing car waiting for it to warm up while she cried because nothing had changed except her. She didn't want to have changed but she had. Something had started to grow in her and been stopped. That wasn't the same as if it had never been there at all. There was a darkening at the white side window and gradually as the ice melted she saw it was his hand, open palm and fingers pressed against the glass, just his bare hand there flattened against the icy pane, until his clear handprint was melted through the ice. Like a wave, he was waving goodbye. He was supplicating, he was trying to reach her, he was holding his warm dear flesh against the icy unyielding glass to make a point. But he couldn't get in and come away with her, he could only give her the farewell sign of love.

Dropping her comb into the sink, Anne makes her way back to her bed. After she has lain there a while she picks up the diary which is lying open, face down, on her bedside table. Just a few pages. Then she will do something.

FEBRUARY 9, 1962

I'm starting an extra class after school on Wednesdays for the high fliers, and the gardening class is now regular on Fridays. If I can persuade students about crop rotation and a more varied diet it should filter quite naturally into village culture. But we must get girls—it's the women who're in charge of the village crops, the women who grow them, sell them and cook them.

I've got through on the radio to the Dutch and organised a meeting for Saturday. Miriam is beginning to make the odd complaint about me having filled up all the free time, but it's impossible to sit idly by when I can see how hugely much there is to do—and how receptive people are to a little encouragement.

The internal politics here are tricky. The clinic works well enough; the Frenchman, Dr Paul as everyone calls him, seems committed and hardworking, if somewhat lacking in social skills. I gather he's been rather dismissive of Miriam's suggestions about offering family planning advice. But the young girl who's interpreting for her has told her the women are very glad now they can see a lady nurse. I'm still finding my colleague Mark a little difficult—I feel he resents me, and although of course I don't blame him, it's difficult to know how to behave. Also I've been forced to realise that he would not have been a good bet as senior teacher; he's often late, which gets the school day off to a poor start, especially when I've made such a fuss with my students about *punctuality. And he didn't bite when I suggested he might like to run an extra class for the weaker readers. He is less committed than I had hoped.*

Karl is increasingly prickly with me; I suppose he feels threatened by someone putting more energy into the work than he. I've suggested to him that we could have a much greater impact for good on the community if we offered classes for adults (especially women): literacy, agriculture, nutrition, practical things they actually want to know. I find myself looking forward rather longingly to his departure. Even the church is less effective than it should be. It's breeze block with corrugated-tin roof and little slits for windows—like being inside an oven—and once the congregation pack in and their mingled sweat and body heat fill the place, it's barely possible to breathe. There are no plans afoot for a new building, although I know perfectly well we could raise some money from England towards this. And Karl himself is a weary preacher. I find it almost painful, the contrast between his slow dry pronouncements from the pulpit and the fervent enthusiasm of his congregation. Even Jacob made a better job of it, on the one occasion I've heard him take the service. He's unprepossessing, a small, bespectacled fellow with grizzled hair and an unhappy expression, but he seems to have been responsible for the majority of adult conversions at church, and there is real power of conviction behind his words. With Karl, it is sometimes hard to tell whether the man believes anything at all.

MARCH 7, 1962

Oppressive heat these past few days—a heavy intense steamy heat which can sometimes make you struggle for breath. Poor Miriam is sick in the mornings. It's a difficult start to the day, knowing the temperature will continue to rise inexorably all morning, trying to cheer and encourage her and get her to rights for the clinic. She has never been good at mornings. I must admit that it is with a sense of relief that I finally make my own way to the schoolroom—not that it's any cooler there, quite the reverse. But the heat generates all sorts of niggling little tensions. We are longing for the rains to clear the atmosphere.

A chap called Okolie came knocking at the door this afternoon, asking for work. Apparently he's worked here before, but been away 'in my mother's country' (which probably means ten miles down the road) for a while. But he is clearly better educated and generally has more about him than the hapless yard boys who usually hang around on the off-chance of work. When I asked what he could do he said carpenter, which is fortuitous since the schoolhouse is in desperate need of bookshelves, and Miriam is complaining of lack of shelves in the clinic as well. I've been meaning to do the job myself but there aren't enough hours in the day. We went to look at the materials in the gardening hut behind Karl's bungalow, and he asked if he could sleep there while he's doing the work. I can't imagine anyone could object but it's rather a miserable billet, between the rakes and scythes and sacks, so I asked Karl if there was anywhere better we could offer him.

He was sitting at his desk fiddling with the short-wave radio, which seems to be broken as often as it is working. It crackled and hissed throughout our conversation. I hadn't got any further than Okolie's name when he said, 'No.'

'I beg your pardon?'

'No, he can't sleep here. And you'd be well advised not to employ him.'

'But he's a carpenter—'

'He's a hemp smoker. And a thief. Last time he was here Mark's bicycle disappeared.'

'D'you know it was him?'

Karl reset the dials on the radio and listened intently. It is a frustrating characteristic of his, to not answer, frequently by pretending to be absorbed in something else. After a minute I said *goodbye and went to find Okolie. He was sitting in the shade under the lemon tree. 'Mr Karl says you stole a bicycle.'*

'Me? Oh no, sir, I never stole it.'

'Did you borrow it?'

'No, sir. I never saw a bicycle. Where I go, I walk on my own two feet.'

'I'm sorry, I'm only asking because—'

'He tell you I smoke hemp?'

'Yes.'

'I don't do that now. Is it Christian, never forgive a man, never allow him change?'

A very good question. I told Okolie I would pay him five shillings for the first set of shelves, and if I was happy with them there would be more work, but that Karl had forbidden him to sleep in the compound.

On Sunday I went over to the Dutch mission, and we talked about their health programme. They've been concentrating on pre-natal and child-welfare clinics, giving each mother a card to record vaccinations, growth rate, weight; they've radically increased the rate of vaccinations in the area, and the cards are enormously popular—almost a status symbol, according to their doctor. There's no reason why Paul shouldn't introduce the same system at our clinic; from what Miriam says, the records are desperately haphazard. She's only able to vaccinate the babies if they're brought in for some other reason. I took one of the cards to show Paul.

It was late afternoon when I got back to Oji Bend, and Miriam wasn't in the bungalow. It was terribly hot and close, my clothes were stuck to me after the long drive, and I drank three pints of juice and water and took a shower. The bucket shower is a wondrous invention; part of the very basic gravitational plumbing system in the bungalow. The bucket fills from barrels stored under the eaves. They catch rainwater in the wet season and are filled manually at other times. The water seems always to be exactly the right refreshing temperature, cold but with the edge taken off it by the heat of the day. I was drying myself when Miriam called to me from the hall and offered me a drink.

I wrapped myself in the towel and went through to the kitchen where she was topping up a couple of glasses with clear fizzy liquid. A lovely tangy smell.

'Tonic?'

'And gin! Present from Karl!' She dropped a couple of lemon slices into each and passed me one. Karl had told us he was tee-total on the first night, but in talking to him that afternoon Miriam had unearthed the reason: the poor chap used to be an alcoholic.

'He's got a cupboard full of unopened booze; he told me to help myself to whatever you and I liked. He's not as bad as we thought, David.'

'Indeed not.' I raised my glass to her and she laughed, but wouldn't be deflected.

'It's easy for us to come in and be critical, isn't it? Actually, he's achieved an incredible amount here.'

'I've never denied that.'

'I think he likes to feel his way, to wait to see what will or won't work, whereas you want to change everything instantly.'

'Look Miriam, when he came here there was nothing. He changed everything then. He hasn't always been like he is now, or the station wouldn't exist.' I drained my glass and suggested we have another on the veranda. It was still as hot but the sky was completely overcast; it felt as if the rains might start any minute. Miriam wouldn't let it go.

'When Karl came here there were no schools at all, now there's Universal Primary Education, so-called. There's a rate at which people's lives can adapt to change, can incorporate it and make sense of it, and if you go faster than that they're just lost—'

'You're saying we should allow another generation of local girls to grow up illiterate because if we get them into school we're changing their lives too quickly?'

'No, but look at his staying power. Look at his loyalty to this community. We can't rival that.'

'I don't want to rival it. I just want progress.' I poured us another drink. I couldn't see why she was so keen to defend him, although I was glad that she had been taken into his confidence. I asked her about the alcoholism.

'It was ten years ago. He was talking about long cycles, about how your sense of what you're trying to do changes, how you realise that you're only God's agent, not God himself.'

'Is that what he's accusing me of?'

'David, please. His faith is incredibly important to him.'

'So it should be, he's a missionary.' The story of his drinking didn't entirely surprise me. It's often those who are weak-willed in some way who become most inflexible and resistant to change. I've noticed that before, it's a way of maintaining control.

APRIL 4, 1962

Terrible storm last night—great slashes of lightning opening the sky, thunder like bombs dropping—and rain which has flattened our seedlings. I thought at least it would clear the air, because it's been stifling this past week. But this evening it's just as humid and tense all over again; another storm must be brewing.

I'm baffled by the difficulty between Miriam and Luke. I suppose it must have originated in that early dispute over whether we could do without a servant. I think Miriam has continued to feel resentful about the whole thing, and perhaps Luke has got wind of that. The trouble is, she's inconsistent; she'll go for a few days completely ignoring domestic arrangements, just giving the nod to whatever Luke suggests cooking, letting him dish up his endless spam and peas and instant mashed potatoes; then she'll suddenly decide to send him scuttling off after all sorts of ingredients he doesn't know how to find. I've explained to her that as far as fresh food goes, we have to adapt to what's available in the market, but she seems incapable of working it with Luke in such a way as to procure the ingredients for any single meal. So she'll send him off with a list of things, half of which are completely unavailable, and then be unable to make (or teach him to make, which is really what's needed) the meal she had in mind.

She was complaining about the fish he had bought. 'Dried fish, the texture and consistency of old leather—what am I supposed to do with that?'

'But he must know how they cook it, there must be a local dish.'

'Fine. You ask him.'

It turns out there's a kind of stew or sauce they put the smoked fish in, cut up small, but he didn't tell Missus Miriam because you must eat it with foo foo and anyway she didn't ask him to buy the pepper to go with it.

'Miriam, you have to tell him to buy what's there. Whatever vegetables are in season. It's not difficult.'

'Why don't you do it? You are so good at everything, after all.'

I hate it when she adopts that sarcastic tone. It reveals her at her worst—spiteful and defensive. 'You know as well as I do that neither of us can go to weekday market, that's one of the reasons we employ Luke—'

'We could manage without—'

'I'm not getting into this again.'

'You want me to give him carte blanche to buy whatever he sees fit and then I'm the one who has to figure out what to make with it.'

'Give him an upper spending limit—say two shillings—and tell him the sort of things you'd prefer, but allow him to use his initiative.'

'You treat me like a child. What d'you think I've been doing? That's how I ended up last week trying to make a Sunday roast out of a scrawny boiling fowl, some yams and a giant melon.'

'You need to be more flexible—'

'*You do it. OK? From now on you do it.*'

I thought she would change her mind, considering how much more time she spends in the house than I do, but no; so I have taken on overseeing Luke's culinary efforts and although the results are a little erratic, it's all done with relative good humour and the minimum of fuss—there's food on the table every night, and Luke at least is smiling again instead of looking pained and anxious. In Miriam's defence, she really is tired, and this can't be the easiest climate to be pregnant in. Though I notice the local women seem to thrive on it—you still see them walking along the tracks with huge water jars on their heads in the final weeks of pregnancy. They have wonderfully straight posture, I'm sure that must help. Miriam will tend to hunch and slouch.

H IS WRITING FLOWS CONFIDENTLY, letters in the middle of words disappearing into horizontal lines, punctuated by the precise verticals of t and I and f; small, even and surprisingly easy to read, given how many letters are unformed. Very little is crossed out. Anne wonders if she is the first person to read the diary. Her mother can't have read it. Poor Miriam. *You are so good at everything, after all.* Anne knows she is a disappointment to him, as her mother was. How can he always be right, and everyone else be wrong? The old helpless anger churns in her stomach, there has never been any way to deal with him but to refuse, to disappoint.

She should do something now. But what? Lying in the dimness staring, she can see that the light does actually increase as the sun moves overhead for midday; it filters down between the side of the container and the wall of her cabin, and manages to creep redly into her room. The sound of the engines changes once, a jacking up of noise, she imagines the captain: 'Full steam ahead!' She thinks longingly of the rail, of standing in the sunshine staring across the empty sea, letting her mind drift. What is she supposed to do now?

She loved him. At the beginning it was simple. She loved Father for his kindness, and she didn't disappoint him. Anne remembers the first time she visited the rectory; she was eleven. Everything at home was strange and terrible. Mum had come out of hospital but Anne knew she would have to go back because she couldn't eat. Her sister, Anne's aunt Laura, was looking after them, and brisk cheerful nurses visited morning, noon and night to do secret things to Mum. Aunt Laura told Anne that her father was coming to see her.

Anne was waiting when his car pulled up, and went straight outside to join him. He had never been in their house, it mustn't be different this time. She had seen him twice a year since he came back from Nigeria; he would take her out for a day around her birthday, usually to some stately home or castle, where they would walk about the grounds and eat a National Trust lunch. And on Boxing Day he took her to tea at Granny and Grandpa Harrington's, and they made a fuss of her, with a carrier bag full of presents and the table spread with fairy cakes and trifle and little silver-foil-wrapped chocolate Swiss rolls.

When she got into the car this time her father leaned across and kissed her. 'I'm going to show you where I live, Annie, alright?'

She knew he lived in Manchester in a place called The Rectory, St Luke's, but she was afraid it was too far away from home. She was afraid that something might happen to Mum while she was out. He seemed to understand that.

'I'll get you back in time for tea.'

As they drove up the M6 she wanted to ask why he was taking her out today, when it wasn't her birthday or Boxing Day. But she didn't want to hear the answer. He talked to her about his parish; there had been a disastrous wet Sunday school outing to Blackpool where they had lost two seven-year-olds, and found them hours later, playing happily in an amusement arcade. He had had to baptise a baby with the name Melissa Marilyn Murgatroyd. Anne told herself he was inventing things to cheer her up.

The rectory was a big old Victorian house behind a dusty privet hedge. The house next door was boarded up, and there was a car with no wheels sitting outside it. He unlocked the heavy front door and let her into a high-ceilinged hall with a cracked black and white tiled floor. 'D'you want to explore while I make us a drink?'

She walked through the cavernous rooms. Thin old carpets lay in rectangles across the wooden boards and shuffled into wrinkles when you walked on them. A three-bar electric fire sat in the open fireplace in the dining room. There was what looked like an old brown door bell on the wall—she pressed it but nothing happened. The kitchen had a rectangular white pot sink, almost big enough to bath in, and a wooden draining board.

'Everything's going to be alright,' he said. 'Trust me.' He gave her a mug of sweet milky tea which she didn't like but drank anyway, and they went into the garden. Anne loved the garden straightaway. There was a little paved area with a garden table and chairs, and the whole of the rest of the garden was planted in neat rows like an allotment, with a path of stepping stones down the middle; in some rows the vegetables grew up tall bamboo sticks. 'D'you like gardening?'

'I don't know.' There was no garden at Miriam's house.

'D'you want to know what I'm growing?'

She nodded, and they walked down the rows, one stepping stone at a time.

'Strawberries—they're over now. Marrows—that's going to be my prize one, see? Onions, carrots, peas, beans. Dwarf and runner. Potatoes. Maize—you know, sweetcorn. Cabbage—' He smiled at the face she pulled. 'Delicious. And you know what's here right at the back?' He was pointing to a wire cage and Anne was suddenly filled with excitement.

'Rabbits? A tortoise?'

'*Look*, silly. Is there room for animals in there?'

There wasn't, the cage was filled with leafy growth. 'I don't know.'

'Something I thought you might help me with. D'you like raspberries?' He unhooked a little wire door in the side of the cage and they entered; she could see the raspberries now, clustered thickly beneath the leaves, red as Christmas. When she touched one it came away neatly as the glove off a finger, leaving a glistening tooth-white cone on the bush. 'I'll get you a bowl.'

They picked the sweet-smelling raspberries together; he held the canes apart so that she could slip in to reach the lower, hidden clusters. She liked the way he called her Annie. 'You used to help me in the garden when you were very little.'

'In Nigeria?'

'Yes.'

'D'you live on your own here?'

'Sometimes. Sometimes I have students or a curate, and they stay here. It's a big house for one person, isn't it?'

'D'you eat all this?' She gestured at the garden and he laughed.

'No, I freeze some of it, but most gets given away.'

'Who to?'

'Oh, people in the parish. At Harvest Festival we make up boxes—don't you do that at your school?'

'We take tins. For the old folk.'

'Right. They do that here too. Shall we go and eat some of these?'

In the kitchen he picked over the raspberries and told Anne to get the cream out of the fridge. It was easy to find because there was nothing else in the fridge but one bottle of milk, a tub of margarine and a slab of cheese.

'Is this all you eat?'

He frowned. 'You've just seen all my vegetables.' He sugared the raspberries and spooned them into two glass bowls. Anne poured cream, and they ate in contented silence. When he had finished he clasped his hands around the bowl. 'Annie. When your mother dies, would you like to come and live with me?'

'She's not going to die.'

He looked at her with eyes that seemed to bore right through her. 'I'm afraid she is. It's very sad, and very hard, but we have to accept God's will.'

Without answering she pushed back her chair and went up

the creaking stairs. In his room there was the big black frock that vicars wear, hanging on the front of the wardrobe; she had forgotten he must wear one of those. His bed was neatly made with a Bible and some other books beside it. The room opposite had a wide window with a little window seat built into it, and faded wallpaper of roses climbing up trellises. It looked out over the garden. In the bathroom was a big old-fashioned bath that stood on claws for feet. The next room had clothes folded neatly in a pile on the bed. There was a photo of an African lady on the desk. Anne went downstairs again.

'We can paint your room. What colour would you like?'

'I like the paper. Who stays in the other one?'

'Steve Obuku. My curate. But he's gone back to Nigeria to visit his family.'

'I want to go home now.'

Her father rose immediately, put the leftover raspberries into a margarine tub for her to give to Aunt Laura, and took Anne out to the car.

Something must be done. All this is just putting off the moment. She must go down and see them immediately. Take paracetamol and antibiotics. Try to work out if such medication is appropriate. See what the man thinks about installing the woman in Anne's cabin. Is it a crime to help a stowaway? If they are caught and sent ashore, might Anne be sent too? To be clanged into a small sweltering cell and forgotten, charged with helping political undesirables? Isn't that possible?

She should find out what their position really is. Why are they fleeing? Are they *really* in danger? (How will she know?) Perhaps they're under threat because they're criminals—drug or diamond smugglers. Perhaps the woman has a bag of opium inside her which has burst. Perhaps . . .

So she will question them to discover if they are worthy of her help. Is that it? To check that they are deserving?

It's all nonsense, she's despicable. She's getting up when

there's another knock at the door. She freezes. The sound of footsteps going away on the deck. She checks the time: 12.30. The steward again, she should go to lunch or it will seem suspicious. She should go to lunch because she needs to eat. And after that she will go straight down to the hold. She is putting the tablets in her pocket.

When Anne goes into the dining room there is only the first mate there. Robbie Boyle the Australian. He is opening a can of beer. 'Hi there. Want one?'

Anne nods. Everything is paid for in the fare. She might as well have beer.

'Quiet, eh. The old folks are eating in their cabin.' Anne sits and takes a swig of beer. She didn't know you could eat in your cabin. That may come in useful. Although she immediately thinks angrily, for what? Since she still has not the inkling of a plan.

'You OK?' he asks suddenly and rather surprisingly.

'Yes, thank you, I'm fine.'

'Good. Thought you might be having trouble sleeping.'

'No, no, it's fine.' Has gossip travelled around the ship about her nocturnal wanderings? She concentrates on making a sandwich, but Robbie seems determined to have a conversation.

'You been on holiday in Nigeria?'

'No, not exactly.'

There's an awkward silence. Anne hacks at a piece of cheese. It's churlish not to speak to the man. 'No, my father died there. I've been over for the funeral and stuff.'

'Sorry to hear that.'

'Thank you.'

Another little silence but easier this time. Anne is grateful for his contentedly noisy chewing. His black and greying hair is tied back in a pony tail which she hadn't noticed before and which seems to cast him in quite a different light. 'Your old man live there then?'

'In the sixties. He came home after Biafra. He was just visiting, this time.'

'He work in oil?'

Again Anne feels herself blushing; horrid, ridiculous, why does it happen? She wishes he wouldn't look at her. 'Missionary.' He must feel she is delivering constipated little nuggets of information. She doesn't want him to know there was a hot happy time when she was little and her parents lived together. She forces herself to ask him a question. 'Have you always worked at sea?'

'Nah. Used to run a riverboat company on the Murray, till I got sick of pulling stupid buggers off sandbars. Been on the big ships seven years come April.'

'Do you stay with one ship—one shipping line?'

'Depends. Been working this route f'ra while now. Decent crew—look out for each other.' There's a little silence. He glances at her. 'You been on many ships?'

'Oh no—this is the first.'

'There's better routes for passengers.'

'How d'you mean?'

He laughs, his teeth are straight and perfect. 'Places to visit. Things to see. Africa's a dump.'

She pours them both a coffee and they swap stories about Lagos, where he once lived for ten months. Anne watches herself seeming normal, notes that he's perfectly straightforward with her. Perhaps her judgement is really quite faulty at present; perhaps Father's death has unbalanced her in ways she hasn't altogether grasped. Perhaps this whole business on the cargo deck is less dramatic than she thinks, and with a more balanced daytime eye she will be able to resolve it simply, seeing it for the little difficulty it is. In fact, she may have jumped to the wrong conclusion about a number of things. As she did when she first met Robbie Boyle. He doesn't have any designs. Any more than anyone else on the crew—they have all been treating her with considerate politeness. That earlier feeling was a little moment of paranoia, of misjudgement. No one is going to take advantage of her. (Silly, embarrassing phrase—*take advantage of*. Anyone would think she was a schoolgirl.)

'I'll just cover these rolls, they're going to get hard.'

Robbie looks at her as if she's mad. 'There's a freezer-full down below—they'll chuck these to the fish.'

Of course. Of course. She's become as bad as Father. She forces her attention away from the wasted food, sits back and sips her coffee.

When Robbie picks up another can of beer and heads down to his cabin ('A cat nap. I was on the bridge at four this morning') with a simple nod, not even a smile, Anne waits till he has gone then follows down the stairs to the third level. Along the corridor of doors, past the laundry and to the top of the container-deck stairs. Halfway down the stairs she stops, waiting for her eyes to adjust to the dimness, searching for signs of movement. Everything is very still: the big dim hulks of the containers, the canyons of black shadow between them. She expected the man to be waiting, but there's nobody. She descends the stairs slowly and crosses the iron floor to the first container, treading softly. But perhaps she should make a noise, stamp on the floor or call out? Of course he won't simply be waiting all day long, how could he have possibly guessed when she would come? Probably he expected her earlier; almost certainly—she was here in the night and went away promising to help. Now it's what? After lunchtime, almost ten hours later. He's been waiting and he's given up, fallen asleep, curled up in the shadows somewhere. If she creeps up on him he may be alarmed, he might think they are discovered, and panic—

But it's impossible to call out, it feels too dangerous, the sound would reverberate around that echoing space, shockingly loud over the background churning of the engines. A calling voice or echoing single clang could reveal her to anyone, not just the black man but maybe someone passing in the corridor—to anyone else skulking among the containers—to a crew member doing a routine check. All her instincts are against revealing herself. She slips into the shadow and moves in the direction of the open box, going left round one container and right round the next, trying to maintain a straight route. What if she can't find them? What if she gets lost? But that's ridiculous, the floor around the stairs is clear, it may take a little time but it would always be possible to locate the stairs again.

Now she's in real dimness, trailing her fingers along the gritty dusty sides of the containers as she threads between them, ears strained for any breath or movement. How many containers has she passed? Five? She should count from here on. It wasn't that far in, surely it must be the next one? She goes round all four sides of the next container, but it is a blank. So is the one beside it. She has missed them. Maybe further over to the left? Every few steps she stops to listen, eyes peeled against the dimness. Nothing. Could they be asleep? Perhaps the woman has suddenly recovered and they are both hidden, sleeping, no longer needing her. Perhaps they've closed the side of the container again—they must know how to do it—perhaps they've shut themselves away in fear of being found. Perhaps the woman has died . . . Anne moves more and more slowly. It is hard to see ahead. Anything could be in the blackness there. Anything or anyone. What is she moving towards? If the man still wanted her help he would be on the lookout for her, she wouldn't have to prowl about hunting in every corner. Perhaps he quite definitely doesn't want her—has decided it is better to remain completely hidden. It is his decision. Anne has come down here with tablets in her pocket and looked for him. She's tried.

With a rush of relief she turns on the spot and moves back the way she's come. He doesn't want her help any more. Threading her way round the blank corners of the giant boxes, stepping into chasms of shadow between them, hurrying now because there is almost the sense of something following—almost a trace of a footstep at her back, not the man, a different person . . . Anne makes herself stop. Listen. There is nothing beyond the continuous revolution of the engines. She moves quickly towards the lighter area—around the side of a final container—into view of the stairs. Halfway up she makes herself stop and turn round, holding her position for the benefit of anyone who may be peering from between the containers. No one moves.

She runs back up to the top deck light with relief—feels the sun on her face like a blessing—and goes through to the rail rather than into the dim confine of her cabin. The sky is cloudless, the sea fretted with little splashy white-frothed waves running before a wind—perfectly clear and lovely. Standing at the rail she inhales deeply and then breathes out all the dark confusion and anxiety of the container deck, the black man, the sweating woman in the dark box. It's over. It's not there.

With the brilliance of the blue waves and their white crests before her, it is possible to consider that it was a nightmare, an anxiety-inducing scenario concocted by her subconscious, perhaps emblematic of some other situation in her waking life.

Which is enough to make her laugh out loud. Does it need a psychoanalyst to make the startling observation that she is a childless woman of thirty-seven? She has had a nightmare that she must save the life of a heavily pregnant woman; how difficult to interpret!

She remembers the day Tim's daughter was born. He phoned her from the hospital, gabbling with exhausted joy; Fiona had been in labour all night. He wanted Anne to rejoice, thinking her love for him could be that selfless. When she'd put the phone down she could settle to nothing. She remembers going out to buy cigarettes, even though she only ever smoked one or two of Tim's; smoking her way through the packet until she felt sick. Eventually she caught the bus over to Father's. He asked her what was wrong and she foolishly told him she was tired from waiting up to hear news of a friend's baby.

'How wonderful. God's greatest gift. When are you going to have one, Annie? I wish you would.'

'Well perhaps you could ask your God to arrange an immaculate conception. It does take two you know.'

He persisted in his tone of ghastly reasonableness. 'But you're an attractive woman, you could be with a man if you wanted. Why are you always so negative?' It was that afternoon he persuaded her to let him buy her a new kitten. Smokey. Her child substitute—it had been possible to joke about it after a while.

Anne fixes her eyes on the horizon. She allows herself fleetingly to touch the other memory, quick as whipping her hand through a flame. OK. She isn't going to cry. Tim's daughter was eighteen months old by then. The shocking blue line on the pregnancy test. Waiting, waiting, thinking it would get easier to tell him. Then panicking at how much time had gone. The dropping in her stomach as she watched Tim's face—dropping like a stone down a well, like a broken lift down the shaft of the tallest skyscraper in the world. 'No Anne—no. Are you mad? For god's sake no.' That was when the baby was killed. Then, not in the muffled clinic with its hot stale smell, where nothing was real and there was no pain. There was no pain. It hurt less than extracting a splinter.

Anne swallows. A handful of gulls are wheeling and diving, squabbling over something in the water; she sees their repetitive circling motion is both random and inevitable, they must dip, they must soar, they are compelled.

It's wiped. It didn't happen. Like this business in the hold now. The mind playing tricks. What is real is the heat of the mid-afternoon sun, fierce but welcome on her face, its dazzle in the water, the freshness of the breeze, which almost tastes of salt, perhaps a very fine spray lifted from the tops of the busy little waves. It is hot enough to burn, she should go and fetch a hat or sun cream, but the relief of standing still now and allowing her senses to fill up with heat and light is so strong she can't tear herself away. The whole episode with the stowaways is receding, a melodramatic story. It's not the kind of thing that happens to Anne. She stands, eyes half-shut, calm and stupefied in the sunlight.

★　★　★

The Malones are at dinner, seated either side of the captain, who seems to have become their close friend. Three officers sit around the opposite end of the table and stare rudely at Anne. All three are grotesque; she wonders if this is why they are friends, they find solace in each other's ugliness. One has a red and lumpy face as if cauliflower florets are trying to poke through his skin; the middle one is bald with an obscene blond-grey moustache sprouting under his wide pink nose. The third has no chin; beneath his button nose and dot of a mouth, his neck begins—he is an unfinished sketch, a half-drawn man. Anne sits herself squarely opposite the captain, thereby entering Mrs Malone's bubble of conversation. 'One thing about travel is it does make you appreciate home, d'you find that, captain?'

The captain smiles inside his stiff creased face; he has a wonderful Mutti, he confides, when he goes home she certainly likes to spoil him. Ellie Malone claps her monkey hands delightedly.

'Of course she does. And she can afford to, because she knows you'll soon be off on your travels again!' Anne finds herself staring at Ellie's lips, which have again bled into the wrinkles around her mouth, like a crimson mouth in a child's painting running wetly into the surrounding face.

'When we get home the children will clamour to see us, won't they Phil? We'll be exotic creatures, not boring old Grandma and Grand-dad.'

'You have grandchildren?' asks the captain.

'Oh we have five, gorgeous little things, three boys and two girls. Bobby's are four and seven, and Carol's are—how old is the baby now Phil, six months?'

Beaky Phil does not respond.

'And two and four, they're quite a handful, she struggles with them sometimes. Do you have children?' Kindly she includes Anne in the conversation.

And Anne can reply almost blithely, 'No, I teach children instead.'

'Oh, wonderful. What a rewarding job. Is it little ones you teach or—'

'Nine- to ten-year-olds.'

'How marvellous. I wanted to be a teacher but my parents wouldn't let me stay on at school, I had to get a job at fifteen. Those were the bad old days weren't they, captain? Oh! You'd be far too young to remember, silly me . . .'

Anne blanks her out but is unpleasantly conscious of too many eyes upon her as she eats: the three grotesques at the end, the hostile gaze of Mr Malone, even the captain's vacant blue eyes as he bends his ear to Ellie Malone. She wonders if she looks strange, if perhaps there is dirt on her face or her hair's on end. Why has she seated herself here right in front of everyone, instead of sliding in unobtrusively beside Ellie Malone? Ellie addresses a remark to the grotesques and they nod politely.

'Their English is good but they are afraid of making a mistake,' explains the captain heavily.

'Oh I know all you Germans have such good English!' gushes Ellie. 'And how well you manage with all these nationalities on board. Where are the oriental gentlemen from?'

'Singapore, the Philippines; the first mate speaks Malay and Filipino.'

'Goodness!' chirps Ellie. Anne declines pudding then realises it would still be rude to leave and sits rigid through another ten minutes, vowing never to come to the dining room again.

After dinner, she lies on her bed reading. The silence is a blessed relief. At night, when there's no daylight outside to miss, the cabin is attractive—well-proportioned and pleasingly blond and blue, the walls and wardrobe are a pale-coloured wood which glows a golden colour in the lamplight. The smell seems to have gone. Or maybe she's got used to it. It's going to be all right.

April 10, 1962

*The agriculturist at the Dutch mission advised me to visit a farm
set up by Norcap, the Norwegian Churches Agricultural Project,
down towards Arochuku. He told me they're doing very good work
there on livestock, annual crops and economic trees. No one else
on the station has any interest in growing food, and since it seems
obvious to me that this may be one of the most important ways in
which we can help the villagers, I've rather taken it on—and I
wanted to get to the Norcap farm before the roads became impassable with the rainy season. I thought Miriam would want to come
with me to see them on Sunday but she said she needed a lie-in.
I might have guessed at something strange then, because she
never normally misses an opportunity for an outing with me. She
insisted I take Luke, who was eager to come, and in the event it
was lucky that he did.*

    *The Norwegians are impressive. They've been bringing young
unemployed men out from the towns, settling them in communi-
ties and educating them in the rotation of food and cash crops.
What I like very much is the comprehensiveness of the endeavour;
they've got an eye on crop profitability, but they're also improving
soil condition and experimenting with crops which will stem the
most prevalent dietary deficiencies—protein and vitamin C. So
some emphasis on maize and rice, and high hopes of a surprisingly*

tough cherry tree (which must have been the one our village
Headman was complaining about—'small round fruits') which
has very high vitamin C levels. We discussed the possibility of my
sending a couple of boys from my class over at planting time, to
learn from them and bring the skills back to the rest of the group.
There's a real feeling of purpose at their station which is lacking at
Oji Bend, and which I would very much like to bring us round to.

I ended up leaving later than I intended, and then an hour or
so along the homeward road, coming around a bend, I was suddenly confronted by two young boys and a herd of goats. It was
very bad luck. The road (dirt track) had been running through
open country, and we'd just come into an area of scrubby undergrowth and palm trees. I can't have been doing more than 20mph,
but even so, I was on top of them before there was time to brake.
Thank God no one was hurt. The boys and goats vanished, leaving
Luke and me about thirty yards off the track, with the car firmly
wedged between trees. I tried to reverse but the wheels span round
uselessly in the soft earth. There didn't actually seem to be any
damage to the car (apart from some hideous scratches) so we set
about finding sticks and stones to put under the wheels. I'd
thought only the day before about putting a proper toolbox with a
little axe and saw into the boot of the car. In fact I'd been about to
do it when Karl summoned me to talk to Obi's parents about why
I'm not entering him for the Standard 6 exam this time—if it
wasn't for that, the toolbox would have been in the car.

As it was, we were struggling; it was already dusk and the vegetation so tough it was impossible to tear branches off by hand. I
found a torch in the glove compartment and, of course, we had a
couple of pints of water; there wouldn't have been any problem in
settling down there for the night, apart from the fact that I knew
Miriam would be worrying herself to death. But Luke asked if he
could borrow the torch and look for help. I wasn't about to let him
wander off on his own, so I went with him on what seemed at first
an utterly hare-brained venture. He struck off purposefully into
the scrub along a tiny narrow path which looked to me as if it had

been made by animals—perhaps the goats. Then he swerved off
right and was suddenly trotting confidently along a much wider
path, in what was rapidly becoming pitch darkness. I could smell
smoke, I don't know whether that's what guided him, but suddenly there were dogs barking and a man's voice calling out. Luke
called back in the same tongue and motioned me to stop. Several
voices replied, and Luke turned the flashlight onto me, shining it
into my face so that I was dazzled.

'Luke—stop it—turn it away!'

'I show them, Mr David, so they can believe we are not thiefs,
one white man car need help.' He swivelled it away from me and
onto the path before us, where half a dozen men were clustered
blinking and staring at me.

He spoke to them rapidly again; one of the men replied in a low
voice, and was then interrupted by another who seemed to be
arguing with him. The discussion ran back and forth and I stood
there feeling rather uncomfortably irrelevant. At last Luke turned
back to me and said, 'They come help push car but they ask this
torch to keep away bad spirit, to walk back home safe.'

I agreed but before I could say any more, Luke passed the torch
to one of the men, who laughed and waved it round wildly, shining it in his friends' eyes so that they shrieked and ducked away.

'Luke, that wasn't the most sensible thing to do.'

They had turned and were striding away from us. Already the
light, shining on the path ahead of them, seemed small and distant.

'No no, they take us to the road. Quicker this way.'

I made out the shapes of huts and a corrugated iron shelter of
some kind; the smoke suddenly intensified, along with a warm
spicy smell of cooking that made my mouth water. Then we were
moving along two sides of a dark field. A second right took us onto
a much wider track, which I recognised belatedly as the road.
Luke called out to the man with the torch and he began to play it
over the bushes to the right of the track; eventually it caught the
metallic glint of the car. There was a lot of excited discussion and
I decided it was time to take control. I asked Luke to translate my

instructions, got in and started the engine. With three of them pushing either side of the bonnet, I put it into reverse and revved it, and after a sickening moment of hissing as the wheels span in the dirt, it suddenly lurched backwards. Once they saw we were in position to go they gave a whooping sort of cheer. I called out to thank them and asked Luke to tell them to visit the mission, and then we were off, headlamps conjuring the track ahead of us, the tiny torch bobbing crazily behind us as they waved goodbye.

It was half past nine when I looked at my watch, and nearly eleven when we finally reached the station. I told Luke he could go straight to bed. I had hoped Miriam would be asleep but when I opened the door she ran at me and flung her arms round my neck. Something extraordinary had happened to the room. It was littered with balloons and streamers, the kitchen table had been pulled out and spread with white sheets, and was laden with all kinds of food and bottles.

Poor Miriam had planned a surprise for my birthday. She'd taken Karl into her confidence and done a special food order, and everyone in the compound was alerted to come over to the bungalow for a feast when they heard the car coming in. At about seven, which was the time I'd promised to be home.

She'd already run the gamut from hating me for inconsiderately staying to tea with the Norwegians to being convinced I was dead in a ditch. She was absolutely exhausted, and I realised, more than a little tipsy, having drunk the best part of a bottle of wine on her own. I ate, and tried to make her eat something, and opened another bottle of wine.

'But why didn't you leave earlier, to drive home in daylight?'

'I didn't know what you were planning, how was I supposed to guess?'

'I wanted it to be a surprise. I wanted us to be able to feed everyone lovely things—I've spent every afternoon this week cooking . . .'

'But why on earth did you decide to do it on a day when you knew I had a long journey?'

'Because you were out of the way. It gave me time to get everything right. Saul and Benjamin moved the furniture for me, I made the trifle and put it in the clinic icebox to set—'

'Sweetheart, thank you, it's the most lovely surprise.'

'I could no more forget your birthday than I could forget my own. Don't you know that?'

I tried to reassure her but she was unstoppable.

'You think I'm hopeless, don't you? You make allowances for me as if I was a child—'

'Miriam—'

'It would never enter your head that I might be capable of making something happen for you all on my own—and now—' tears streaming down her face—'now it's all wasted.'

I couldn't get to the bottom of why she was so upset. I kissed her and she clung to me and I poured us both more wine, and gradually the snuffles and tears and kisses led to touching and an intensity that hasn't really been there since she first became pregnant.

We invited everyone to lunch the next day to eat up what had been saved; the trifle was past hope but the ham was still excellent, most of the savoury food was fine, and even the birthday cake, once I'd given it a furtive de-anting. Miriam was pale but she said she felt all right. I was pleased to see Karl making an effort to talk with her. It's interesting that he goes out of his way to be kind to her whilst maintaining this quiet hostility towards me. It certainly has the effect of mitigating my dislike of him: much as, I suppose, a parent finds it difficult to dislike anyone who is kind to their child. A situation of which I suspect he is rather manipulatively aware.

I worry about Miriam. She hasn't settled here as well as I have. That hysterical reaction to my lateness is symptomatic. Emotionally she's not at all stable. She's sometimes overwhelmed by homesickness, and she's had problems sleeping from the start. First it was the mosquito nets, and after that the heat and lack of air; she still says she feels stifled at night.

I wish she found it easier to make friends. But she's the only white woman, and the easy friendship and banter I can have with Luke or Okolie or the Headman in the village would be difficult for her—they're all rather nervous and polite with her, and she doesn't have the knack of putting them at their ease. She seems to get on well enough with the women in the clinic but I suspect she always hides behind that professional competence. If she ran a women's childcare class once a week she'd get to know some of the women properly and then I'm sure they'd accept her. But she's resistant to that suggestion, partly because of tiredness (which is fair enough) and partly I think because she really is afraid of emotional intimacy.

I suppose I knew before we came out here that I was the stronger partner in the marriage. But the situation is different now. There are so many claims on me, so much needing to be done; and the knowledge that if I'm an hour or two late because I'm helping a student or advising Okolie or visiting parents in the village, Miriam will be feeling abandoned, weighs me down and makes me reluctant to return to the bungalow, even though I know that my delaying will increase her unhappiness. I can only pray all this will be improved by the arrival of the baby; that the child will steady and fulfil her.

Things would, of course, have been easier if Dr Paul had been a friendlier character. In the beginning I left it entirely to Miriam to deal with him since he is her colleague rather than mine. But when it transpired, in our second month here, that she still hadn't had any proper conversation with him beyond purely practical issues, I determined to tackle him myself. At that point I really thought some of the fault might be Miriam's; I know her shyness can seem like haughtiness.

I went and found him in the clinic one afternoon after Miriam had finished work; he was sitting stooped over the counter there writing in a big notebook. Considering he's a doctor, he doesn't look very healthy. He's as thin as a rake, with rather sallow skin and lank thinning hair.

24/196

'Hello, Paul, can I have a word?'
He nodded, rather impatiently, I thought.
'Sorry, you're busy.'

'Patients' notes. What can I do for you?' His English is excellent, but his French origins are still perceptible in the slightly odd emphasis he gives to certain words. He's funded by some obscure French charity and we haven't been able to work out anything of his history. Feeling rather stiff and ill at ease standing there, I leant my weight against the big medicine cabinet and crossed my legs, but he immediately motioned me away. 'Careful please, it is not very strong.'

I gave a little laugh and deliberately sat astride the patients' chair. 'It's too hot to stand up!'

He didn't respond to my friendliness, so I was forced to carry on.

'I was wondering, you know, how things are going with my wife in the clinic?'

'Did she ask you to speak to me?'

'Lord no, of course not. Just between you and me, eh, I wondered how you're getting along.'

'Fine. She's a capable nurse.'

'Oh, good. So there aren't any problems.'

'Has she indicated that there are?'

'No, not at all. I mean, I know she's a good nurse. I know that sometimes people can find her a little shy, a little reserved, but—'

'She is extremely polite and competent.'

'I'm pleased to hear that.'

There was a silence during which he stared at me, clearly waiting for me to leave.

'I gather you're not keen on the idea of a family planning clinic.'

'These people are interested in having as many children as possible.'

'Not very good for the women, eh?'

'Most women breastfeed for two years. They don't sleep with

their husbands until the child is weaned. Contraception is perfectly irrelevant to them.'

His tone was almost aggressive, but I was determined to be pleasant, so I told him how much I admired his thorough knowledge of Ibo culture, and invited him to dinner.

'Thank you but I prefer to eat alone.' The silence lengthened and he didn't so much as blink.

I suddenly realised that I was actually imposing upon the poor fellow, he really does find it difficult to talk to people. I don't think he even knows he's being rude. He's simply a loner, and it's our bad luck—Miriam's bad luck in particular—that she's been saddled with him as a colleague. But at least I know the problem isn't with her, and I was glad to be able to tell her how highly he values her work.

Although of course she was prickly about it.

'How d'you know?'

'He told me.'

'When? You must have asked him.'

'Indirectly. I just asked him how you were getting along.'

'You've got no right to interfere. It's my work. I'm perfectly capable of dealing with Paul on my own.' She'd been working on the little herb garden she's attempting to grow in the shady area between the bungalow and the banana trees, and she was delightfully sweaty and grubby, with a streak of earth across her cheek and neck where she'd swatted at some insect.

'You're irresistible when you're angry.'

'Pig!'

I hugged her, and we were able to laugh together then. But I'm not letting this women's childcare class idea go—she needs to make some friends.

ON THE DAY BEFORE Mum died, Anne remembers the hospice nurse asking her if she wanted her morphine topping up.

'No thank you, I'm perfectly capable of doing it myself when I need it.' *Perfectly capable* is recognisable in a way that that earlier *emotionally dependent* is not. For a moment Anne considers the novel proposition that Father might sometimes have been wrong. Wrong about Miriam. Wrong about herself?

Was he wrong when she dropped out of art college? If he hadn't pressurised her so much to stay, if he hadn't argued and insisted—perhaps she would have been able to argue *herself* into staying.

But it was precisely because he wanted her to stay, because he thought it best, that she had to leave. Was that him being wrong or her making him wrong? Surely it was her acting, as ever, to disappoint him?

The day she went to tell him. She hadn't been home to the rectory for weeks, hadn't known that the kitchen walls would be covered in her rejects. He'd Blu-tacked them up, different prints off the same plates, over-inked, under-inked, paper creased, stuff from a pile that he'd found on her floor and asked if he could have.

'They're mistakes, Dad, they're no good.'

'I'd like to look through them, if you're done with them.'

He'd taken the rubbish and tacked it up as if it was good.

She was tired of it; her head ached from the fumes of the chemicals in the print room. Her lines were stiff and thick, her prints black and blobby. She was sick of being obsessed by a technique she couldn't master. Other students produced glowing canvases of colour or witty postmodern comments on art—a fire bucket was one that got commended, and a pencil that had been sharpened right away into fine coils of shavings that stretched the length of the room. She knew the images she produced were derivative. The teachers were embarrassed by her, she was sick of apologising for herself.

'I've left college, Dad.'

'You what?'

'I've left college. I'm going to apply for teacher training in the autumn.'

He insisted that they get to the bottom of it. 'Why don't I come along with you to speak to these tutors? If none of them even *like* engraving—'

'Etching, Dad. There's no point. I don't want to do it.'

'You did want to, you wanted to a year ago, what's happened to change your mind? You've made great strides these past few—'

'No I haven't, Dad. Let it go, OK.'

'You can't just give up at the first little setback. What would happen if we all did that?'

'I'm stopping doing something I'm no good at, that there's no market for anyway, and I'm going to do something socially useful. You should be pleased.'

'You're short-changing yourself, Anne. You've got a talent and you're turning your back on it—'

As she left the house he was still speaking. When she got back to her room he rang on the corridor phone. He persecuted her for days, so that her resolve hardened to adamant, and she wouldn't have gone back to her course if the lecturers had lain down and wept before her.

What if she had finished the course? Might things not have worked out better? Might she not have ended up with one or two pieces of work she liked; with a skill that she wasn't afraid to return to from time to time? Impossible to be an artist, of course, but not impossible to learn a technique and sometimes get pleasure from using it. Instead of giving up and being nothing. A teacher. Anne suddenly sees that the thought continues: if he *was* right that she should have continued—well, he could only be right then due to being wrong earlier. Because initially he'd been against her doing art. Which was one reason why she did it in the first place . . .

Anne puts a postcard of the ship (supplied free with one sheet of writing paper and two envelopes, in the drawer of her bedside table) into the diary for a bookmark. What she has done is not enough. She did check in the area where the open container was. She did check, all around. But even so. The stowaways may shut themselves in and sleep all day. That would be safest, the best way of avoiding anyone in the crew. Maybe they have slept all day and the man is right now creeping out to look for her. Maybe he assumes Anne can only visit them at night. Maybe her earlier relief, her jumping to the conclusion that they really don't need her, is simply a confirmation that she is irresponsible and cares for nobody. What if they are waiting for her now, this minute?

Suddenly convinced that this is true, Anne runs to the door, then stops again. Surely the whole thing is a misunderstanding—something which would be clear immediately to someone else? What if she's simply making a mistake? She's a terrible fool, an idiot who can't see in front of her eyes.

No. She'll have to go and look again. With a spasm of rage she acknowledges there will be no peace until she does. She slides her feet into her trainers. A wave of utter weariness washes over her. This afternoon, the heat, the dazzling light, the space— all that is null and void. She puts the tablets back in her pocket, leaves her cabin—waiting at the top of the stairs to check that nobody's about—and heads down to the container deck. Completely unsurprisingly, the Nigerian is waiting at the bottom of the stairs. He nods and beckons hurriedly when he sees her, then turns and she has to almost run to catch up with him. Past the containers, to left, to right, this is exactly the way she came this morning. Round a corner and another corner— and they are at the open container. It yawns blackly, there is no candle stub tonight. Anne catches at the man's arm, wanting to postpone the moment when she must see the woman. 'What's your name?'

'Joseph.'

'I'm Anne.'

'Anne.'

'Is she any better?'

He shakes his head. He's turning out his pockets—he passes her a nightlight then flicks a lighter over it, holding it steady till the wick flares up. He takes the nightlight from her and Anne follows him into the box. The woman is bad. Her face seems more sunken, her mouth half-open, gasping at the air.

'I have antibiotics. Here.' Anne drags them from her pocket and presses one through its foil. 'A drink?' The man sets down his nightlight and tilts a five-litre water container so that water sloshes into its upturned cap. He passes the cap to Anne, but the woman is flat on the floor.

'You'll have to lift her up a bit.'

He kneels beside the woman and slides his arm underneath her head and shoulders, raising her a little; Anne leans forward and puts the tablet between the woman's cracked lips, then tilts the thick plastic screwtop to her mouth. Water flows in, and down from the corners of her lips. But the woman gasps and struggles a little and does swallow—and even swallows two mouthfuls more, when Anne offers the water again.

Joseph lays her down and moves away.

'D'you know what's wrong with her? How long she's been ill?'

There's no reply. She can't really see his face. 'Why have you left Nigeria?'

'I was writing for a newspaper. They arrested the editor, they set fire to our offices.'

'But you can claim refugee status, if you're in danger—'

'Not till we are in England.'

'But on the ship—'

'No. Not on the ship.'

Anne climbs to her feet and follows him out of the box. She's sure he's wrong; all she needs to do is take control of this situation and it can be resolved happily for all concerned, all she needs to do is persuade him to trust her. There is a sudden grating sound behind her, as if the woman is choking. Hurriedly they lift her and Anne wipes her face with something from the floor, a T-shirt. Through its folds she feels the hard lump of the tablet straight away. There is nothing but the tablet and watery bile. The woman starts to breathe again, dragging lumps of air down her throat; the sound fills the box. There is a bad smell, she needs washing.

'She can't stay here.'

The man doesn't speak. If the woman can't keep the tablet down, it can't cure her.

'Let's take her up to my cabin.' It may not do any good, but at least she can be cleaned, at least she can be propped up with pillows, at least Anne can make some attempt—

'You tell nobody.'

'OK. Nobody need know. I'll keep the door locked.' Better to do something than nothing. Joseph slides his arms under the woman's shoulders and starts to lift her. Anne realises he expects her to take the feet. Are they going to walk through the ship with the woman's body slung between them?

'Wait. Can't we carry her on something? In something?' There isn't anything. A roll of carpet, Anne thinks, ludicrously; that's how they carry bodies out of houses. A linen basket, a box of some kind . . . a coffin.

'She's not heavy. I can carry her.' Joseph moves around and slides his arms under the woman's shoulders and knees; straightens up slowly. He holds her in his arms like a child.

'Can you manage?'

He nods. Anne grabs the blanket with an idea that she can hide the woman under it if they meet someone; ridiculous, since the woman's ragged breaths will give her away wherever she is. They make their way quickly to the stairs. Joseph rests against the stair-rail while Anne runs up to check the corridor is clear; then he follows her along the corridor surprisingly swiftly and quietly, to the next set of stairs. There is nobody there, but after the first flight he is gasping for breath.

'Give her to me—here –' Anne takes the weight in her arms, not much more than a large child, gets up the next flight, and he relieves her again for the last. There are shooting pains in Anne's arms and legs. She opens the door to the deck and darts ahead to unlock her cabin. Joseph staggers in and drops the woman onto the bed. There is a long moment of gasping and breathing. Anne feels her heart beating in her chest like the wings of a bird that can't get airborne.

Then Joseph reels to his feet and back to the door. 'Don't tell.'

Anne nods and he has gone. She doesn't even know the woman's name. Anne fills the little washbasin with warm water and dips in the hand towel. Clothes, take off the woman's clothes. First lock the door. As she undoes the buttons of the big man's shirt the woman is wearing, Anne suddenly thinks of her father's body. Did someone undress him, wash him, change his clothes? Someone at the undertaker's, it would be somebody's job. She couldn't have done it. But she is doing this. It is easier with a stranger. As she wrestles with the thin limbs and soiled garments, Anne notes that she is trembling with exhaustion, but simultaneously dreads the moment when she has finished; when she must simply lie on her bed and listen to the woman breathing or dying. Step by methodical step she finishes undressing her. The sharp scent of urine fills the air. Anne eases a towel under the naked body. The woman's stomach is big, skin stretched tight; as Anne rolls her back onto the towel she sees the shape of the belly shift and realises with a lurch of shock that the baby is moving, it is only a layer of skin away. It is close enough to be watching Anne.

She crouches beside the bed. She never felt hers move. It could have grown inside her like this woman's baby, been awake and moving while she slept—had a life of its own. A life of its own. Something wordless fills her mind, as if she is biting with her gums, biting with toothless gums on something very hard. When the feeling recedes she kneels up and waits a while, letting the vibration of the ship fill her emptiness. Soon she is able to get on with her task.

The rest of the woman's body is skinny—only this bloated sac of a belly. Anne raises one thin foot and gently wipes it with the wet towel. Start at the feet and work up. She can make herself do this. If the woman's eyes flickered open for a moment and took in a strange white woman wiping her limbs, raising and lowering her legs—that would be a different matter. But she's sleeping, she doesn't know, it is possible to have compassion for the anonymous body that contains the wriggling shape of a child. When she's done, Anne pulls a T-shirt of her own over the woman's head and wraps a towel around her lower half. There's no point in dragging knickers on and off. Raising the woman's head and shoulders and bracing them against her own shoulder, she pulls down the covers—then drags them from under the woman's back and buttocks, so she's lying on the bottom sheet and Anne can pull the covers up and over her. At last the woman is clean and decent and in bed. I could pay for her, Anne thinks wildly; pay her fare and then she's simply another passenger sharing my room. I'd call a doctor to my room-mate. Nothing to do with stowaways. Anne could pretend that they came aboard together; that she is astonished the captain didn't know she was there; that the steward can't have cleaned her room very thoroughly if he never even noticed . . .

She picks up the dirty clothes, the shirt and wrap-around skirt and underwear, and shoves them in a plastic bag. They can be washed in the morning. Turning off the lights she opens the cabin door and wafts it back and forth a few times to let in some fresh air. At last she shuts and locks it. It seems to her the woman is breathing more quietly; though when she feels her forehead, it is still just as hot. With the end of her toothbrush she crushes another tablet in a glass and mixes it with water; props a couple of pillows under the woman's head and dribbles the mixture into her mouth. She splutters as it hits her throat and about half is spilled—but equally, half is swallowed.

Anne allows herself to fall back on her own bed. Her mind is a little circle of space surrounded by clamouring questions. If the woman goes into labour . . . if the woman becomes sicker . . . if the woman regains consciousness and panics . . . Every scenario leads to danger. For a moment though Anne can be peaceful, just for a moment.

She imagines she is a patient being cured by a Victorian doctor. Leeches suck her blood till they are sated and drop off, to be replaced by hungry new ones. And the patient, draining of blood and colour, gradually becomes lighter, paler, more insubstantial, until she simply floats and drifts away whitely into the ether, no longer weighted down by that cargo of rich red blood.

She must have been asleep because the retching and gasping seemed to be coming from far away. Now they are closer. She sees the watery solution she forced the woman to swallow earlier. She feels almost ready to cry. If the woman can't keep water down she will die quickly. Also the baby. A double death. Crawling from her bed Anne wipes the dribble and offers a teaspoonful of plain water. The woman swallows three teaspoonfuls in all. Anne puts the water down. She is stuck in her room with a sick woman who has a baby trapped inside her. If only she could go away and leave the steward to sort it in the morning.

If she could think of any way out of this, how happy she would be. But the way out will be as bad as being in here. The way back is as bad as the way forward. Anne twists the cheap metal teaspoon in her hands like a key.

The hours between four and seven seem to pass more quickly. She must be ready when the steward knocks. She showers and dresses hurriedly, and feeds the woman six spoonfuls of water. When he knocks for breakfast she is standing ready; opens the door a crack and slips out to join him. She has £10 folded ready in her hand. 'Morning. I wanted to ask you, would it be alright if you don't come into my cabin any more?' She holds out the money, the man stares at it in bewilderment. 'I'd rather make my own bed and so on, I hope you don't mind, I'll keep it clean and tidy in there—it's just, I'm a poor sleeper, so sometimes I sleep in the day . . .'

The man is still staring at her as if she's mad. Is £10 not enough?

'Here, please take this.'

'You don't want your bed making?'

'Thank you, no. I prefer to do it myself.'

He looks hurt.

'I—I'm not complaining or anything, you've been very good at your job—I just prefer to do for myself, that's all.'

The steward takes the £10 and marches off. She has offended him. Utterly, utterly incompetent and useless. What would Father say? 'You've got enough to do without coming and picking up after me. Prefer my own mess, to be honest, know where I've left things.' Easy, friendly, why can't she be like that? He knows the steward will want to do what he wants, that the steward will be glad to humour him. Whereas Anne knows the steward will have no desire to humour her; indeed, it is she must humour him.

She can't face breakfast; she'll sit in her room till it's over then sneak in for some fruit and a coffee. But when she looks at the woman she wonders if she should be fed? Not if she keeps vomiting. Also the woman can't be left in case she goes into labour. But if she does go into labour what use will Anne be? Anne stumbles out of the cabin, locking the door behind her, and finds her way to the rail. There is low cloud on the horizon; the sun is hidden but it's still warm, there are large slow-rolling waves. Staring at the even waves and their grey impassive emptiness, Anne thinks of Lowry's painting of the sea, how the water fills the whole canvas and gives nothing, no promise, no direction, just an implacably other place, a desert of water, lacking all meaning. How long must this voyage go on? Already it feels interminable. With irritation Anne realises someone is coming.

'G'day. Thought I might find you here.' The Australian—the first mate. He has heard something. Someone saw them last night, staggering up the stairs. The steward has been to him about Anne's suspicious desire to keep him out of her cabin.

'What is it?'

'Just letting people know—bit of rough weather up ahead. We'll hit it tonight. Tail end of a cyclone.'

'Oh.'

'You get seasick?'

'No. I don't know. I mean a cross-channel ferry is the most I've ever—'

He smiles. 'I reckon you'll feel the difference.'

Anne thinks of the woman rolling and thrashing around on her bed in a rough sea. Being sick. Going into labour. Robbie comes to lean on the rail beside her.

'You don't eat breakfast?'

'Sometimes.'

'Well, make sure you have lunch. Like I tell the new boys, chucking on an empty stomach's no good.' He is kind. He knows what to do.

'Thank you. Do you have a moment?'

'Sure.'

'I—I just wanted to ask something.'

'Go ahead.'

'I wondered if you had ever been on a ship that had stow-aways?'

He is looking out to sea; after a little pause he says, 'Uh-huh. On this route, Africa–Europe.'

'What happened?'

'Depends on the captain. The captain'll want to get 'em ashore as quick as he can.'

'But when you were there—what actually happened?'

'The first time, they weren't discovered, the buggers ran ashore at Tilbury and we took the bloody rap.'

'Were they allowed to stay in England?'

He shrugs.

'And the other time?'

'We put them ashore at Abidjan.'

'Were their lives in danger?'

He laughs. 'They think they'll get rich in England. They got no idea.'

'If there were people whose lives *were* in danger, really, they would be allowed to stay on board, wouldn't they?'

He glances at her as if she has suddenly said something inter-esting. 'Sure. Genuine refugees.'

'And if they needed help—say medical help—what would happen?'

Again he glances at her. Then he shifts his position, turning to lean his back against the rail, folding his arms. 'You been exploring?'

She has given them away. No, he's guessed. She still doesn't have to tell him anything. 'Is it true there's no doctor aboard?'

He's staring at her, a slight smile around his narrowed eyes. 'That's what they tell the passengers. But we have a medic who can deal with most stuff, the crew need that.'

Of course. If there's a medic then the woman can be helped. No need for airlifts or turning back. Everything can be solved on board. She realises Robbie is waiting for her to speak. His smile has become mocking.

'You wanna tell me? If there's someone here who's crook—'

'They mustn't be sent back.' It comes out in an embarrassed blurt. 'I'm sorry, I agreed not to tell anyone, so I have to ask you to promise.'

'Of course.' He's leaning closer to her now, somehow surrounding her back, his voice is lower and more confidential. 'These types can be terrified. They don't know where to turn for help.'

'Yes. That's it. You won't tell anyone?'

'Trust me.' He lays his hand on her arm and gives a little squeeze. 'We'll keep it between you and me, OK? The captain's got no choice, he'd have to send them back. But if I deal with it myself . . .'

Joseph must be satisfied by this, surely?

'OK?' He smiles at her. 'Don't look so scared.'

Anne imagines falling against his chest and bursting into tears. He knows what to do. He will look after things.

'When did you find them?'

'Yesterday. The day before.'

He slides his hand over hers on the rail. 'You done good, kid. They on the container deck?'

'Yes.'

'How many?'

'Two. Well, one really that needs help, she's very ill.'

'A woman?' He's surprised.

'Yes, she's pregnant, but there's something wrong.'

'OK. You tell me exactly where they are. No need for you to go down there again.'

'She's not down there, she's in my cabin.'

There is a silence. It occurs to Anne that he will perhaps think she has helped them to come aboard—that she is in some way responsible for their presence. So she tells him how she first saw Joseph outside the laundry, how they carried the woman up to Anne's cabin. Robbie listens attentively; his hand still covers her own, the ends of his fingers making little soothing stroking movements across the backs of her fingers. 'OK. Let her stay in your cabin for the day, she's safe there. I'll bring the medic this evening when nobody'll notice.'

'Thank you.'

'Don't worry about the crew. They'd do anything for me.'

'Thank you so much.'

'No worries.' He grins and steps back from the rail, loosing her hand. 'Glad to be of service.' He winks and she blushes instantly, she can feel the stupid heat flooding her face. 'You're pretty when you blush.' He's gone before she can even register the words. Then a second, longer blush engulfs the first.

The day passes interminably slowly; every hour on the hour Anne feeds the woman a few spoonfuls of water; once she changes the towel between her legs. Then she sits back on her own bed and opens the diary.

May 5, 1962

The trouble with Mark Udom came to a head last week. I've lost count of the number of mornings I've had to go and settle his class until he rolls along at eight or even later. I've bent over backwards to be friendly; discussed every change I'm making in school in minute detail with him. But there's always a difficult atmosphere. Often he'll deliberately disregard some instruction I give him; I've asked him to set his class a regular weekly comprehension, and so far this term he's done one. And there are three bright girls who had a good attendance record in their class last year, who have completely stopped coming to school after six weeks with Mark. Girls are the very last ones we need to lose. I've asked him twice to check with their parents but I don't believe for a moment that he has done.

When he didn't turn up on Friday I was stumped. My class were doing a practice exam, and although I set his class some work when I realised he wasn't there, they were restless and giddy, and there's not enough room to put them in with mine. Jacob saved the day, appearing quietly in the doorway and offering to take Mark's class. It turned out Mark had told him he was going for an interview at a government school, where he'd get paid twice as much. I don't see how he could get an interview without a reference from me, or why on earth he told Jacob rather than me that he was going. When he rolled up on Monday morning I told him he'd behaved unprofessionally and he went straight to Karl and handed in his notice. Good riddance, frankly, I don't see why I should carry someone who's driving away the very students we should be doing most to help. I've got three trainee teachers on placement from the end of the month—if they're any good I'll ask one to stay.

MAY 16, 1962

I've had a run-in with Karl about the shelter for the clinic. If I was him I'd be delighted to see signs of initiative and responsibility from others on the station, but not Karl. Miriam has several times mentioned the problem of the patients having nowhere to queue; they cluster around the clinic, hugging the shade as it moves around the building, and at midday they desert to sit under the banana trees behind the church. Now the rains have come they sometimes huddle in the church itself. I had a word with Luke a while ago, and he said he could get me four volunteers for a couple of days, so we started to erect a shelter. It's basic, not much more than a thatch on poles, but better than nothing. Karl came out just as we were raising the thatch, and asked me for a word. Apparently he should have been consulted. I said I hadn't thought it important enough to bother him with, and that produced one of his long pained silences. I was already half out of the room when he finally said, 'I'm not sure you appreciate how things work here, David.'

'What d'you mean?'

'We've had an undertaking for government money to build a new clinic with waiting room.'

'I know, but—'

'If we continue to be patient, that funding will materialise. If in the interim we improve our own facilities and create a waiting room, they'll be at perfect liberty to build the government clinic elsewhere.'

'But it's only a shack, anyone can see that. I gather from Miriam that your government money was promised eighteen months ago. It could take as long again before—'

'If we have a waiting room, we have a waiting room.'

There was a silence. I could hear Luke shouting at my volunteers, telling them to lift higher. 'What d'you want me to do? Send the men home?'

'I'd be grateful if you'd discuss things in future before rushing in.'

'Right. Sorry. I will.'

As I walked back to the clinic I could see they had started to secure the thatch, and one of them called out to me triumphantly, 'What you think, Mr David?'

'Good work. I think you're doing a very good job.'

Touchingly, on hearing this, they redoubled their efforts. It would have been utterly destructive to have stopped them. The contradictions, anyway, in Karl's position, are pretty striking; of course it should be a government clinic, not a mission one. But would they prefer to take over a dilapidated, run-down place, or buildings that the community are renewing and are clearly committed to? When Paul leaves, a government-trained midwife will supposedly be put in to work alongside Miriam, and take over solo when we go. They won't get another doctor out here in the back of beyond. But if Karl was fighting for the place, letting local politicians know how vital it is (it's not possible to drive to hospital for four months of the year, for heaven's sake), why shouldn't they upgrade their plans and base a doctor here as well? Instead of which, he waits passively and the place deteriorates around him.

One delightful side effect of this thatching work was that Ukabegwu's father invited me to the boy's coming-of-age celebration. It's the first time I've been invited to one of their feasts, and I feel I have been accepted as a friend. Traditionally the villagers (perhaps only the males?) class themselves in age groups, so all those born within a certain period of time celebrate their coming of age together. Ukabegwu and the other boys were decked out in coloured scarves and strips of cloth, with strings of cowries and bells around their arms and legs; they danced through the village followed by a chanting mob of relatives and well-wishers, and in particular a group of very lovely girls who darted gracefully in and out of the dance to wipe the boys' sweating faces with their handkerchiefs. I asked the Headman what the relatives were singing; the boys' praise-names, he told me. They shout out rhetorical questions about the boys: 'Who makes the earth shake when he walks?' 'Who is as strong as a tiger?' and each answers with their own boy's name. As I watched these energetic young men and beautiful happy girls I thought sadly of our culture's equivalent: a 21st birthday perhaps, where everyone stands around awkwardly getting drunk.

Towards the end of the evening Ukabegwu's father asked me some detailed questions about the church. I'm pretty sure he's interested in converting, which would give me tremendous satisfaction—to have reached the father through the son. He already seems familiar with a number of Bible stories, he told me with pride that he knows Jesus can multiply bread and fishes. He wants to know where the land of milk and honey is! I shall ask Jacob to offer him some religious instruction.

In general Karl maintains a noticeable distance between himself and the Nigerians in the compound, even Jacob—but especially the servants. Which I know is very much a characteristic of his generation. The fact that he can remain untouched by Independence and the changes of the last few years feels rather dangerous, as if a partially sighted man is steering the ship. I've been made particularly uncomfortable by his treatment of his houseboy. Saul is a shy, silent soul, who seems to go about his duties in a permanent state of apprehension. I've never seen Karl speak to him other than to give an order. Our boy Luke is irrepressibly cheerful, and since I've helped him with the cooking, is always ready for a chat with me about his sister's children, the size of his uncle's yam crop, and so on. Indeed, I'm *glad to say he's not afraid to bring his problems to me.*

A couple of weeks ago he asked if we could talk. He solemnly told me he wants to get married but can't afford the bride price her family are asking, and will I advance it to him out of his wages? £75 is the asking price; a quite incredible sum for a man like Luke. I told him the most I could possibly give him in one go is £25, and he seemed to accept that. I wrote down the figures for him—his weekly pay, and what it will be if I take out 5s a week repayment—that it will take him nearly two years to repay me. Then we shook hands and I promised him his £25 next week when my pay comes in. His fiancée is sixteen and to begin with will stay on with her parents in the village. (Just as well; she certainly couldn't share that hovel he and Saul sleep in. I shall have to suggest to Karl that we get a new hut built for the happy couple.) It was pleasant to see the huge grin of relief spread across his face.

It's a small enough favour, yet it seems to have earned me his complete devotion. Complications as well, though; on Sunday morning after church he asked me eagerly whether I would be willing to make the same arrangement for Saul.

'But Saul is Mr Karl's houseboy.'

'Yes, sir.'

'Then he must ask Mr Karl himself.'

Luke shook his head. Apparently Karl makes a point of never advancing wages. I should have thought he would be able to discriminate between reasonable and unreasonable requests; however, it's not for me to meddle in affairs between him and his houseboy. It does make me think again of an idea I mentioned to Miriam a while ago, though, of setting up a little savings society here on the mission compound, that members (and I'm thinking particularly of the staff) can save with and take loans from, at a minimal charge. It would be an excellent way of inculcating better money-management, and of preventing people like Saul and Luke from spending all their pay the day they receive it. (Miriam tells me they give most of it to their relatives, and it's true that last

*week Luke even had to ask me to carry over his 5s repayment to
next week, because his sister needed new clothes for her children,
to go to her brother-in-law's wedding.)*

JUNE 20, 1962

*Poor Miriam was wretched when I came in tonight, streaming
with sweat and plagued by flying ants which had somehow again
got into the bedroom. I suspect she left the door open, although of
course she denies it. I swatted the lot then bathed her face and feet
in cool water. When she was comfortable I read to her (Anna
Karenina) until she felt she could sleep. Then I came out here on
the veranda to write this and admire the reappearance of the
stars—we've had nothing but rain for the past week. The lamp has
been put out three times by insects, that ecstatic final frenzy of
fluttering as they approach the flame, and then the sudden sizzle
and stink of burn, and the guttering to dark. It is almost a welcome
punctuation. I've sat here each time in the new dark watching the
shadows of the palms emerge against the sky, listening to the frogs
croaking by the pump. I feel at peace here now, indisputably—it
was the right choice to come. What we can do here, the difference
we can make, is something that will be with us both forever.
Already that early talk of 'Let's take stock after six months' feels
irrelevant. My trainee teachers are as eager as my students and
since there's a constant demand from the college in Umuahia for
rural placements with experienced teachers, I can keep Mark's
class going simply with trainees (scrupulously supervised, of
course) and spread the teaching skills faster and further. Paul's
going to stay on till Miriam's had the baby, and they seem to be
making good progress with the child vaccination programme.*

*As for the church itself, if I can get four volunteers at the drop
of a hat to build a shelter for the clinic, I'm willing to bet most of
the congregation would lend a hand over something as important
as a new church. Karl's weary caution strikes again: the school*

committee already takes money from the villagers and provides a team of volunteers to keep the school buildings in repair. If we ask for volunteer labour for a church, he claims the villagers' goodwill could be exhausted.

But what an incredible opportunity to pass on building skills to half the population of the village! If we could get student brick-layers and carpenters from the technical college at Umuahia, they could teach the boys in Standard 6 and their fathers and older brothers. We could have a church that would also be an object lesson in how to build—in which the villagers themselves would be able to feel real pride. Likewise the cassocks, altar cloth, etc. I suspect the Mothers' Union would leap at the chance to do some sewing for the church. We asked Miriam's mother to put out feel-ers after some old sewing machines and she's collected two treadles and two electric for us; they're shipping to Lagos over the summer. Miriam can teach the women how to use them—a new skill in the village!

The Mothers' Union are astonishingly enthusiastic: you can't go into the church without falling over two or three of them sweeping and polishing; they hold sway entirely over the organi-sation of the Sunday school, christenings, Easter, all the major festivals. Karl has given them a considerable amount of power which would be a very good thing but for the fact that they're in a state of enmity with the non-Christian women in the village. Miriam's coming across some of the traditionalists in the clinic and they're quite intimidated by characters like Perpetual Ikobi and Catherine Anoka; accusations have been flying around about some traditional women's ceremony for initiating a new wife into the village (involves her making payment and giving a broom to the pagan village wives, I can't get to the bottom of it but the married Christian women want to substitute a Christian version so they can be paid too). And now there's an argument brewing over which women can join the Mothers' Union. Officially it is only those who lead Christian (ie. monogamous) lives, but a couple of the prime movers are first wives of men with several wives. Karl should have nipped this in the bud—much too difficult to extricate them now.

It's a pity Miriam isn't willing to interest herself more in all this; as a man I'm rather in the dark, but I get the sense that the women run and control much more of what goes on in the village than we realise. Certainly they grow most of the food and sell the surplus, it's they who support their children, often they who supply the school fees, whilst maintaining an appearance of utmost deference to their husbands.

I should note here with shame that in one respect at least I judged Mark Udom unfairly. I blamed him for the fact that several girls had dropped out from his class, but Miriam now tells me she has learned, from women at the clinic, that when girls begin to menstruate they are secluded for up to three months—confined to the parental home and given special education in women's matters. Since the girls in Mark's class are mostly twelve to fourteen that is almost certainly what happened—and he would of course have been too embarrassed to explain it to me. I'm very sorry we weren't able to get on better, Mark and I, it's a great pity our relationship started off on such a difficult footing.

I'm haunted rather by that extraordinary child-like quality in some of the older girls; a kind of dare-devil shyness, which makes European females of their age seem old and staid in comparison. Is it because they're so sheltered, the least thing out of the ordinary sends them into an ecstasy of wide-eyed giggling excitement? Teaching them fills me with energy: I suppose it's the delight one feels in being able to show things to a child for the first time. They do seem to have an almost prelapsarian innocence.

JULY 2, 1962

Okolie completed the first set of bookshelves successfully, and came back last Monday to start the clinic shelving. I left him to it, but then Karl informed me in passing that 'your friend', as he

calls him, was up to his old tricks. I went to check on the garden-
ing hut and found Okolie sitting against the wall, eyes closed.

'Okolie? Okolie? Are you all right?'

It was clear he had been working; there were several planks
lying around on the grass, they had been cut to length and sanded.
I couldn't really object to him sleeping, it wasn't as if I was paying
him by the hour. I turned away but as I did so I heard giggling.
Looking back I saw that he was watching me under his lowered
eyelids. Then he put his finger to his lips and giggled again.

'What's the matter? Okolie?' *It was obvious immediately that*
he was under the influence. When I shouted at him to pull him-
self together he began to sing under his breath, watching me
craftily all the time. There wasn't much I could do so I left him to
it—trust Karl to have found him in that state.

When I walked back past the shed an hour later he wasn't
there. I concluded he'd probably curled up somewhere to sleep it
off, and went back to my work for the afternoon. In fact, I have to
admit, I forgot about him. I was teaching the grammar school
entrants later that afternoon, and after that dealing with the
man from Umuahia Generator stores, who I'd asked up to look
over the compound. Installing a new generator is something Karl's
been talking about since we arrived. A constant supply of elec-
tricity would dramatically improve life here, especially in the
clinic where a proper fridge would mean they could keep a much
wider range of drugs to hand. The current diesel-powered 'light
plant', as Karl calls it, is a nightmare. It's solemnly switched on
at six and off at nine every night, but generally conks out after
less than an hour anyway. It's only fit to power up the radio and
whet our appetites for proper light—and sometimes it doesn't
even manage that. With reliable electric lighting, Paul could
better conduct the odd emergency operation at night (that poor
woman brought in with a ruptured uterus, Miriam ended up
standing holding a torch in each hand while he worked); evening
classes become a more realistic proposition, and we could begin to
teach the use of electrical tools and sewing machines.

By [the time I'd shown him round and we'd discussed size, installation costs, etc, and taken the whole thing to Karl for his blessing, it was after seven and quite dark. I simply went back to the bungalow, ate with Miriam, and fell into bed by 9.30.

Saul came knocking at the door as I was having breakfast next morning, to report that a thief had been in the night. Turns out Karl had asked him to fix a broken door handle; he'd gone to look for a screwdriver in the garden hut and found half the tools missing.

I hurried out after him. The hut was exactly as I'd seen it the previous afternoon—planks scattered across the grass, door wide open, no sign of Okolie. The toolbox was still there but a lot of the smaller stuff had gone: hammers, spanners, screwdrivers, pliers. I got Saul to help me clear up and lock the shed, and was then obliged to go and tell Karl. I have no doubt it gave him great pleasure to inform me (without even looking up from his book) that this is exactly what Okolie did last time he was employed here. I told him I'd pay for new tools myself if I couldn't retrieve them.

I could hear the clanking of the old treadle sewing machine when I got back to the bungalow; Miriam busy making some little sheets and a tiny nightgown for the baby out of one of our old cotton sheets. She's resourceful about that sort of thing, I must say. And just as well, given the state of our finances. She was in a good mood as she showed me the nightgown, very pleased with her notion of little ties at the side to avoid the need for buttons— so when I'd admired it I told her about the business with Okolie.

She put the gown down. 'What are you going to do?'

'Karl's attitude from the start has been the man's a hemp smoker and therefore evil and we should send him packing.'

'Maybe Karl doesn't have enough faith in his own ability as a Christian to believe he can turn Okolie around.'

'That's why I want to give him a second chance.'

She smoothed the gown on her knee and folded it up. 'You're right.'

I thought later that night how lonely Karl must sometimes

*feel. Miriam and I may have our differences but at that bedrock
level of faith and understanding we are completely at one. She
believes as passionately in the transforming power of Christ's
love as I do. In fact the same thought was in both our heads,
because we knelt and said our prayers together that night, which
we haven't done for a while, and thanked Him for the gift of each
other.*

JULY 15, 1962

*Okolie came back a couple of days later. He was waiting, very
shamefaced, outside the schoolroom when I finished teaching. I
let him in after the class had gone, so that we could talk privately.*

'I'm sorry, Mr David, please forgive me.'

'You must bring back the tools.'

*'I can't. I sold them. I don't know what it is, a kind of devil
comes over me.'*

'Where's the money?'

*'I spent it.' He opened his arms wide in grief. 'I spend every
penny on hemp for me and my age-group. I am so bad.'*

*There was a slightly theatrical element to this display which I
disliked very much—and I also thought he was far too complacent
in his expectation of forgiveness. So I played the hard man for a
while, telling him that Karl wanted to call the police, talking
about how he was hindering the work of the mission, that we
have no money to replace the tools and so on, and pretty soon he
was weeping. I left him to stew for a while and when I went back
he begged me to tell him how he could redeem himself. Miriam
had made the suggestion that he could do some work for us,
preparing the baby's room and making a cot, for which we would
pay him—which money could then be used to replace the missing
tools. The problem was the tools would have to be replaced before
he could do any work; also he could hardly be expected to live on
nothing whilst he was working. I couldn't see any way round*

other than to dip into our emergency-fares-home fund, so I told him to come back the next day after I'd had a chance to talk to Miriam.

We were both anxious about spending some of that money. It is a safety net, and I think Miriam particularly has a sense that if anything goes wrong in the later stages of her pregnancy—or indeed, once the baby is born—we could use it to get home quickly to good hospitals. I reminded her that a character like Okolie has very few chances. Without our help, he'll almost certainly end up in prison. And in our hearts we both know that if we need to go home, God will provide. After some discussion she agreed, and I gave her a kiss. We decided we would tell Okolie he could sleep on our veranda while he did the work. Then I had to go and inform Karl.

'I told you I don't want him on the compound.'

I made it clear that the mission would not suffer financially in any way from my personal decision to take responsibility for Okolie.

'The money's not the point. What sort of an example does this set? The man smokes, he steals, he betrays our trust—and far from being punished, he's rewarded.'

'But a demonstration of forgiveness—'

'Makes us look like fools. Read your history. It's exactly what went wrong on some of the early missions: bleeding-heart missionaries taking in slaves, adulterers, crooks—making a church out of the outcasts the decent Africans despised, and then expecting them to queue up to join it.'

We parted on very bad terms, with Karl categorical that at the least hint of any further trouble he would get the police on to Okolie. 'You can't help people like that. Save your energies for those you can help.'

I bit back the reply that sprung to my lips: 'What if Christ had behaved in that way?'

THE WOMAN IS STILL ASLEEP. At lunchtime Anne locks the door on her and takes her washing down to the laundry— then goes and eats with the captain and a handful of officers. They are preoccupied by the weather, which will apparently be worse near the coast; there is talk of not calling at Abidjan, of pressing straight on to Europe. The captain is called to the radio and, nodding their excuses, the officers swiftly follow him. Anne sits alone at the table. She is disturbed by the leftover food on their plates. Father again.

It was only a few days after mother's death; Anne had just moved in with him. They were eating together at the kitchen table. When she'd finished she pushed a couple of forkfuls of mashed potato to the side of her empty plate.

Father looked at her without moving. 'What's that?'

'What's what?'

'On your plate.'

'Potato.'

'I hope you're not thinking of leaving it.'

'I'm full up. And it's cold.'

'You eat it before you leave this table.'

She was so shocked that she did. At home she and Mum had always left the end crusts of sliced bread, but when she did that at the rectory, he ate them. Every loaf was eaten to the end, even if it was three or four days old. Leftovers, no matter how minute the quantity, were scraped into little plastic boxes, put in the

fridge and eaten the next day without fail. Fat that came out of
frying bacon and sausages was poured into a jar and used to fry
the onion for the following night's spaghetti. Bones of fish,
chicken, any meat, were boiled to make stocks. Vegetables were
scrubbed not peeled, and no matter how bad, no food was ever
thrown away. She had to empty her cat's dish surreptitiously,
when the milk had soured, hoping he hadn't noticed. She used
to wonder if it was because he said grace—something to do
with not being able to throw food away once it's had God's
blessing. Because he never showed anger over anything else,
she became desperately anxious to do as he wished over food,
and learned to clear her plate scrupulously and even mop it
clean with a slice of bread, as he did. He never changed—she
remembers a pub lunch they ate together a few months ago,
where big chunks of cheese were served with the bread.
Watching him in silence as he rolled the leftover cheese in a
serviette and slipped it into his pocket. To this day she has to
assess and mentally weigh up the amount of food she will put on
her plate before serving herself, because getting it wrong—
taking more than she can eat—will be bad. It is better to go
hungry than to have too much.

Before she returns to her cabin Anne goes to the rail. There is
a strange feel to the weather, the sky is a hazy metallic grey, still
and close, and the water almost greasy, its swell sluggish.
Everything is in slow motion, arrested, waiting for the main
event. For a moment she is seized by terror at the foolhardiness
of the ship, ploughing its way across this greasy sea towards the
storm, its white wake blazing unabashed.

Back in the cabin nothing at all has changed. The woman
lies, mouth half open, eyes closed, sucking at the air. Perhaps
she's in a coma? Perhaps she can't be anything more now than
just a life-support machine for the creature inside her, which is
growing and moving and developing all the time she lies so still.
Her presence in the cabin makes a mounting pressure in Anne's

head, it will be hard to bear it until this evening, thank god she doesn't have to endure it any longer than that. She thinks of Robbie's kindness, his competence—and his sudden whispered remark about her prettiness.

In the evening, time speeds up. After crawling from three to four and four to five it is suddenly rushing towards seven; she has not prepared the woman for the medic's visit, she hasn't fetched her clothes up from the laundry, the cabin isn't tidy. Too late to fetch the clothes now, he may come while she's out of the cabin. Did he mean before or after dinner? And what about Joseph? He will be waiting to hear from her—

Suddenly there's a knock at the door—earlier than she expected. During dinnertime, in fact. Of course, she realises in a rush, that's sensible, all the officers are in the dining room. Anne opens the door a few inches and Robbie steps forward out of the darkness.

'It's OK.' He comes straight in and moves to look at the woman; the medic is behind him. Anne is surprised to see he is in the grey crew overalls, she had expected him to be dressed like an officer. Robbie nods to him and together they bend over the woman, clasping the bedding round her, and pick her up.

'Isn't he going to examine—?'

'Don't worry.' Robbie repositions himself so he is supporting the woman's head and shoulders. 'We're taking her down to sickbay. More facilities there.' He nods to her to open the door for them, and before she can speak again, they're gone. The woman has gone, the bed is empty, stripped bare, just a creased bottom sheet and dented pillow.

Too late, Anne thinks she should have followed them. She opens the cabin door again but they're gone, they must have already negotiated the door at the top of the stairs—where is the sickbay? She should have gone with them to open doors, and so she can explain to Joseph where his wife is. But now there's nothing but the empty deck. She closes her door and sits on the bed. That's it then. No longer her responsibility. And

Robbie didn't even look at her, just came to get the woman. Of course. He has a job to do, what did you imagine? She stares vacantly at the empty bed.

There's a quick knock at the door and the handle is twisted. Before she can stand up Robbie has come back in. 'Alright?' He's breathing heavily, as if he's run to get here—his face and hair somehow full of wind and energy. Is it the storm, she wonders in confusion, is the storm beginning? She stands up and he comes straight to her, smiling into her face. 'Alright? She's safe now, she's in good hands.'

'Has the doctor already seen—?'

He puts his hands on her shoulders and gives her a slight shake. 'She'll be right. He'll take a look at her. If she needs drugs, he's got 'em. OK?'

'If he *can't* help her . . .?'

'He'll get someone who can.'

Anne nods dumbly.

'He'll do it for me, I look after my men. So cheer up, kid.' He pulls her to him and wraps his arms around her in a big comforting hug. For a moment she is gratefully enfolded like a child in the kindly warmth of it, her face buried in his shoulder, then she becomes aware of the pressure of his body, the whole length of it, against hers. She starts to shift and he hugs her more tightly to him. She can feel the shape of his penis stiffening against her hip. She jerks her head back and his face is a blur, his lips crushing down on hers.

There is a moment, Anne remembers afterwards, a moment quite soon, where he breaks away and holds her nearly at arm's length again, staring into her face.

'Alright?' he asks with a grin. They are both quite still, then she gives a little tiny nod. And he is on her like a starving man, clawing at her clothes, pushing her onto the bed with an infectious urgency which makes it hard to disentangle and remember afterwards, she can't stop feeling shocked, she can't quite believe it was her.

Afterwards he looks at her and laughs. 'How're you doing? Better?'

Anne laughs herself, her face as strange to it as her body is to the sudden intense pleasure he has given her. He gives her buttock a gentle slap. 'Nothing to beat it, mate. Nothing to beat it.' He stirs and shifts himself from the bed.

Anne feels a ripple of embarrassment, of shyness, even fear. What on earth has she done? Already he is a stranger, the big man groping around the floor for his clothes. His legs and chest are covered in thick black hair, he is utterly unconcerned by his own nakedness, or by her watching.

When he's dressed he sits on the chair to lace his shoes. 'The man,' he says.

'The man?'

'Stowaway, the other one. Where do I find him?'

It's an unpleasant reminder. 'I haven't seen him today. Can I bring him to the sickbay?'

Robbie shakes his head decisively. 'Too dangerous, he'd be seen. Tell him to meet me, I'll come to the container deck.' He consults his watch. 'Can you find him now?'

Anne feels a great reluctance to go anywhere. She wants to lie and digest what's happened—maybe sneak to the dining room for some cheese and biscuits when the coast is clear, then sit on her own and go over the last hour carefully. Nothing like this has ever happened before. But it's true she has to speak to Joseph. He will be worrying. 'Yes. I'll get dressed and go.'

'Tell him to meet me at eleven. On the container-deck stairs.'

'OK.'

'You want me to visit you again?' A knowing smile. Anne is flushed with embarrassment again. How can she have done it with a man who uses this kind of innuendo? He makes her think of a gigolo. He comes back and crouches beside the bed, placing his hand at the back of her neck, stroking. 'Tonight? In the morning?'

Anne laughs with embarrassment. She doesn't know what to say.

'You want me to come back?' He pulls her head closer to him.

'I—yes.'

He lets her go. 'Good.' He pats her thigh approvingly then turns away. He goes out with his head held high (Anne realises with horror that the door wasn't even locked) and shuts the door behind him without looking back. Slowly and reluctantly Anne begins to dress.

When Anne gets halfway down the container-deck stairs she stops and waits, eyes searching the dimness for any sign of movement. There is nothing, and she goes on down slowly, ears straining after a footfall or a breath that might suddenly stand out from the background noise of the engines, eyes peeled for a lighter shade against the background blackness. At the bottom she stands perfectly still, waiting, and then Joseph's shadow does detach itself from that of a container.

'You're alone.'

'Yes.'

'Come.' He moves quickly between the containers, away from the light. It is not in the direction of the box the woman was in. After a minute he turns to face Anne, his breathing harsh. The feeble light makes a gleam on the planes of his face, forehead, cheeks, nose, chin, a black mask in the darkness. 'Who did you tell?'

'It's alright—only the mate—he's keeping it a secr—'

'I asked you not to tell.' He whispers with such force her face is spattered with the hot moisture of his breath. 'Where have they put her?'

'She's alright, she's in the sickbay, a doctor is looking after her.'

'We will be killed.' He is close to tears.

'Listen. Joseph, listen. You're wrong.'

'They came down here today. Two of them with sticks. Searching for me.'

'Today?'

'Yes. You told them I was here.'

'But he wants to help you, he wants to show you somewhere safe to hide.'

Joseph turns away, leans his back against the container and slides down into a squat. 'You are wrong.'

Anne crouches beside him. 'Listen. I told the mate. He's promised you'll both be safe. He says it's the captain who would take you back, so he's taken your wife to the sickbay secretly. No one else knows you're here.'

'Why should the mate protect us? You don't understand anything.'

'But the doctor is treating your wife.'

'Where is she?'

'In the sickbay, I told—'

'Where is it?'

'I don't know. You can see her yourself; he's said he'll meet you here at eleven.'

Joseph raises his hands to his head in an attitude of complete despair.

'Joseph?'

After a while he lowers his hands and turns to her. His face is wet. 'Listen to me. You won't see Estelle again. Neither of us will.' He talks over her as Anne starts to interrupt. 'Listen. Do you know there are fines for carrying stowaways?'

Anne shakes her head.

'When a ship takes immigrants into UK, the government fines the shipping company.'

'But refugees—'

'Even legitimate refugees. Yes. And the company passes the fine on to the sailors.'

'These sailors?'

'Yes. So the crews hate us. Because they will lose money.'

'But the mate has promised to take care of—'

'To avoid the fines, the sailors would kill us.'

This is paranoia. Anne wonders if he is mentally unstable. What can she say to calm him? 'I'm sure she'll be alright—'

'It's in their interest to get rid of us.'

'Joseph, listen. He's taking great care to keep it secret—'

'Of course. D'you think he wants the whole ship to know he is a murderer?' Suddenly he freezes. She can hear nothing except the thundering of the engines.

'What?'

But he raises his hand to his mouth, finger on lips, then rises silently and disappears around the corner of the container. Anne sits unmoving in the darkness. She hears nothing suspicious. She gets up and creeps back between the containers towards the light at the stairs. As she draws near she sees a pair of legs slowly ascending the upper stairs and moving out of sight. Dark trousers. Impossible to make out any more in this light. Robbie? Following her? A passing crewman checking the cargo? The medic, even, come to tell Joseph he is a father. Who knows? Joseph's information sits in her mind like an unwanted meal, square on the table before her. It will not go away but she doesn't have to eat it. Mechanically, silently, she climbs the stairs; when she reaches the top, the corridor is empty. The ship is a drawing by Escher, she thinks, all these corridors and stairs leading in and out from one another, a conundrum with no beginning and no end. In her cabin, she sits on her bed for a while, staring at the other empty bed.

OCTOBER 16, 1962

The baby was born last night. A girl, perfect, 6lb 10oz. I cried when I saw her. Paul called me in straight after the birth and passed her to me wrapped in a white towel. Her wet black hair was plastered to her head and her eyes an unfathomable velvety grey, staring unseeingly, blinking at the lamplight. I knelt by Miriam's bed and thanked Him, my heart so full I could hardly speak.

It's been a week of anxiety. Miriam's waters broke last Sunday, and Paul examined her and was confident that labour should begin fairly soon, but by Tuesday when she'd felt no more than the odd twinge, we were beginning to wonder if we'd made a mistake. As she explained to me, once the waters have broken, there's a danger of infection, and the birth needs to follow soon. But the notion of driving her down those horrible bumpy roads all the way to hospital at Enugu, expecting her to go into labour any moment, didn't appeal to either of us. She believes Paul is as good as any hospital doctor, and we made the decision months ago that she would have it here, knowing full well that if we did want the hospital option, she would have to go in a week early precisely to avoid that sort of journey. By Wednesday she was quite low, and suffering with numbness in her legs from the way the baby was lying. I hurried back after classes, to read to her and massage her legs, and went to find Paul in the late afternoon when she finally dozed off.

'I can do an internal to try and get her started.'

'D'you think that's best?'

'I'll do it in the morning.'

I suppose I was looking for reassurance, but Paul doesn't do that. I went back to the house, where she was still dozing fitfully, and told Luke he could go. We'd arranged that if I needed him in the night I'd ring the bell; he can hear it from his hut. Then I sat in the kitchen and prayed for guidance. Maybe Karl was right, maybe I should have persuaded her to go to the hospital. For some reason I was tormented by a sense of guilt, I remember begging God to punish me rather than Miriam, if we had made the wrong decision out of pride, to let me alone suffer the consequences. A foolish prayer, since our happiness is so inextricably tied up in each other, and the only real thing that would cause me suffering would be if some harm came to Miriam.

I must have dozed off with my head on the table, because the next thing I knew was Miriam calling me from the bedroom, her voice high and panicky. The contractions had started; she said she'd been calling me for a while, though it can only have been a minute or two at the most.

I pulled her up in the bed and made her more comfortable, then went out and rang for Luke. While he ran up to wake Paul I brought extra lamps into the bedroom, and riddled the stove and made it up so we could heat some water. Miriam was frightened, her eyes were huge, and I had to wipe the sweat off her face and neck, but I think I knew then that everything would be fine. The labour had come on in answer to my prayers; He was with us.

Paul examined her and told us it would take several hours yet, and went back to his own bed. And I lay next to Miriam, wiping her face, reading to her for a while, even dozing off again. Her contractions had slowed down. I got up at five and made her some tea, but she wouldn't let me send for Paul again till seven, and when he came he shook his head and said, 'A long way to go.'

I wonder why it is that childbirth should have become such a slow and difficult business for European women? The Headman's youngest wife was at the river washing clothes in the early morning before her child was born. I met the Dibia on the path back from their compound at noon and he told me the baby had already arrived. It's as if Miriam's body doesn't know what it's supposed to do, as if that primitive knowledge has somehow been lost in the refinements and cosseting of our civilisation.

Luke was given instructions to fetch me from class at the least change, but it went on like that for the whole of the day, and by evening I could see she was exhausted. It wasn't until 11 p.m. that the contractions speeded up, and when Paul came back again he sent me out of the room.

I sat sweating in the steamy kitchen with a pan of water simmering on the stove, listening to Miriam's gasps and Paul's quiet voice instructing her, begging the Lord to let it be all right, to bring us through the darkness to the light of day. Such a curious sensation to be that man, straining his ears for the sounds of his wife's pain, his child's first cry. I had an unshakeable image of a black-suited Victorian gent standing with his back to a roaring fire, rocking backwards and forwards from his heels to his toes while his wife's screams sounded weakly above. A cliché and yet I was in it, and I knew it was more real than any other moment of my life. If I could have given my strength for hers, I would have.

When Paul called me at last I didn't know what to think or expect, and the sight of that tiny, red-faced creature made me weep like a child. Miriam utterly exhausted, managed a flicker of a smile for me before closing her eyes.

And now we've all slept; in fact Miriam and baby Anne (Anne Felicity, grace and happiness) are still sleeping, and I have taken today off to tend them. Luke, beaming with joy, has brought us a gift from his fiancée, a bundle of leaves ('ogisiri', I haven't identified it yet but he has promised to show me where they grow) which are supposed to give protection from infection to both mother and child. The tradition is to line the baby's bed with them. Miriam was so pleased by this I think it may be a turning point in her difficult relationship with Luke.

Karl called this morning to offer congratulations and pointedly remind me that he had recommended hospital. Since in the event he could see as well as I that hospital had not been necessary, I didn't respond, but asked him to say a prayer of thanks with us, which he did graciously enough.

DECEMBER 4, 1962

The Harmattan is raging this week—the sun is quite misted over and it's that cold gritty wind that gets into your eyes and every nook and cranny. It dries your skin—sandblasts it, in fact, as Miriam pointed out. My lips are cracked and sore, despite liberal applications of Vaseline. And the Africans seem to be rendered utterly miserable by it.

But the teaching continues to go well. There's a group of six very bright boys in Standard 6, all easily capable of grammar school and indeed university. The difficulty is persuading their parents to let them go to the grammar. It's in Enugu so they have to stay with relatives there or board, and the expense is beyond the reach of some of these families—£60 per year. Obi and Isaac will be fine, both their fathers have good farmland and Obi's father is an important man in the village, he carves the ceremonial masks. But the other four are all problematic in different ways. John is the only son in a Christian family and his father depends on his labour in the fields. Okwuekwu and Nwosisi are brothers whose father died last year, and his relatives have been very generous in letting them complete Standard 6. And Simon simply tells me his parents won't let him go away.

Not only are they all bright and able, they have the added

closeness of all coming from the same age-group. And in school there's a healthy rivalry between them. Obi sets a standard in maths and Simon in English which the others all strive to attain. If they can move on together as a group there'll be no stopping them.

I started by going to the village school committee, and they discussed the whole issue very seriously for more than an hour. They're keen to send boys to grammar school; only three from the village have gone in the past, and they know it is the key to better employment. But they can't possibly afford to finance six. The most they could offer is £10 per student.

So I went with Simon to see his father. As soon as we entered the compound I was mobbed by a dozen youngsters, mostly naked despite the wind, who all wanted to touch my clothes or beg a coin or a sweet. A tall skinny woman in a faded wrapper came out of her hut and shouted at them, but they didn't take much notice. Then Simon introduced me to a man who looked far too old to be his father. He ceremoniously gave me a kola nut to break, and when we'd both eaten a segment I explained that I want Simon to go to grammar school.

He replied very briefly to Simon, who translated for me. 'He says I must be a palm tapper. No more school.'

I asked why but the old man waved his hand at Simon, indicating that Simon could explain to me himself.

'My father cannot climb the trees now, it must be my job.' The old man cut in impatiently. 'My father says he has many valuable palm trees and an excellent crop of yams.'

It was one of the poorest-looking compounds I had ever been in. Simon looked uncomfortable and I saw that it was a mistake not to have brought a neutral interpreter. 'If Simon goes to grammar school—don't you have brothers or other sons who could tap the palm trees for wine?'

Simon translated very hesitantly and, I thought, at unnecessary length. The old man gave no reply at all, simply sat staring at the wall above my head. At times the Ibo insistence on maintain-

ing face strikes me as downright hypocritical, but I restrained my impatience.

'If we can get a grant—if the mission can pay for Simon to go to grammar school—would you permit it?'

The reply began while Simon was still translating my question. He switched to English seamlessly. 'This household is blessed with many riches, the finest yams, the strongest palm trees, the most beautiful daughters. If the son will go to grammar, this is also riches.'

'So we have your permission to send Simon to grammar?'

'My father says, the son will be an important man in the village. He will bring great wealth and honour to his family.'

I nodded, Simon relaxed and smiled, and the old man and I shook hands.

I assumed this sort of situation must have arisen before, so had no hesitation in asking Karl if there was a grant or a hardship fund Simon could apply to.

'No.'

'Well how can poorer students go to grammar school?'

'They can't.'

'There isn't any funding available for bright students in rural areas?'

'And I haven't got anything in the mission budget.'

'Couldn't we lend the family the money and ask for it back when he gets a job?'

'There isn't the cash spare to do that.' And he picked up his pen again.

I was damned if I was going to see that boy held back for the want of a few miserable pounds. Miriam and I talked about it over dinner and we had a brainwave: to set up a sponsorship scheme through our church at home. We could ask church members to make a regular commitment to funding the education of individual students. It would be satisfying for them because they'd get progress reports on how their student was doing. And if a sponsored student ends up going to university in Britain then there is a ready-made contact group who would be eager to meet him and offer him hospitality. I was so pleased with the idea that I wrote that evening suggesting it to the education secretary at the CMS.

A few days later, when I was up early in the schoolroom doing some marking, Karl appeared and asked me to explain the scheme to him. 'Miriam mentioned it, but she didn't go into detail.'

I didn't know Miriam had spoken to him. He sat in Nwosisi's desk, facing me; in the morning light his face was sharp and angry. He must have just washed his hair and beard because it seemed extraordinarily white and fluffy. He looked like an image of the unforgiving Old Testament God. I outlined our idea to him.

'There may be some aspects you haven't considered.'

Of course, and naturally it would be Karl who could point them out. I was busy, a new trainee was starting that day, I needed to get through the marking before my class arrived, and in my own defence I was probably also rather tired, since Anne has taken to waking around midnight every night as fresh and chirpy as a bird at dawn. Miriam doesn't seem to have any patience at all at that time of night, and after she's fed the baby I usually end up pacing round the room with her over my shoulder for an hour or more, since movement is the only thing that settles her.

So I may have answered him rather sharply. But I also think it's high time this whole issue of his passive resistance to me was dragged into the light. 'Karl, what have I done to offend you? Why is it that every improvement I suggest, you reject?'

He sat there in silence for a moment then he slowly pushed the chair back, levered himself to his feet and walked out of the room. I tried to carry on with my marking, but it was obvious I'd have to go after him. I caught up with him at his door.

'Karl, we need to talk about this. We need to pull together.'

He was staring so intently at something on the floor that I couldn't help looking to see what it was, but there was nothing there. 'You are an exceptionally arrogant young man.' And he shut the door on me.

When I went home for lunch Miriam called me laughingly from the bedroom, to come and look at Anne. Miriam was bathing her in an enamel bowl, and Anne was kicking and splashing, a look of utter astonishment on her tiny face.

'When did you tell Karl about the sponsoring idea?'

Miriam looked up at me, her smile fading. 'He called by yesterday afternoon. Why? What's the matter?'

'Why didn't you tell me?'

'Because it wasn't important. He came to see if I wanted anything for Anne, when he places the shopping order. He was being kind. I don't know why you dislike him so much.'

'He's just told me I'm exceptionally arrogant.'

She scooped Anne out of the bowl and wrapped her in a towel. 'I don't know why you two rub each other up the wrong way all the time. I don't understand it.'

'Because he's incapable of listening to anyone else's ideas.'

She dried Anne's face then passed her, bundled in her towel, over to me. 'You dress her, I'll go and see him.'

She was gone a long time. I dressed Anne and played with her for a while then put her down for a sleep. I tidied up the mess of baby clothes Miriam had left littered all over the floor. For someone who objects to having a servant, she certainly leaves him plenty to do. I ate the soup Luke had made for us. When Miriam came back she seemed rather subdued.

'Well?'

'He made a good point about the sponsorship actually, which is that we get extra funding for the clinic from our UK church donations. People only have so much to give, and if we start asking for education sponsorship we're going to lose out on the clinic.'

'I don't believe that. It will attract a different kind of donor, not just the routine collection plate givers. What's the harm in trying, anyway?'

She sighed. 'He's cautious. But after he's weighed up the pros and cons, he is open to new ideas.'

'Such as?'

She didn't know. 'We should have talked to him before we wrote to England. That's all. He feels as if you're doing stuff behind his back.'

'Only because he slaps it down if I tell him about anything first.'

If Karl thinks I'm giving up on this idea, he's got another think coming.

MARCH 25, 1963

My poor diary; I always imagine it's only a few days since I last wrote, but weeks and weeks fly by. A quiet evening when I could simply write seems an unattainable luxury. Indeed, it's only a disagreement with Miriam which has given me this hour of solitude tonight. It's so hot and close that sweat from my fingers is running down the pen, and the side of my palm is leaving a damp smear across the paper as I write.

We have had a serious difference of opinion over Okolie. I'm disturbed by Miriam's attitude, and can only hope that over time she might come to see how uncharitable she's been. The cot and little table he made for Anne are both well-crafted, we were pleased with them, and when he turned up last week again in his roving way, looking for work, Miriam was very happy with my suggestion that he should make Anne a playpen. She's starting to crawl now, slowly but with incredible persistence. Miriam has caught her twice at the top of the veranda steps. We drew him a diagram of the type of thing, an open-topped wooden cage really, where she can play safely. He thought it would take him a day or two, and asked for money in advance to buy some cane, which we agreed would be strong enough for the 'bars'. I know he was around during the afternoon looking for scraps of wood in the gar-

dening hut and working on the frame, then I didn't see him in the
evening. We assumed he'd found a better place to sleep than our
veranda, and thought no more about it. But around 9 p.m., after
I'd told Luke he could go, and Miriam was nodding off in the
armchair with a dozy Anne still clamped to her breast, there was
a sudden urgent knocking at the door. I was surprised to see Luke
again, standing on the veranda looking utterly woebegone. 'My
bedroll, sir.'

I followed him over to the close dark little hut he shares with
Saul. The ledge he sleeps on was bare, his sleeping mat and blanket vanished. 'Where's Saul?'

'Still at Mr Karl's.' Saul's bed had not been touched.

'Is anything else gone?'

Luke glanced into the basket he keeps at the end of his bed,
checked the little pile of clothes on top of it, and his candle stump
and Bible. 'No, Mr David.'

I couldn't understand why anyone would take his bedding,
which can hardly be considered valuable. The sleeping mat is
useful of course, but it's nothing more than woven palm leaves.
The women in the village make them, they're not hard to come by.
And blankets are not really necessary at this time of year. I wondered initially if it was some kind of prank on the part of Saul or
one of the others. But Luke shook his head. 'That Okolie. He ask
me today for a blanket and I tell him he must ask you.'

'He never did.'

'No, sir.'

I fetched the torch and we went round the compound together,
shining it into likely corners where Okolie might be holed up. I
fully expected to find him in the gardening shed, but he was
nowhere to be seen amongst the piled wood and implements; the
playpen frame he had started making was balanced neatly on top
of the workbench.

I took Luke back to the bungalow and asked him if he'd like to
sleep on the sofa for the night, but he shook his head mournfully,
so I gave him a couple of cushions and a spare blanket to lie on

and told him we'd sort it out in the morning. Miriam was still awake when I got into bed, and wanted to know the story.

'Oh, that's it. That's it, he's not working here again.'

'Well let's wait until I can sort it out with him in the morning, shall we?'

'No. That's disgusting, David. If he'll steal from someone as poor as Luke, he's shameless.'

'Luke'll get a new mat and blankets, I'll make sure of that tomorrow.'

'That's not the point. Yes you can replace the bedroll, like you replaced the tools he stole. The point is if he'll take a sleeping mat from Luke he'll take anything. I'm not having him here around the baby. He's untrustworthy.'

'I really don't think he'd have much use for a baby.'

'Don't be so stupid. You can't have someone wandering in and out of your house who doesn't care about how what he does affects other people—'

'Last time you agreed with me that he should be given a second chance—'

'Yes but not a third. Karl's right. It's not fair to the others.'

'Miriam, are you seriously saying it's impossible to forgive a man for borrowing another's bedroll?'

'You know as well as I do it's not borrowing. He's traded his own bedroll for hemp, and doesn't think twice about nicking poor Luke's in its place. He knows he can get away with it. You're not helping him.'

'I reduced him to tears over the stolen tools—and there was no trouble at all last time, when he was making the cot.'

'Fine. He's a reformed character.'

'Clearly not. But it would be surprising in a way if he didn't lapse from time to time. You think forgiveness should be finite, do you?'

'I think you can't see when you're being strung along.' She was incapable of listening to reason, and I ended up sleeping on the sofa myself, just to get a bit of peace.

Things were still strained between us in the morning. I was also angry to find that I couldn't have a shower. Miriam uses far too much water with Anne; before she was born the barrels only needed refilling once a month. With sensible use, the last refill should have carried us through to the rains. I asked a couple of the yard boys to refill the barrels for us, and went over to the schoolroom without speaking to Miriam. When I came home for lunch she was standing defiantly on the veranda waiting for me. 'I've sent him away. He had the face to turn up in the middle of the morning and start ferreting about in the garden shed.'

'He's got the base of the playpen in there.'

'I told him if we see him here again we'll call the police.'

'Did you ask him about Luke's bedroll?'

'He denied it. Which isn't surprising since he's a liar.'

'Give a dog a bad name. Why didn't you send him to me?'

'Because I was perfectly capable of dealing with him myself, thank you.'

'If he did take it, I could have got it back off him. What's the point in just sending him away? What good does that do?'

'Well I did. And that's the end of the story.' She went stamping off to Anne's room and shut herself in there while I had my lunch. How is it that when Miriam takes things into her own hands she always makes a mess of them?

We've spent the evening separately, she with Anne indoors and me out here on the veranda. I am still very angry and disappointed in her.

ANNE WAKES WITH a strange terrible feeling. Something is pushing her down. Pressing on her lungs and throat, pushing against her windpipe so she can't draw breath, forcing her weight back like lead against the bed. Sweating and gasping she tries to reach the lamp—as her fingers find the switch there is a jolt and she starts to fall, back, back, back, the hard bed falls away behind her, the room is creaking and straining, objects slither across the floor. The storm, she realises at last. We are in the storm. Things have fallen off the table onto the floor. Her clothes and shoes tumble from one end of the room to the other. She is on her feet and staggering to the bathroom before she knows why, and is sick as soon as she reaches the basin. She stands groggily over it, hands clasping either side, trying to swill the lumps down the mean little crack between the raised stainless steel plug and the hole it slots into.

Robbie said there would be a storm. Robbie.

What on earth has she done? Suddenly in a head-to-toe flush of shame she recalls Robbie smoothly producing a condom at the necessary moment. With practised ease, she tells herself. How many female passengers has he practised on? What on earth possessed her?

This isn't necessary. It isn't necessary to make such a fuss. No one has been hurt. Other people do it, they do it all the time. Why must she always be subject to this ridiculous inquisition? It *doesn't matter.*

For a moment there is blessed silence in her skull. She moves away from the sink. You can do it again, if you want, she tells herself calmly. Why not? There's nothing wrong with Robbie. He's been kind, over the stowaways, more than kind, he's a decent man.

But then stopping again in the bathroom doorway, hands gripping the sills as the ship plunges down, no Anne no, seeing the way it is leading. Don't persuade yourself that you like him, don't start to do that. If only she could disconnect the hideous computing weight of her mind, its leaping from point to point, its automatic responses; if only she could proceed simply, on the surface. And now as the ship begins its sickening upward heave Anne finally manages to locate the real source of her distress. Joseph.

How could she have forgotten? She falls to her knees in the doorway. Joseph said. It wasn't a dream. Joseph is real. His wife is real. His wife was in that bed. She raises her head to look at the other bed, and is unpleasantly shocked. It is neatly made, with the blue flowery cartwheel cover stretched smooth right over it, as it was on the day Anne came aboard. But they took the woman in the bedclothes, they carried her wrapped in the sheets, the bed was stripped—Anne saw it. She crawls to the bed and pulls back the cover, touches the ironed, turned-down sheet. When did the steward make this bed?

She crawls back to her own rumpled bed and gets herself onto it. Why did she tell Robbie? She told Robbie because she thought he could help. But now Robbie has taken the woman away, and wants to find the man. Why? Either to kill them—or to help them. Which is after all much more likely. It is more usual to help people than to murder them. Joseph is overwrought.

Her clock has fallen off the bedside table and she has to squint at her watch for a while before she can make out 4.21. She has to see the woman who she knows was in that bed only a few hours ago. To find the woman, she has to speak to Robbie.

She struggles into her clothes; the ship is moving irregularly, rising and tilting and falling sometimes more deeply than others. Once or twice it feels as if nothing will stop it, it will simply go on pitching downwards, while objects rain to the floor. To open the door onto the deck is to enter a howling lashing spray-filled world where it is hard to snatch a breath as the wind rushes by; clinging to the cabin wall and to fixed objects along the way, she makes it to the stairwell. Once she is inside and the door shut, the absence of wind is an extraordinarily voluptuous warm silence.

'Hello.' Mr Malone is sitting hunched on the top step of the stairs, both hands clasped tight around the handrail.

'Are you alright?' He doesn't look it.

'I wanted some air . . .'

Grabbing the other handrail Anne wedges herself onto the stair beside him and both of them concentrate, as the ship falls away beneath them.

'Air,' he repeats, after the thump has juddered up through all the metal stairs and up each vertebra of their spines. 'Stupid. Came out on deck, now I can't open the cabin door.' His long face is white, either side of the livid birthmark.

'Shall I try?'

He bows his head defeatedly, but struggles to stand as Anne does; clinging to each other they drag themselves away from the gaping stairwell and are then flung viciously against the outer door. He seems dazed and staggers even when the ship has righted itself.

'Hold on to me. Put your arms around my waist.' It is the same as instructing a child. With his weight at her back Anne heaves open the door and leads them both out into the wild dark. The Malones' cabin is the twin of hers; as she grasps the door handle she is afraid they'll both fall in flat on their faces, and bellows to him to hold the door jamb. But needlessly—he's right, the door won't open.

'It's locked.' The wind whips the words out of her mouth and she has to turn to face him, back pressed against the door, to scream into his face, '*The key?*' The ship lurches and flings his bony frame against her as he delves into his pocket; after a long moment of horrible pressure in which it is hard to draw breath, balance returns, and as his weight rocks away from her his hand produces the key.

The lock turns, the door flies open. Anne and Mr Malone stumble into the dark cabin and together force the door shut in the teeth of the wind. In the sudden silence Mr Malone flicks a light on. Ellie lies in one of the twin beds, her thin pink hair plastered to her skull. Mr Malone sits groggily on his bed.

'Is Mrs Malone . . .?'

'Sleeping tablets. Nothing wakes her.' He draws a breath and straightens his back, plants his feet solidly on the floor. 'Thank you.'

'It's OK.' Anne starts to move but the ship is diving again; she is forced to sit abruptly on the floor, bracing herself with her knees, back against the side of Mrs Malone's bed.

'Where were you off to?' Mr Malone asks.

'I was looking for the sickbay.' She shouldn't have said that.

'Feeling sick? I've got some tablets here.'

'Yes. Thank you.'

Leaning over on his elbow, he extracts a packet from the drawer beside his bed, holds it in the air a moment then tosses it towards Anne. It falls short, less than halfway across the floor between them. Anne crawls forward to reach it. She is distracted by a strange movement of Mr Malone's.

'Here,' he says urgently. 'Here.' He is fumbling in his trousers. Behind Anne, Ellie Malone sleeps quietly in her bed. Anne on all fours stares in astonishment at Mr Malone as he pulls out his semi-erect penis and offers it to her. His mouth is an oblong of darkness. 'Good girl. Here.'

Anne gets herself out of the room and across the howling space to the stairwell with surprising speed. She thinks afterwards that she must have left the Malones' door open. Good, he'd find it hard to close. One of Goya's monsters; leaning forward out of the shadows, gape-mouthed.

There is no point in even thinking about this, it is irrelevant, a tacky little sideshow. The issue is Joseph, his wife; the thing is to find Robbie. Malone is just a senile old man. He was shocked, confused by the violence of the storm, probably hardly knew what he was doing. But even as she banishes it she can't help an incredulous sob of disgust. Is it her fault? What awful signals is she giving off? Is it because of what happened with Robbie, can he smell it on her, like a dog?

She swallows her revulsion, forces herself back to the task before her. She must find Robbie. Where will he be? The bridge? The engine room? Surely not asleep in this. She starts down the stairs, gripping the handrail tightly as the steps yawn away beneath her feet. She doesn't know where she is going. At the bottom of the first flight she hesitates then lunges through the double door into the corridor. A small slight crewman in his grey boiler suit is coming towards her, zig-zagging from side to side. He is no bigger than a child. He stares at her blankly.

'Can you tell me—' She breaks off as the ship does one of its impossible plunges—unable to finish her question till the descent is done. It ends with a sickening jolt which makes the iron floor clang and shudder. '—where's the sickbay?'

The child-sailor stops, bracing himself against the ship's movement. His expression is puzzled; he looks Filipino, perhaps he doesn't speak English.

'Where is the doctor? The place for sick people?'

When he opens his mouth his teeth are brown and crooked with dark gaps between them. 'No, no, there is no place. You must stay in the cabin.'

'It's not for me. I have to visit someone who is very ill.'

He's frowning. He shrugs, already moving off. 'Sorry. No doctor on this ship.'

Lurching, Anne turns to follow him. Someone more senior; this boy's probably new. He moves quickly away from her along the tilting corridor, turns left and disappears. When she reaches the door she thinks he went through, it's unmarked. It might just be his room—or a toilet—god knows what it is; she can feel the nausea stirring in her stomach again. Suddenly the door opens and Robbie himself comes out, almost bumping into her. 'What d'you want?'

'Robbie, please, can you take me to see the woman?'

He keeps on moving down the corridor. She has to hurry alongside him, her hand on the wall for balance.

'For Christ's sake, go to your cabin, I can't help you now.'

'But it's important.'

'Where's your friend? He didn't meet me.'

Why is he so abrupt? 'I don't know.'

He stops for a moment. 'I've got stuff to do. It's not safe for you wandering about in this, you could fall.'

'I have to see her—'

'In the morning. I've got men to look after—go back to your cabin.' He has taken her elbow, he's steering her to the stairs. As she steps up, clinging to the handrail, he gives her a light pat on the rump. What does he mean by it? Patting her as if she understands—what? There must be a sickbay. Why would he lie to her?

She gets back to her cabin before she vomits again. It's a relief to lie down even though the bed tilts and drops alarmingly, even though everything around her is creaking and slithering and falling. Sleep will be impossible but at least she doesn't have to keep her balance, dragging herself up stairs, lurching down corridors. This is all nonsense, misplaced anxiety; she is inventing a new problem each time an old one's solved. The first mate is dealing with it. She doesn't worry that he might let the ship sink in the storm. The stowaways are his department, now, none of her business.

It seems to Anne that she doesn't sleep but lies in a queasy daze, her body tilting first one way then the other, her blood and brains and thoughts sliding up and down her like sand in an

egg timer. There's Tim bringing his smiling face close to hers—
closer, yes, he's going to kiss her, and her heart lifts like a kite in
the wind—but it's Robbie. It's not Tim at all. And there's
Joseph's mask hanging in the black air between containers, his
whisper blasting at her 'They're going to kill us,' and the puzzled
polite child-face of the Filipino, 'No doctor on this ship.' There's
her father taking Robbie by the shoulder, 'I appreciate you're
busy old man, just tell me where I can find this sickroom and I
won't bother you again' and Robbie nodding subserviently,
there's her own hot gasping body clamped to Robbie in a
spasm like some sort of female devil. She watches with appalled
fascination; there's the child in the dark womb clamouring in
fear, kicking and punching at the blind sides of the sac as his
mother's body slides and flops uncontrollably with the lurching
of the ship . . .

Robbie is in her room. He's bending over the bed.

'How did you get in?'

He laughs. 'Through the door.'

'But I locked it.'

'Nah.'

She knows she did. She's scrabbling to get up. 'Can you take
me to the sickbay now?'

'What's the big hurry?' He's sitting on the edge of the
narrow bed. He hands her a glass of water and she drinks
thirstily. 'You manage to grab some sleep? Did you puke?'

'Yes. Has the storm ended?'

'For the time being. We're inside it—this afternoon we pass
out of it, it'll be choppy again then. But no worse than it has
been.'

'The doctor—'

'You worry too much. Hush.' He puts his hand on her arm,
strokes it; he is looking into her face. 'Why didn't the other one
meet me?'

'Joseph? I think he's scared.'

'What did he say?'

'He's anxious about his wife.'

'I was going to take him to her.'

'If I could tell him I've seen her, reassure him—' Again she starts to get up.

Robbie leans closer in. 'Sure. You want to go now?'

'Yes.'

'Now?' He is leaning closer, his hand has closed over her arm, she can feel the heat of his breath on her cheek. 'Now?' He's brushing her ear with his lips.

'I want to go—'

'Now?' His hand is sliding up her arm. He brushes her nipple lightly through her T-shirt. 'How about in a little while?'

There is no chance to reply because he has put his lips on hers. Anne is confused. Joseph's wife, I have to let Joseph know where she is. But Robbie—he's kind and warm, of course the woman is well, all that is nothing but paranoia. If I said no right now, he might be offended and stamp out of the cabin slamming the door, not take me to the sickbay after all. If we do this (she's slipping already, knows she will) he'll take me to the woman afterwards, it will be fine, we'll go there very soon . . . She's not causing this to happen, it's not her fault. Robbie is in control. But she gives permission.

Anne is floating like a helium balloon. Someone has let go of her string. She's floating up, higher and higher, tilting and veering one way then the other, spinning in the wind but always ascending, steadily, the ground diminishing far beneath her. She dreamt that Robbie came to her room, there was something a little awkward she needed to ask, a favour of some kind it niggled her like a splinter in her finger, but then she had forgotten it because little niggling things hold you down. Once you are rising up and up through the air above the toytown landscapes you get a sense of proportion, you know things are unimportant and can be left behind, there is all the world and no need to cling to what you are, you can change, you can escape.

She has been dreaming. It is Robbie beside her asleep, the air whistling through his nose as he breathes, a slick of sweat down their sides where they lie pressed against one another. What time is it? She can't understand why her clock isn't on the table. She still has the feeling of the balloon in her head, rising and rising. It is bitter to be here in this dark cabin with sweaty skin stuck to hers, the bulk of a hot body clogging the bed, the weight of everything inexorably descending again; she must see the woman, she must talk to Joseph, how long have they slept? She heaves herself away from Robbie and crawls off the end of the bed, finds her watch in the bathroom. 10.30. Morning or night? It must be morning, but when did he come to her room? She doesn't even know, it seems the night went on forever, with nightmares and anxious wanderings about the ship—did she really speak to Joseph? Did he really say they had come after him with sticks? More likely it was a nightmare, perhaps Robbie has been here all night, she's got confused because they made love again, she has dreamed the pitching storm and the rotten-toothed sailor who denied there was a doctor, she—

'Hello?' Robbie is stirring. As she goes back into the room he hauls himself from the bed and switches on the lamp. His face is bleary with sleep and dark with stubble. 'What's the time?'

'Ten thirty.'

'I'm late.' He starts pulling his clothes on in a rush.

'I'm ready, I'll come with you.'

'Not now. I'm on duty.'

'But the sickbay—'

'What?'

'Just tell me where it is, I'll go on my own.'

'No one's allowed in—how d'you expect me to protect her?'

'Robbie, please.'

He's ready, buttoning his shirt as he moves towards the door. 'Get this bloke to meet me, I'll take you both to see her.'

'When? What time?'

'Seven thirty. The container deck.' He's gone, pulling the

door to smartly behind him. Anne feels a terrible sense of loss.
He should have taken her to the woman. It was agreed. He
didn't even look at her as he went out. Angrily she asks herself,
what does that matter? Looking doesn't matter at all, what matters is that more and more time passes and he doesn't take me
to the sickbay. It's my own fault, I should have insisted. I should
have made it clear that had to happen first, before anything else.

What was it then? A trade-off? She wouldn't have had sex
with him if he hadn't promised something? Sordid, disgusting.
Rage bubbles up. What does it *matter*? But indignation is batted
aside by the next question. Does Robbie like me?

She minds if he doesn't like her. Crass as it is, it feels essen-
tial, a game he should at least pretend to play. But does she like
him? Why is *she* doing this? For instant gratification? Or for
some unseen, long-term goal? For Christ's sake—

OK. She has a choice. She can choose what happens next.
She will decide if she wants to sleep with him again. She will
get a purchase on what is happening instead of being swirled
along like a leaf in a flooding gutter.

She showers, dresses, helps herself to coffee and a banana
from the empty dining room—then puts on her jacket and
goes to the rail to look out over the edgy sea. It seems strange
that there are little choppy excitable waves and yet no wind, she
doesn't see how the two can go together. The sea and sky are
weirdly empty, there isn't a single gull, no sign of life anywhere.
As if they have churned into a zone where nothing else
comes—she imagines the circle of storm around them like the
rim of an upside-down glass, they are captive under its bell-
shape, captive and exposed.

She is trapped on this ship.

Suddenly she imagines talking to someone on land.
Someone real, outside this, someone who could listen and
advise and make sense of it, who would be able objectively to
see what she should do; who could even, if they thought it
necessary, contact the authorities—police, immigration, who-

ever. She could ring Tim. With a shock she remembers that's
not possible. The connection with Tim is broken. When she
broke it he hissed in her face: 'What the hell d'you want? What
d'you think you want?' She said goodbye and his lips curled
between a snarl and a sneer. 'This is crap. I'll see you next week.'

She returns to her cabin and tips out her bag to find her
mobile. There was nothing to do but turn him off. But she can
use it now, surely she can ring someone else? She has a horror of
the torrent that will pour out when she turns it on, his messages,
questions, anger. It is only the conviction that it won't work
anyway which makes it possible to switch it on. The little green
light blinks at her, yes it is charged. But searching, searching. She
knew it; nothing. Perhaps on deck? She takes it through the containers to the rail but there's no change. Of course there's no
signal, they are far out of range. Her foolish and temporary relief
is swamped now by fear. They are out of range.

Is it possible to contact anybody from this ship? There's no e-
mail, no phone, no post; there'll be a radio, but where? On the
bridge, or somewhere under the eye of the officers. It would
only be used by passengers in an emergency. Nothing can be
said to anyone ashore. Until whatever is going to happen has
happened. In a world of mass communications and ceaseless
babble, she is as cut off as if she were already dead. And no one
knows where she is. Only Matthew Afigbo, but Matthew is in
Lagos; how long would it be before he realised she hadn't
arrived home?

Unnecessary thoughts; result of lack of sleep and too much
emotional upheaval. She is used to a quiet life, where events get
plenty of digestion. Her life seems to have been put on fast-for-
ward. Too much is happening. She conjures the image above her
desk at home, Munch's drypoint etching, *Girl in a Nightdress at
the Window*. An inspired gift from Father. She sees again the rec-
tangle of daylight that the girl carefully stands back from as if to
avoid contamination, the avid tilt of her head as she stares at the
world outside. The simplicity of the picture's stillness. A watcher.

April, 1964

A year since my last entry! I can't believe how the time has flown. But how appropriate that it is tonight, after all, that I've found time to pick up my pen again. It's after eleven and Miriam's asleep but I'm utterly awake, and full of the kind of excitement I used to feel on Christmas Eve as a child. Outside the rain makes a happy drum roll of anticipation on the roof, swirling away the dust of the day, flooding and gurgling down the gutters and drains, filling my ears with its energetic music. A great day for the mission! Today we got permission to go ahead with the new church building. Of all the things I've managed to achieve in the five months since Karl left, I must say this is the one that gives me greatest pleasure. It is such a huge symbol of hope—of growth and renewal. Everyone is already lifted by the news, and on the back of it other projects become more and more possible. A group from the Mothers' Union are going to a big meeting in Onitsha, to discuss Sunday school teaching and Christian women's issues. Most of them will never have been so far from home. It's not so ridiculous now to consider a secondary school here—I'm willing to guess it'll only be a month or two before those boneheads in the education department revise their opinions and decide nothing would suit them better than to attach their names to a burgeoning success story. The work goes on, God's work goes on.

And I rejoice and thank Him.

Miriam was oddly uninterested in the news. Anne's still not well and seems to be absorbing all of Miriam's attention. Paul is quite confident after a battery of tests and results from the hospital that it was simply gastroenteritis, not anything more sinister (Miriam talking wildly about cholera and typhoid last week) and although the poor little mite is thin and pale as a ghost, she is at least keeping liquids down now, and has spent the better part of the day sleeping peacefully. It has been worrying, but she's on the mend, He has listened to our prayers—and I can't help feeling it's time Miriam considered returning to work. It's true there has recently been a succession of incidents and illnesses, but nevertheless Miriam has a job and a duty here as a nurse—a vacancy we would probably have filled if we had realised how long she would be unavailable for work. Things are standing still at the clinic; we were talking about outreach work a year ago and there has been almost no progress on that front. Partly down to Paul himself, I know, but I can't in all honesty expect him to be pushing new projects forward when he's close to leaving himself and the only assistance he has in Miriam's place is the formidably lazy Mrs Katanga. He'd be better off with an untrained girl who had a bit of energy and enthusiasm. But I'm not in any position to advise him while my own wife is still at home every day.

An oddly touching little incident this afternoon, after the women's Reading Class. A delightful session, as ever, with lots of banter and laughter alongside real concentration and clear progress; and at the end, Amoge came up to the desk and asked if she could speak with me. I saw the others raising their eyebrows and giggling at her, and she simply stood there for a while, staring stubbornly at the floor, trying to ignore their silliness. I felt a sudden sympathy for her. She's been one of the more confident ones in that group, and I suppose I may even have thought her a little overloud on one or two occasions. But now as she stood there tongue-tied and they trooped out gig-

*gling and whispering behind her back, I did feel rather sorry for
the girl.*

*And rightly too, as it turned out. I don't know what it cost her,
in terms of pride, to come and lay her heart bare to me, but I do
feel privileged to know that my students really do see me as friend
as well as teacher. Her situation is very sad. I knew she was married, but I didn't know that she has been so since the age of
fourteen (not unusual here) and that her husband has now asked
her for a divorce because she hasn't given him any children.*

*'And have you had—you and your husband are . . .' I made a
mental note to ask Miriam to have a chat with her, to make sure
all was well. But I'm glad to say Amoge felt no awkwardness on
the subject, and also managed to put the matter with great deli-
cacy.*

*'My husband visits my hut at night. But I am barren as that
Bible lady. Rachel. I am no good for wife.'*

*'You couldn't take care of someone else's baby and bring him
up as your own?' I've heard of this business before, of course, in
the village, that infertile women are rejected and returned to their
families—but where there is some degree of attachment between
the husband and wife, as I assumed there must be in this case, it
seemed worth gently exploring alternative solutions—indeed, I
thought that was why she was telling me about it. But she had a
different plan.*

'Can I come to work on the station? And live here?'

*I had a sudden vision of her life as an infertile woman:
returned to her family, who would reluctantly refund her bride
price; henceforth regarded as unmarriageable, a family skivvy,
never at the centre of things. And she is so young and bright and
pretty. 'But what can you do, Amoge? We already have the houseboys—'*

*'I am strong, I can do anything. Cooking, cleaning, your
schoolroom is not clean every day.' She glanced at the muddy
footprints in the doorway—of course it's true. Luke comes over
here to do it a couple of times a week, when he's not too busy—*

but recently with Anne's illness, Miriam has wanted him on call at the bungalow. Poor Amoge looked so hopeful.

'It would be lovely to have it cleaned every day, my dear, but there are no wages for a schoolroom cleaner.'

She stared at her feet, crestfallen. Close up, her skin is like a black tulip. Then I had an inspiration. Although I've raised the subject several times, Miriam has still got absolutely nowhere with the business of looking for a woman to take care of Anne. Luke is wonderful with her, but Luke has other work. And Miriam and I have both come to see now how naive we were to imagine that Miriam could have Anne by her in the clinic, in the midst of all those germs and diseases. I could almost sense God's hand in this.

'Have you ever looked after children?'

'I bring up my little brother from a baby, when my mother died. He is eight years old.'

I hadn't realised how much sadness the poor girl has had in her life. Her mother died in childbirth when Amoge was eleven, and as the only girl in the family she singlehandedly brought up the baby, besides cooking and fetching water for her father and brothers. No wonder she doesn't want to return to the family home.

'Amoge, let me talk to my wife and see if we can come up with some work for you. I can't promise anything, but I will think about it.'

Experience has taught me to be wary about promising employment now, having been besieged by every single member of Luke's extended family, and endlessly by parents of Standard 6 students, expecting—even assuming—that I can easily find them employment on the station. There are no more wages in the kitty; but once Miriam's allowance starts to be paid again (as soon as she gets back to work) we can take a little out of that for childcare. And if Amoge could share Mrs Katanga's hut there'd be no expense there at all.

I saw her eyes fill with grateful tears, and she bowed her head for a moment. Incredibly graceful, the way these girls hold them-

*selves so straight and upright—when she bent her head it was like
a flower swaying in the wind. It's carrying the water on their
heads, of course, that gives them such wonderful upright posture.
I hope the installation of that new pump in the village won't
result in a generation of slouching, round-shouldered western-
looking women; we would be doing these villagers quite a
disservice.*

*I'm tired now and rambling, time to go to bed. It was a lovely
ending to the day, though, both the knowledge that she felt able
to tell me her troubles, and the thought that Miriam may thereby
be encouraged to return to work the sooner.*

So, to bed; to dream of our new church!

NOVEMBER 20, 1964

*Harvest festival—on a rather grander scale than Karl ever envis-
aged! It's always been a delightful occasion, of course,
masterminded by the Mothers' Union—they come with their
yams and cocoyams, breadfruit, eggs, with bananas and oil and
palm wine. And this year we contributed three baskets of wonderful vegetables grown here by the students. There's always been
singing and dancing and genuine thanksgiving, but this year I
persuaded the Headman to introduce an element of Ibo culture
and permit a masquerade. I've seen the masks in use once at a
funeral—extraordinary, terrifying things, created by the village
carver and completed with headdresses of cloth, feathers, palm
leaves and raffia grass. They believe the men who wear the masks
are each inhabited by the spirit of one of the ancestors—so their
movements become strange and jerky like puppets, a performance
by (literally) the possessed.*

*Apart from a few mutterings from the Mothers' Union, Jacob
has been the only one to raise objections; 'You approve of ances-
tor worship? You think it is a good Christian thing?'*

I tried to explain that remembering and honouring the dead is an important part of any worship; that God loves celebration. But poor old Jacob is cast in Karl's mould; anything different, anything which allows the extraordinary energy and creativity of the villagers to bubble up—is dangerous. I can't convince him that by joining their ceremonies to our own Christian festivals, we strengthen both. As Miriam said to me afterwards, the masquerade was thrilling. Not a word you would use to describe many English harvest festivals!

All the women had brought food, and we lit the braziers Luke and Saul had made so they could cook. Mounds of foo foo, great golden heaps of gari and wonderful spicy sauces. The Headman's first wife gave me her speciality, ogiri isi, made from fermented melon seeds. After dark the men settled to drinking palm wine, Anne fell asleep over my knees, exhausted by the day's excitements, and Miriam came to sit beside us. 'David? Can we go home for Christmas?'

I was astonished by her request. At that moment of completion, of celebration of what had been achieved here in the year, all she was thinking of was going home. 'Why d'you raise it now?'

'Because I want Mum and Dad to see their granddaughter before she grows up.' I realised that, manipulatively, she was approaching me when she thought my good mood might make me more likely to agree to her request.

'You didn't enjoy today?'

'Today was a real Christian Ibo festival, of course I'm proud of today. But that doesn't stop me thinking about my family and friends.'

'This is our family, these are our friends.'

'I'm not asking you to leave them—just take a holiday. You promised, David.'

I waved to Amoge who smilingly came and took Anne to bed, then I went across to help the boys put out the braziers. The children had collected up the palm-leaf plates and put them to burn; they were sizzling, little clouds of smoke rising through the clear *windless air towards the glittering stars above. This is a wonder-ful place to be, my work here a privilege. It grieves me that Miriam cannot feel the same.*

December 1964

A long conversation this evening with Jacob, who's been telling me more about the old beliefs. I'd been trying to get my class to interview their parents about the oda, or shrine, which used to be found in every traditional compound; also about whether many of them still really believe in reincarnation. But we've hit a bit of a wall—there's clearly still a superstitious reluctance to talk about such things to outsiders. And perhaps a rational enough desire to hedge their bets by continuing to subscribe at some level to the old, despite converting to the new. Jacob was talking about the first boy the village sent to grammar school, only four or five years before we arrived. A Christian family, but before he left his father had the Dibia cut him under the arms and rub in some powerful concoction to prevent him being poisoned by people who might be jealous of his success. He still has the scars, apparently.

Jacob of course is very hardline on all this: 'Thou shalt have no other God but me'; a text he has actually used for a sermon, a couple of months back. I don't entirely agree with him but my respect for him has increased since Karl's departure. He has risen admirably to the challenge of the new responsibilities I've given him. Now there's a student teacher in the village, he keeps respon-sibility for the Bible class, Sunday services and church work generally, and I organise visiting preachers for him once or twice a month. His steady, detailed knowledge of the village families has led him into increasingly useful work with them; today he had to attend a diocese meeting and asked if I would visit in his stead a family who have converted recently and whose little girl is dying of leukaemia. She's been at the hospital for a couple of months now, but there's nothing they can do, and Paul arranged for her to come home to die.

The mother is very quiet, but the father full of questions: if he had converted earlier, would Jesus have saved his child from getting ill? If God takes her to Heaven will she get older there or still be a little girl when he himself goes to Heaven as an old man and meets her? What if she doesn't recognise him? If Jesus truly loved them surely he wouldn't take away their greatest treasure?

The notion of a Love that expresses itself by testing the endurance of the beloved feels peculiarly abstract and unhelpful (though interestingly close to the behaviour of some of the local gods, according to Jacob—there's one called Ulu that showers misfortune upon its favourites; must be pan-cultural, I guess, the idea that there has to be some reward for great suffering—or indeed, some point; or that the victim must be endued with special powers in order to be able to bear it). But what's needed here—as ever—is a sympathetic listener, not a sermon. They are a steady, well-liked couple and have only the one child. The whole village is unsettled with their distress, and also by the sudden death last night of one of Tedum's goats. The most likely explanation is a snake bite, but when anything of this sort happens the old superstitions seem to seep through to the surface, like inky writing soaking through fresh blotting paper.

ANNE HAS BEEN STALLING AGAIN. What she must do is go and reassure Joseph. She makes her way down to the container deck, stopping on each level to glance up and down the corridors in case 'Sickbay' is signed anywhere. She could, of course, ask another officer. But might that create suspicion? They might even take her there and step into the room with her. Then the woman would be discovered. Idiotic thought. Joseph is not on the container deck. At least, he does not appear when she waits at the bottom of the stairs. When she walks towards the containers it seems to her they have been moved, they are not as they were before—but anyway, she knows he has abandoned the box where he stayed with his wife. What if Robbie has been searching down here? What if what Joseph said about Robbie is true? She's not going to think about that, nor the woman with her gaunt sleeping face, nor the live baby wriggling in her stomach, there's no need to think of any of that. She waits ten minutes before deciding he's not here. She is in some repeating-nightmare syndrome, a not-funny *Groundhog Day*, where she is doomed to come up and down these stairs perpetually in search of stowaways who on balance aren't there and quite possibly never existed.

She remembers putting the woman's clothes in a washing machine. Proof that the woman exists (worryingly so: if someone else should find them they would guess at the woman's presence; the clothes could hardly belong to either of the western women aboard).

The laundry is empty, its hot clean smell reassuringly familiar. But when she checks the washing machine where she put the clothes (only yesterday, wasn't it? Only yesterday afternoon) it's empty. Nothing in the baskets, nothing piled anywhere. Only some clean wet clothes scrunched inside the next machine—crew overalls, she recognises the grey. So where are the woman's clothes?

Perhaps there never were any clothes.

But she knows that's not true. Either they have been taken by someone like the captain, as evidence of a stowaway. Or Robbie himself has spotted and removed them, perhaps returning them to their owner. Would he have told Anne that? He might not have remembered. She scours her memory for *anything* he has told her about the woman—anything about what was wrong with her or how she is improving—but there's nothing.

She has to search for the sickbay. She walks the lengths of the corridors on this deck, checking all the doors for signs. Besides Laundry there is Linen Store, which she tries to open (why? Why try and open the one door she knows is not the one she wants?) but finds to be locked, and one unmarked door which swings half open, but contains nothing more interesting than a couple of toilets and shower cubicles. In the stairwell she meets a tall pale sailor with eyes as light and colourless as glass. She risks asking him for the sickbay, but he only looks incredulous and then rather afraid. He glances around as if someone else might have heard her, then puts his fingers to his lips.

'Do you speak English?' Anne asks. But he shakes his head so that his off-white hair flops from side to side, and runs quickly up the stairs. She follows him slowly, and goes on up to the open air—then doubles back to the little top-deck library. Perhaps there is a plan of the ship here. But the library is empty and sterile-feeling, there is no catalogue or place to look things up, only random selections of books along the walls. She slumps into one of the leather chairs, feeling the vibration of the engines through her elbow on the big wooden table; the slow vibration, the slow voyage, how many more days to go?

The door pushes open and Robbie comes in. 'I've been looking for you.' He doesn't smile.

'Yes?'

'Bad news. The female stowaway—her condition deteriorated. The medical officer felt he had to tell the captain. And the captain's angry. He doesn't think she could've come aboard on her own; he's ordered a search of the boat to find her accomplice.'

'What will he do with them?'

'He'll turn back to Abidjan to put them ashore. But the cyclone's moving inland, we'll have to wait for it to clear.'

'What shall I do?'

'You must tell me where the bloke's hiding so I can get to him first; then I can tuck him away somewhere the captain won't think of looking. Otherwise he'll get sent back.' His voice softens now, he pulls up a chair next to hers and takes her hand between his. His hands are warm and dry and leathery, the feel of them is reassuring. Anne draws a deep breath.

'It's serious, kid. My mob'll make a very thorough search.'

'Is it true—' He is kind. He is on Joseph's side. 'Do the sailors sometimes try to kill stowaways?'

Robbie stares at her unblinkingly. 'Where d'you hear that shit?'

'I—I heard there are fines . . .'

'You think the crew are a bunch of psychos?'

'No. No, of course not.' Anne wishes she hadn't said it.

Robbie turns her hand between his and begins to trace the lines in her palm, like a fortune teller. 'Of course there's more than one crew who would *think* it, perhaps. You gotta remember, some of these sailors aren't educated. I look after them like they were my kids.' He glances into Anne's face, suddenly kindly, it seems he wants her to understand. A wave of relief washes through her. 'What have they got, most of them? Maybe a shack somewhere with a girl in it, and a kid. They work their butts off, weeks on end at sea, to be able to take a present home to the girl and sit in the shack with her eating a bowl of rice. Why should the Africans steal that off them?'

'You mean, because of the fines?'

'The fines, sure, why should my boys suffer because the Africans want a free ride?'

How much are these fines? Would Father's flat raise enough? 'Maybe I could pay, Robbie, I could get the money for Joseph and his wife—'

'It's not the point.' She feels the chill of his anger again. She's said the wrong thing. 'Why should anybody pay? The Africans' lives are worthless. In their own countries they massacre each other, the ones at the top of the heap stuff their riches in Swiss bank accounts, the ones at the bottom starve. And they want to crawl out of their own cesspit to the west, where they can guzzle our food and grab our houses and cars—'

Anne has taken her hand out of his. She is pressing herself back in her chair, away from him. The force of her legs pushing against the table foot makes her chair suddenly squeak back an inch over the polished floor.

Robbie raises his eyebrows and smiles. 'What the crew think, kid. Survival of the fittest.'

'You think it.'

'Nah.'

She wants to go. But she should argue. 'It's racist filth. What *we* did to Africa—'

He starts to laugh. 'The cruel colonists? Spare me the history lesson.'

'You're disgusting.'

'What the *crew* think. People who haven't had the benefit of a western education.'

'And what do you think?'

'If they can get to Europe, good luck to 'em. But it's my job to look out for my boys.'

'By *killing*—'

He shakes his head theatrically slowly, as if she is very very stupid. 'For god's sake. I've told you so you can understand why this shit happens.'

She gets up to leave. She doesn't want to hear his poison, she doesn't want to contemplate what may have happened, what may be going to happen.

'You gonna shoot the messenger?'

He's been playing games with her from the start; she gave the woman to him, she held the door open while he carried her out of the cabin.

'It's not what I think, OK? I've lived in Africa. I have friends there.' He told her that before, that first lunch when they talked about Lagos. He is smiling; cajoling her. But laughing at her too. 'If I thought that, would I tell you?' He reaches forward and grabs her wrist. She has to take a step towards him, she will fall if she doesn't. He grins into her face. 'Tell you I'm an ignorant racist bastard, would that be the way to impress you?'

Anne doesn't know what to say. She doesn't trust her own judgement any more, she's veering about like the ship in the storm, not knowing anything, not knowing what is true.

'Come.' He is patting his knee, pulling her down.

She thinks of the last man she has had dealings with, Matthew Afigbo in Lagos; his kindly solidity, his tactful placing of the bribe on the bully's desk, the calm orderliness of his life as he saw to her father's burial and visited his parishioners. There are people who are calm and solid, whom you never have to doubt, good people whose intentions are clear. This man is not like that.

'You know what the penalty is, if one of us consorts with a passenger?'

'What d'you mean?' She allows herself to be pulled onto his knee.

'If any of us takes a shine to a passenger?'

'No.'

'Dismissal without pay.'

'Why?'

He shrugs. 'Bad for discipline.'

She remembers wandering the ship looking for him; accosting him publicly outside that engine room or whatever it was. 'Why didn't you tell me?'

'Because I like you.' He smiles into her eyes. His hand, which has been holding her, suddenly slips between her legs. 'Don't you believe that either?'

'I don't know.' She's scared. She doesn't know. He has all the power, he is helping the stowaways, he says he likes her, he touches her. 'Anyone could come in.'

'Let me worry about that.' His fingers are sliding under her clothes, his lips are pressed against hers, Anne is slipping. His lips brush her ear. 'Do you trust me?'

It is breath coming out of her. 'Yes.'

Supporting her weight, he stands. 'Come here. By the door.'

'We can be seen through the window.'

'Nobody passes. Here. Against the door, like this.'

Anne is in a daze, a swoon. He likes her. He could be dismissed without pay. He is hot and quick and certain, he knows what to do with her, she can let herself be carried along, until suddenly they're done and she is crying helpless floods of tears as if her whole head had melted. They slide to the floor.

'Hush, hush, what's the matter?' His hand is lightly over her mouth, he wants her to stop howling. 'Don't cry, what's the matter?'

She has to fight to control her breath. 'I'm sorry. I don't know. Sorry.'

He gives a little relieved laugh. 'Well stop then, you baby. Here.' He starts to wipe her face with his shirt, he is helping her up, pulling up her jeans and fastening them neatly, dressing her like a doll. He sits her in the chair while he tidies himself. Then he crouches beside her. 'You alright? I didn't hurt you?'

'No. Of course not.'

He nods. 'OK. Now, you going to stop thinking I'm some kind of psycho?'

'Yes.'

'What I want you to do, before we hit the storm again, you take me down to sort things out with your friend.' He helps her up, she is as uncoordinated and gangly as a newborn foal, as if her limbs have been taken apart and just put together again. He leads her along the corridor to the stairs, and she disentangles her arm from his hand. He is risking his job, she thinks.

Down one, two, three flights. She motions him to wait at the top of the container-deck stairs, and herself creeps halfway down. 'Joseph? Joseph!' she hisses, not daring more than a whisper. Her eyes scan the dimly lit area, the black shadows, the blank planes of the containers. He is nowhere to be seen. She moves on down and into the shadow of the area where they last spoke. Freezes and listens—nothing closer than the below-deck racket of the engines. Turns back and heads between the containers towards the place where the woman lay. She is moving, it feels, quickly and confidently now, knowing Robbie is at her back to keep her safe. She whispers Joseph's name again and listens, but still there is nothing. And she is forced to turn and make her way slowly back. Robbie is standing staring in her direction. As she steps into the lit area and he sees she is alone, he turns and begins to ascend. There is something oddly familiar about his dark legs, moving up the stairs.

At the top Robbie opens a door—the first of those blank green doors. She half expects to see the winter park with its smooth-barked trees and people hurrying home, but it is a little cubicle of a place with a single bunk built into the wall, a functional steel sink, a mirror-fronted cupboard. Something vaguely surgical about it, perhaps just the sink. She has a sudden sickening memory of that clinic, a white cloth draped over a stainless steel bowl. Robbie closes the door behind her and turns angrily. 'Where is he?'

'I don't know.'

'Why doesn't he come out to meet you?' His eyes are cold and sharp. She doesn't want him to look like this. She wants him to smile at her.

'I don't know. Robbie, I really don't know. The first place they were in where the woman was, that container's gone. I couldn't even find it.'

'You're lying. You know where he is.'

'No I'm not, why should I?'

There's a moment's silence. Anne takes a step towards Robbie but he steps back, hand on the door handle, ready to leave. 'As soon as you find him you let me know. Understand?' And he does go, quickly, angrily, just like that, just as if he hadn't wiped her tears on his shirt or dressed her as tenderly as if she were a child, or told her that he liked her.

Anne feels the shadow of her former fear. She thinks of a kind of torture (but can't remember the name of it) where the victim is subjected to an offer of freedom then renewed captivity, to hope then despair. Her tired brain fixes it: Pavlovian dogs. Behave in a certain way to get a reward. But then the experimenter administers an electric shock instead of a reward. The dog does its trick, gets its reward. Does its trick, gets its reward. Does its trick, gets a shock. At random. Quite soon the dog goes mad. It no longer knows how to behave.

When Anne has returned to her cabin she showers and goes back to bed. There doesn't seem much else to do. The ship is already beginning to heave up and down on the rising sea, they are re-entering the edge of the storm. She doesn't know what the captain is planning to do about the woman, or if they will call at Abidjan. If she stops believing Robbie she will go mad. He said he would take her to the woman, she remembers that, but 'not in the middle of the day'. Tonight then. She dozes uneasily for a while, and then switches on the lamp.

August 28, 1965

A long gap. The days are too full, there's been no time to keep a record of the time. Full and happy, with a greater sense of service and contentment than I've ever had before. Happiness writes white; *a pleasing little saying Miriam told me when I was bemoaning my abandoned diary.*

Though it's not quite unhappiness *that now prompts me to put pen to paper. Not unhappiness at all but unsettled-ness, I suppose—and of course the sudden resurgence of time. Miriam and Anne have been in England four weeks now, another two to go. It has been liberating, knowing that if I want to I can stay on in the office after supper until my whole desk is clear, and come back to the house at midnight without having to face Miriam's weary questioning or silent hostility. Lunchtimes likewise, I've been able to do some useful extra work with Peter before his entrance exam, by keeping him half an hour after class in the mornings.*

But it would be ridiculous to pretend I don't miss them, Anne in particular. She's at a delightful stage right now, full of curiosity about everything, dashing about the station like a little monkey, vastly entertained by the discoveries she makes along the way. In the kitchen she's been into just about every cupboard and drawer she can find; she managed to eat half a jar of the Vaseline poor Luke keeps under the sink for his sore heel. He took her to Miriam in tears, afraid she might be poisoned, though of course there was no effect whatsoever. She has a family of tiny dolls Amoge has made for her out of scraps of old material, and spends hours in whispered conversations with them, or rather, whispering their conversations for them, enacting little dramas. Amoge has taught her some songs and ditties which they chant together and then Anne claps and laughs in sheer delight. She is an absolute ray of sunshine about the place. And I miss her tugging at the blankets and wheedling her way into the warm space between me and Miriam in the bed; and her imperious insistence that only I should cut up her food at dinnertime. She's the darling of the whole station; there's not a person here (not even Paul at his most curmudgeonly) who doesn't smile to see her, and the houseboys are terrible, slipping her sweet things and treats whenever they can. Luke is putty in her hands—she makes him take her across to the clinic on his shoulders, pulling at his hair if he doesn't gallop fast enough.

She's in grave danger of being spoilt and I've told Miriam I think we should have another, not just because it would persuade Anne that she's not the centre of the universe, but to provide her with a playmate. But Miriam is rather resistant; says she wants to get involved with the occupational therapy work at the old leprosy settlement, on top of her work in the clinic here, and that anyway I hardly have time to see her and Anne now, so how would another child fare? One of Miriam's convenient illogicalities, since she knows I manage my time quite carefully, and would make sure I adapted to the needs of a little addition to the family. It would be truer to say that she would have difficulty adjusting her working hours etc to suit another child. I'm not sure she realises how lucky she is in Amoge, who is endlessly patient with Anne, and who could easily, I'm sure, be persuaded to take on another, younger charge.

Which brings me to Amoge. I suppose she has been preying a little on my mind these past few days, in a way that she wasn't before Miriam went away. It's funny how it's appearing in a slightly different light in Miriam's absence; again, perhaps only the effect of having a little time and space in which to consider. But Amoge herself has interpreted Miriam's absence in a way which I am obliged to discourage.

There is something rather odd and contradictory in the very fact that I am now (while Miriam is in England, and clearly can't be affected by my behaviour in any way) afflicted by little pangs of guilt, which I never really felt while she was here. And which I know in themselves to be unnecessary; my love and commitment to Miriam are as strong as the day I married her. If any proof were needed, it lies in the fact that now, when I have unlimited opportunity to spend time with Amoge, I'm actually seeing rather less of her than I was before.

Recently I have prayed to Him for the strength of mind to end it. Really Amoge should be sent away, but I haven't the heart to when Anne is so devoted to her, and indeed while Amoge is so useful to Miriam herself. It's not as if it has been anything Miriam could really be hurt by; she would have more justification in being jealous over the amount of time I spend coaching my grammar-school entrants than in those little snatched half-hours with Amoge. Thanks to the ever-vigilant Mrs Katanga, we've only ever done it once in Amoge's own bed (the occasion when Mrs K visited her sister in hospital); mostly we've been confined to our hurried early-morning encounters in the schoolroom, which punctuate Amoge's sweeping up and my inspection of the trainees' marking, and general planning for the day. Miriam isn't even awake then, it's time stolen from no one but myself.

And Amoge is incorrigible. How could any man resist? Even sitting here calmly writing about it I still find myself excited by the memory of that first morning in the schoolroom; of her sweeping her way industriously up and down between the desks, bottom swaying from side to side, until she suddenly became aware that I had been distracted from my work by her movement; of the way she straightened and looked at me then dropped the broom and began to walk slowly towards my desk, fingers deftly unthreading the buttons on her blouse. Coming round the side of the desk till she was standing only inches away from me, opening her blouse and standing there perfectly still, smiling at me, waiting for me to touch.

It has been innocent enough; two of God's creatures delighting in the bodies He has given them. It's not as if Amoge has a husband she is betraying, or indeed, as if anything is being taken away from Miriam. Miriam and I still have relations, and I might even say that my little encounters with Amoge have rather added spice and interest to the marital bed.

But Amoge has got the wrong idea about Miriam's absence. Partly I'm afraid from Miriam herself, who actually told Amoge how angry she was that I wasn't going on leave with them. I don't know why she can't see how utterly inappropriate it is for her to talk to Amoge, a servant, about her disagreements with me; or indeed to talk to anyone one else about a matter that should be private between the two of us. Apparently she told Amoge I'd promised when Anne was born that we would take her home to see the relatives, and she has had to wait and beg for three years for me to agree. Now I've let her down again, proving I put everything in the world before her.

Miriam knows that since Karl's gone I've not only taken over his job in name but actually made it into a far bigger job (despite the fact that all the preaching is, of course, done by Jacob and the visiting pastors); should I disappear for six weeks while the new church walls are going up? While my trainees need help and constant supervision? While my Standard 6 class is only two months away from their exams? While the whole difficult business of the profits from the market stall remains unresolved? While Paul already has to juggle his clinics and rely on everyone for extra help because of Miriam's own absence? While the Mothers' Union are in some strange and as yet unexplained state of offence, with half of them refusing to speak to me, and neither Perpetual nor Catherine prepared to tell me what's behind it?

But all that's beside the point; the problem is that she chose to complain of me to Amoge. Who's a simple girl and could find only one explanation for my unwillingness to accompany my wife and daughter to England, viz herself.

Which led to an encounter which was, I think, even more distressing for me than it was for Amoge. I met with her in the schoolroom a few times in the first weeks of Miriam's absence, and arranged to pick her up on the road beyond the village in the car one afternoon, so that we could have a slightly more leisurely tryst in the open air, but that is nothing different than has happened while Miriam was around. Last Friday, in the third week of Miriam's absence, I was up very late in the office, trying to finish off the accounts. I think it must have been after eleven when I finally stumbled across to the house. It had been raining heavily all evening, drumming on the roof; I was half stupefied with the noise of it, and didn't bother to pick up the umbrella—so I was drenched to the skin when I got to the bungalow. I collected the lamp Luke leaves burning for me, and headed straight for bed. Except that lying in the bed (on Miriam's side of the bed, to be precise) was a completely naked Amoge. I was so shocked I couldn't speak, and she began to smile and writhe in the bed in a way that reminded me vividly of the snake Luke found in the generator hut. At last I found my tongue.

'Get out. Get out of that bed now.'

I don't think she heard me over the rain, because she rose to her knees on the bed, flaunting herself at me, still smiling and stretching out her arms. I put down the lamp and grabbed the nearest thing to hand—my own dressing gown—and wrapped it around her shoulders. 'Not here. Not here in my wife's bed, Amoge.'

She understood me well enough then and within a moment the smiles were replaced by tears. 'But your wife gone England,' she kept repeating through her sobs. 'Your wife gone England.'

I ushered her out into the sitting room, then gathered up her clothes and handed them to her. Opening the door to the deafening beat of the rain again, I ran over to the office to get the umbrella for her. The whole sky was flickering with continuous lightning, and through the streaming rain the empty compound was weirdly stark in the light. When I ran back with the umbrella she was gone, leaving me to a rather troubled, sleepless night, wondering how on earth I had let things come to such a pass.

And by the time dawn began to creep redly up the eastern sky, I had decided that I should definitely finish with Amoge. I don't want her thinking she can take that kind of liberty. I certainly don't want her to imagine that I in any way view her in the same light as Miriam. I can see that I am at fault; the girl is younger than me, impressionable, perhaps even genuinely fond of me. It was she first played the temptress, but it is clearly my responsibility to end it, to save both of us from straying further.

I was reluctant to meet her first thing next morning, so I avoided going over to the schoolroom till 7.25, when I knew my pupils would be gathering. And in fact, by dint of avoiding the schoolroom first thing, and thanks to the fact that Amoge is not needed to look after Anne, I managed to avoid bumping into her for a couple of days. But this morning I decided to grasp the nettle, and went to the schoolroom at 6.30.

She was already at work polishing my desk, but when I walked in she froze. I closed the door quietly behind me, and went to my chair. 'Amoge my dear, sit down. We have to talk about this.'

She sat at the front desk, eyes already swimming with tears, hands clenched on the desk in front of her, like a child waiting to be told off. I was filled with remorse.

'I'm sorry if I upset you the other night. I wasn't expecting you to be there.'

'You don't like me.'

'You know I am very fond of you, but—'

'But not good enough to come in your house.'

'You do come in my house, you look after Anne, I trust you with my child.'

'Your wife is gone but you don't want me.'

'Again, not true, you know perfectly well that I want you—'

'Here.' She spat it out with contempt, gesturing to the schoolroom as if it was some kind of pit. 'Like dogs.'

What on earth did she imagine could happen? 'I can see that this has all been a mistake. What we should do now is kneel together and ask God's forgiveness.'

'You finish me?'

'I'm married, Amoge.'

She sat in silence. I found myself staring at her hands, the nails were biting into the rosy flesh of the palms. I waited for her to speak but nothing came.

'You know I love my wife and child. I've never led you to believe anything different.'

'You make love me.'

'Yes but I can see that was a mistake, now. I can see that we should have resisted that tempt—'

Abruptly, she pushed her chair back and stood up. Before I could finish she had run out of the room. I picked up her cleaning things and put them away neatly in the cupboard. I was mystified by her. She can't have imagined in her wildest dreams that there could ever be anything more between us.

This evening I've resisted going to seek her out. What on earth is there to say? I feel sad for her distress, for whatever delusion she has been labouring under. I pray God will soothe and comfort her, and that He will, out of His great love and generosity, forgive me for my part in this sin. But it is painful to feel that she is angry with me when I don't fully understand why. I don't want things to be awkward with Amoge when Miriam and Anne return.

SEPTEMBER 5, 1965

I haven't seen Amoge all week, and was disturbed by her absence from Reading Class. I nodded to Theresa, who usually sits with her, to stay behind. The whole class was, I thought, unusually subdued and quiet. Perhaps they picked up the mood from me. 'Theresa, where's Amoge?'

'Her father's compound.'

'Has she left the mission?'

Theresa shook her head.

'She's just visiting at her father's?' It was not unreasonable, given that she had a holiday from her work caring for Anne.

'Yes Mr David.'

'D'you know when she will be back?'

Theresa looked at her feet, there was a silence.

'Can you tell her, can you tell her my wife and Anne will be back on Sunday, and I'm sure Anne will want to see her then.'

Theresa nodded then dashed out as if she were afraid I might bite her.

I decided to leave it at that, and spent the rest of the evening going through the market stall finances with John Matefi, who has, I am sure, been fiddling the books, though it is hard to put my finger on the spot. He was clearly rather alarmed at the amount of detail I was willing to go into, so with any luck I will have frightened him off trying the same trick again. If it continues dry I shall be able to get off early tomorrow to Umuahia to pick up clinic supplies and the stained-glass window design which Mr Nwodo promised to have finished for me—a real treat to look forward to.

A S ANNE CLOSES THE DIARY she is aware of a horrible feeling of emptiness. She wishes she had not read this. When did she last eat? After a while she opens the door a crack and rain lashes in on her. It's dark. She's puzzled about how to get food, then remembers the steward and rings for him. He's a long time; she turns the closed diary over in her hands as she waits, the texture of the cloth binding rough beneath her fingers. It is the same neat even writing, the same certainty, unfurling line after line across the page. The same conviction, in everything he does. Yes she has always raged, but a part of her did believe in him. The steward knocks and after an awkward conversation goes away and returns with the bread roll and water she requested. Sitting on her bed nibbling the bread and sipping the water she thinks yes, she is in jail. But Robbie will come soon, he will have stopped being angry. He will come soon and take her to see the woman, and then she will try to find Joseph again. It will be all right. It will be all right.

When she's finished the bread she puts on her English winter jacket and lets herself out onto the deck, needing to escape the cabin, wishing she could escape the ship. She stands at the rail under the pitch-black sky gulping lungfuls of rushing air, relieved to be distracted by pepperings of hard wind-blown rain and spray, her mouth full of the taste of salt.

She senses rather than sees the shape at the rail beside her. A small figure, no bigger than a child; between the gusts of wind there seems to come a sound of sobbing. Anne moves close enough to touch the little cold hand on the rail—Ellie Malone, it can't be anyone else. 'Are you alright?' she shrieks.

But she can't hear a reply. Ellie is sodden; taking her by the unresisting arm, Anne hauls her back to her cabin. In the light she is a mess, her few strands of hair plastered to her pink skull, red swollen eyes, black mascara streaks across her withered cheeks, her almost lipless mouth a crimson smudge. Anne guides her towards the bed and as the ship tilts Ellie collapses onto it. Fighting gravity, Anne staggers up the floor to the bathroom and fetches Ellie a towel.

'What is it?'

Ellie dabs her face and wraps the towel like a shawl around her neck. 'I want to go home.'

'The storm?'

Ellie shakes her head. 'I want to see my daughter.' It is a wail, and Anne moves awkwardly to comfort her.

'Won't you see her when you get back?'

Through sobs Ellie gasps, 'I want to see the children opening their presents.'

Anne sits beside Ellie and puts her hand on Ellie's arm. She's puzzled what to say. 'I thought you liked Christmas on board ship?'

Ellie shakes her head. 'I hate it. I hate it. False cheer. Frozen food. Getting drunk with strangers.'

'But don't you and Mr Malone always go away?'

Ellie nods. She blows her nose on Anne's towel and composes herself. 'He doesn't like me spending time with the children. He wants me to himself.'

Anne visualises Mr Malone's beaky birthmarked face and staring eyes, and suppresses a shudder.

'He says we should live our own lives now.'

'But surely . . .'

'What?' Ellie looks Anne in the eye.

'Can't you stay at home on your own?'

'He won't go away without me. If I stay at home he stays to make my life a misery.'

'But if you tell him you don't *want* to go . . .'

Ellie looks at Anne in silence for a moment, then gives a little laugh. 'Easy to tell you're not married.'

'I don't understand.'

'He doesn't like the grandchildren running about, interrupting his routine. They make him feel old.'

'So you have to exile yourself to the middle of the ocean?'

'D'you know what he'd be doing if he was at home? Watching to see where I went. Listening to see if I spoke on the phone.'

'Jealous?'

'Of his own children. He won't have them in the house overnight.'

'Why d'you go along with it?'

'We've been married forty-six years.'

Anne doesn't know what to say, and Ellie's voice rises defensively. 'He's nice to me when we come away. He just doesn't like sharing me.' She rises unsteadily and staggers to the bathroom where she dabs at her ruined face with the wet towel. 'Will you help me back to my cabin, dear? I expect we'll all feel better after dinner.'

Anne guides her through the wind and rain to her cabin, then returns and sits on her own bed, staring at the opposite wall. She tries not to imagine the Malones in their beds. Robbie must come back soon.

But time passes. Dinnertime (when she was sure he would come), 9 p.m., 10 p.m., 11. Is it the storm? Is that what's keeping him busy? The ship is lurching up and down but no more violently, it seems, than it did before. Should she go and look for him? The hated vista of the stairways and corridors opens in her mind's eye. She can't bear to go staggering down and along those corridors again, constantly off-balance, peering this way and that for a door, a sign, risking his anger again and also of course the danger of getting him into trouble—no. Her whole body weighs like lead, the bread and water churn in her stomach like the workings of a cement mixer. She can't read on. She can't go out. There are things she can't think, she mustn't begin to imagine. She holds herself in suspension. Eventually this will end.

At 3 a.m. when she has given up all hope and is lying semi-conscious, flattened by the ship's bucking and dropping, the door flies open with a blast of cold wet air, and Robbie is there. 'Where is he?'

Anne is bewildered.

'Where's the stowaway?'

'I don't know. I haven't seen him.'

'You're lying.' He comes in, letting the door slam shut; suddenly to her amazement he is yanking open the door of her wardrobe, groping about inside. Striding into the tiny bathroom, kicking the side of the shower, crouching to look under the beds.

'Robbie I told you I don't—'

'He's not on the container deck.'

She is struggling to get up, panicking. 'Are we going to Abidjan?'

'No. Where is he?'

'If I see him I'll tell you. Take me to the woman Robbie, please . . .'

He gives a final glance around the room. 'Not now. I want to know where he is. Tonight. You understand?' Another blast of dark wind like a cold hand slapping her face, jolting her out of her stupor, and the door slams shut.

Anne has got her legs out from under the covers—she is on the edge of the bed, feet braced against the floor, ready to stand up. But what for? He looked in the wardrobe. He was looking under the beds.

Her bare legs stretching in front of her seem white and thin and as if they don't belong to her, as if they couldn't hold her up. The second toenail on the left foot is bruised, she notices. Why did he look in the wardrobe?

Because he wants to find Joseph.

Why does he want so badly to find him?

Suddenly, completely without warning, Anne's stomach leaps up her throat and she vomits. The spasm is violent, her nose and windpipe are blocked momentarily, she has to struggle for breath. She leans forward over the legs that don't belong to her, gasping and staring at the pale splatter on the neat fleck carpet.

It can't be true. Robbie is kind; when she first told him he promised to keep it a secret. He's not like the captain—the captain would send them back. In the library—look, in the library, he wiped her tears on his shirt, he dressed her as if she were a little child. Didn't he say he liked her?

He wants Joseph.

Now—yes, because something's happened. There's some danger she doesn't understand, he's impatient with her for being slow, that's all it is . . . it doesn't mean what you're thinking. It doesn't mean . . .

She forces herself to her feet, like a stiltwalker she can go step step step to the bathroom. Wipes her legs with the towel, rinses her face and mouth. The trip back to the bed looks a bit far, she pulls down the toilet lid with a bang and sits there.

It doesn't mean what precisely?

You have to think this.

OK. If Joseph was telling the truth. If Robbie wanted to kill them. From the start? OK, from the start. If Robbie wanted to kill them from the start, from when Anne first mentioned their existence—why would he take the woman out to the sickbay?

That's easy. So he could dispose of her when it was convenient. He came back to Anne's room. After he'd removed the woman, minutes after, full of strange energy—intensity—she thought the storm, something's happened, an electric current—and he came to her—

It's cold here, she will go back to the bed. But walking is too hard, she crawls up the hill from bathroom to her tilted bed on all fours, and has to wait for the ship to right itself momentarily before she can raise her limbs against the downward pull and get up onto the bed.

She forces her mind back over the minutes the incident took. The other man, the 'medic', was a crewman, she was surprised by his boiler suit at the time. Together they lifted the woman like a sack between them. Anne opened the door for them. She had barely closed it when she realised she should have gone after them, and looked out to the stairs where they should be. They weren't there. They'd gone very quickly, she remembers she was surprised, because it would have been hard for them to open the door at the top of the stairs. She sat on her bed and stared at the woman's empty bed and wondered what to do. She felt regretful he had not looked at her.

What did Robbie and the sailor do? They lugged the woman out of the cabin and round between the containers. They shouted out to one another in the wind, counting as they swung the body higher over the rail. They flung her into the sea, in the dark. They patted each other on the back and laughed, exulting at how easy it was. And Robbie came back to fuck Anne.

Anne is cold again. She must have been sitting still a long time, her legs are stiff when she tries to uncurl them. She should have pulled the blanket over her. All this must be true.

From the start? From the very start?

She remembers the first lunchtime when she talked to Robbie. Remembers clearly thinking, he's not flirting with me at all. I imagined it, I simply made it up. Then the next time— yes, she asked him about the stowaways. He guessed, he knew what she was saying. 'You're pretty when you blush.' He said it to make her tell him more.

Each time she asked to see the woman he put her off with sex. She refused to believe what Joseph told her. Even in the library, when she had heard the racist venom from his very lips—even then minutes later she was opening her mouth and letting his tongue inside . . .

It should be possible to die of shame.

SEPTEMBER 19, 1965

I can't face my class this morning; my hands are shaking like an old man's. My eyes fill with tears at the slightest thing.

I must set it down. I must examine it, to try and understand why He has allowed this to happen.

Begin at their return. Yes. They came home on the Sunday morning. I drove up to Enugu the day before, so I could be at the airport bright and early. Anne squealed with delight to see me and even Miriam, who had been angry ever since I said I couldn't accompany them home, was warm and smiling, kissed me fondly and clung to me. All through that long drive home we talked. Back at the bungalow I had instructed Luke to prepare chicken and vegetables and a huge fruit salad. He welcomed them, all smiles, and we ate and they talked on, pouring out news of friends and relatives. They had even met up with Karl, now apparently happily training missionaries for overseas service. Anne proudly recited to me the lists of her newly found grandparents, aunt, uncle, cousins—and pets; Miriam tells me she was much taken with cats (I had never noticed till now that we have none here) and loved to follow them around the big English houses. Through Miriam I managed to get a glimpse of how strange and wonderful it all is to Anne, the cold paved streets and terraced houses, the red brick and grey stone, in contrast to the lush green sprawl of the compound here. And when Anne couldn't keep her eyes open any longer, I carried her hot chubby little body to her room and tucked her up, and Miriam and I fell into bed with a warmth and pleasure we haven't known for months.

It's strange. I have never cried like this before. Dear Lord, help me understand Your will.

I was busy on the Monday, of course, up and at my desk before Miriam was awake; she was going to take a couple of days to sort things out before going back to the clinic—and Ebitu's father came to see me at lunchtime, so what with one thing and another I didn't see Miriam to speak to until the evening. It was delightful to be able to sit with her on the veranda again, sipping a cool drink, talking through the events of the past month. I had entirely forgotten to ask whether Amoge had come for Anne, but Miriam herself suddenly mentioned the girl. 'Amoge was late this morning,' she said.

'Oh?'

'I could tell something was wrong so I asked her.'

'Yes?' I was being annoyed by mosquitoes; I had to step into the house for a bottle of repellent. 'Yes?' I said again, using some and passing the bottle to Miriam.

'The silly girl has only gone and got herself pregnant.'

I became aware of Miriam repeating what she had said and asking if I had heard. 'Yes. I must say I'm surprised. I thought she was infertile.'

'I guess her ex-husband'll work it out, when his new wife doesn't conceive either.'

I was conscious of the silence. 'So what did you advise her to do?'

'She must get married, obviously, but she won't tell me who it is.'

I had finished my drink. I got up and refilled our glasses, and popped my head into the kitchen to tell Luke he could go when he'd finished cooking, I would serve it up myself. I remember standing for a moment in the hallway not wanting to go back onto the veranda, I remember thinking how foolish it was that such a little thing (and one that should, by rights, be joyous) could present itself as such an unpleasant problem. When I forced myself to go out again Miriam was still sitting, staring at the last of the pink light in the sky above the palm trees.

'It's so beautiful here. You know I missed it? Even though I've spent all that time here, missing England.' Her voice was sweet and low.

I bent down and kissed her neck. I knew how lucky I was to have such a wife. She turned to me.

'We'll have to do something, David. I feel we're almost in the role of her parents now. We'll have to help her sort it out. Can you have a word with her and find out who he is?'

'What if he's married?'

'Well—I know the church doesn't approve, but quite a few of the village men have two and three wives, don't they?'

There was another silence, which Miriam broke. 'What really bothers me is—maybe it's stupid—I was afraid of something bad, to cause her to be so upset, something shameful, like maybe her brother or her father—'

'Oh no. No, it couldn't be.'

'I think she's more likely to tell you than me.'

My heart sunk even lower at this evidence of Miriam's faith in me. 'Shall we eat?' I asked her, and we went in to dinner.

I had hoped to avoid Amoge for a while, until I had had time to consider the situation and decide what might be the best course of action, but early the next morning I had to examine the church walls with the builders, then teach, and spend my lunch hour making the radio report which I had neglected to do on Sunday because of Miriam's return, then work with the gardening class, and it was while I was in the middle of showing them how to make a compost heap that Amoge suddenly appeared and announced that Miriam had asked her to talk to me. I told the lads to continue with general weeding, and took Amoge into my office.

'Miriam tells me you're pregnant.'

'Yes.'

'Who is the father?'

There was a little silence as she stared at me.

'You haven't slept with anyone else?'

Her eyes widened as if I had hit her.

'You told me you couldn't have children. If I had imagined there was any danger of that I would never have—' I didn't want to speak harshly. It was very difficult, her standing there looking at me as if she imagined that somehow I could find a solution.

'Please don't cry. Do you think we could find you a husband from the village? I'm sure there are men who would like a skilled second wife like you. Mr Ikedi, for example, he's a kind, steady fellow . . .'

The tears ran down her face.

'Amoge, what do you want me to do?'

'You should marry me.'

'Don't be ridiculous. You must marry a village man or—' The radio suddenly crackled into life. I must have left it on after the lunchtime call-in. It was Mr Nwankwo, the preacher for Sunday, wanting to know if he could arrive a day early and take a Bible class the night before, and needing directions. I was busy with him for a few minutes. When I finally switched off, Amoge had wiped her tears and composed herself. She began to speak.

'I ask to work in the compound for you. Because I like you. They all know I am your woman.'

'Who? Who knows?' I was appalled.

'The women. They see you talk me after class, they see you give me special station work.'

'But I did that because I was sorry for you, because of your divorce.'

'Now I am shame. You kick me out. I have white baby, who will marry me?'

If I had thought of it before it might not have struck me so brutally then. But I had not considered the colour of the child. 'You must leave. Today. You can get a lift in the stores van to Umuahia this afternoon.' I reached into the desk for the cash *box but the lid came off as I was lifting it out and coins fell and rolled all over the desk and onto the floor. I was flustered and I pushed a handful towards her, I don't even know how much, her eyes were boring into me. After a moment she stepped forward and swept the money into her hand. She walked out of the office.*

I had to finish things. I had to return to the gardening class, I had to check off the stores delivery which arrived soon after, I had to help Luke with the generator which was cutting out again. A long-running dispute between two boys in Standard 5 had been taken up by both families and I had promised to cycle into the village before dark to talk with both parties. And all the time the trouble was churning in my mind, Amoge, Miriam, Miriam, Amoge, distracting me from my work. It was quite dark by the time I had to cycle back to the station and I couldn't stand the turmoil in my mind a minute longer. I leant my bike against a tree and knelt down in the darkness there and then to pray for guidance. And my prayer—I thought—was answered. It became clear to me, as I knelt and reflected, that I must make a clean breast of things to Miriam. Indeed, I felt a wave of relief. I must beg her forgiveness, and after that peace and a return to normality would become possible. There should be no secrets between a man and his wife. I had done her wrong.

A part of me, of course, was still reluctant—knowing, foreseeing, the distress and confusion that might be caused; but I could see it was His will I should confess, and when I got on my bicycle to head for home again, it was with a slightly lighter heart.

I was late for dinner as it was, and Anne was tired and whiny throughout the meal. Miriam asked me why Amoge hadn't come to give her her bath but I simply said I didn't know, and left Miriam to put the child to bed while I sat at my desk trying to work out how best to explain myself. When she came in at last with a cup of coffee I asked her to sit down. 'I need to talk to you.'

I watched her balance her own coffee on the arm of the sofa

*then she turned to meet my eyes. The colour drained out of her
face like water through a sieve. 'Amoge.'*

*'I need to talk to you about it,' I repeated carefully, but she was
staring at me open-mouthed, as if I had turned into some kind of
monster.*

'It was you.'

'It's not what you think, it's not—'

*Quite suddenly she launched herself at me, flailing out with
her arms, hitting my face, knocking things from the desk. The
coffee sloshed across my diary. She was screaming dreadful
things, words she would never use—'Bastard, bastard, fucking
bastard!' I had to grasp her wrists and force her away from the
desk.*

*'Stop shouting. You'll wake Anne.' I let her go and she stopped,
shrinking away from me into the chair. 'Miriam listen to me.
Calm down. It wasn't important.'*

*She was still staring at me with that terrible look on her face.
'You wouldn't come to England. You wanted to be with her.'*

*Even in the heat and distress of the moment I noted how sin-
gularly women's minds function: that both she and Amoge should
find the same reason for my staying, though the real reason must
have been crystal clear to both—my work.*

*She was beside herself. I tried repeatedly to explain; to point out
how trivial a matter it had been, to let her know that Amoge herself had acted the role of seductress, that nothing could have been
further from my mind when I suggested we employ the girl—but
no. Miriam wanted to put the worst possible construction on
everything, I was complete and utter villain, I had planned it all
months in advance. After a while I saw it was pointless to continue, and I walked out onto the veranda leaving her to calm down.*

*A long period passed. My senses were so painfully alert I could
hear her sniffling and gulping from the back of the house. I could
even hear Anne murmur in her sleep. The sound of the frogs at the
pump was almost deafening. I was filled with terrible weariness,
at the thought of the talking and arguing and explaining there*

was still to do—at the way it would distract me and rob me of energy for my work. Then as I sat on the steps with my head in my hands I suddenly remembered Amoge. The ugly crash of the petty cash onto the wooden desk echoed in my ears. I began to run across to Mrs Katanga's hut, praying that Amoge had simply hidden the money under her pillow and fallen asleep. I had only wanted her gone to protect Miriam from knowing. But Mrs Katanga, roused eventually by my calls, told me furiously that she had gone, gone that afternoon and taken a bundle of her things with her.

I made my way slowly back to the bungalow, sick at heart, determined to go after Amoge at first light. Miriam was waiting on the veranda, I saw her outlined against the glowing light in the window. She stood quite still as I came up the steps. Then she hissed at me, 'Been to visit your bitch?' and something hard came swinging at me out of the darkness.

I was in my study on the floor when I woke up. It was daylight, and the side of my head was throbbing—I don't know what she'd hit me with, perhaps a piece of wood. When I tried to sit up my vision blurred and I felt sick, but after a while I managed to prop myself in a sitting position against the wall. The house was quiet. I was thirsty. I pulled myself up slowly on the furniture and went out into the hall. All the curtains were still drawn although the sun was high in the sky. I made my way to the kitchen but Luke had not put out any juice for breakfast. I poured myself a glass of water from the jug and sat at the table trying to work out what had happened. It was midday. My class would have wasted their morning. Luke should be here; had Miriam and Anne breakfasted without me? Gradually the wretched debacle of the previous night came back to me. There was blood on my shirt, so I crept to the bedroom to look for another, leaning against the wall as I went. But when I opened the door I lost my balance anyway, and fell. The room had been ransacked. My clothes were strewn across the bed and floor, ripped and trampled upon. The wardrobe doors *hung open, it was empty, all Miriam's clothes and shoes, gone. The suitcase was gone from the top of the wardrobe.*

I think I was still sitting there gawping when Luke came in in the afternoon. Tutting and fussing, he helped me into a chair and fetched water to bathe my head.

'Where are they?'

'Sir?' He pretended to concentrate on dabbing at the wound.

'Where are they?'

'Missus Miriam tell me I must take her.'

'Take her where?'

'I say, where is Mr David but she tells me you agree, I must do what she ask.'

'I'm not going to blame you. Just tell me where they are.'

'Enugu.'

She woke him at eleven—it must have been straight after she knocked me out—and told him to drive them to Enugu. Did she drag me into the study on her own? And leave me lying there, hurt? I can't bring myself to believe it of her. Luke told me she put two suitcases into the car, and took Anne, asleep and wrapped in a blanket. And she took turns with Luke to drive the six-hour journey to the airport; gave him £10 for petrol when they arrived and told him to have a rest and something to eat before he drove back. From Enugu of course, she could fly to Lagos. And from Lagos to London.

I was befuddled and drowsy with pain; it took me a while to work out that I must go after her. I must catch her before she got a flight. I asked Luke to make me some coffee, and had a proper wash and changed. The compound was eerily quiet when I went out, no one around the school, the church site deserted; the men must have stopped work because they saw I wasn't there to chivvy them. The stillness of the place struck a kind of dread into me and I resolved that I must start to train up a good assistant as soon as possible, to ensure that work could go on if ever I was ill. My trainee teachers, of course, all move on to other schools. Jacob is a good, almost a saintly man, but not a leader. He has no grasp of the practicalities of running the station. I need to train someone young. I had noted before that Karl's failure to do this made him believe he was indispensable, and I saw that I had perhaps fallen into the same trap, purely through pressure of work.

My head was full of these thoughts and I was even working out who might be a suitable candidate, perhaps Joshua who is currently teaching Standard 5 for me, or Stephen, a bit of a plodder but utterly honest and reliable. I have driven over the planks at Ubibi corner (bridging the deep ditch where the road has subsided) scores of times—in rain, in darkness, practically in my sleep. But as I was driving towards them I suddenly knew—and I slowed right down, to take the utmost care—that I would not be able to steer the car over them. I slowed to walking pace. I edged the front tyres onto each plank, held the wheel steady, crept forwards in a straight line, already knowing the thing to be impossible. I was even waiting for the horrible splintering sound and lurching crash, as the rear left tyre slipped off the edge of its plank, and the back of the car skewed downwards at a shocking angle.

(My head so full of spinning thoughts, my pen can't keep pace, but to experience that terrible dread on approaching a bridge I have previously crossed unthinkingly, blithely, reminds me of the loss of Faith. Loss of Faith makes what was simple and easy, difficult. It reduces an able, confident, active man to a hesitant, craven fool. I must have Faith. I will have Faith. I know these are His tests.)

It was impossible to open the driver's door because it was wedged against the ditch. I crawled across and got out the passenger side, and tried to inspect the damage. There wasn't much to be seen but the car was lying at a hopeless tilt, back tyres in the bottom of the ditch, like a kitten trying to crawl out of a bucket. We would need ropes and a lot of strong men—maybe even a towing vehicle. I started to walk back to the village.

It was after dark by the time we got it out, and the rear section of the exhaust had been crushed against the underside of the car. I limped back to the station with it. I had anyway given up the idea of following her to the airport. It seemed to me that she must come to her senses, that she must realise very soon how extreme an overreaction she had made, and I was fairly confident also that once she had a chance to consider what she had done, she would be anxious to know that I was not too badly injured. I thought it more than likely she'd return to Oji Bend in the morning. I even dismissed my original notion of radioing through to Sarah, the CMS nurse at Enugu, to ask her to intercept Miriam at the airport. I would have had to tell Sarah why, and the fewer people that knew, the better. I was certain Miriam would come to her senses. I ate the food Luke put in front of me, swallowed a handful of aspirins and went to bed.

And I was up in good time for school the next morning. In fact I myself swept and tidied the classroom before my pupils arrived. I was a little disturbed by the high level of absentees, but it would have been logical for them to fear that I might be away again, and of course many of them have a long journey on foot. The smallness of the class, and perhaps their shock at the sight of my injury (I had removed Luke's bandage, which seemed to me to dramatise the damage; there was a large bruise, certainly, but only a superficial scratch had drawn blood, I could see the whole thing would be fading by the end of the week) caused my students to be unusually quiet and withdrawn. I could even hear Joshua's low voice explaining equations in the next room. I missed the usual display of eagerly waving hands when I asked a question, and by the end of the morning my head was aching again. After I'd dismissed them I sat at my desk in a daze, trying to remember what I had to do next. Luke had made tomato soup for lunch, a particular favourite of Anne's. Alone in the bungalow, I found I had little appetite. I had returned to my office to make a start on the small pile of letters and messages on my desk, when I suddenly realised what it was I had been forgetting. The church building. The men had been absent from their work yesterday when I set out in the car, I had not even checked on them this morning.

The site was deserted. The walls are finished, and they have erected the scaffolding to enable them to work on the roof, but *nobody was at work. I couldn't understand it. I went over to the clinic to ask Paul if there was a traditional festival of some kind going on, and it was only as I pushed open the door that I realised he would be wondering at Miriam's absence, this being Wednesday (or perhaps Thursday, I can't remember) when she should have returned to work. He was busy examining a child of about Anne's age, a thin naked boy whose pregnant mother was sitting anxiously watching. He completely ignored me but I am used to his (lack of) manners by now, and sat down to wait. He fired a number of questions at the woman and seemed annoyed by the responses she gave. Rather abruptly, I thought, he dismissed her, although she was clearly wanting some medicine for her child, and pointed hopefully to a number of bottles on the shelf.*

'Can't you treat him?' I asked.

'He needs meat. She says only her husband can have meat in their family. There's nothing wrong with the boy that a better diet wouldn't fix.'

This is the work the Norwegians are concentrating on: the introduction of plants which are high in protein, and which villagers can be persuaded to grow themselves, in order to improve their basic diet which, in this area, is seriously protein-deficient. My gardening class already know about maize, and the value of stewed mulberry leaves, but I suddenly realised what a useful pincer action could be achieved if Paul in the surgery was also giving out information about ways of growing food that would improve their health—or perhaps sending them to me so that I could give them the information; or ideally, I could have small packages of relevant seeds ready to hand out with instructions . . . Paul asked rather impatiently what I wanted.

'Sorry. I've just come to say that regrettably Miriam won't be able to return to work this week as—she's been very suddenly called back to England. We had a radio message to say her mother is dangerously ill. She'll return as soon as she possibly can, and in the meantime I suggest we use her allowance to employ whatever help you can get locally.'

Paul was staring at me. He didn't speak.

'Is that all right?'

'OK,' he said.

'Also—I was wondering if you know what's going on in the village—some kind of festival or something?'

'Not that I know of.'

'Well the men didn't come to work on the church yesterday, and they're not here today either. I'm a bit puzzled . . .'

Paul turned and walked down to the other end of the surgery, where he began to sort through a number of medicine bottles, placing some in the icebox and some in the sink.

'You don't know where they are?' I asked.

'They're at home in the village.'

'But why aren't they at work?'

There was rather a long pause as Paul unscrewed a couple of bottles and poured their contents down the drain. They smelled unpleasant.

'Paul?'

'Two of Amoge's brothers are on the building team.'

I watched him rinse the rest of the bottles, then I thanked him and went back to my office.

Clearly it had been foolish of me to imagine that the thing could be kept secret. In fact if what Amoge had said was true, the womenfolk at least had known almost from the start. My class tomorrow would be no bigger than it had been today.

I knelt down and prayed for guidance. While I could see that Amoge's brothers had every reason to be angry with me, I couldn't see the logic of their withholding their labour from the church—which is for the benefit of the whole community. If they wanted to punish me, they should come and challenge me, not seek to obstruct the building of God's house. I found it hard to batten down my growing anger, and imagined the satisfaction it would give me to visit them and put them in their places by offering £25, or whatever insulting bride price they would have expected for

Amoge as a second-hand wife. If any man had come and paid for her, the transaction would have been as simple as selling a pig.

Almost immediately I was overwhelmed with shame. I was insulting my own beliefs and those of others. Of course I would never pay for a woman. Never treat her as a commodity which could be bought and sold. Nor, indeed, do the villagers. I knew full well that a man who ill-treats his wife can expect an angry visit from his in-laws, who will always have her welfare at heart. My thoughts had become as cynical and callous as those of a hardened sinner. I couldn't understand how it was possible, in so short a time, for me to have fallen so far.

Or for others to judge me so harshly. Nothing I had done before seemed to count—either with Miriam or with the village. After years of my support and love, in an instant Miriam believed me to be bad, horrible, unworthy of love. In an instant all the work I had done for school and church was wiped out.

My mind was spinning like a coin, two sides chasing one another round and round and round in a blur. On the one hand I knew that the whole situation was ridiculous—utterly ridiculous. What is important here is God's work, teaching and spreading His word, changing people's lives, improving their diet; this is the work to which I have devoted myself, this is the work that must continue. In the scale against it, what has happened with Amoge is a grain of sand, a mote of dust. On the other hand, I can see that the whole edifice is in danger of tumbling for that single mote.

Suddenly I realised that I must go after Miriam. She wasn't coming home from the airport. She would be in Lagos—or even back in England by now. Thinking badly of me, hating me. I had to make her understand what a mistake it was, I had to have her beside me, to help me carry on. I had to prove to her that I loved her.

I ran back to the bungalow to pack, and put a couple of shirts and some trousers in my old holdall. I went to the cupboard in my study where we keep the little safety-deposit box, to get my fare. Its door was swinging open. It was empty.

For a while I sat at my desk. I thought perhaps we had been robbed. Perhaps, in hurriedly taking her fare, she had left the box unlocked and someone (not Luke, surely?) had filched the rest of the money. I couldn't believe she would have taken it all. But the fact was, I couldn't go home. I couldn't pay my fare.

I realised I was sweating profusely. I got up to get a drink of water, and noticed, as I did so, a slip of paper on the floor behind the door. It was the sheet on which we keep a tally of what goes into and out of the deposit box. I picked it up and glanced at it. Miriam had entered the withdrawal of her and Anne's fare. Underneath it she had scored a line and beneath written £0/00s. I sat down and carefully studied the paper. Then I copied the figures onto an envelope and did the sums again. From the original amount we put away was subtracted payment to Okolie (work on Anne's room, and to buy new tools); payment to Luke (new bedroll); payment to Simon, Nwosisi and Okwuekwu for first year grammar-school fees; withdrawal of £25 for Luke's bride price (I had forgotten this, having originally supplied it out of my own monthly salary, then finding it impossible to manage that month on so little); payment to Mr Nwodo for church window designs; payment to Amoge for the past six months' childcare (originally intended to come from Miriam's wage, to which she objected as part of the general argument that arose when she went on leave, saying that I should pay an equal share. In order to silence the argument swiftly I had simply taken it from the deposit box, intending to sort it out with her when she was in a more reasonable mood). There were a few other little items on the back of the sheet as well; and I saw, when I had subtracted them all, that Miriam's maths were correct. When she had taken her fare, there would have been no more than £10 left. And she had given Luke £10 at the airport. My fare was entirely spent.

I heard Luke come into the bungalow, he lit the lamp in the hall and its soft glow was visible through the open doorway. It was already dark; either no one had remembered to switch on the gen-

erator, or it was broken again. I went through to the kitchen to tell him not to worry about food, and he stood for a moment looking at his feet, then nodded and padded out and down the steps again. I had decided it would be best to write to Miriam. I took the lamp with me into the study and settled at my desk.

I spent a long time composing the letter. I explained to her that what had happened was a silly mistake, nothing more, and that I had always loved her. I reminded her that everything we had worked for together on the mission was more important than the petty feelings of either of us, and that she was putting God's work here in jeopardy. I begged her to borrow the fare from her mother and return, and told her I didn't know how I could carry on without her.

When I had finished I felt a bit better. I wanted to post the letter immediately, I even thought of driving with it through the night to Enugu, until I remembered the state of the car. But the clinic deliveries were due sometime in the week, so I could give post to the driver then, to take back to town. Or to the visiting preacher at the weekend. Either way, it would be en route to her shortly.

I realised I was very tired. In the kitchen I found a packet of rich tea biscuits, which I ate before going to bed.

Next morning there wasn't even enough water for a wash—the barrels had run empty again. I couldn't understand how we'd run out so soon after the rains—there must have been a blockage somewhere, leaves in the pipes. There were no yard boys about when I went across to school, so I couldn't organise to get them refilled. There were only nine in my class. My head was aching savagely. I taught them for the morning and told them they could go home at lunchtime.

I realised that I was very unhappy with the way Miriam has behaved. She must find her own peace with God; she will have her own conscience to deal with. I have always known she was excessively jealous, and far too dependent on me. Perhaps she will learn from this unhappy experience and become more self-reliant.

Perhaps in the long run our marriage will even be strengthened by it. I can only hope so, and pray that God will help her to a better understanding of the true nature of love, and of the necessity for forgiveness. It is her departure which has brought the worst of the opprobrium upon me. A wife should stand by her husband; in the village it is considered a wife's duty to conceal her husband's weaknesses, whether he be impotent, poor or unfaithful. In protecting him she protects herself. Together the couple are strong. This is the meaning of marriage.

I had to stop thinking about her; I had to turn my attention to the mission. The ship I had captained so successfully up till now mustn't be allowed to be endangered by her behaviour. I decided to ask Luke to go down to the village and ask Abachie, who has emerged as the natural leader of the church builders, to come and see me. I thought long and hard about my class, and decided that I would entrust each of those who came in, individually, with the task of calling on two of their absent classmates and telling them that school was continuing as normal, that I had noted their absence, and that they would have extra work to catch up on if they did not return quickly.

As I was walking back across the compound I saw Jacob heading for the clinic. I called out to him and he turned with obvious reluctance and came back to speak to me. 'Jacob. Reverend Nwankwo is coming on Friday evening and has offered to run the Bible class, is that OK with you?'

'Of course.' He didn't meet my eye.

'Have you heard anything in the village about—are people talking about me?' I don't know why I asked him this, it was the last thing I wanted to know.

'I do not listen to gossip; should you carry a man about like an exhibit for sale in the market?' He glanced into my face, and then to my surprise he asked me to step into the old church with him. It was empty and as dark and hot as ever, I found it hard to catch my breath in there. He walked calmly before me to the altar rail, then knelt, so I knelt beside him. In a quiet dignified voice he *prayed to God to help His servant David—to help me in my time of difficulty, and to give me the humility to carry out His will. He prayed for forgiveness of sins for everyone on the station. After we had continued to kneel in silence for a short while, he patted my shoulder kindly, then got up and left the church.*

Humility has always seemed to me the least attractive of the Christian virtues. What is there to admire in humility? What changes and improvements has humility ever made? It's that craven effeminate side of Christianity: bow your head and turn the other cheek. Isn't anger a decent emotion? If I allowed myself to be angry (I am angry. I might as well admit it) then isn't that anger the fuel that generates the energy to force me to rebuild my life? The voice in my head which talks to Miriam is angry: see me trying to repair the damage. You think you can destroy the mission, you think you can smash my work. But you can't, see?

But the layers of my mind are slippery and transparent, like cellophane. I can see the self-deceit, for example, when I take the idea of humility which I know to be necessary, and exaggerate it, twisting something which is in fact good until it appears only bad, so that I needn't give it credence. The notion of humility embraces all that I ascribed to anger, in the way of energy and doggedness. Humility says I must accept my punishment but continue to strive zealously to do my duty. To teach, lead, help, convert. Humility never said I should stop doing those things.

Cast in old-fashioned terms, the devil is tempting me. Laying his subtle arguments before me; sucking the value out of things. Humility; love; steadfastness; forgiveness. Working his nasty twisted magic on them till they all seem hollow, worse than despair itself because at least in despair there's no tricksy suggestion of hope. Whereas love, the word love conjures warmth and kindness, open-armed forgiveness, understanding—above all, understanding. And Miriam's love . . . how could love go? How can understanding end? How in the course of a day can a person suddenly say it's gone? And His love too—if it was love, that gave me this mission, gave me Miriam and Anne, gave me a life which I delighted in and which was dedicated to His service—has His love also ended? Like switching off a light? For one human error?

He refines us in His fire. Here I am, never tested before now—crumbling like a shoddy wall at the first pressure. So that I must hate myself, feel that I am worthless and deserving of His neglect.

When I've lost myself entirely in the circularity of it, I cling on to the necessity for action: I will write again to Miriam begging her forgiveness, I will teach my class each day even if they dwindle to half a dozen, I will recruit a new reading class, I will go and see Amoge's brothers. I will act with humility.

8 P.M.

But I had forgotten about the water. Luke met me on the bungalow steps and told me about it again.

'Couldn't you get some of the yard boys to fill the barrels for me?'

'No yard boys today, Mr David.'

It was true, there was nobody about. And I had let my class go. 'Well, we'll have to do it, Luke—you and I can do it together.'

He looked very disgruntled at this, and in fact it took us the rest of the afternoon. I hadn't quite realised before the brute idiocy of having to haul buckets of water from the pump to the bungalow, then up the ladder to the eaves. It must be possible to rig up some sort of piping system—even a hose would be a start—but I haven't got round to thinking about it before. Right now it was the last thing I needed, my shoulders are stiff and sore, and I am literally trembling with exhaustion. And we didn't even fill them beyond halfway.

TIME PASSES. What is there left to think? Anne's father is no worse than she might have expected. She herself is responsible for the death of a woman and her unborn child. She must go out into the ship and find Joseph, warn him. Of what, she asks herself? He already knows. Quite probably another crew member has already found and killed him.

Nevertheless she will go out into the ship; sitting here any longer is impossible. The storm is lessening again as she leaves the cabin, the wind has dropped a little. Hugging the cabin wall she edges round towards the lit stairwell; descends mechanically, both hands clasping the rail tightly. Where to look for him? If he has been scared away from the container deck, he could be anywhere—under a bunk in an empty cabin, in some space between decks, some part of a ventilation or ducting system . . . what hope has she, really, of finding him? He may not even be there any longer. If she finds him she will take him to her own cabin and lock the door upon the two of them and not let anyone in until they dock at Tilbury. She remembers Robbie letting himself into her room. He has a key, of course. She cannot offer Joseph any protection. He is better off on his own.

She makes a slow round of every deck, past every closed blank door, greeting the three sailors that she passes, meticulously peering into those rooms she is allowed to

enter—the library, the games room, the dining room.
Everywhere is deserted. When she gets to D deck she waits,
listening; checks the laundry room. The corridor looks different but she can't place what it is. Then as she moves towards
the container deck she realises that the doors at the top of the
stairs are closed. She has never seen them closed before. She
approaches warily, Robbie may have left a guard or watchman,
it may be a trap. But there is nobody. And the doors are locked;
she cannot budge them. So if Joseph is down there he's captive
and there's nothing to be done.

Back along the corridor, back up the stairs. On deck the
rain has stopped, everything is dark and wet and slippery. She
makes her way to the rail. She can hear the voices of her class
singing earnestly, sweetly.

> 'Now the day is over,
> Night is drawing nigh.
> Shadows of the evening,
> Steal across the sky.'

How can she go back to her class? How can she stand in
front of the children?

> 'Now the darkness gathers,
> Stars begin to peep,
> Birds and beasts and flowers
> Soon will be asleep.'

She stands dumb and senseless as a post, hands clenched on
the cold rail. Gradually, from a great distance, she considers what
she could try to do. If she went to the captain and told him the
truth (how much does he already know?) and asked him to
force Robbie to produce the woman . . . and if he couldn't, then
put him under arrest. It wouldn't work. Either because the captain would not believe her (why should he? Against the word of

his first mate) or because the captain's response would anyway be the same as Robbie's—kill the stowaways, get rid of them. If only she had kept the woman's clothes. Her hands on the wet rail are beginning to ache with cold. The pain is a relief. She won't move, she'll stand here till her legs are weak and her hands numb, even frozen to the rail, she will stand here stubbornly until something becomes possible.

From under the massy weight of black cloud in the sky gradually comes a grainy pallor which lies diagonally across the sea; specks of light in the thick darkness, specks which when multiplied together make patches of lighter grey against the black. It is those etched gargoyle faces—that skeleton arm (like a swimmer's, she realises, lifting out of the black sea) of Goya's *Nada*, the message brought back from the grave. Above the appalled and eyeless messenger hang the malevolent, idiot, grief-stricken faces of those who must peer through swirls of black, through impenetrable layers of darkness, to read his dreadful message. Every speck of whiteness on the paper serves only to deepen the dark.

Slowly the etching fades. Cold grey dawn spreads like lard across the sky. There is no suggestion that a sun has risen, no trace of pink or yellow; if it has risen it is behind so many layers of cloud that it is leached of all warmth and colour. The waves smash against the side of the ship. They are too small to cause much inconvenience now, but they hurl themselves angrily, petulantly, as if the very presence of the ship is maddening to them. Something hisses behind Anne.

Her turn is slow and stiff, and at first she sees nothing but the container behind her back. Then looking up, she sees a head peering down from the top. Joseph. Instinctively she glances about—nobody else in sight. His finger is to his lips and she nods. Leaning further over he whispers, 'I need water. And food. Tonight. Leave it here –' pointing to the crack between his container and the next. Before she can nod the head is withdrawn. He's gone.

Stiff with cold she stumbles back to her cabin. At breakfast she can get bread and fruit. A bottle of mineral water, they are in the fridge in the dining room. He is alive. If she could feel anything, she would be glad.

But the woman, Estelle, will be dead. And the baby? The baby inside her, how long would it live, after the mother's death? They cut living babies from dead victims of car crashes, Anne has heard of that. They cut living babies from living mothers too. Not now, she tells herself. Concentrate. Estelle's baby wouldn't drown. It lives in fluid, its lungs don't work till it's born. For a moment she imagines the baby floating and playing happily in the depths of the ocean, a mer-baby, a sea-child, able to go where born humans can't, a creature still at one with its original watery element. Then she thinks of the mother's lungs filling with salt water. The weight of it, dragging the body down. The little astronaut's feeding tube that nourishes the baby, the umbilical cord that links him to his mother—slowly becoming null and dead, devoid of sparkling oxygen, heavy with salty water. She imagines the baby clutching at the tube as his body realises it is being poisoned. Struggling to detach from his doomed spaceship, convulsively demanding oxygen, ripping from the placenta, beating his head against the womb entrance that holds him captive. But there's no response. The flesh is dead and already getting cold. The tomb won't open.

At some point in the day (she must have forgotten to go to breakfast. She must remember the food and water. It is the only thing she has to do) the lock on her door is turned from the outside and Robbie comes in.

'You have got a key.'

He's putting it in his pocket. He doesn't care if she knows. 'Where is he?'

'I haven't seen him.'

'You know, and you're going to tell me.'

There's a silence. What's he going to do? Hurt her? Kill her? He moves towards her and she backs till she can't go any further, the bed is behind her knees. He puts his hands on her shoulders, pulling her towards him, bringing his face close to hers. She remembers the exact feeling, the shock, the excitement, the pleasure. The taste in her mouth is bitter; her voice a frightened whisper. 'You killed that woman.'

'You don't know anything.'

'I'll go to the police when we land.'

'Really. And they're going to believe you? Everyone on board knows the kind of woman you are.'

She stares at him. What does he mean?

'A slag,' he supplies. 'Out for revenge. Because I don't want you.'

'But you—' She can't help herself. Don't speak to him. *Everyone on board knows.* Of course. She walked into it.

'If you know where he is and you're not telling me . . .'

'What will you do? Throw me over the side as well?'

'You're a fantasist. No one's been thrown over the side.' His lips are curled with contempt. After a moment he turns and leaves, his lie hanging dully in the air. Anne slowly rises and relocks the door, putting a chair by it. It won't stop him but it will give more warning. Then she sits on the bed and leans her head against the wall.

October 1, 1965

The Bishop. He arrived at twelve this morning, in his jeep. I have known, of course, that he must arrive—that he would arrive, any day. But it was still rather a shock to see him. I have changed my mind so often over what I would tell him and how I might explain the situation, that a part of me was convinced he already knew. And every question seemed to lead to a trap gaping open before me . . . within minutes I knew that I had to tell him the truth.

The Bishop: I realise now how much I had conspired in making him the slightly ludicrous figure that he was. How much it had flattered my own vanity to believe him powerful. How when I showed him the increased numbers of students getting their leavers' certificate, and how many teacher-trainee placements I had overseen, and discussed the quantity of reading books I'd need for next year, and the amount and variety of vegetables we were getting out of the station gardens, and the dimensions of the new church (oh yes, how bleakly simple it looks now, all bigger, better, bigger—pride gathering itself for a fall) I delighted in the notion that he was powerful, that his was the voice that might relay my triumphs back to Onitsha. I needed him to be powerful. And yet in the very notion of his powerfulness, I found a place to mock him. I could think of him as worldly. Whereas I knew I had loftier, more idealistic values. I was doing the real thing, in the

villages, on the ground. He was only travelling around the country gathering news of those victories on the ground—aggrandising
himself and his diocese. I could simultaneously despise him for his
dedication to aggrandisement, and yet use him shamelessly as an
audience for my own achievements. And delight in the irony that
I, the white man, was doing real work with the people whilst he,
the black man, cut off by his superior position, could only peer
over my shoulder.

Now in the unthinkable silence and emptiness (and shabbi-
ness, I suddenly saw—the house has become shabby and dusty
since Miriam left, even though Luke still comes in every day. My
books are piled on the dining table in squares of dust, dead insects
lie in little heaps beneath the lights) in the silence and emptiness
of my house I told him as simply as I could that Amoge was pregnant and that Miriam had not been able to forgive my failing and
so had left me.

And the self-important, puffed-up little man (whom I have
mocked, in the past, for those very qualities, whilst simultaneously needing him to have those qualities, which in turn reassured
me of my own superiority)—he sat and listened to me in sober
silence and then spoke so thoughtfully and kindly that I was
ashamed. 'What d'you want to do?' he said.

'I don't know. I've been trying to keep things going here, but I
haven't had much success.'

'Would it help if we separated out the problems?'

I agreed; I didn't even know what he meant.

'There are two problems, aren't there? One is this station.
Over the past three years you've restored vigour to this mission.
You've improved the school and made it a useful training school,
you've created an agricultural base, you're building a new church.
You've won the trust of the villagers.'

'But I've lost it now.'

'Well, maybe. But we should also consider that whilst they
have stopped trusting you, they will not necessarily have stopped
trusting in what you stand for. The church.'

I saw then that he would take the mission off me.

'David.' *He was pushing something at me, some white thing.* 'It's all right. David? Listen.'

I found it was a handkerchief. My face was wet with sweat. Luke never mended the fan, after Miriam left; it worked itself loose and stopped every other day. I offered the Bishop his handkerchief back but he indicated I should keep it.

'Your work has put new lifeblood in this mission. The work was good, the work must continue. I am going to relieve you of your duties immediately. I am going to put someone new in here; a young Ibo who's been teaching at our school in Onitsha, and is also a catechist. Full of energy, full of zeal, a young man who will carry on your work with conviction and enthusiasm.'

The sensation of loss—as I discovered repeatedly after Miriam left, particularly in the night, when I lay alone in bed, unable to sleep—the sensation of loss is very like falling. Slipping downwards through dark air fast, so you can't catch your breath and your stomach seems to churn weightlessly in air. Sometimes if you can't anchor yourself it makes your head spin and there are feelings of nausea. It is an unsettling feeling, loss. Panic is a similar feeling; controlling the breathing is the key to it. Once I can take six deep breaths I know I can beat it.

The Bishop put his hand over mine on the table. I remember clearly seeing the gesture and finding it surprising, even rather suggestive and amusing—I could hear a voice which might have been my own and might have said something like, 'The Bishop fancies me after all, darling'. I could have said it, laughing, to Miriam. But I wasn't speaking. His hand in fact was quite dry and cool, not very human at all, but strangely reassuring. It anchored me. 'The second problem is you. What will happen to you. I could recommend that you go back to England but—'

I started to object but he shook his head to silence me.

'I think God has work for you still in this country. Difficult times are coming, we need every soldier in Christ we can muster. The mission school in Umuahia lost two teachers last week: one joined the army, the other, a Fulani, has gone back north. At the same time, the refugees from the north are seeking school places for their children here. To begin with, let me post you to the school to bridge that gap.'

North, south, I had only the vaguest sense of the troubles to which he referred. I was sick with loss. 'If I'm not fit to teach the children here—'

'No one has said you're not fit. Only that the villagers are angry. You are God's representative here; if you're not above reproach . . .' He waited quietly, then resumed. 'In a new place, you can start again. You can redeem yourself.'

There was a silence when he finished. From a long way outside myself I watched my tired mind scrabble from one hopeful plan to another. If I could persuade the builders to start again, if I could encourage the best of my pupils to take the Standard 6 exam then their results would show—if I could talk to the women in the reading class and explain—if I could persuade Miriam to come back. But all I could see was the compound that morning when I woke up late and found Miriam and Anne gone—the silent building site, the quiet empty school, the absence of petitioners at my office door. A dead place. I was suddenly hit by a wave of exhaustion, and it seemed as if it would be easy to do what he said.

Luke came into the room. He looked at the Bishop. 'Would you like dinner, sir?'

'No thank you, Luke, the Mothers' Union are waiting to speak to me. If you can call everyone on the station together in the schoolroom for six o'clock, I'll say a prayer with you before I go.'

'Yes sir.' I saw Luke glance at me under his lowered lids, the way a dog does when it knows it's behaved badly. Last night I had to ask him what the women were doing. I think they were from the Mothers' Union, I could hardly recognise them in the fading light. They came into the garden just before dark, with palm leaves and fern tucked into their clothing, carrying twigs. When I called to them they ran away. He told me it is nso ala, the earth is angry with me. Then he quickly left the room.

OCTOBER 2

It's 5.30 now, still perfectly dark, and the rain's soft percussion on the roof. The earth's crust, I have read, is composed of gigantic areas of solid matter called tectonic plates, floating on the hot molten rock underneath. Over time, infinitely slowly, they move upon their fluid bed, a few inches perhaps in centuries. And gradually, inexorably slowly, two of them will move closer together, compressing the lava between them. Until suddenly it erupts. Volcano, earthquake, tidal wave—in a day the surface of the earth is changed. That's what has happened here. A slow movement. A sudden fall.

I am a man who's stubbed his toe on a pebble, and fallen headlong down a well.

ANNE WILL HAVE TO leave her cabin to find some food. It would be better if everything could stop—thought, movement, bodily functions—but nothing stops. She's been lying in bed for a long time but now she has to get up to pee. And walking to the toilet, she is dizzy with hunger. Her throat is parched. The body just keeps going.

There is murky light in her cabin-prison; must be day. She doesn't want to see anyone, shrinks from the idea of their eyes on her. But calling the steward is beyond her. If she just creeps quickly to the dining room, grabs a handful of food, she can be back here in minutes.

She pulls on some clothes from the floor and moves the barricading chair. It feels cold on deck, the sky is grey. They must be quite far north. There's a strange noise—she hesitates outside her door a moment, ears straining. It's a rhythmic sort of banging and a roaring like the wind in the storm, only there's no wind—the roaring stops for a couple of beats then starts again. She makes her way to the dining room. Realises as she opens the door on a babble of noise and abrupt silence, that it's a mistake, they're all there, it must be meal time. She starts to pull the door to again without even looking up at them.

'Miss Harrington!' It's the captain. Something bright orange on his head, he's waving at her oddly. 'You are feeling better! You must join us!' A chorus of other voices, they are all turned to her, a set of grotesque masks straight out of Ensor, grossly protruding features, leering mouths, gaping eyes. Ellie Malone, nearest this end of the table, looms closer, crowned in lime-green, coming unsteadily to take her elbow and guide her to the empty seat. 'You must come and join us!'

Who are they? Officers she's never even seen, grinning and nodding in party hats. A glass of wine is pressed into her hand, the captain flourishes a carving knife. Ellie smiles beatifically, and pulls up her hat which has slipped right down over her baby-pink head. 'We're having such fun!'

As she raises the wine to her lips Anne sees along the length of the table, Robbie, on the other side of the captain, watching her. Their eyes meet. The wine hits the back of her throat and she coughs, spattering the white tablecloth in front of her with red wine. There's a momentary hush, like when she opened the door, then laughter and calls, a man is thumping her on the back, Ellie refilling her glass. Suddenly a plate heaped with food is placed in front of her.

'No—no —' She tries to pass it on, there is far too much, panic is rising in her throat.

'It's for you! Eat up!'

She won't be able to eat it all. But she'll have to try. There are candles on the table, their light glinting on the glasses and cut-lery, and the rising crescendo of conversation and laughter around her makes her giddy. She must start to eat quickly, she's afraid she'll faint. The officer next to her laughs insanely; there are hootings and brayings from one end of the table to the other. She pushes the food into her mouth, dry white meat, a roast potato, her hands are shaking, is she dribbling? How long since she's eaten? Mr Malone is staring at her with his dead eyes; she remembers he waved his ancient penis at her, he thought she was asking for it.

There is a pretence that she's been ill, Ellie Malone asks repeatedly if she's feeling better, but her questions are punctu-ated by high foolish giggles as if she already knows the answer.

Everyone on board knows the kind of woman you are. Instinct urges Anne to flee but she can't leave her food. She shovels it in, feeling their eyes on her. She is sitting at table with Robbie. A murderer. He put his hand between her legs . . . She freezes, willing the half-chewed food on down her constricting gullet. Not here. Not now. Just swallow. She can feel her face is on fire.

She remembers the rotten-toothed Filipino and the other one, pale-eyed, who couldn't tell her where the doctor was; frightened of her, afraid to speak, thinking perhaps she was after them too; backing away with the common knowledge that she was the mate's. She's so thirsty she drains her glass in three gulps and a man's tilting the bottle over it. As the room slides and dives she recalls that it's wine, what she must drink is water. Looking along the table for it she sees that the men wear white shirts and jackets, the captain even has a bow tie. What is it about? They keep glancing at her; she realises she is only wearing her jeans and the T-shirt she sleeps in, and that it is splattered with red wine. Her hunger is sated. But there is so much left on the plate. She sets down her knife and fork, and is able for the first time to properly see what's there—turkey, roast vegetables, cranberry sauce, Brussels sprouts. This is a particular meal, she knows what it is. Ellie Malone leans across suddenly, snatching at something beside Anne's plate, brandishing it under her nose. 'You haven't got a hat. Pull!'

As Anne stares in blank stupidity the man beside her takes her hand and places it on the sausage-shaped object—a cracker, of course, she shrinks from his touch but he pats her familiarly on the back, 'You need to get into the spirit.' Of course they will all think they can touch her.

'Pull! Pull!' Voices shouting at her—she pulls the end of the cracker and it rips apart, spewing its contents across the table to shrieks of laughter. Someone fishes a small tight parcel from a glass of wine; peels off the rubber band, unrolls and shakes the hat. 'Here you are. Good as new.' A red paper crown is pulled down over her forehead. She tries to take it off.

'No no!' The captain, playfully shaking his finger. 'You must wear—it is Christmas!'

Opposite her someone lights a cigarette. The drifting smoke conjures Tim and her eyes are smarting with tears. She must leave the food on her plate. No matter what. She has to get out of the room. As she makes her escape, bellowing laughter and yelping voices are still resounding in her ears. She blunders through the containers to the rail and looks up automatically to where Joseph was last seen. Is he still alive? Starving? She has twice left food and water. But what's the point in pretending she can help him? She has brought him nothing but disaster. She doubts he could stay up on deck now anyway, it's too cold. Anne has barely glanced at the iron-grey sea and she's shivering, teeth chattering, nipples frozen stiff.

She moves back to her cabin. It's Christmas. Three and a half weeks ago, she was making cards with her class; stained-glass window cards out of coloured cellophane. It's Christmas.

NOVEMBER 12, 1965

At last the scales have fallen from my eyes. At last I can under-
stand what's been going on.

My writing is as big and loopy as a child's. It is still very
painful to hold the pen. The little finger remains in a splint, but
less swollen now. After I'd read her letter I punched the wall. I've
never been violent in my life before.

Who knows what you'll find once you scratch the surface. A
violent, blaspheming man. A hypocritical whore of a woman. The
missionary and his wife.

She replied to my letter. She has been very unhappy. No one can
understand how terrible this has been for her, except Karl. Karl who
has been to visit them. Karl who kindly bought a present for Anne
my daughter. *Karl who has advised her to write offering forgiveness.*

I never saw it before. I can see it now. Crystal clear. Now my
unhappiness at leaving the station seems like the time a patient
spends under the anaesthetic. Numb, dreaming, idiotically obliv-
ious to pain. A fool, till he wakes up. Miriam with Karl.

From that very first night—oh yes, from the beginning—when
she criticised him, I can still hear her sharp voice, 'You must find
that very depressing,' and I, a cheery buffoon blandly seeking to pro-

tect her, to kindly and foolishly protect my poor wife from the old man's possible anger, asked him to excuse us both for our tiredness. And he cut me dead. Replied straight to her. 'Yes, sometimes I do.'

As if I didn't exist. That was the start. A dialogue between the two of them, with me the eager blind overworking pup they kicked about between them.

Now it all falls into place as neatly as a child's jigsaw. My first birthday here. She wanted to make me a birthday surprise. And she wanted Luke out of the way. Of course. She wanted to spend the morning in bed with that white-haired, wrinkled old bastard. She wanted him to fuck her.

Yes. And when they'd had a good long morning at it they hosed themselves down and arranged the birthday tea in a hurry. Only I didn't come home on time and she suddenly thought I might be dead. No wonder she was drunk and hysterical when I got back. Guilt, relief, rage, a crazed stew inside her. And then I—she and I—on the floor . . . Did she still have his spunk inside her?

Every instant of every day is reconfigured by it: now I understand his antagonism, now I understand her self-appointed role as peacemaker, now I understand why she went to calm him down after he'd called me arrogant (and how exactly did she calm him? While I dried and dressed our baby and tidied up and ate my lunch alone, for that 30–40 minutes, how exactly was my wife soothing the old missionary, my boss, her lover?).

The broken fingers were quite good at first. I don't know what now. If I press harder as I write, a thread of fire runs from the little finger to the elbow. But the pain is beginning to make me nauseous rather than oblivious. It's the detail, I'm afraid. It always comes down to the pornographic detail, doesn't it, the extra detail that I don't need my resourceful mind to supply. My wife with her lover.

Even if I can blank that for a moment, there's all the rest, buzzing like a cloud of hornets round my head, crawling up my nostrils and into the corners of my mouth, sitting on my eyelids, inserting their tails into my ears, crawling under my collar, stinging here and there till I'm so maddened I don't know which way to turn. Every moment of memory is poisonous; my left hand clenches and unclenches involuntarily, as if I could squeeze it around his scraggy neck. Squeeze until it goes as limp as a strangled chicken's. All the time I tried and worked in good faith, and then when I worried about hurting Miriam by telling her about Amoge—all that time they were together, laughing at me, waiting for me to fall –

How they must have laughed. When I played into their hands, refused to go on holiday with her—leaving them free to meet and plot together in England. She even told me that she'd seen him there, what sort of a frisson did that give her, that hilarious little atom of honesty, she had seen Karl in England? Presumably she'd parked Anne with her mother and gone to him, abandoned herself, with a little pause for breath here and there to further plot my downfall. How convenient it would be if the fault were mine. How much better it would be if she could appear the injured innocent. And the deep hot joy for him, of knowing I would be destroyed, that every effort I'd made on the station would be smashed to dust once it all came out.

Did Miriam know? That everything I worked for would be smashed? The school, the church, the evening classes? I suppose she must have done. She must have done, in casting her lot in with him. And yet he had the arrogance to hate me. While he was screwing my wife and injecting my life with poison, he didn't even have the decency to feel guilt or shame, no, he brazened it out, making his partiality for her and his dislike of me obvious to the whole station—

And I even welcomed that. I even welcomed his kindness (as I saw it) to her. Thought the better of him for it, was glad that poor Miriam had someone to talk to.

ONE DAY THEY ARE approaching land. The movement of the ship is different, the engines no longer straining. Anne doesn't know how many days have passed. She left another bag for Joseph, with rolls and cheese and two bottles of water, but she doesn't know if he took it or one of the sailors found it. Maybe Robbie found him. Robbie has never returned to her room, which makes her think Joseph was found. Why else would Robbie leave her in peace?

Anne remembers her mum's friend Karl. An old man with white hair, for Anne's birthday once he gave her a Nigerian bangle of tiny coloured glass beads sewn onto a soft leather backing. Is it true? She supposes it must be. Every bad thing is true. It's why Father never came to visit, even when Mum was ill.

They are approaching land and it will be time to get off the ship. The voyage is going to end. She crams objects into her case. Father's first-aid box, it won't fit. She remembers there's another case, his, in the wardrobe. These objects belong to an ordinary life. Will it be possible to pick them up and walk off this ship?

She goes out, blinking in the glare of the white daylight, her breath cloudy before her face. It is very cold; dirty snow on the edges of the estuary, clouds of black smoke and white steam rising from the industrial sprawl further up river. The landscape seems extraordinary.

Slowly the ship moves up, into place; turns, changes direction, drops the power of its engines. There are other ships, and tug boats, there is a quayside, the land is close enough now to make out people. Two cranes stand poised to welcome them. It happens in slow motion.

Once they have docked a gangway is lowered, gangway and steps. She watches crewmen heave them into position. You can get off this ship. Shuffling and blinking like an old person she drags her cases to the gangway. Nobody helps, she feels the eyes of the crew burning into her. A slag. The captain is in the Malones' doorway, he is shaking both their hands. Anne can't quite believe she will be allowed off. Will she really be let to walk free?

When she gets to the ground she is trembling. There is a roped walkway to follow, she is obliged to pass through customs. One of the cranes is already dipping and bowing its giant hook towards the ship, men on board are calling and gesturing to the crane driver, to line it up with a container.

She knows Joseph's dead. But if he weren't, how could he get ashore? Up at the customs-house wall she sets down her cases and stares back at the ship. Robbie is visible, standing at the top of the gangway. He is talking to someone, he moves aside and the Malones come down and along the roped walkway and pass before her into the customs house. Robbie is still standing at the gangway. Of course. He will stand there for as long as it takes to catch Joseph trying to get ashore. If Joseph is still alive.

Anne picks up her cases and walks into customs. Out again the other side. There is a wide empty area like a car park, and a couple of taxis waiting. To her right is a Portakabin with a sign saying POLICE. What can she tell them? There was a pregnant Nigerian woman. And a man. They asked me for help but I betrayed them. I don't know where they are, I think the first mate killed them. I don't have any proof. Yes I had sexual relations with the first mate. Yes I am a piece of filth.

Anne raises one hand to summon a taxi. That first gesture of Joseph's, in the corridor outside the laundry. Please.

The taxi takes her away from the docks. She cannot stop shaking.

PART II

BEFORE THE END OF the Christmas holidays, Anne returns to work. In her classroom snowmen and angels still hang dispiritedly from the lights, and the walls are covered in new verses to old carols. She stops to read one.

> Away in a buggy, no house and no home,
> Baby Jesus cried for his Mum.
> All the cars going past on the road
> None of them stopped
> To give him a ride.
>
> By Jason Williams

She pulls out the staples and collects the dusty sheets into a pile; strips the dangling decorations from lights and window frames; pins up a bright new calendar. There is plenty to do: the work she set for the last week of term hasn't been marked, the cupboards and drawers need clearing out, there are new schemes of work to plan. She and Jackie, who teaches Class 4, eat their sandwiches together at lunchtime, and she exchanges descriptions of Lagos for tales of the snow-bound farm in Wales where Jackie and her family spent Christmas week.

Anne finds herself remembering the Christmas Matthew Afigbo spent with Father and her at St Luke's, when Matthew was a student. It was the year Anne started teaching. Matthew wanted to see snow, so on Boxing Day the three of them drove to north Wales, into Snowdonia. It was a cold dry day with fleeting sunshine and scudding clouds; on the tops of the mountains the white cloud shifted and coiled like fitful smoke in the wind. The tops were snow-covered and Father wanted them to walk up from the road so that Matthew could stand in the snow. Anne, watching the moving, shape-shifting clouds, which billowed heavily down the mountainside obscuring everything in their path, then as suddenly thinned, dispersing in the clear blue air, suggested it might be dangerous.

'Rubbish,' said Father. 'It's practically clear.'

'Yes but look how quickly it can come down—it's not as if we've even got a compass.'

'You don't need a compass to tell up from down. If we find ourselves in cloud we simply come down.'

'But—'

'Why are you so timid, Anne? We're not infants.' He strode off ahead of them, and she and Matthew had no option but to follow. Quite quickly the path became steep, there were loose rocks and rubble to climb over, you had to look where you were putting your feet. Once, Anne slipped, half-twisting her ankle, and Matthew put out his hand to steady her.

'Thanks. I don't know how you put up with him.'

Matthew smiled his slow shy smile. 'I'm thinking this is my fault.'

'It's not you that's so far ahead up there that we can't turn back. If the cloud comes down he'll vanish.'

'You want us to stop here?'

Anne shrugged. 'What's the point? If he gets lost we'll have to go up after him anyway.'

'We could just sit and wait for him to find his way down, like the man said.'

'He'll be cross with me for keeping you back from the snow.'

'Well I'll tell him these stones are too hard for my feet.' Calmly Matthew turned around and surveyed the view, selected a boulder and sat on it. Anne glanced up—Father was out of sight—then perched on a stone beside him.

'I'm sorry about this, Matthew. I shouldn't have come. He'd have taken better care of you on his own.'

Slowly, Matthew shook his head. 'He thinks everything of you, you know? He told me you're coming home for Christmas, he was so happy.'

Anne was shocked into silence. Matthew glanced at her and laughed.

'It's true. You know the man can't show it.'

'Thank you. You must think we're ridiculous.'

A small shower of pebbles skittered down from above, and they could hear the sound of Father's boots descending. 'There you are. Thought I'd lost you. It's a bit boggy up yonder—why don't we drive on and find a place where the snowline's closer to the road?' He moved on past them and down without waiting for a response. Matthew winked at Anne and rose to follow him.

Later in the afternoon they did reach the snow, and built a snowman to prove it. Somewhere, she has the photo of Matthew and the snowman. On her way home from school Anne buys a postcard of a snow-scene and sends it to Matthew, thanking him for all his kindness at the time of Father's death.

It is perfectly easy to function; especially when term begins, and her class arrives to mill around her with excited stories and requests and anxieties and all the hot close busyness of their twenty-eight urgent young lives. At home Smokey is ecstatic to be out of the cattery, winds herself round and round Anne's legs, purring welcome.

On Sunday there is a memorial service for Father at St Luke's. She is asked if she wants to speak about him, but they quite understand when she doesn't. She puts on the grey skirt which is not quite right over the hips, and a white silk blouse which she rarely wears because it is too smart, and the olive-green wool jacket which is her smartest jacket but doesn't fit under her coat so has to be worn without, and is cold, in the biting winds outside the church. All his parishioners, it seems, are there; a bishop conducts the service. Kind things are said. Afterwards, people she has vaguely known for years come and touch her arm and express their sympathy and say, if there is anything they can do. Some are genuinely upset. He was loved, he will be missed. She thanks them and shakes hands, preoccupied by the various discomforts of her clothes. Afterwards she throws the skirt away.

That night her eyes are jittery with tiredness. She switches on the TV but its harsh noise and rapidly changing pictures make her headache worse. She turns it off, and is sitting blankly stroking Smokey's warm weight across her knees, when the phone rings.

'Hello?'

'Anne. It's me.' Tim.

She waits, listening to the open line between them.

'I just heard about your father. I'm really sorry.' A little pause.

'Thank you.'

'Shit. I don't know what to say. D'you want to talk? Shall I come round?'

Anne waits because no answer is coming to her lips. The silence grows.

'Anne? Anne? Are you there?'

'It's OK Tim. Thank you.'

'I'll come round now.'

If only it was possible to just keep the open line. To not speak into it, to not clutter it with words. To just keep that open breathing connection, the gentle pop of his drawing on his cigarette, the sound of his silence. The knowledge that he is there.

'Better not. But thanks.' She makes herself put the phone straight down. She stares at it sitting smugly on its cradle, counts to twenty, picks up the receiver and leaves it off the hook.

The biggest problem is sleep; she goes to the doctor for sleeping pills but the old one has left and the new one is irritatingly inquisitive. Has she tried exercise and warm milk? Would it be better to tackle the root of the problem? If this is about her father's death, maybe she should talk to someone about it.

'I don't want to talk about it. I just want to get on with my job.'

The doctor sits quietly, watching her. His patience embarrasses and exasperates her; he reminds her of Father, sitting there knowing everything. Eventually he turns to his computer and taps in a prescription. As the printer whirrs he leans back and smiles broadly. 'Fair enough. I'm giving you enough for two weeks. If we're just talking about a disordered sleep pattern, that should nudge you back into routine. If it doesn't do the trick we'll think again.'

Anne takes the prescription without speaking, angry that he is amused at her expense. But when she takes a sleeping pill she finds her bed rising and pitching beneath her, seasickness swirling in her belly and a cold sweat breaking out all over her body. It is not even a dream, it is just the sensation—the symptoms—of being back in the ship. She will not give Dr Munro the satisfaction of returning to him, and spends a lot of nights lying in bed waiting for time to pass, eyes closed, mind blank, periodically reminding herself to unclench her fists and take deeper breaths. Sometimes when she is too tired to keep it at bay, the image of Robbie Boyle bursts into her mind and her eyes smart with contemptible self-pity: then she gets up and paces the house until she's wearied herself to numbness. One weekend soon she will go to Father's flat and start clearing it out. It will have to be sold, of course.

Anne can see the space her life inhabited before she went to Lagos. In Reception the children play with thick wooden alphabet jigsaws where the shape of each letter can be slotted into a gap next to the appropriate image, the C-shaped slot beside Cat, the hollowed S by Snake. But Anne no longer seems to slot into the old Anne shape.

It's summer. Walking home from school Anne feels the warmth of the sun pricking her skin. In her house the air is baked stale;

she walks through to unlock the back door and sit on the doorstep. Her tangled garden is full of the scent of the pale climbing rose which dangles over from next door. Among the knee-high grass and dandelions a patch of vivid blue cranesbill and a straggling fuchsia with its elegant crimson bell-flowers are sole survivors of last year's flowerbed. A bee moves slowly into and out of earshot, bumbling around the roses.

It is the final week of term, and she is already feeling nostalgic about her class. Not just individuals—not just Lauren Palmer with her bright curious eager face, or Darren Beswick with his interminable deadpan explanations which now reduce the whole class—including Anne, and Darren himself—to tears of laughter; not just individuals but the whole innocent group of them. She's never had a class who were so open to things—who liked her so much. Maybe that's all it boils down to, she thinks, playing with a handful of grass seeds. They like me so I like them back. A mutual admiration society. But even if it's that base, it's still worked; they've done better than anyone expected in their SATS, and the slower readers—especially Kirsty and poor crushed-looking little Micky Carter—have made great strides. She will be sad to see them go.

She takes off her sandals and rolls up her trousers to feel the sunlight on her legs. Sports day tomorrow, then end-of-term concert, school disco, clearing of walls and desks and shelves, the final flurry of cards and little presents and tearful farewells—and then the holidays.

There will be work to do for next term, gabbles her mind, but she stops it. She has worked. She has done nothing but work these past six months, work and the clearing and selling of Father's flat are all that she has done. Around those two activities she has slotted a regimen of eating and resting and occasionally sleeping, a weekly shop, a yoga session, thrice-weekly visits to the swimming baths. She has persuaded the quizzical doctor into giving her more sleeping pills, which she takes irregularly when the tiredness becomes a liability. She has looked after the machine of her body and it has functioned. She has not been ill once.

Now in this unaccustomed heat there is a strange feeling of luxury: the soles of her feet rest on the baked stone of the path; Smokey materialises, rubbing her side lazily against Anne's hip, butting at her elbow for attention, vibrating with her own pleased purr. Anne is sitting idly, she realises. She is sitting idly, smelling the roses and the hot stone, hearing the bees and the distant calls of the children in the park, Smokey's fur soft under her fingers. She has not sat idly for a long time.

Below the level of thought, things have changed. Anne imagines something at the bottom of a pond. Under layers of mud it begins to cohere; microscopic in size, particles fuse, cells join, under cover of water and darkness a chemistry begins. With infinite patience something small and shapeless starts to form and work up through the mud. When at last it separates from the pond floor in a slow-motion cloud of the fine silt it so closely resembles, it doesn't rise but hangs motionless in the water above the site of its own emergence. It has the exact weight of water, it has no direction. When something, maybe the inpouring of a rain-swollen stream, sends a shiver of current through the pool, the thing is nudged sideways into weeds. There it lodges, trapped between leaf and stem, occasionally given another gentle nudge upwards by a new influx of rain or melting snow. It hangs between the fronds like some dirty misshapen fruit, dangling with its own weight, idiotically bound by the laws of gravity. Tiny beads of oxygen pearl off the weed and shoot up like stars through the water around it.

When, after an age, it has worked its slow way up the leafy ladder of weed, it slips unnoticeably from under the final leaf into a reach of clearer water, blue-lit by the sky above. And now, encouraged, it gathers speed. With nothing else to snag it, it accelerates towards that flat day-bright surface, the pond's lid. Suddenly it's powering unstoppably through the water, to emerge at last into air with a splash, tearing the water into a ragged display of flaps and shreds and droplets which rear vertically glinting like shattered glass from the stretched meniscus then fall back and vanish again into the silvery whole. The thing from the bottom is there, arrived, in daylight. It floats on the surface, visible and insistent.

The voyage must be answered in some way. Joseph and Estelle may be dead and gone, but the ship—the crew—Robbie Boyle—still exist. The thing can't be ignored, after all these months it is here now, bobbing unavoidably on the surface of her consciousness.

She could criticise herself for having taken this long but what's the point? This is how long it takes. Every decision she's ever made. Leaving art school; the abortion; finishing with Tim. It's not to do with will, it's about gathering necessity, a movement slow as the growth of plants, as the ageing of her face, something which can only become apparent over time, over a long time of infinitesimal but continual transition. Reversal, in fact: art student—not art student; pregnancy—not; being with Tim—splitting up; keeping the voyage secret—exposing what happened. A seed—a tree; a smooth-cheeked baby—a wrinkled crone.

How precisely to do it is questionable. The most straightforward thing would be to go to the police, as she failed to do the day she landed. But she imagines the glazed incomprehension of the man on the desk she might talk to: *We've got a right one here.*

No, it needs to be someone who is aware that such things happen, someone who has the grounding at least to begin to believe her. Since she is making an accusation—of murder—the best person must be a lawyer. The only lawyer she knows is the harassed awkward man who gave her Father's will and handled the sale of his flat. A man constantly interrupted by phone calls and messages, his ruddy face furrowed with concentration on too many tasks. It would be impossible to speak to him. She could ask him though for the name of a lawyer who deals with refugees.

Anne speaks to Mavis the receptionist in the morning, and Mavis rings her back at lunchtime with the names and numbers of two firms. Both are in London; there is no reason not to ring the first one first, and without allowing herself time to think, Anne does so, making an appointment for the following week.

The brief spell of summer yields to persistent grey skies and on-off drizzle. Anne goes out to clear the garden anyway, working until her clothes are sodden and her bent back too stiff to straighten, yanking up handfuls of the tall coarse grass then attacking its knotted roots with a fork. Her gardening gloves are coated in mud and wet through; at night she leaves them on the boiler and in the morning they've stiffened into two black hand casts. The physical sensations, of wet and cold, of exhaustion, aching muscles and the pleasure of a hot bath, are novel. She is happy to be mindless.

At the law firm she is ushered into the office of a surprisingly young woman. Anne has rehearsed her lines on the train: she is disconnected as she relates the story of Joseph and Estelle; of the way she revealed their presence to Robbie Boyle; of Estelle's disappearance, and Robbie's determination to find Joseph. She does not admit her own relationship with Robbie at this stage—she doesn't want the woman to despise her, or to think this is about revenge. Of course, it will have to be told in the fullness of time.

The woman ('call me Caroline, please') is quick and sympathetic. She is continually flicking her lank blond hair back out of her eyes, a movement which makes her seem nervous but is, Anne realises, completely automatic. Behind that nervy manner the lawyer is utterly composed. She gives Anne a warm smile. Terrible things happen on ships. She describes a recent case to Anne, two Africans found dead at unloading, suffocated by the chemical cleansers used in the containers. Nobody knew they were there—it was claimed. It is rare for refugees to come in like this now; most come over from France, in lorries on cross-channel ferries, or through the tunnel. The conversation shifts rapidly to what evidence there is for Anne's story.

None of Estelle; she vanished. Even her clothes from the washing machine. None of Joseph—after that cold meeting on the upper deck, Anne never saw him again. Caroline flicks her hair. 'Have you considered the possibility that he may have survived?'

'I don't see how he could.'

'But you thought the mate was still looking for him.'

Anne shrugs.

'Give me the name of the ship and your arrival date again. It's worth a check.'

'How can you check?'

'If he claimed asylum.'

But . . . if Joseph has indeed remained invisible and survived the cold and hunger of the deck, eluded the hunters, somehow spirited himself onto land—surely he will have disappeared like a grain of sand on a beach?

'You said he intended to claim asylum. He will have been interviewed by Immigration. His application will be on file. There's a process.'

'OK.' Anne recites the necessary facts. 'But I don't believe he got ashore.'

Caroline nods, writing efficiently. 'It would still make sense to check; and I could put out some feelers about that ship, the captain and mate, see if anyone's come across those names in the context of stowaways. I can check if they've paid carrier liability.'

'D'you think there's a case?'

Caroline smiles quickly and flicks her hair. Anne realises the interview is over. 'I'll know better in a week or two. Shall we say August the tenth, same time?'

When Anne checks her watch, she finds she has spent twelve minutes with the lawyer. Going home she is glazed with disappointment, although rationally she knows nothing else could have happened. She has been humoured and dismissed. You knew from the start, she tells herself, there's nothing to go on. Even less, when you admit to sleeping with Robbie.

The intervening ten days are slow. She is slipping into inaction, lying in bed watching the sky through the window, watching clouds reshape and move slowly from one side of the frame to the other. Staring at the forms of wardrobe, mirror, corner angle, till they are imprinted on her memory. Eating dully, with no appetite, because it must be done—drifting through the days as aimlessly as a dandelion seed on the wind.

When she returns to London she determines to tell about Robbie and herself immediately; it was stupid not to do so before. How can the lawyer advise her if she doesn't know all the weaknesses of the case? Given that nothing will happen beyond the movement of cash from Anne to the lawyer, she might as well be as economical with her time as Caroline is surely being with hers.

But Caroline is full of smiles, flicking her hair excitedly. 'Good news!'

'What?'

'Your friend landed. Joseph Oleweyu made an asylum claim at Tilbury on December the twenty-eighth.'

Is that his name? It sounds so distant, so official. Anne struggles for a response. 'Are you sure?'

'I've checked with the Immigration people at Tilbury. They don't like telling us but I'm handling another case from there, so he knows me.'

'Joseph's alive?'

'Indeed.'

'Where is he?'

Flick of the hair and a more business-like smile. 'I can't tell you that, for obvious reasons. If we gave out asylum seekers' addresses—'

'Of course.' He's alive. He's alive and in England and she has wasted seven months in the dark trying to digest responsibility for his death. The change makes Anne giddy.

'I tell you what I could do,' offers Caroline. 'I could write to him and give him your number. Then if he wants to get in touch it's up to him.'

Anne nods. She wonders if he has already instigated a case against Robbie. 'They granted him asylum?'

'Temporarily. He'll have had a screening interview and filled in an SEF form; it could be up to a year before the Home Office pronounces.'

'But he's not in detention somewhere?'

'No, he's free.' Smile and flick. 'He's out in the world.'

This journey home is very different. Anne feels light, as if she might float up from the damp pavement, as if she will bob against the roof of the carriage on the train.

Her light-heartedness at Joseph's survival transforms the days. She looks at her house, which is choked with furniture and boxes from Father's flat, things that were too difficult to make decisions about or get rid of. Because there is so much junk she hasn't cleaned properly; there is a closed, musty smell to the place. His furniture is no good—the old oak dining chairs, the dark dressing table with oval mirror were OK in the rectory but out of place in his flat and equally so in her own small rooms. Able to be decisive at last, she phones Emmaus and gets them to take the whole lot away in their van—chairs, table, ugly standard lamp, chest of drawers. Her living room becomes spacious again.

She'd cleared his bookshelves wholesale into boxes; now they can be sorted. The theology can go to charity shops; the heavy reference books she'll keep, the sparse and erratic fiction (Chinua Achebe, Stephen King, *Anna Karenina*) likewise—and then there are more diaries. A cardboard box full of blue cloth-bound volumes, years of his life like unexploded bombs. It is as if she had found pornography under his bed. What is the point of keeping them if she won't read them? But this is slowing her, making her dull and heavy again, it's one box for god's sake, it'll fit in the cupboard under the stairs. She drags out the junk and pushes the box right to the back out of sight, it slots in neatly under the second stair.

Late on Saturday afternoon she takes two bags full of clothes and kitchen stuff to Age Concern. And over her tea she looks through the review section of the paper and thinks about going to an exhibition. It is months since she went to a gallery; she has a sudden, delightful, childish sense of anticipation.

It is when she is getting into bed that she notices the blue NIGERIA diary—on her bedside table along with her other books from the voyage, they have sat there at the bottom of the pile all this time, undisturbed by her weekly heap of library books, the crime and travel that have been helping her through the nights.

She must put NIGERIA away under the stairs, along with the others. She extricates it and puts it on top of the pile. She can see the edge of the ship postcard, marking her place. A cold creeping in her entrails; she forces herself to turn away and pick up the colour supplement she's brought upstairs for bedtime reading. Gazes, glazed, at the bright pictures until her sleeping tablet kicks in.

On Monday morning she phones the lawyer and is told she's busy and will call back. But the call is not returned. Anne finally gets through on Wednesday. Caroline is embarrassed. 'Yes I have made contact with Joseph, and he's getting along fine. I'm afraid he doesn't want to talk to you.'

Anne considers. Why should he want to talk to her? The she-devil who gave them away to the mate—who said she would protect Estelle and failed—

Caroline speaks briskly into the silence, Anne senses her desire to get on with other work. 'You shouldn't feel upset about it—obviously, from his point of view, it was a traumatic experience and he's trying to put it behind him. The main thing is, he's alive and well.'

'Yes.'

'I'm sorry—'

'Do you know what he's doing about—what happened on the ship?'

Impatience in Caroline's voice now. 'No. Quite possibly nothing. I've given him your number, if he needs your help he'll ask for it.'

'Right. Thank you.'

'No problem. You'll have to excuse me now.'

'Of course.' The phone clicks down.

Anne goes out into the humid sunshine and walks along the old railway track. He is alive, that's the thing not to lose sight of. Still she is bitterly disappointed. And equally, angry with herself. Did you really think you'd be able to have a friendly chat and explain away the disappearance of Estelle and her baby? Or agree together to go to the police and prosecute Robbie Boyle? That that would make it alright? It's better than you deserve, to know he's not dead.

She walks ferociously fast, noticing the sputnik shapes of conkers growing amongst the darker leaves, the reddening berries on the rowan, the mindless productivity of nature. Its stupidity is maddening.

Joseph doesn't need Anne. Is he himself charging Boyle with murder? Or has he got another plan, another way of avenging Estelle? Pointless thoughts which circle like crows; she wills herself to shake free of them and turns for home. This afternoon she'll go shopping and stock the fridge. Ring someone—Jackie, or Izzy from yoga, see if she can persuade them out for a drink. Pretend she has a life.

Back in the house she brushes Smokey aside and goes upstairs to change her shoes. Sitting on the bed, wriggling her feet into sandals, her glance falls upon the NIGERIA diary. She picks it up, there are only a few pages left unread. Why not? It's not as if she's likely to find out anything worse. The energetic anger which fuelled her walk is making her reckless. Kicking the sandals off again, she swings her feet up onto the bed and hunches over the diary.

February 1967, Enugu

It's over. The bad time is finished, and I thank God for delivering me. I've emerged from the valley onto the uplands again. He tested my Faith, to strengthen it.

Refugees from the north are pouring into Enugu. Many have fled with no more than the clothes they stand up in. A declaration of war is expected daily. And here in one day I can do more for these poor people than I could in a week on the mission: sorting and distributing clothes and bedding from overseas, helping people to make contact with far-flung relatives, planning their journeys for them, ensuring that the sick are seen by a doctor and that those who have no relatives and nowhere to go are at the very least provided with basic utensils and transport to the camps; and praying with them. Above all, praying with them. Reminding them of His love and care to them, helping them to see that His purposes are working themselves out, and that they, like the Israelites, are being tested to produce a finer harder brighter metal, an independent Christian nation.

I can see now that what happened at Oji Bend was necessary; a part of His plan. That I had to be broken to be made whole, that I had to abandon my pride and give up the thing which seemed most important to me, in order to be able to truly serve Him. The loss of Miriam and Anne was necessary. Because all the missions are closing now, all staff except medics have been flown home. If

I had remained at Oji Bend I would have been sent home with them.

He had another plan for me.

When I look back over that year now it is as if into a chasm, a dark pit where I stumbled about without direction, blinded by my own distress. I left Oji Bend initially for the school at Umuahia, where I taught Standard 4 and 5 classes whose teacher had gone to join the army. The Bishop himself arranged for me to stay with Peter, the mission secretary. For a while I lost all sense of God, I even blamed Him for what had happened, for making a joke of me—for using my patience and hard work to build up His mission, then wantonly letting it be destroyed. He seemed to me cruel, arbitrary, faceless. My distress was nothing to Him.

After a while a new teacher arrived, and I started accompanying Peter on his visits to far-flung schools, where he talked about God's goodness and encouraged them to form Bible classes, and I distributed books and leaflets from our van, and gave practical advice to teachers of reading. We ranged across the whole Eastern Region. Some schools were already closing; every day there were stories of attacks and atrocities in the north. Those with relatives in the north begged them to return, the trains and buses were packed to overflowing. Hostility towards whites (after all, the architects of this bundled-together, ill-proportioned, Muslim-dominated nation) increased and we were frequently challenged at roadblocks, on one occasion even being taken for government spies.

So self-obsessed and lost in my own wretched darkness was I that the rumble of approaching civil war for a long time seemed no more than an outer manifestation of that inner conflict; it was even with a kind of perverted satisfaction that I learned of murder and genocide, of innocent men incarcerated in prison, of the exodus of foreigners and the breakdown of communications between factions. The disorder of the whole seemed to me no more than a reflection of my own cracked vision. When the *schools were closed and it was suggested that we should leave the country I laughed. I had nothing to go home to England for. If there was danger here I would embrace it, run towards it with my arms open wide.*

And that's when, finally, He chose to speak to me. When I was so furious and crazed with my own pain, my own disappoint-ment, my overwhelming ego, that I resembled nothing more than a two-year-old in a tantrum. Herbert's beautiful words came to my mind soon after:

> But as I rav'd and grew more fierce and wild
> At every word
> Me thought I heard one calling, 'Child',
> And I reply'd, 'My Lord.'

Peter and I were on our way back from Nsukka, passing through Enugu, where a refugee train had arrived. The main road was impassable. People wandered up and down, dazed and dis-tressed, calling for their relatives. Individuals stood guard over pitifully small piles of possessions: a chair and two blankets; a bundle of clothes, a cooking pot and a rolled mattress; a Bible and a goat—and beside the road, laid down as they had been unloaded from the train, was a row of wounded Ibo men from the tin mines near Jos, who had been attacked by their Hausa and Fulani workmates and didn't dare to go to the hospital up there. Their wounds had been tended by a nurse who was on the train, but in those crowded filthy conditions there was little she could do, and a couple of them were nearly dead. Peter offered the van to ferry them to hospital, and I took the water container from the back and carried mugfuls to each in turn. I was crouching to prop up one young man whose leg was a mass of blood-sodden rags—I was holding the cup to his lips—when a child materialised beside me; a little girl, no bigger than Anne, staring at the water mug. When the miner had done I offered it to her and she drained it. As I came back with fresh water for the next man she was still standing there, staring at me. 'Run to your mother,' I told her, but she didn't move, only stood there watching as I watered each of the men. Then an ambulance appeared, and Peter and I helped to lift the wounded into it. We helped some more into the van and Peter drove off after the ambulance to hospital. When they'd gone, I noticed she was still there, sitting on the ground, intently drawing in the dust with a stick. The initial hubbub of refugees was filtering away. Some had been claimed by relatives and were heading off purposefully into town or along the tracks to outlying villages, their possessions balanced on the women's heads. Others were settling in the rough grass by the roadside, making little fires to boil up water and cook a handful of ground yam. I asked the station master to tell her to go to her mother, but she answered him rapidly and defiantly, and he told me her mother and father are dead. Peter returned from the hospital and began tugging at my arm; he and his wife were flying out next day and he needed to get back to the house.

'But we can't just leave her—'

'What are you going to do? How many thousands of orphans d'you think will be coming out of this?'

We got in the van and drove off and she didn't even look up, absorbed in her dust picture. That night when I went to bed I knelt and prayed for her, and afterwards I realised it was the first time since Miriam left me I had felt another's pain more keenly than my own. In the morning I locked up the mission secretary's house and drove Peter and his wife to Enugu airport and went straight on from there to the Presbyterian church in town. We knew they were already spearheading relief work in Enugu, and administering monies from the Christian Council's Refugee Fund. I offered my services and by the end of the day, was in my new role as Refugee Reception worker. I knew He needed me again; I knew that I could serve.

It seems to me now that perhaps human ties—family, friends, close attachments of any kind—are not really compatible with service. That His injunction to His disciples to 'Leave all that you

*have, and follow me' is a practical instruction, referring to much
more than simply material goods. Monks and nuns who devote
their lives to His service make a difficult decision, once, which lib-
erates them forever after. Even before Miriam became Karl's
whore she was always a drag upon me, always jealous of my time;
even my darling little Anne distracted me from the task in hand.
When His work is pressing, everything else must be put aside. I
am one thing now: His servant. I am happier and more at peace in
all this turmoil than I have ever been. The only person I know
from any past life is the houseboy Luke, who came to me at the
mission secretary's house a couple of months ago, beaming with
pleasure to have found me again. I have been touched by his loyalty. He says little about Oji Bend, only that he doesn't like the
new boss. He heard from her brother that Amoge is far away in
Lagos and has given birth to a daughter. But we don't talk about
any of that, neither of us wants to look back. It is possible, now,
to live entirely in the present.*

OCTOBER 1968

Umuahia, Biafra. (Evacuated Enugu one year ago.)
   *What I saw today makes nonsense of everything. We've been
managing—we thought we were managing. The ICRC and
Caritas flights are coming in nightly now from Fernando Po to
the Uli airstrip. Which remains miraculously usable, despite the
bombing. We're getting it out on lorries to the hospitals, to the
food distribution centres, to the camps. Tons of food a day.
There've been rumours—there are always rumours. Rumours that
we're winning, that the Feds are deserting, their ranks decimated
by self-inflicted injuries; rumours that we're losing, that since
we lost Bonny and Port Harcourt and the oil, France has abandoned us. Without the oil Biafra is of no interest to anyone; we all
know how little the world cares about genocide. Rumours that
we've lost Aba, Owerri, Okigwe. We know Biafran soldiers fight*

barefoot, with sticks against mortars, because we see them brought into the QE Hospital. Rumours that we're starving.

In the middle of it, in the thick of it, supervising the unloading and loading and counting and weighing and checking and signing and accounting for, the spot checks by OAU supervisors, distracted by beating off the political parasites who think they and their families and their families' families have more right to food than the next man, and the desperate robbers in the bushes by the roadside, and the cheats and thieves and lorries that arrive with short measure, and the arguments over the always insufficient medical supplies, there hasn't been time to look beyond the next immediate task . . . I knew there were rumours. And with no petrol; with the army roadblocks and the bridges down; with the absolute hatred now against the English whose bombs and bullets are ripping apart young Ibo men, justified hatred which makes me the target whenever I am amongst Ibos who don't know me (fear? Was that really my excuse? I don't think so. I can think badly enough of myself without latching on to that explanation)—no, it was obsessive overwork, pure and simple. All four of us from the Joint Church Aid, trying to make the relief operation from Uli as effective as it could be—all four are responsible. Each of us is responsible. I am responsible.

Rumours of starvation. Finally today I went over to the Queen Elizabeth (where the wounded soldiers now lie on the floor in rows not only beside but also under the beds occupied by earlier admissions) once the lorries were loaded up, and got in the van with the mobile medical unit. There were reports of typhoid at one of the camps out towards Igbere forest. When we got there it was bad but no worse than others: hordes of clamouring hungry distressed people, women holding up their skinny babies, children fighting to get close enough to beg a morsel of food, a strip of cloth, an empty bottle, anything, rubbish—and flies and general stench. In the beleaguered hospital tent two women were giving birth, and there was a queue of the usual complaints—anaemia, oedema, scabies, sepsis, and the typhoid suspects, of course—

and the doctor introduced me to a pale gaunt-faced young man
who was digging through the supplies we'd brought.

'Hubèrt Girard. Médecins Sans Frontières—there's a camp
where they've been bringing them out of the forest.'

His English was as poor as my schoolboy French, but I estab-
lished that he was working in a camp of 900, that most of them
were starving. He needed anti-malarials and insulin for a diabetic
member of their team, and anything else we could give him. I
helped him load up his battered Austin 7 and we drove for
another hour and a half along a track which the bush was doing
its best to reclaim, twigs and branches whipping at our windows.
The camp was a recent, breeze-block building, unfinished—perhaps intended as a primary school. Some inmates stood in the
yard watching incuriously as we pulled up. No quick movement
here. No run for the vehicle, no pushing and shouting and calling
and begging. The youngsters watching us had bellies like melons
and arms and legs of twigs. Their heads and hands and feet were
too large for them. They had great sunken eyes with flies at their
lids, and limbs too lethargic to swat them away. They moved as if
underwater. Men, women and children, all ages, they'd come out
of the refugee camps in the forest. A woman sat on a desk with a
tiny motionless creature clamped to the empty sac of her withered
breast; a boy with a belly swollen as a gourd stared at me then
slowly began to lick the gleaming empty sardine can he held in his
hand. Most were naked but all clutched an empty tin or bowl or
jar, kept hold of it all the time so as to be ready for the sudden
miraculous appearance of something to put in it. Tins in memory
of corned beef. Of spam. A teenage boy leant against the wall, his
arms dangling uselessly to his knees. They had come out of their
sockets—muscle wastage—and were attached by no more than
the flaps of skin. The weakest lay patiently on palm mats, waiting
for death. Not a sound, not a cry, not a murmur of complaint, in
this camp of living ghosts, dying quite pointlessly with absolute
dignity.

The doctors had drips and injections but no food; they were

selecting the children with a chance of survival, for a feeding pro-
gramme. Those that were too far gone were being left to die.

If we tried to stretch the food further—the ICRC stuff that
comes into Uli by night—all that would happen would be that more
people would starve more slowly. The choices become absurd. There
are food mountains piled up for us in Lagos and Enugu. Dried milk
and eggs for the children with kwashiorkor. In the territory we've lost
the starving are getting fed. There's a Red Cross feeding station out-
side Enugu now where they have three meals a day—one of the
pilots told us. Bulgar wheat porridge and corn-soya milk foo foo,
dried stockfish and vegetable soup. Ward masters spoonfeed the
weakest. But Ojukwu won't let the food be sent in to us; no land cor-
ridors, 'the Nigerian war machine could roll into the Biafran
heartland'; no daylight air corridors for the same reason; no relief
supplies via any Federal Nigerian city because the food might be poi-
soned. (Another rumour: arsenic in salt, milk and sugar which came
to us via Nigeria.) The solution we came up with was for the OAU
to organise relief supplies by sea and up the Niger, to be unloaded at
Oguta. It would work. We were told the suggestion had been passed
to Ojukwu, but there's been no response. None of us is in control,
none of us is in possession of all the facts, none of us knows how this
can end. On the radio Ojukwu talks of extermination.

There was nothing to say. What could I say? Who knows how many
are dying in the forest? Hubèrt drove me back to the mobile med
unit. They gave us food with the staff—a thick soup of spiced tinned
vegetables. We ate shamelessly. We took a boy with a burst appen-
dix with us back to the hospital, but he died when we got there. The
drivers brought over the signed chits from the feeding stations.

What do You want me to do, Father? I'm lost now; Your plot is
too terrible to follow. What use is the finger-in-the-dyke of the
food drops, the supply lorries, my busyness? Aren't we just agents
of misery? Prolonging the suffering, stringing out the hope? If the
aid stopped and the thousands who surely will die anyway simply
lay down and died now, it would be over. Is it better to die by star-

vation than the sword? Have You simply made us the agents of greater suffering?

My own steadiness astonishes me. There have been no tears, no faltering. I have gone like clockwork through the day. I'm writing now in the hour before the Red Cross plane. I have no desire to sleep. Perhaps that's all He wants. A machine; an automaton; a servant who asks no questions, who assumes no responsibility. One who simply serves.

But I did that once before, as I thought. I served, I worked and served, and everything was wrong. Something to do with pride. Is it the same again now? Am I beating against that same old blindness? I peel my eyes for a glimmer of light, in this unfathomable darkness He has sent us.

Their empty tins haunt me, the gleaming licked-clean metal. Myself, I've eaten twice today.

The pages that follow are full of lists: lists of quantities of dried eggs, flour, oil, dried fruit, tinned goods, milk powder; figures which are totalled then divided, page after page of his neat orderly writing, thousands and thousands of tonnes of food, divided and subdivided under incomprehensible headings, sometimes just a letter, C or W, sometimes what looks like the name of a place or person.

She flicks through them impatiently until she comes to another entry. It is the last in the book.

MAY 1969

Mbano. We have retreated here, since the Feds moved on Umuahia.

Working today from my bed (blanket and cushion in the corner of the upstairs room I share with my five-strong relief team). If this is malaria it's unlike the earlier bout. Waves of dizziness and delirium followed by great clarity. I can't stand up but right now

*my mind's as sharp as a machete. Racing, flashing, seeking work.
Calculating and recalculating; the current number we must feed
in the Province. 30 hospitals and sickbays, predominantly
wounded soldiers and children with kwashiorkor; 20 outpatient
clinics; 82 child-feeding centres (approx 400 at each); 60 refugee
camps (around 1,000 each), and the 25 substores for the num-
berless uncamped refugees. Totals a minimum 500,000 to be fed.
At the rate the food lorries come from central store, how long
will it take them all to die? The children are going first of course,
at the end of the month in round figures knock out say 20,000
children. But others who've been surviving on their own supplies
will by that time have run out and be looking to us . . . The Red
Cross are stopping their food drops, that'll clear a swathe. The
end advances like darkness at sun-fall. In the night He will give us
His peace. The cost of salt was 3d a cup. Now you can't buy salt.
Only on the black market. 30 shillings a cup, Luke told me. Being
purified by fire, they are His chosen people. After two years of the
Blockade, a new tyre costs £100. For many vehicles tyres are
unnecessary. The old van still drives on its rims, till the end of
each month's petrol allocation. I am told it would be £25 a gallon
after that. My old friend Okolie sells it on the black market;
Miriam was right about him. He's a rich man now.*

*I am in the spot where the world melts down, the crucible into
which humanity is poured for recasting. Each body forms in the
usual way, the round head, long torso, kicking arms and legs, to
swell into grotesque starved parody of that shape before stiffening
into stillness and rotting down again. Skeleton women give birth
to skeleton children whose bellies bloat with dreams of food, then
shrivel up in death.*

*We do not feed the soldiers; no relief supplies for active com-
batants. In a way they are more fortunate. Abruptly killed, or
wounded by the bombs, their lingering is shorter. His purposes are
beyond our comprehension. His word runs like crackling bushfire
among the ranks of the suffering, His word of Hope. Turning at
the end to God, their faces relax into joyful smiles. They offer*

Him thanks, holding out their hands as trusting children to the Father who will lead them on.

He gives me strength. Not loaves and fishes, for which I've wept and prayed, not loaves and fishes, that is not His plan; but strength to pass on His word to the most needy in the soldiers' hospital—in the neurological unit where most lie brain-damaged or paralysed, rotting with bedsores, starving; many are reborn, many filled with His joy. My young friend Ben, his whole back an open putrefaction, bubbling over with happiness, whispering up to me, 'What joy I experience these days through His love!'

The noon-day light, it's coming through the cracked board at the window. It makes my eyes water. A sliver hot and sharp as a blade. Dear God. Dear God.

He does hear my prayers, yes, even to loaves and fishes. I forgot. The cassava leaves. Because what kills them is lack of protein, that's the cause of kwashiorkor. No cattle have come to us from the north since the first days of the war, and by the end of the first year every living beast was eaten—goats, chicken, bush meat, rats, even insects—not a creature stirs. In the old days I saw cattle coming south once, a living sea, pouring down the road, thousands upon thousands. They would kill them as soon as they got here; this is not country for cattle, tsetse fly country—the Headman told me that.

But cattle are a memory now, meat is a memory. Loaves and fishes. Yes. Protein. In cassava leaves. Poisonous when plucked, but boil for 10 minutes with the lid off the pot and the poison evaporates, leaving protein. A miracle. It can be grown anywhere, cassava. The agricultural team moves from village to village, demonstrating its cooking. Hope in the face of despair. In the villages they are eating dirt.

The hunger must end. The war must end. When there is nobody left to starve. In God's time, when God wills.

How many thousand have I seen die? Luke tells me to keep to my bed, and fetches me water. But I will not die. Not till the task is over. Not until every single soul that I can save has been gathered in to Christ, not till then will He grant me rest.

How clearly I can see it now. In this tide, this flood of suffering humanity—how petty each one's concerns, for his wife, his home, his chickens, his cooking pot. How the tiny dramas of each individual life—who fathered whose children, how many more yams one grew than another, who is richer, poorer, wiser, stupider—of how little account is all this. We are ants. A train of ants pouring from the ant hill into the world, consumed by fire, swirled away by flood, crushed underfoot, we are nothing in the face of the vastness of the universe. Only one thing matters: that we should turn our faces to the Lord. He alone can give us meaning, in life, in death. Nothing else matters. We cling to life as ants do, wanting it for itself, fastening upon scraps of food. But if we turn to Him, he will gather us all in at the end.

The mistake we make is to give importance. The mistake I sometimes make is to see—sometimes to see a child, a single child. To see her wizened old monkey face, her spider fingers clutching in spasm at empty air, her bloated belly a mockery of pregnancy, of further life which can never flow from her. To be filled with debilitating grief for that single child, for the smile that will never lighten her face, for the step she will never take, for the word she will never speak, the game she will never play. It is of no help. The individual vision is no help. I have a job to do. The food must be distributed—in inadequate amounts, to thousands, never to a single child. We are ants, we can't see the universal pattern. He knows that baby girl, He knows why she suffers, He has blessings prepared for her. And I have His work to do, and strength from Him to do it, strength I mustn't waste in pointless tears.

If there is anything after this war, after this great hunger and great slaughter, I shall devote my life properly to Him and take holy orders. And no longer concern myself with food for the body, a concern doomed to disappointment, because how can all be fed? But only with eternal food for the soul. I thank Him, that I have learned to say, Thy will be done.

ANNE REMEMBERS WHEN he came back from Nigeria. Mother took her to see him in hospital. It was the week before Anne's birthday—she must have been seven. He cried at the sight of her and she was revolted by his skinny yellow face and the black gaps between his teeth. His hands were like a skeleton's. She was terrified that he would want to come to her party, that her friends might see him and know he was her father.

She folds her arms round the diary and hugs it to her chest. If he had told her this, if she had known what had happened to him—but the thought stops there. What? She would have understood him better? She never even asked him about Biafra.

She tries to imagine him coming home to England—seeing his plump healthy daughter, his lost wife, his friends and relatives all as if through a thick glass wall. It must have been hard for him not to despise us, she thinks, not to find us vain and petty and selfish, not to be disgusted by our profligacy and waste.

Of course. He was. *I hope you're not thinking of leaving that.* Would it have helped if she had known? She would have thought more kindly of him, at least. She remembers with shame small moments of rebellion: cooking herself too much pasta when he was out, and burying the leftovers in her garden; pouring a disgustingly thick leek soup down the outside drain.

But he hid it very well. He made himself seem OK. She

remembers worrying what he would be like the next time she had to see him, when he was first due to take her out from Mum's house. But he seemed normal then, a thin normal man. He made her laugh by telling her about the eccentric people on his course who wanted to be vicars. He didn't cry or talk about anything embarrassing. He asked her to admire his new false teeth.

She sits for a long time hugging the diary, remembering how he was, how he chose to be. Dedicated to God. She sees he needed it to be true.

Anne goes down to the kitchen and puts the kettle on, then changes her mind and opens a bottle of wine. It is one of the half dozen he gave her last birthday. She needs something to ease her. She feels small and selfish and wrong. So what's new? Hasn't he always made her feel like that? But now she is also wrong for minding, for blaming him for making her feel bad. Since what he has lived through excuses him much, and all her griefs are self-imposed.

She tries to go back to the beginning. To when she first moved in with him. At the start it was happy—she's always remembered that, she enjoyed living in his house. It seems to her she didn't really register Miriam's death; it was simply a relief to be away from gnawing anxiety, from nurses and doctors and hospital smells, and people whispering and crying in corners. She didn't have to be anxious or sad or careful in his house, she didn't have to think about the terrible thing that was going to happen because it had already happened. Her mother was dead.

And he was very kind to her. He let her have a kitten. He was full of projects and plans; he would teach her about gardening and give her her own plot to plant as she wanted; they would redecorate the rectory, room by room, and Anne would choose all the colours; they would learn Italian together, listening to tapes, so they could go on holiday to Florence next year. He got her a place at the girls' grammar rather than the local school, which had a poor reputation, and when she started at

her new school he helped her with her homework and taught
her essay planning. She was surprised and embarrassed that he
wanted to say prayers with her at night, because her mother had
stopped doing that years ago. But it wasn't too bad; he did all
the praying, she just had to listen and say 'amen'. When he
asked God to comfort her for her loss she felt mysteriously
important. God moves in unfathomable ways, he told her, His
plans are beyond our comprehension. Comprehension meant
not just the reading test you do in English, but also 'understanding'. If there was a plan of God's, if it made sense
somewhere for her mother to be dead—then that was a relief
and she didn't have to worry about it. Father seemed quite
confident of this.

Everyone looked up to him. People were always ringing up
or coming to the rectory, asking his help and advice; he would
take them into the sitting room (calling to her to make them a
cup of tea) and close the door, and she would hear the serious
murmur of their voices from the kitchen. In church it was
impossible to look away from him, everyone's eyes were drawn
to him magnetically, and at the church porch he always knew
exactly what to say to each one—who to take aside for a quiet
word, who to make a joke with, who to silently clasp on the
shoulder with a serious sympathetic glance.

In the evenings she often had the rectory to herself, and sat
at the big oak dining table with her homework spread right
across it, sharing the heat of the three-bar fire with Misty, enjoying the knowledge that Father was out there planning the old
folk's outings or talking young couples through the seriousness
of their marriage vows, or helping a harassed single mother to
work out her benefits entitlements. The busy vicar making the
world a better place. A superhero, Anne tells herself wryly.
Super-Vic. But the memories bring waves of nostalgia. When
he came in he would make them both cups of cocoa and sit at
the opposite end of the table telling Anne about the people he
had met, glancing through her homework, suggesting a word

change here or a correction there, his calm kindness spreading like incense across the room.

There is the sudden loud interruption of the phone. Anne stares at it without moving for three rings. It will be Tim. She will not be able to refuse to see him. If only he would leave her alone. With deliberate slowness she sets down her glass, with deliberate slowness approaches the phone, lets it ring until she has counted twelve rings. Deliberately she picks it up.

'Hello?' A male voice, hoarse and deep and accented, bewildering her ear.

'Hello?'

'Anne Harrington?'

'Yes. Who's speaking please?'

'Joseph.'

'Joseph? Joseph! Thank you!'

'Why do you want to speak to me?'

'Joseph, I'm so glad to hear you! I was afraid you were dead—when she told me you were OK I couldn't believe . . .' Anne falters into silence. There is nothing coming back down the line. He knows he is alive. No thanks to her. 'I'm sorry—I just wanted to—I hoped we could meet maybe—'

'For what purpose?' His voice is cold.

'To—to—I wanted to tell you how sorry I am. Sorry isn't enough. I should have done what you said, I was trying to help—I never imagined –'

'No.'

'I know there's no point in saying I'm sorry. I'm sorry. But maybe I could—if there's anything you need—any way I can help you –'

'What? What do you imagine you can do?' She can hear the beeps, it is a payphone running out of money.

'Joseph I'm so sorry –'

'There is nothing you can do for m—' The line going dead clips the end of *me*. Anne replaces the phone and stands watching it. Dial again. Please. After forty seconds she realises she could ring him back and dials 1471. It will be engaged, he'll be trying her. But the ringing at the other end goes unanswered.

After a while she returns to her chair and her wine. What did she expect? What *can* she do for him? Reinvent the past? Unpick that first moment at the ship's rail when she allowed Robbie Boyle to slide his fingers over hers, when she offered up Estelle like a pound of meat? What can she decently do other than promise never to intrude on Joseph's life again, to spare him the contamination and foulness of her presence, to allow him the remote possibility, at least, of forgetting he ever had the misfortune to meet her?

She gulps at her wine to flush the bitterness from her mouth. Everything is sour in the end, no matter how sweetly it begins. And Father now—now she knows what he lived through . . . Her own pettiness stifles her but what choice did she have, other than to oppose him?

Looking back, it seems to Anne there was a period in her teens when she was almost in love with him; proud he was her father, basking in his reflected importance, delighted by his kindly interest in herself. It was only gradually that things changed.

They did learn the Italian he promised—she still knows the odd word. But they didn't get to Florence because the church was running activity holidays in France for inner-city children, and a couple of the holiday leaders dropped out. Father had to run one in Brittany; Anne couldn't be the other leader because she was too young, a self-contained blonde woman from the choir went in that role. It was a bad week for Anne since the children all knew each other and decided she was posh. She watched her father teasing them and chivvying them into doing what he wanted, throwing himself into football and swimming and canoeing with them, playing raucous games of charades in the evenings; and she felt left out. She dreaded the approach of bedtime, when she would be doomed to the room she shared with five other girls, all of whom spent the night speculating in graphic detail about the (joint) sex lives of their camp leaders.

'Can I sleep in your room, Dad? Please.'

'Of course you can't, don't be ridiculous—a great big girl of thirteen. What will the other kids think? Try to be more friendly, Annie, they're good lads and lasses at heart.' She was afraid to greet him at breakfast in case he noticed her blushing for him.

On the final night there were team games and Anne was the last to be picked for anything.

'You must throw yourself into things more,' her father told her on the way home. 'It doesn't matter if you do it wrong, as long as you have a go.'

Anne pours herself another glass of wine. It seems to her the world has always been full of people who know what to do. That she may be the only one who still hasn't learned. It was that year, or the next, that a youth club was started at the church and he pressurised her into going. 'It's time you got to know some of the kids around here. The others'll be just as shy as you—everyone's shy at your age.'

Anne went a few times, rigid with embarrassment, and stood with some girls she didn't know, watching boys playing table tennis. At Christmas there was a youth-club disco, which was packed, and Anne found herself dancing with a tall skinny youth who asked her if she wanted to come outside for a cigarette. She had practised smoking with her new friend Maddy at school and was glad of a chance to display her skill. They leant against the wall sharing his cigarette in nervous silence, and then he asked her if she wanted a snog.

Ten minutes later her father had found her pressed against the wall at the back of the building, with the tall youth's hands under her clothes. Since more than a dozen members of the youth club were there as well, most in much more advanced states of undress, Father couldn't do any more than clap his hands and tell them all to get back indoors sharpish. But he made his disappointment with Anne clear as he drove her home. 'You should respect your body, Anne. Didn't your mother teach you that?'

'I wasn't doing anything, I was only—'

'Do you know the boy? Do you like him? Does he care about you?'

'Dad I'm not trying to *marry* him.'

'How can you kiss someone you don't even know?'

'It wasn't just me—everybody was—'

'That doesn't mean you have to be a sheep, and follow the rest of the flock baaing all the way to the chopping block. You should never do anything that doesn't feel right.'

'I didn't *do* any—'

'Your body is a temple.'

For the first time, Anne answered Father back, in her head. 'Bullshit.'

She remembers she was glad she had kissed the skinny boy, because she'd never snogged anyone before and she needed to learn. But she was ashamed that Father had caught her, and even more ashamed that she did so calculatingly need to learn. It would be a thousand times better to be full of self-respect and only ever kiss the person you were in love with, but all her friends had already been with boys. What if no one ever liked her or tried to kiss her again?

Anne closes her eyes. Tim. He liked her and wanted to kiss her. After the abortion he was kinder than ever. But she was lost. She didn't know what she'd done or why. Was the abortion for him or for herself? For him, of course, it was what he wanted. And for her because she couldn't have borne his displeasure. But hadn't she just used that? Used the idea of his anger because she was scared to go it alone, because it was easier to believe she wanted a baby and he was preventing it than to own up to the fact that she herself was scared: scared to tell Father (what a joke), scared to lose Tim (whom she would now banish anyway), scared above all of the minutes and hours irrevocably ticking away as the thing from which there could be no turning back grew unstoppably inside her, preventing her from thinking? It seemed to her then that if there could have been a week—one week where everything was arrested, one week outside time where she could clear her head and get everything in perspective without the baby developing any further—then perhaps she would have been able to decide to have it. But as it was, with days of growth mounting up, all she could feel was panic, all she could think of was making it stop. You can always get pregnant again, she told herself. This decision is not it forever. But then she must not be with Tim. And how could she stay with him anyway, now everything was unbalanced between them? He had made her give up the baby but was pretending he was kind. She had given it up for love but it made her dislike him. He would only ever do what he wanted. She had not before pictured that as cruelty.

Half stupefied with the wine, Anne gets up to make some food, opening the kitchen door to the early evening damp. The garden looks raw, half-dug, the tiny lawn yellow and uneven where she has cropped it with the shears. She was waiting for it to dry so she could use the lawnmower. The garden is a mess, nothing is ever finished, why can't she do things properly?

She is halfway through a bowl of pasta when the phone rings. She runs to it. 'Hello? Joseph?'

'Tim.'

'Oh.'

'Who's Joseph?'

'No one. It doesn't matter.'

'Who the hell is Joseph?'

'Tim, please—'

'I want to see you.'

'Tim I want you to leave me alone.'

'I'm not going to leave you alone. I'm coming round tomorrow. Lunchtime. You'll be in?'

'I don't want—'

'I'll see you then.' The phone clicks down, Anne returns to the table. She has a terrible craving for a cigarette. Her pasta is cold, she had barely warmed the sauce anyway. She picks up her bowl and takes it to the bin. Stands there for a moment paralysed, then goes back to her place at the table. Pulling up her chair she slowly begins to put forkfuls of the cold pasta into her mouth.

When she's finished Anne goes to bed. Leaving her lamp on she lies looking up at the pictures on her bedroom wall. Prints Father's given her over the years, knowing what she likes. Munch's *Girl in a Nightdress at the Window*, her favourite of all. *The mistake I sometimes make is to see a child, a single child.* But he gave importance to her. Far too much importance. Scrutinising her exam grades and reports, checking up on her work; vetting where she went out and how late she stayed; deliberating for weeks over her A-level choices.

She studied in her room after her O levels, and when she heard Father come in in the evening she would go down and have cocoa with him in the kitchen so he didn't come to find her upstairs. He didn't see her art until the end of her first A-level year, when it was on display at parents' evening. 'So this is all yours, Annie?' He stepped forward to study the crouched and broken figures, the empty room full of dark fingers of shadow, the black night seascape with its faintly glimmering beach. Then he moved on in silence to the other students' work. In the car going home she couldn't resist asking him what he thought.

'They're rather gothic, aren't they? A bit dark and gloomy for my taste—a touch of colour would be nice here or there. But I'm glad to see something creative is coming out of all this teenage angst.'

Looking back, it seems to Anne that this was the comment that decided her. 'I want to go to art college.' For a long time he didn't listen, calmly driving her up and down the country to university open days so she could consider all the alternatives. 'Art is a hobby, not an academic subject. You can do art anytime.' When she got her college place he capitulated. She came in from school one day and there was a pile of art books on the table—heavy library tomes full of glossy reproductions. He told her he wanted to understand what she was going to do. It was as if he'd never said a word against it. She remembers clearly the confused, twisting feeling it gave her. Pleasure at his interest and attention, excitement at being able to show him her favourites: Dürer, Rembrandt, Goya, Munch, sweet Samuel Palmer and Blake. And fear of him knowing them. She needed to keep him out; these were hers, the one thing she knew and he didn't. It was pathetic—other kids needed to keep their sex lives or their drug-taking from their parents. Anne needed to keep her art a secret.

By the time she started her course he was already suggesting subjects she might like to draw, and planning them weekend trips to exhibitions in Glasgow, London, Liverpool. And she was thanking him and railing against him, and never able to get it right.

The night is long. Two or three times she falls into a fitful dream. Father lies ill in bed surrounded by sackfuls of food which she must eat; they are in the hold of a ship, someone is looking for them, it will never be possible to hide so much food, she shouldn't have it with her.

When she opens her eyes it's murky dawn; two hours later the sky is still no lighter, choked with thick dark cloud. She gets up at six and makes herself a mug of tea, and takes it up to drink in bed. It was her loss of faith that really divided them, she supposes. That must have seemed like the worst thing she ever did to him, the greatest rejection of all.

Her friend Maddy first pointed out to her that having a vicar for a father was totally embarrassing. But Anne would have got there on her own. To go to church and stand with your eyes closed whispering to a dead guy with a beard nailed to a wooden cross was totally *primitive*, said Maddy.

And Anne, watching her father's rapt earnest face in church on Sunday, found that she agreed. She reached for that happy feeling of importance Father had given her when he had asked God to comfort her, and realised that the happiness had come from Father's attention, not from God at all. She hadn't gained any understanding of Mum's death—she hadn't even thought about it. God had done nothing for her.

Over the following days she watched herself; waiting in the evening for Father to come home and make cocoa and tell her about God's goodness in helping to reconcile a pregnant teenage girl with her estranged family; or about the incredible efforts that the Sunday school had put into fundraising to buy a computer for a village school in Nigeria—watched herself slipping away, turning into a wraith, moving out of the charmed circle. One Saturday night she could no longer put off telling him that she wouldn't be coming to church in the morning. He stared at her for a moment then burst out laughing. She was wrong-footed. 'What's funny?'

'You being a teenager. Alright, fine, don't come to church. But I hope you grow out of this phase quickly, Annie, because God loves you and you need Him in your life.'

'I don't *believe* in him, that's what I'm telling you.'

'You're very young, you don't know what you're talking about. If you don't come to church, I want you to sit quietly somewhere and think about what religion means to you.'

'It doesn't mean anything!'

'You're being a silly girl. I'll pray for you.' He left it at that, treating her with a gentle kind of pity, occasionally reading Bible passages to her, even more occasionally entering into a debate about meaning or morality, and then berating himself for bothering, because she would surely grow out of this 'rebellious teenage phase' very soon.

He did put pressure on her, as she grew older, to join in the do-gooding aspects of church life. 'You don't have to believe, to know the value of helping others. There are a hundred wonderful things you could do with your summer. Work in an orphanage in Romania, or run a play scheme in Walthamstow —look through this booklet.'

She wasn't good like him. She didn't want to do good. She sat in her room doodling, hearing the phone and the doorbell ring and his clear, confident voice: 'God bless you, my dear. I'll be over right away. Has the certificate been signed? Do you have the name of an undertaker?' and 'Come in and sit down. Your boy's young and thoughtless, that's all, you must give him another chance. What you need is a nice cup of tea.' All these people. Being helped. She hated the way he always knew what was best for them. If she had gone on his do-gooding holidays what use would she have been? Anne can still feel that black stubbornness in her heart.

Occasionally she overheard him making excuses for her. 'I don't think Annie'll be able to help with this year's fête. She's got an awful lot of school work now.' Or, 'Anne's thinking things through. We'll see her in church again soon, never you fear. She'll sort it out.' Did it hurt him, really? It seems to Anne he never took her seriously and therefore he couldn't be hurt. He was disappointed, of course, that his daughter wasn't there in church supporting him, demonstrating her belief in the family firm; disappointed that she wasn't going to be a missionary or a Mother Teresa or the first female bishop. But he never gave up; that was one of the maddening things about him. All through her adult years, right up to his final departure for Lagos, he still seemed to think she'd see the light, was still waiting for her to grow out of her 'rebellious phase'.

She remembers a bitter argument; it must have been last autumn, they were blackberrying together. He'd asked her about religious education of the children at her school, and she was describing their assemblies.

'And d'you tell them you're a heathen, Annie?'

'You still can't respect my views, can you? I'm an adult woman and you still think you can patronise—'

'*Respect your views?* For pity's sake. You don't believe in anything. What is there to respect?'

She was so angry she had walked off from him and hidden
herself in the wood. The anger, she knows, was with herself as
much as him, because she didn't have an answer. He always
made her wrong.

In the middle of the day there is a knock at the door. Anne is
still lying in bed. She listens to knuckles rapping against wood;
to the door handle being tried; to the letterflap clicking open
and Tim's voice calling: 'Anne? Anne? Anne! Open the fucking
door!' It goes quiet but then she hears his footsteps under her
window, he has walked round to look into the front room. He
raps on the glass, hard, she is afraid it will crack. Then the phone
begins to ring. It stops after twenty; there's a pause and then it
starts again. Anne puts her head under her pillow. Eventually it
is quiet. She lies and watches as the afternoon sky darkens into
evening.

There is nothing she has to do. No children to teach, no
work to do. She allows herself to go down. Like Estelle, she
thinks; sinking down into another element, where everything is
slower and darker, where at the bottom you can hardly see at all.
It's quiet there, just a dull distant roaring from the pressure;
things glide past silently, they loom in on you shockingly fast
but then they're gone again, it's as if you're nothing, if you just
stay still.

She can't stay still enough to entirely avoid the images that
crash in on her from time to time, the giant waves, the moving
foetus under the stretched skin, Robbie Boyle's smiling face:
'Don't you trust me?' Father moving through the camp of the
starving.

But mostly she stays blank, curled under her duvet, eyes following the shapes of the clouds. When she is hungry she finds
something in the kitchen—a tin of pears, some Ryvita, a
spoonful of marmalade from the jar. She notes with vague con-

cern that the pile of tins of catfood is going down; one day she will have to get more for Smokey, but not yet. There is nothing to do and nowhere to go and anyway she is no good. Everything is more peaceful after she thinks of unplugging the phone. She watches light turn to dark, dark turn to light, she watches the *Girl at the Window* until blackness obscures her, and blackness until she reappears. She lies as still as she can.

She is disturbed at last by Jackie hammering on the door and not giving up. Shouting at her through the letterbox. 'Anne. If you don't let me in I'll break the glass.'

Jackie takes her to Doctor Munro. He laughed at her once, she remembers, but now he treats her with extraordinary and undeserved kindness. His name, he tells her, is Victor. 'If there isn't a friend or a relative who can stay with you for a while, I'm going to get you into hospital. Alright?' A part of her that is left outside is quite cunning. That part knows there is nothing really wrong. She will get well again for the start of term, she knows she will get well when she has to. But she lets him arrange things anyway, and she takes the pills he gives her.

'You'll feel better soon. I guarantee.'

Dr Victor doesn't know, but he means well.

And in hospital the waves are quelled to a slow swell, oil on the water, a slow sluggish swell and the looming faces indistinct, barely visible, no longer able to touch her. She sleeps at last a dull and dreamless sleep. She is numb.

PART III
4 Years Later

ANNE HAS ALREADY finished work and is tidying up her paints and threads when Vic calls upstairs. 'Dinner in five minutes. Drink?'

His voice is light and neutral; she freezes for a moment, trying to gauge it. He has cooked, he's offering a drink, perhaps it will be OK. 'Lovely. I'll come down.' Hurriedly she stabs needle and pins into the pincushion, dunks her brush in the jar and heads down. He is opening the wine and looks up at her, smiling pleasantly as she enters.

'How's it going?'

It's true. He's fine. She allows her tightness to relax a little. 'OK. I'm nearly done. D'you want to have a look after dinner, and tell me what you think?'

'Sure.' But as he passes her a glass the doorbell rings. 'If it's a patient, I'm out.'

Shutting the kitchen door behind her, Anne goes to open the front door. It is Vic's mother. 'Oh, you are in then. I did try phoning but—'

'Hello, come in, what number did you call?' His mother always rings on the surgery line.

'That wretched answerphone.'

'Vic! Vic, it's your mother.'

He comes into the hall frowning. 'We're just about to eat. D'you want some?'

'No, you go ahead. I had mine an hour ago.'

Anne ushers Mary into the kitchen, offers wine ('Oh no, not for me') and a cup of tea, relieves her of the plastic bag she's been clutching.

'That's why I called—I've only popped in for a minute really, just to drop off that.'

Anne moves to put on the kettle.

'I've been going through the boxes in the wardrobe.'

'So what have you found?'

'This.' Mary delves into the bag and pulls out a short yellowing lacy garment, at first Anne thinks a veil. Then realises it is for a baby.

'Your christening gown, Victor! I thought you'd like it.' Mary gives a little laugh. 'I thought it might encourage you.' Anne keeps her eyes on Mary and the gown. There is a short silence.

'That's lovely,' she says. 'Who made it?'

'My mother. Look at the work in that—I knew *you'd* appreciate it.' She passes the gown to Anne; it is stiff scratchy lace with a satin underskirt, creamy but yellowed with age in places, the sleeves are doll-sized.

'Yes, it's lovely,' she repeats stupidly. Vic is slamming dishes onto the table; surely he isn't going to serve up now, can't he wait till Mary has gone?

'All hand-sewn,' Mary says defensively, as if someone has complained of its not being. 'They don't wear that sort of thing these days.'

No, thinks Anne, they wear comfortable soft cotton babygros. Turning, she carefully drapes the gown over the back of her chair.

'Trouble with clothes like that,' Mary starts up again suddenly, as Vic bangs down the saucepan, 'is they never get much wear. Like wedding dresses.'

Vic drags out a chair and sits at the table. He stares aggressively at Anne. 'You eating or what?'

She moves to the table, trying to rearrange her chair so her back isn't to Mary. 'Come and sit with us, Mary. Are you sure you don't want any?'

'What is it?'

Anne looks at the mixture Vic is dolloping onto his plate. 'Red pepper and kidney beans.'

Mary shakes her head. 'I like to try new things but I've never got on with those kidney beans.'

'What new things, mother?'

'What?'

Anne bends her head over her food.

'What new things d'you like to try?'

Mary's voice rises in pitch against his sarcasm. 'New recipes. Some of the things Anne makes. That cheese and celery bake.'

He doesn't bother to reply, shovelling more food into his mouth.

Mary pointedly addresses herself to Anne. 'Doesn't take them long to grow out of it, anyway, even if you could use it again.' Grow out of it. The notion of a baby growing strikes Anne as repellent. Large and swollen in the sweet doll's dress, its puffy wrists bulging out of the sleeves, its flesh cut into redly by the bias binding around the neck. The satin would be pulled tight across its chest, you wouldn't be able to undress it, you'd have to carefully slit the garment off it with a razor, like you do when someone's injured. Obscene, that business of children increasing in size. She thinks for a moment of her neat doll figures in their boxes. Sewn into their clothes.

'It's my exhibition preview next Monday,' she tells Mary brightly. 'Would you like to come?'

'Not if it's late.'

'No, it's at lunchtime, it's only in the library.'

Vic raises his head. 'I'll give you a lift, if you're here for the end of morning surgery.'

The relief that washes through Anne is also guilt: gratitude to Vic, even love, with an undertow of immediate guilt. It seems to her the guilt is more about her earlier feelings of exasperation with him than about Tim—but the knowledge that she will see Tim on Friday creates a feeling almost of panic, of simultaneously wanting to hide everything from and explain everything to Vic, of terror at her own foolhardiness and of how it could be interpreted. It's nothing, she tells herself, by Friday night it won't exist.

'It's not paintings, is it? The exhibition?' Mary asks suspiciously.

'No no, it's the little boxes, the ones you like.'

'Doll's houses.' Mary nods her satisfaction. 'I'll come then. You want to watch your eyes, you know, doing that fine sewing, you want to watch you don't strain them.'

'My eyes are fine, thanks.'

Mary folds her empty plastic bag and rises to her feet. 'I'll be off then.'

Anne pushes her chair back.

'No no, you stay where you are, I don't want to disturb your tea.'

Mortified, Anne sits chewing as Mary locates her coat and puts it on, and refolds the plastic bag and lays it on the chair arm. 'There's some stuff of your father's in those boxes.' Anne wonders if this is what Mary really came to tell Vic.

'Burn it.' He does not look up from his plate. Mary folds the bag again, puts it in her pocket this time, and leaves the room. Anne listens to her fumbling with the front door.

'Vic?'

'What?'

The door bangs shut. 'Nothing.'

When he has finished he puts his plate in the sink and goes into the other room; the TV begins its noise.

The christening gown still lies across the back of the chair like someone crucified. Anne folds the stiff little sleeves in to the centre and rolls it up and shoves it in the bottom kitchen drawer with the tablecloths and tea towels. Then she begins clearing and tidying the kitchen. A pile of letters and papers has accumulated at one end of the table; slowly she sorts them into three piles; for the recycling bin, for her desk, for Vic's. At the bottom of the pile is her red temperature-graph book. Has it been there all that time? She checks the last date. Three months? Has no one cleared away for three whole months?

She puts the book on her own pile, then moves it across to the recycling heap. It is rubbish. It is finished, that.

Back in her workroom Anne rinses and dries her brushes, and puts the last box up on the shelf with the others, the doll's houses as Mary calls them. Behind her the door opens and Vic comes in.

'You asked me to look.'

'I thought you'd forgotten.'

'No.' It is as if his mother never came. He walks slowly along the row of boxes, pausing briefly to peer into each tiny room. 'What have you decided about glass?'

'I'm not using it, Vic, the reflections are too difficult.'

'You're wro-ong!' He turns to her with a grin, as if he's caught her out.

'Go on.'

'Protection. All it needs is someone putting their great grubby hand in to touch something and—*also*, by the way, protection against dust. They'll get dirty, they'll fade.'

'But I *want* it to feel as if you could put your hand in and move stuff about. I don't want it sealed off.'

He gives a little hum, his 'do what you like but I think you'll see I'm right in the end' hum, and comes to a halt in front of *Hospital*. 'This looks better.'

'I've taken the red off.'

'Yes, he's lost in snowdrifts, isn't he?'

'A kind of shell, I thought, with echoes. Like brackets. He's bracketed off.'

'It's good. All the whiteness is more terrifying.'

Before, her work was slight. His attention invests it with power and meaning. 'Thank you.'

'You know what I think you should do?'

'What?'

'The boat.'

'The . . .?'

'Your cabin. The container. Scenes from the boat.'

Anne stares at him.

'You must have thought of it.'

'Yes.'

'Well why not?'

Anne sits down and puts her elbows on the desk. He can ask and she can reply. It is possible to speak of it; he speaks of it—as something real, with a single question yanking out a thread from the dark knot inside her. She feels an impulse to kneel at his feet and beg forgiveness. 'I don't know. Sometimes I think I should, and then I think it may not make sense to people; it may require some kind of explanation which I wouldn't want to have to give.'

'That's not an argument. You'd make sense of it. Like these'— he gestures to the boxes.

'I don't want to do it as therapy.'

'No.' He comes to the desk and leans against it, facing her. 'It wouldn't be, would it? It might have been if you'd done it back then. But now . . .'

Anne stares at her fingers. She has thought of doing it. Has she even been waiting for this suggestion? For permission? Suddenly he bends so his face is on a level with hers, and grins. 'You're beyond therapy, in my opinion. So it'll have to be art.'

Anne laughs and raises her lips to his. There is always this moment. This moment when she knows this is real and the other isn't: this is the real Vic.

Next morning she has just started sewing the last figure for *Waiting Room* when he suddenly opens the door. It is ten to nine.

'Haven't you got surgery?'

'Yes. I forgot to tell you—I made us an appointment for today. Two o'clock.'

'An appointment?'

'With Hargreaves at the clinic.'

She must have misheard; she was thinking about Hargreaves earlier, and now she thinks she's heard the name, when Vic is really talking about something else altogether. She stares at him.

'You can make it?'

'Two?'

'Yes.' He's gone, rapidly clicking the door shut after him. Carefully, Anne tucks her needle into the doll's arm and puts it down. What is the appointment for? It can only be to ask for further treatment. But they haven't discussed it. It has been let slide, the whole thing, into what can only be assumed to be (surely by both of them?) giving up. Into defeat and silence and a long brittle dangerous mood out of which Vic occasionally surfaces to astonish her with kindness.

Walking to the window and staring down into the murky January street, still hardly light, Anne struggles to latch onto a sensible thought. He must have made the appointment a week ago, at least; he hasn't forgotten to tell her, he hasn't wanted to tell her. Maybe she has made it impossible for him to. And his rages of the past few days (consider also the days leading up to his making the appointment, those moments when he was deciding to pick up the phone now—now—and then not doing it) all have a different flavour, in the light of an appointment having been made. How unfair she has been.

But what is the appointment *for*, that's what she really needs to know. Another attempt? Another month of medication and bloatedness and fuzzy-headedness, of Vic continually furious, of offering herself up to bright lights and probing fingers and long needles, of intimate exposure and utter failure? Hasn't he understood that she doesn't want it any more? A punishment is a punishment; once the point is made, why keep repeating it?

I could do it again on my own, she thinks dully, it's only me.
I suppose I could go on doing it indefinitely, in a way it doesn't
really matter (thinking of the women who actually mind their
feet up in stirrups while the gynaecologist ferrets, of the women
who find the pain or fear of the needles overwhelming); none
of that really matters, none of it really hurts or offends, I don't
mind being a lump of meat, I *am* a lump of meat. No, I could
put up with that if I had to but—

Not Vic. Not a renewal of that venom. Because as they are,
surely, over time it will dissipate. Only last night, only twelve
hours ago in this room he smiled, joked, looked at her work;
starting a new cycle will return them again to the crucible of
his anger.

Crouching down by the windowsill so she can't be seen from
the road, Anne watches patients arriving for surgery. One old man
with a stick moves at a brisk pace up to the house then stands,
staring at it, bracing himself to enter. How can something which
began so kindly and simply turn into such cruel complexity?

She remembers how she went to visit Vic. He was Dr Munro. She
was better, it was after her breakdown. He had been kind. She
needed to ask him—she trusted him more than the hospital
doctors—whether it could happen again. Whether that kind of
depression could sandbag her again.

'Yes.'

She waited for him to tell her how to stop it.

'I could arrange for you to see a counsellor.'

'What would they do?'

'Ask you questions. Try to help you to understand a bit
better what it was all about—'

'No.'

As if talking about it would help. As if describing what she
had done on the ship, wilfully done and allowed to happen, as
if revealing herself in all her shame to another person could
make one iota of it better. No. It must be carried, carefully, del-

icately, secretly, inside herself, the hollow of what had happened, balanced like a brimful glass, because one drop of it could dissolve her.

'Alright. But if it was a choice between hospital again and talking to someone—'

'It wouldn't help.'

'OK.' He sat back and smiled at her, making a steeple of his long fingers with their bitten-down nails. There was a silence.

'So—if it does happen again . . .' she persisted.

'Pills.'

'Is that bad?'

'Of course not. It's treating a chemical imbalance with chemicals. It's adding a spoonful of sugar to an impossibly sour apple pie.'

'But would I—'

'Anne, I can't tell you what's going to happen. But if it does come again it doesn't have to get so bad. If you pick up on the signs, you can come for help sooner.'

She must be trying his patience. 'I'm sorry.'

He was looking at her with a little frown. The silence lengthened and Anne wondered if the appointment was over. 'Well. Anything else you want to ask?'

'No. Thank you.'

'OK.' He smiled. 'Good luck.'

Clearly she was supposed to leave. But wouldn't there be another appointment? If he'd said 'good luck' it meant he thought she was better. She knew she was. But better on a narrow footbridge, better on a tightrope. If she began to wobble, then what? 'D'you really think I should see a counsellor?'

He was looking at her for a moment quite intently, and then suddenly he pushed his chair back and stood up. He was turning away from the desk towards the window behind it, so that his dark shape was silhouetted against the light. He raised his hand to his face, perhaps to his eyes, Anne couldn't see. 'I don't think it can do any harm.'

There was a silence, Anne considering the harm that it could do. It was a crime. Murder. At worst she could be told it couldn't be kept confidential, she would have to tell the police. She might have to go back to the ship, identify Boyle and the sailor who helped him carry the woman. Be disbelieved. At best she would simply have to tell the tale to someone who would listen sympathetically then tell her everything would be alright now, which would be nonsense; harm, in fact. A confessor is what I need, she realised, and the privacy of the confessional. That's the only thing that would help, confession and penance. Crawl to Canterbury on your bare knees. Scourge yourself, fast and pray for forgiveness.

He turned back from the window. 'I had a breakdown when—when my marriage ended. My wife Tanya left me. I didn't want to talk to anyone.' There is a silence, she has a sense of him choosing his words. 'I understand your reluctance. I honestly can't advise you. Most people find it helpful. That's all I can say.'

Doctors sit behind their desks and know everything. They never stand up. They never talk about themselves. 'Thank you.' Anne couldn't see his face because of the bright window behind him. She started to ask, 'Was it—?' and he replied instantly—his voice was light and open now, almost surprised, as if he was surprised to hear himself say this.

'I knew. I more or less knew what it was about and I didn't see how someone else poking about in my conscious or subconscious could help me round it. It was *my* problem.' He sat down again, his voice became rather dry and humorous. 'That's not you, though.'

'Not exactly.'

He folded his arms and sat back in his chair, looking pleased, and somehow full of energy, as if he was just about to make an excellent suggestion. 'The very fact that you have come out of it *without* wanting to talk to anyone seems to me to suggest that you'll handle it, whatever it is. If you made the analogy with a physical wound: a gash will often heal itself without any intervention, without stitches or antibiotics. A body which is fundamentally healthy will heal. I presume the same goes for the psyche.'

If it would heal . . . what would that mean? The vial of acid would be lidded over, sealed in, no longer dangerous; it would always be there, it could never go away, she couldn't empty it—but if there was a lid on it, if it was safely stowed, then . . .

The phone on his desk rang and he picked it up; there was a brief conversation about a prescription. As he put it down he glanced up at Anne and smiled. 'I really ought to see some of my other patients.'

'I'm sorry.' Scrambling to her feet in embarrassment.

'Hang on.'

She stopped. But he didn't say anything else. Confused, she turned to look at him, but he was studying the computer screen intently as if looking for something. As she turned back towards the door he spoke.

'A suggestion.'

'What?'

'Perhaps you should change doctors.'

Anne came back to the chair she'd just left. What had she done wrong? Why was he casting her out? 'Why?'

'I just wondered. If we might, if you and I might be able to talk about these things—if you wanted to—if I wasn't your doctor.'

'If you weren't my doctor . . .'

He shrugged. 'As friends.'

She stared at him.

'Not as doctor and patient.'

'Oh.'

'Not if you don't want, of course.'

'No. Fine. That's fine.'

'Good.'

Anne scuttled from the room.

Two days later a card arrived with the name and address of a Dr Gray on it. Underneath was written:

We could continue our conversation on Friday evening at 8.30
if you are free? The Royal Oak on Bridge St is quiet.

It was signed Vic Munro. The handwriting was open and flowing, rather beautiful.

That Friday morning Anne woke with cramp in her calves. She sat on the edge of the bed rubbing her legs, knowing that she had understood something in her sleep. It was the same. Like Boyle. She'd met Boyle and thought he was flirting with her. (I didn't think Dr Munro was flirting when I met him. No, but I was half-mad.) But then Boyle had thought she was flirting with him. He took it as an invitation. As the doctor had done. Had he taken it as an invitation? Had it looked as if she was flirting? But this wasn't a date. It was a conversation, it was two people who had an experience in common meeting to talk about it. And he was older than her—wiser. But what if? It was too difficult to articulate, it made her revolted with herself. He wouldn't, obviously, of course he wouldn't want to touch her— but because the thought was in her head it couldn't be erased now and so would make her self-conscious and taint their conversation. What if she didn't even know what signals she was giving off?

She sat through the evening in her bedroom, watching it get dark. The anxiety was growing inside her stomach. It had to be controlled, it had to be prevented. She put her right hand to her mouth and closed her teeth over the fleshy part on the back of the hand, between the base of the thumb and the first finger. It was a nice neat mouthful, plenty of stretch in the skin, it was possible to bite down quite hard into the flesh. She bit for a while then studied the results. An oval of deep white dents in the flesh, turning to blue as she watched them. She could concentrate on that, on making the little marks permanent, on biting down but not breaking the skin, on keeping the pressure even. When this hand was done she could do the other.

Next day it was OK. Everything was clear. Of course he had wanted her off his list; it would be a liability for a doctor, a slightly deranged woman who seemed too needy. He might even have been afraid that she would accuse him of some impropriety. He was quite right to ask her to change doctors. She wasn't aware that she had been embarrassing, but how could she know? For a period of time in hospital she had scarcely known what she was doing. She didn't need a doctor anyway. She wasn't going to be ill any more.

The fact that he never sent her another card or tried to contact her again proved that he had simply been trying kindly and politely to get rid of her. He was a kind man, he didn't want to make her feel bad.

A month later, she saw him in the supermarket. He was halfway down the aisle, studying a packet. She moved on quickly to the next aisle. The sense of him at her back (assuming he was going up and down the aisles, not just to a couple of isolated purchases) made her panic and she left without several of the items she'd intended to buy. Then as she was waiting at the bus stop he drew up to the kerb in his car. He had automatic windows, the one on the passenger side rolled down without him moving, and he spoke, hardly turning his head to her. 'Want a lift?'

Anne got into the car and put her shopping on her knee.

'I owe you an apology,' he said, as he steered the car out into the traffic. 'I behaved unprofessionally. I'm sorry.' His voice was light and neutral, it wasn't angry at Anne or himself.

'I don't understand.'

'Yes you do. That's why you wouldn't meet me.'

There was a silence. Anne felt him glance away from the road at her, but she kept looking straight ahead. What could she say?

'I'm sorry. I've never done that before.'

Anne remained silent, twisting her fingers in and out of the shoulder straps of her bag.

'Aren't you going to speak to me?'

'I don't know what to say.'

'Well —' He half-laughed. 'I don't know. Tell me you accept my apology or something. Tell me you don't think I'm a complete prat.'

Anne opened her mouth to speak. 'I don't think . . .' The sentence died. It was important to be clear. 'Can you help me?'

He glanced at her, longer this time, then back to the road. The indicator clicked on, he was turning. 'If I can I will.'

Would it be a mistake to ask this? Would it imply some other meaning? She couldn't see how it would. 'Explain to me what I did.'

'What you *did*?'

'What did I do that was inappropriate? That made you see I wasn't right?'

He slowed the car and stopped it. A residential street, houses with drives and gardens. He kept his hands on the wheel, staring ahead. 'I didn't think you weren't right. You were fine.'

'If people just humour me—if I'm giving off strange signals, or doing something without even meaning to—it would be better if you—'

'For god's sake! You didn't do anything strange. You didn't give off any signals.'

'You wouldn't ask me to find another doctor for no reason.'

'My dear child.' He leant his head against the steering wheel in an attitude of defeat. 'You hadn't done anything. It was me. I was interested in you. And then I thought, she's my patient, I can't talk to her about myself, we can't discuss mental illness. And the selfish solution seemed to be for you to get another doctor so that I could talk to you properly.'

Anne brushed the side of her hand against her lips. She mustn't bite it while he was there.

'That's why I apologised. You'd been ill—you were vulnerable, the last thing you needed was sudden abandonment by your doctor.' He turned to Anne and almost shrugged—shrugged off some layer of himself—and began to laugh. He had an infectious, wheezing laugh. 'You should see how many letters I've thrown away. You'd be amazed.'

She had glanced up once at his bright face but now kept her eyes on her twisting fingers. She felt herself to be some kind of emotional cripple, limping behind him.

'I thought I might be able to help you. I liked you. That's why I'm trying so cackhandedly to apologise.'

'But . . .'

A long silence.

'Yes?'

'But did you—did you think you liked me—because of something I'd done?'

Now he was silent. A woman was coming down the pavement pushing a pram. They both waited till she'd passed. 'I don't know what you mean. What sort of something?'

'Something—I don't know—inappropriate. Did you think I liked *you*?'

It felt as if that was the right question at last, the clear question she should have been asking all along. But his reply came slowly and with difficulty. 'If I had thought that you liked me, would that have been inappropriate? If a patient likes a doctor it's not real, it's clouded by the role; I couldn't tell what you thought.'

'You didn't think I was –' she forces Robbie Boyle's phrase through her teeth—'throwing myself at you?'

'*Throwing* yourself? No!' He laughed. 'I thought *I* liked you. Which was inappropriate. For a doctor and patient. Not for two people but for a doctor and patient. Especially an older doctor and a younger patient.'

'That's the reason you asked me to leave your list?'

'Yes, didn't you get my note?'

'The Royal Oak, 8.30 p.m.'

'Yes.'

'Yes.'

'So you know I wanted to see you.'

'I didn't go.'

There was a moment's silence then he began to laugh. After a while Anne started too, although she didn't know why it was funny. When they stopped he turned the ignition and drove on slowly. 'What would you say if I asked you again?' His voice was light and springy, full of energy and laughter, mocking their situation, the way it was necessary to disentangle all this and yet the recognition that of course the disentangling of it was vital. He was waiting for her to speak. She imagined something immensely complex and sensitive, a radio telescope gently swivelling its huge dish a few millimetres across, a few millimetres up, to position itself most perfectly in the universe to catch the vibrations and echoes of a distant star. He was waiting to draw in and process whatever scattered sense she made.

'I'd probably say yes.'

He laughed quietly to himself. 'Such enthusiasm.'

And so it had happened; easily, happily, he had entered her life. He had filled her with hope; she had been able to tell him everything. And then they spoke of children.

She remembers the day, three summers ago: the heather was just coming out vivid purple across the moors. They followed the steep little track up to the right from where the road ends at Mossbrook, and then turned left over the stile and up the footpath towards open country and the reservoirs. Heather was branching out over the narrow sunken path so that they were brushing past it, disturbing myriad insects, small wasp-striped flies, fat bees, little tortoiseshell butterflies which danced in the air in front of them. Vic was ahead, walking faster than Anne, and when she stopped to extract a twig which had jammed into her sandal she was suddenly aware of the larks babbling overhead; of all the sounds in the valley—the dull rumble of traffic, the whine of insects, the looming then fading roar of a plane approaching Ringway—and up ahead, startled by Vic, the football rattle of a grouse. The prickling heat and discomfort of the moment (especially her feet, dust and grit from the path had got between her soles and her open sandals) and the heady vastness of the air and sky with all their sounds was vivid. A moment of happiness. When she looked up the hill for Vic he had vanished over the crest or into the heather, it was impossible to tell, and she scrambled on up the hill after him; one of those hills where the crest keeps receding in front of you, so that just when you think you're there, you find you have further to go.

After a bit he appeared, walking back down towards her. 'Want a rest?' There was a little island of rock in the sea of heather; Anne sat, and he stamped down the heather in front of her to allow them a view.

'It's my sandals.'

He glanced down at them briefly. 'You should have worn proper shoes. Anne?'

'What?'

'Shall we have children?'

She remembers looking at him, how easy it was simply to look at him quizzically and make him laugh; his delighted, gleeful laughter. 'What, now?'

'Yes.'

'This minute?'

'There's a catch.'

Inching off the rock she lay back on the prickly heather, shading her eyes against the brightness of the sky. 'I thought there might be.'

'I've got a very low sperm count.'

Anne remembers the sudden stillness they both fell into, suspended animation, as she realised he was serious, and that he was waiting for her reply.

'You've been tested?'

'Yes. Tanya and I wanted children. We had all the tests.'

'Can you have them at all?'

'Oh yes. But it would have to be by IVF. The sperm needs a helping hand to the egg.'

'OK.'

'What do you mean, OK?'

'If you're asking me, OK. Let's do it.' She remembers the clarity and joy in her mind, that she could know so absolutely and immediately that it was right.

'You don't know what it entails, yet.'

'Well I know other people do it; it can't be that bad.'

He laughed and she realised from something in the sound that he was close to tears, and sat up so they could put their arms around each other.

Anne looks at her watch. Nearly ten. Will Hargreaves want to examine her? Better have a shower just in case. And get this last doll finished.

It is one when Vic calls her from downstairs. 'You lunching?'

She isn't hungry, she feels sick. 'I'll come and have a coffee with you.'

'We should leave in twenty minutes.'

'OK.'

In the kitchen he is sitting at the table with a sandwich, reading the paper.

'Surgery busy?'

'Not bad.' He doesn't look up.

'Coffee?'

No reply.

'Coffee, Vic?'

'I said no thank you.'

'I didn't hear you.' He turns the pages of the paper.

'When did you make the appointment?' Wishing she wasn't speaking. Why can't she just keep quiet?

He stands up, brushing crumbs to the floor. 'Monday, Tuesday, I don't know. Does it matter?' He goes upstairs.

Anne drinks her coffee then puts on her coat and stands by the front door waiting for him. He isn't in the bathroom any more, what's he doing? It is half past one. 'Vic?'

'What?' Irritably, from the bedroom.

'Shouldn't we be going?'

'I'm waiting for you.'

'But I'm standing here in the hall.'

'How am I supposed to know that?'

'You said twenty minutes.'

He runs down, clumping on the steps; his face is hard and set. 'Where are the car keys?'

'Here.'

They are out of the house, they are getting into the car. But it's ridiculous, she tells herself, I don't even know what we're going for. It is not possible to ask him, she will simply have to hope she can pick it up from whatever Hargreaves says. Surreptitiously she raises her hand to her mouth and sinks her teeth into the familiar bite mark. At the end of the road he turns left.

'Vic?'

'What now?'

'I thought we were going to see Hargreaves?'

'We are.'

'But isn't it the other . . .?'

A fractional pause in which he could concede, then, 'We can get there this way, can't we?'

'It will take longer.'

After a minute he says, 'Why didn't you tell me, if you noticed I was going the wrong way? What's the point in telling me after I've turned?'

Anne remembers an article she once read about a relationship phenomenon in the States; Submissive Wives. The idea behind it was the woman had to agree with everything the man said or did no matter how stupid, and then he would feel good and like her. She wonders if it is possible that a person could like you for patronising them. Could dishonesty be the basis of a relationship? But isn't it, she asks herself? Isn't it? Going to an appointment I don't want and don't even know what for? Playing along with that? Isn't it the same? And lying to him about. Concealing. Tim.

There's nothing to conceal. Really.

There's no point in the thinking, the thinking is all specious, what is done is what counts; they are going to the clinic. Vic is taking them to the clinic, at the very least she should honour him for that, at the very least she should acknowledge its difficulty, rather than carping about what she has or has not been told.

Entering the muffled, silent world of the clinic, she feels as if they have hardly been away from it. Everything about it is intensely familiar: its distinctive smell—not unpleasant, a particular kind of polish or air freshener, she supposes, but somehow enveloping, inescapable; the empty corridor and waiting room; the nods and smiles of white-coated staff calmly circulating in purposeful motion; the helpless passivity that overwhelms her and makes her own movements slow and timid. All hurry, all natural activity, is slowed in that thick heavy air, slowed perforce, so that patients (patients? Clients, she tells herself, customers) move from the start as if drugged, tranquillised, barely able to transport themselves from the reception desk to the waiting area.

Vic grabs *The Times* from the coffee table and puts it up around himself; Anne sits back in her chair, breathing. It is necessary, of course. The staff must exude competence, and a kind of mystique. Why else would anybody pay them? They do have some control; some women do become pregnant. And those women come in here for check-ups, joyous and benevolent, loving the calm steadiness of the place, feeling that something in its peacefulness has communicated itself to their innermost core, that they carry a part of it inside them. Do they? Anne wonders. She knows she will always be an alien here, struggling to breathe, moving against resistance, unable to believe. It's your own fault, she tells herself. It's like any magic or religion. If you believed in it, it would work. You need faith.

But faith in what? The power of money to buy what they want? In the strength of Vic's desire for this? In the doctors' skill to make it happen? In herself, in whatever it is she wants? No, she doesn't have faith in any of these, why should any of them work? In the thick bright air, between the clear pastel walls, surrounded by the peaceful solidity of the furniture and the calmly confident gestures of the smiling staff, she sees herself a dark and trembling shadow, thin, without substance, a negative.

Estelle's baby she imagined underwater. Yes. Floating and moving in that element, surviving there without air as he had lived in his mother's womb, his movement slow and graceful, his tiny hands raised to his mouth in wonder as coloured fish swam by; he would be upright, like a sea horse, his huge eyes filled with delight. But that was a sop. A dream to comfort herself, like a child sucking her thumb. And even if he was there, down there at the sea's bottom, even if he was there or here (are there children's ghosts swimming here, in this thick still air, waiting to attach themselves to living women?) she could never have him. She could never have him, because she had caused his death. She knows that calmly and absolutely, not even with any grief now. It is too late. When she remembers that undersea world, Father is there too. She did not put him there but she should have done because he too is peaceful now. The slowness of movement, the gentle breathing of the sea, swaying plants and whole shoals of tiny glittering fish in one motion, is fitting to his state; he could belong there where she couldn't stay, he and Estelle's baby and indeed Estelle herself.

Vic turns the pages of the paper rapidly, furiously, as if he would tear them; so much noise and movement here is shocking. With a sudden little jolt Anne realises she thinks of it as death. A place of death. A funeral home might be like this. Might it? She has never been to one, it is a stupid thought, it is time to focus, to know what she is doing and what she wants, not to be swamped in hopelessness.

An Indian couple come out of Hargreaves' room, the man

corpulent and besuited, behind him the woman, tiny in a green and gold sari, her face frightened. She leaves the door to Hargreaves' room open and after a moment Vic rises and puts his head round it.

'D'you want us straight away or . . .'

'Yes, yes, come in Vic. Hello Anne, you're looking well.'

Hargreaves' polished desk is wide and empty, apart from the discreetly angled computer to his right; he leans back in his chair, folding his arms, beaming at them with expansive pleasure. As always, Anne notes his moustache. An odd touch, surely, for someone who has to be clean and sterile and conduct delicate operations. The moustache gives him a slightly raffish air, almost, with his black hair and dark eyes, a bandit—but maybe other people like it. It is a sign of vanity, she supposes, which in moderation can be an endearing weakness. He rocks forward on his chair now and lays his hands on the desk before him, big long-fingered capable hands, suddenly Anne imagines them pressing either side of her waist, skin on skin; the heat of it. She swallows. He is a big athletic man, bigger and solider than Vic; is that why he's so successful? Is that why women flock to him for fertility treatment? Because he's the ideal mate, the man who can give them babies? His power is sex, she realises. Everything he does is sex. What he advises, what he charges, the intimate procedures with bowls and syringes, the light in his eyes—all, sex. All I need to do, she realises, is fuck with Hargreaves. And I would have a baby. It is as simple as that. He knows it and so do I, all of this is simply . . . a waste of time.

Vic is saying something. Making a joke about Hargreaves' poor results. And Vic knows it. Her stomach contracts. Of course he does. Vic knows it too and has to sit here knowing what we all know, making jokes and paying money and exposing and humiliating himself, to try to make a child happen. It is a flash flood: the rushing water scouring out the debris, suddenly washing the earth bare. Love. I don't know what love is, she thinks. Most of the time now I hate him. Then this.

But they are saying. Hargreaves is saying. Holding up one hand to Vic—trying to stop him talking?

'Let me just run through the possibilities—we haven't exhausted them yet, not by a long way. And then if you're still both absolutely certain that this is what you want . . .'

What? That what is what we want? For a moment she thinks the pair of them might even have seen her thought about having sex with Hargreaves; which is impossible, of course. How hard it is to breathe in this room, she must focus on what Hargreaves is saying, she must listen and understand. The air is so thick it is hard to breathe unless you are accustomed to it, that's the problem; she has a sudden vision of Delacroix's *Experiment with an Air Pump*, the intent illumined faces, the dying bird in its bell jar, its silence.

'You've gone two rounds of IVF, the first with GIFT, the second with micro-manipulation, sub-zonal insertion. It would be perfectly possible to repeat either procedure and for it to result in success; we've just had a couple successful on their fifth try, after almost no hopeful signs. As you know, it can happen at any time.'

Vic is tapping his foot rapidly against his chair leg; Anne resists the impulse to lean over and stop him. Hargreaves' job to deal with it. Not mine.

'Secondly, there is the other micro-manipulation technique left to try—'

Vic is shaking his head. Hargreaves ignores him.

'—direct injection. I know you have reservations but this now has a forty to fifty per cent success rate—'

'No.'

There is a little pause.

'Can I ask why?'

'It's unnatural.' Vic speaks lightly; as a little frown gathers across Hargreaves' forehead, Vic begins to laugh. The more Hargreaves looks puzzled, the more Vic laughs; the sound is irresistible and Anne is drawn into it too. Hargreaves smiles politely, with enforced patience, waiting for them to stop.

'A strange word to use in these circumstances.'

'Yup.'Vic nods, still grinning, still enjoying himself; now I'm his supporter, thinks Anne, now I want him to succeed, to blow Hargreaves away. 'Yup. But all these things are relative, don't you think? At various stages and levels of complexity your work involves making it easier for the sperm and egg to get together so that fertilisation can occur –'

Anne wonders if Hargreaves will be irritated; but he knows Vic's a doctor, she reminds herself. And this is the irresistible Vic—the light, reasonable, fascinated exploring voice, leading you along the twists and turns of his idea, beguiling you, seducing you into listening.

'– of which GIFT is rightly the favourite since all you do is mix them and fire them back into the fallopian tube; then IVF itself, watching fertilisation occur in vitro before placing the embryo in the womb; then subzonal insertion, cracking the egg if you like—inserting a few sperm inside the zona pellucida, so they don't have to batter their way in; but this one's different. If you inject one single sperm into the centre of the egg, you are actually fertilising it. You are removing every element of chance and choice. You create that embryo. Which is qualitatively different from any of the other procedures: it isn't *allowing* fertilisation to take place, it isn't making fertilisation possible; it's grabbing the egg and the sperm by the scruff of the neck and ramming them together. If you like, it's egg rape. What if you make a monster? What if you make a psychopath? Should anyone other than God have so much responsibility?'

Hargreaves smiles patiently. 'You're being romantic. But it's not my job to persuade you.'

Vic grins. 'Oh but it is. Think of the cash!'

Something in his tone—its lightness, its self-mockery, his clear recognition of his position vis-à-vis Hargreaves, makes this not offensive but wonderfully funny, and for the first time in the consultation Hargreaves breaks into surprised and unreserved laughter, slapping his hands on the desk.

'Indeed. How right you are.' Still smiling, he turns to Anne. 'What's your position on all this?'

Warmed by the laughter, she is able to answer easily, almost without thinking; 'I agree with Vic.'

Hargreaves nods. 'Well then. The procedure for AID, as you know, is straightforward. Anne gives details of her cycle to the nurse, goes onto Buserelin and fertility injection routine—'

'Is that necessary?' Vic's voice suddenly sharp, the humour gone.

'Well it makes sense to maximise Anne's fertility in preparation for the insemination.'

Insemination. The word drops through into Anne's consciousness. He is talking about AID. Artificial insemination by donor. Vic has brought them here for that? He must have done, since everything else is rejected. He is agreeing to donor sperm. It's hard to grasp. She needs to understand. Does he mean it? But the argument is going on. Vic's voice is pressing, insistent.

'Are those injections standard? Is that what you usually do?'

'Yes.'

'Why can't you just do the insemination when she's about to ovulate naturally?'

Hargreaves smiles patiently. 'My wife showed me a magazine article recently which described a turkey baster and a cup of fresh semen as being the only items needful for DIY insemination; and of course that's true. What they didn't give were the success rates. If you're going to take the decision and go through the process in a properly regulated manner—and indeed, pay for it—then surely it makes sense to create optimum conditions?'

'Not if the patient responds poorly to the drugs.'

Hargreaves glances from Vic's face back to his computer screen and, after a tiny pause, continues smoothly.

'You're worrying about Anne's reaction to the drugs. Obviously the problems that occurred first time round—the ovarian hyperstimulation—will be avoided. From the look of it —' he leans towards the screen, clicking on the mouse—'yes, on round two when we dropped the perganol from the cocktail, and lowered the whole dosage—there weren't any problems?'

He glances at Anne and she nods. The first time was pretty much lost in a blur. They'd given her the Profasi, collected seven eggs, fertilised one and replaced it—and then she'd started vomiting. Straight away, much too soon for pregnancy. And her stomach had swollen up like a balloon, she remembers; a horrible parody of pregnancy, in the first week of implantation: nausea and a swollen belly, getting bigger and bigger till she could hardly breathe. Ovarian hyperstimulation syndrome. Vic had driven her to hospital in the night and they'd put her on a drip. They told her her ovaries had overreacted to the perganol. Next time she should have a lower dose. And no, by the way, she wasn't pregnant.

After a silence which Hargreaves rightly takes to be consent, he makes a steeple of his fingers and resumes. 'The only other thing you need to do is fill in the donor form.'

'What's that?'

'It's just for details like colouring, religion, and so on.'

'Really?' Vic's voice is delighted. 'Religion?' He turns to Anne. 'Can we have a Muslim fanatic? Or a Mormon? What about a nice Jewish boy?'

Hargreaves looks pained. 'Some people do take it seriously— we have to comply with the law, obviously—you wouldn't want sperm from a donor with a different ethnic background.'

'No? No little black piccaninny, then? No lustrous Oriental?' He isn't being funny any more. Anne feels his pleasantness fade and die like a sudden burst of sunlight on a March morning chased by cloud; it has returned to cold and grey. Hargreaves tries to be jovial.

'Well the idea is to match the child to the parents; someone from another ethnic group might rather give the game away.'

'But it's not my child.'

'Biologically, no, of course.'

'If I can't have my own surely the least I can have is what I want?'

Hargreaves glances at Anne. What does he think she can do? She looks at her hands.

'The only thing I forgot to mention is the counselling, of course. You'll both need to see the counsellor.'

'Why?'

Vic stands and moves across to the window. His voice is still light but charged, poised for attack. Anne knows that whatever Hargreaves says now—

'There are issues you'll need to think about. Like when you tell the child, how you explain its parentage.'

'And how *do* you explain it? To a five-year-old? How much detail do you tend to find is helpful? Do you describe the guy in the cubicle jerking off for a tenner a throw?'

There is a silence. Vic glances from Hargreaves to Anne and smiles. 'Sorry, have I been offensive?'

'Everyone has to see the counsellor,' Hargreaves says matter-of-factly. He stands up. 'And if you want to talk to me again . . .'

Anne moves forward to shake his hand. 'Thank you.'

Vic nods at him and pushes out of the door in front of Anne; Hargreaves moves quickly to hold it open for her.

'Good luck,' he says quietly and kindly, and Anne nods mutely. Don't be kind to me. She follows Vic blindly through the waiting room, catching the second door as it swings back in her face.

When she gets to the car he is gunning the engine, staring round out of the windows. 'Why does it always take women so long to get out of a place?'

She tells herself not to reply but then her mouth opens. 'I think we should have seen the receptionist. I must make an appointment with the nurse.'

He stops the car abruptly. 'I'll pick you up in half an hour. I need a coffee.'

'Right.' She gets out of the car again. It is so clearly pointless. She bends to the open door. 'Vic?'

'What?' Impatient.

'If it makes you so angry just to talk about it—'

'I'm not angry. I'm bored, it's like the bloody safety drill on a plane. Pointless routine.'

He starts to accelerate and she slams the door quickly. Do you not think it odd, she asks him in her head, that I should have to go back and make the appointments while you have a coffee? But that is a stupid thought, it would be nerve-racking and difficult if he came with her. If even making appointments is difficult in his company, why am I trying to have a child with him?

Back in the unruffled atmosphere of the clinic, the sleek receptionist gives Anne an appointment for counselling, and tells her the nurse is waiting for her now. Anne has forgotten, of course. After the doctor you see the nurse. When she emerges forty minutes later she has charts, instructions, a timetable, even the supplies of Buserelin. She had forgotten the efficiency of the place; once you enter the door you step onto the conveyor belt. It will require a positive effort to get off it.

There is no sign of Vic. She hesitates for a couple of minutes, then crosses the road and walks away from the clinic as fast as she can. At the corner she stops, folds in four the papers she's been given, packing them into her shoulder bag along with the Buserelin. The instinct to hide them from Vic is very strong. The physical reality of the brown bottle in her bag, of the dates the nurse has inserted on the papers, have given her a flash of insane hope. What if it works? It is as if she's been given the key to a wonderful secret.

She remembers all the hope there was. Vic's kindness. Starting to draw again. His passionate interest in her art; the decision to stop teaching for a while and devote herself to painting and making full time. Her sense of—yes, of resurrection. She has hesitated over this word before, it is so clearly Father's, but it is the only one appropriate. She was res-urrected, there was a coming back to life, to which indeed

Father contributed, in which he was even instrumental, in the arrival of that last heartbreaking diary. Remembering, she is filled with nostalgia for the simplicity of those feelings. The clear sharp grief, the flood of love, her tentative steps into her new life, the sense of possibility. The diary marked the turn.

It was not long after she and Vic got together. It must have been a Saturday, because he was at her house when the post came, a thin book in a padded envelope, airmail from Nigeria. Inside the blue cover, a letter from Matthew Afigbo.

December 19, 2000

Dear Anne,

I hope you had a pleasant trip home and that all is well with you. I have been thinking of your father, who was with me this time last year. This diary was by his bed when he died. Forgive me for not passing it to you straight away, but I was not sure what to do for the best. I knew he was looking for someone while he stayed with me, and I was afraid you may be upset to learn of it. But I have prayed for guidance, and I believe now that you have a right to this information. It would be wrong of me to hold it back.

I know you will be able to forgive your father, he was a good man. There are things in every life that are not for us to judge, that only God can understand.

I pray for you Anne, and hope that your life will be peaceful and happy, and that one day we will meet again.

With warmest wishes,

Matthew

She couldn't read it while Vic was there, just the sight of its plain blue cover, the shape and weight of it, started a trembling in her stomach. It can't hurt you, she told herself. She put it on the table and walked round the kitchen looking at it from all sides. She wondered about burning it. If he had wanted her to know whatever it was, surely he would have told her?

Vic made her a cup of tea and kissed her and left for ten o'clock surgery. She paced about the house until something somehow slotted into place and she was able to draw her chair up to the table, pull the diary towards her, open it up and crack back the covers so that it would lie flat on the table before her. When she did open it she realised it was hardly used. He had only written on the first few pages. There was an old creased manila envelope in the front, not addressed. She placed the envelope on the table, and started to read.

November 29, 1999. Lagos

This is a hard place to come back to. For the first time ever, I think, I feel old; grateful to Matthew for showing me the ropes; slow to grasp things, assaulted on all sides by random bombardments of memory which almost halt me in my tracks.

Amongst the Nigerians I knew at Oji Bend, one in particular springs to mind now. The father of my student Ukabegwu. He converted to Christianity in the same spirit in which a man buys shares on the stock market. Expecting benefits, looking to increase his profits. Wanting milk and honey. When his pagan neighbour's goat bore twin kids and his only one, he came to me to complain. When his second wife died of a snake bite, he left the church in a rage.

I imagined, perhaps, a settled peace. In old age, a comfortableness with God. Instead of which, certainty drains away. I am assailed by doubt. I find myself envying Matthew his confident pronouncements from the pulpit, his easy warmth with his parishioners. As my body becomes less flexible, more rigid, so I fear do my mind and spirit. And I think of Karl, for whom I felt a young man's contempt and anger—Karl who mistrusted change and feared the new, who needed to retain control of what was happening, because if he didn't he would be blown away like an old dried husk. Karl of whom I was then so furiously jealous.

I imagined a relationship with God as cosy as a forty-year-old marriage; warmth, familiarity, no need any longer to question or defend: acceptance.

Instead of which, my mind runs on unpicking the past, unpicking certainties, seeking clarification, wondering if what I believed to be His will was His will. Or whether I ran along false footpaths, while He watched as dispassionately as He might watch a foolishly buzzing fly.

I can feel a kind of separation. The wheat from the chaff? I can hear my own voice, expounding to my new Bible class (yielded up gratefully, I think, by Matthew, who has more than enough to do) His message from His book, judiciously weighing their suggestions and replies, resolving difficulties, answering questions. With sure, mechanical ease. Inside my heart other questions bubble, rising to the surface again and again, irrepressible. Not even questions, but faces. Miriam. Amoge. The child that Anne was when we were here. The child of Amoge.

For a few days I didn't even understand why I was staring at every half-caste woman I saw who looked to be in her thirties. I knew and didn't know that I was looking for her. That I have come here to find a needle in a haystack.

I can't have flown into Lagos at night before. Or maybe I don't remember. The blackness of the sea, the curious soft warm glow of the city, resolving itself as we circled lower and lower into individual pinpricks of flame-coloured light and the yellow glare of scarcely moving lines of headlights. 'Power cut,' I heard the Nigerian behind me sigh quietly to his companion before I had registered that what I was missing was fluorescent street lights, domestic yellow windows, the electric blare that is any modern city at night. A moment of wondering whether the airport has its own generator, and then the acid-drop white of the runway lights marking out our path.

The woman who checked my passport smiled and said, 'You are welcome!' with such warmth that I was suddenly convinced it was her. But then I looked at the angry woman struggling on her own with two suitcases and a toddler, and the busy girl at the car-hire *desk, and the thin girl who forlornly held up a name board for a passenger she hadn't met—and as the close warmth and smell of the place and the deep husky voices of the women percolated through me and finally transported me here, back to Nigeria more surely than eight hours' slog on a plane had done, I realised that every sense was alert for her. Matthew had sent me his driver and he picked me out of the seething mass at Murtallah Mohammed and led me to his car. We crawled out onto the six-lane highway that now connects the airport with Lagos Island, and joined the queue in the fast lane. In the slow lane, cars which had become irritated by the wait to reach the airport (all three lanes on the other side of the road were stationary) tore past us in the opposite direction.*

I could see in the darkness now that the flame-coloured lights were indeed flames—kerosene lamps, the driver told me, a tin, a wick, some kerosene. Yes there are fires, of course. When we stopped at traffic lights the shadowy movement at the roadside resolved itself into hundreds of milling individuals, most of whom rushed out into the traffic with trays of oranges, boxes of cassettes, ice-cube trays, food and drink of every description—the first to reach the cars seemed to be small children on skateboards, resolving into legless men on wheels, eagerly holding up a packet of cigarettes, a begging bowl, a newspaper.

'Don't let down your window,' my driver instructed sharply. There was a girl with a huge tray of sliced fruit on her head, standing quite still in the crowd. But she was young, far too young, no more than seventeen. When we came to the bridge there was the blackness of the sea again, and only the line of light of headlamps and brake-lights connecting us across it to Lagos Island. I felt as if I was falling, falling and staring, looking into the darkness for one face.

DECEMBER 1, 1999

And that, I suppose, is what it's about. The reasons I have given others, given myself even, are all true enough. But that unspoken one is central. Yes I've come back to see how things have changed here in the last twenty years. Yes I've come back to make a per-sonal bridgehead between St Luke's and my old curate Matthew Afigbo's Lagos parish. Yes I've come back to touch the heat and sweat of the place, to reach again the young man that I was, the exhilaration and trauma of those times.

But somewhere here I have a daughter.

Interesting how things change in complexion, slowly, like a planet slowly revolving and turning towards the light. At first I didn't want anyone to know about Amoge and her child because I was ashamed of my adultery. Now I keep it secret because of the shame of having done nothing about them for so long.

Now, when it's too late to offer help or support, what right do I have to chase after them? To ask forgiveness? To ease my own pain. Selfish again.

Long hours of prayer here, in Matthew's ugly brick church, wrestling with my own motives. As ever, what there is to do, in practical terms, feels clean. The link that I can make between our two parishes, our two countries, can do nothing but good. Matthew is immensely grateful for the two gap-year students we've recruited; he will place one as an unofficial assistant to the chaplain in the children's ward of the local hospital, and the other directly in the church school. And their reports back home, and individual family contacts that each makes, will encourage others to come. The paranoia about asylum seekers makes traffic the other way less likely, but I shall travel back with Steve Adeyemi, both of us wearing our best dog collars and mildest looks, in the hopes of getting him in for a short spell at least, and again, once we can produce evidence that our church's Nigerian visitors do return, perhaps they'll get a less boorish reception from Immigration. Matthew himself was so bruised and humiliated by his last attempt that he is unwilling to try again. Communication and assistance between our churches can only be for the good.

It is in the other areas that motives appear murky. Visiting the old diary as I visit the place, the man I was seems fragile and deluded, pitiful in his isolation. Now it seems to me the only good that I can point to is in the links between individuals. What else can stop us tearing each other to pieces like wild animals, bombing and shredding the flesh of young men, starving children by the thousand? I have used Him, the notion of service to Him, to excuse my own negligence. I have only accepted personal responsibility when it has been foisted on me by external events— as care of Anne was by Miriam's death. I thank Him for the opportunity that gave me. Not for Miriam's death, I could never have wished that she should die; but it is out of that tragedy that I know and love my daughter. One of my daughters.

The presence makes the absence the more noticeable. Now I know what the loss of the other daughter means.

DECEMBER 8, 1999

Incredibly, I received an answer to my letter to Amoge's brother. Carefully written in pencil on a page of lined paper cut from an exercise book.

Dear Revd Harrington,

My sister is dead June 1990, we fetch her home for the burial. Her girl is gone overseas. You can ask the lady where Amoge use to work. Mrs Anene, 20 Elizabeth Avenue in Ikoyi district.

Yours,
R. Otanga (Mr)

Matthew got a man from the church to drive me there on Sunday afternoon. A wealthy suburban house hidden behind high wire-topped walls. We were kept waiting outside the locked gates while the guard relayed my name to his employer, and came back and forth to the car with a series of questions about my business. Matthew had reckoned on my dog collar winning me entrance, but in the end the man was satisfied only by my offering him my passport as proof of identity. My driver shrugged it off. 'Robbers. Everyone expects armed robbers in this place.'

Mrs Anene, a beautiful black woman running to fat, was sitting in a large and curiously empty lounge, on a white sofa. She motioned me to sit in a huge white armchair facing her across a bare glass coffee table. She was perhaps in her fifties, richly dressed, very gracious. She ordered a young man to fetch us drinks and dismissed my driver to the kitchen.

When I told her I was looking for Amoge's daughter she turned her painted mouth down at the corners and fluttered her eyes in distress.

'I loved my Amoge. She was more like family than servant, to me. Twenty-three years, she stayed with me. When she was sick I thought nothing of the doctor's bills. I told him, call again, doctor, if you can give my dear Amoge any relief, if you can prolong her life by a single day, you must call again, and never mind the charges. That's how I am with my servants, reverend.'

I nodded, and asked again after the daughter.

'Lily, yes, a beautiful girl. The first time I saw her in her mother's arms, I said, that child is a real beauty.'

Lily. I had not known her name.

'There are not many people in my position who would take on an unmarried servant with a child. Where I can help my fellow creatures, especially if they are worse off than me—then I do. It's my nature. Yes. Sometimes my trusting nature has led me into trouble, but still I believe in helping others.'

'And where is Lily?'

'She was well treated in this house, I can tell you. Any little bits and bobs she wanted for her games—I saved her my cotton reels, and Amoge made her a snake from them, I remember—excuse me.' She dabbed at her eyes. 'How fond Lily was of that little snake! And scraps of cloth from the sewing. Amoge used to make tiny families of dolls, just the size for doll's house. Very clever, very pretty little pieces of work, all in matching clothes. They were so good I got her to make some for my sisters' children at Christmas.'

'And where . . .?'

'Amoge was so proud of her. A very beautiful girl, fine pale skin, light as a model. I said to her mother she could have her picture in the magazines, a girl with light skin like that.'

'And . . .'

'Amoge wanted her to go to England. She had her heart set on it; she turned to me for help, of course—I was her closest friend. And I did my best, reverend—'

She stopped abruptly when the boy returned with our drinks, chiding him sharply for being so slow, then turned back to me with a smile. 'I put as much effort into that girl's future as if she were my own daughter; and I succeeded in finding her a position in Italy.' There was a moment's silence as we both sipped our juice.

'Do you have an address for her?'

'Oh no. It was all a long time ago you know. A long time since poor Amoge died, and four–five years before she died, Lily flew away.'

'But Amoge must have written to her.'

Mrs Anene smiled at me. 'She was only a village girl. She hadn't mastered the art of writing.'

But I knew she had. I had taught her. She could read and she could write. 'Do you have any of her things still, something which may give me a way of contacting Lily?' Her name was sweet in my mouth.

'No, no. How could I keep things all these years? I have to clear the room for my new servant. Why do you want to find her, reverend?'

'I have a message for her from her father. There's something he wants to give her. A gift.'

'Her father? Lily's father?'

'Yes.'

She hesitated. 'He was a white man.'

'Yes.'

'You know him?'

I nodded.

'I have one small envelope belonging to Amoge.' She rose and *left the room. I strained my ears to follow her but in that thickly carpeted house the sound of her was soon gone. It was quite a long time before she returned, holding a creased manila envelope. She handed it to me. Three flat bits of paper inside. The first, Amoge's death certificate. The second, Lily's birth certificate. April 21, 1966. Her mother's name. Her father's name, David Harrington. When I saw my name my heart jumped in my chest. As if the certificate made it real—what I have known for thirty years, as if I could never really know it until now. The third I recognised when I unfolded it. A Sunday-school certificate from the mission. Amoge's name was entered in my own hand. I must have sat staring for longer than I thought. Mrs Anene, who had not sat down, held out her hand for the envelope.*

'You've seen my passport, Mrs Anene?'

'You must forgive me, we learn to be suspicious here.'

'No, no—the name.' I held out the birth certificate to her, and pointed to 'Father'. She glanced at it then up into my face. 'I need your help. Please. I have to find my daughter.'

Mrs Anene closed her eyes for a moment, then perched on the edge of her sofa. She stared in silence at the floor.

'Please help me.'

'The only thing I have—perhaps—is the name of a woman connected with it.'

'With?'

'Sending girls to Italy.'

'Girls? A group of them went together?'

'This was a girl with no father, no money, no education. Not content to clean floors like her mother.' Her tone was sharp with anger.

'I know.'

'Anything could happen in Italy. You understand? It was her choice.'

'Yes.'

She went out into the hall; she left the door open and I could see her pull out the top drawer of an elegant long-legged desk, and take a thick old address book from it. She copied something slowly onto a sheet of writing paper and brought it back to me. 'This lady had some connection—with sending girls to Italy. I knew her many years ago. Now I don't see her.'

My hand was held out for the address but she was finding it hard to pass it to me.

'She is not the type I like to associate with. She is completely changed now.'

'Thank you, I am very grateful.' I took the address. She was still holding the paper so tightly that it ripped in the corner as I pulled it from her. I asked her if she would pray with me and we both knelt on her thick white carpet and asked Him for forgiveness. The manila envelope was like a flame in my hands. I thanked her again and departed.

DECEMBER 11, 1999

I haven't slept well since I came here. The heat troubles me more than it used to. It seems to sap all my energy. In the old days I think I used to almost revel in this climate, in the way I could keep going through it. When others were overwhelmed I felt a triumphant kind of pity. For Miriam, for her complaints about sleeplessness and feelings of suffocation—I saw it as yet another sign of her innate weakness, she could never cope with anything as well as me.

Now as I lie here sweating and aching in all my limbs, with the thick warm darkness pressed into my face like a heavy blanket I can't throw off, forced to rebreathe my own used hot air, she is another grief.

I have had to sit up and turn on the bedside lamp. My bed was spinning and falling through the darkness. I realised I was hyperventilating. In a while I shall read my Bible. But for now, the steady progression of my pencil across the sweat-dampened paper calms me. She is another grief. Of course.

I never saw her again. Even when I knew she was dying. It suited me to believe she had betrayed me.

How clear and easy it all is now. Is this the wisdom of old age? It dawns on me that I now know, with absolute certainty, that Miriam was never unfaithful to me. (How long have I known it? Did I know it last year? Did I know it before I left England? Did I know it yesterday? Impossible to say.) But it has arrived in my head tonight as a fact, as much as my age, as much as the existence of my two daughters. Miriam was never unfaithful. It wasn't in her nature. All that awkward friendliness with Karl, the apologies she made for him, her attempts to explain him to me, were for me, to help me. When she wrote me that letter, even then, she was still wanting me to understand the process she herself had gone through, and even, what I owed him. If there had been the least suggestion of anything between them she would never have written in that way. Because then she would have been able to see how I might interpret it. As it was, her innocence made her oblivious.

If I know that now, didn't I know it then? In part, yes. I could believe that under the guise of helping me and smoothing things between me and my—could you call him boss? why not, in the interests of simplification: the power relationship was the same—in the guise of smoothing the difficult relationship between me and my boss, she in fact gave herself to the older and more powerful man. But even as I felt the slicing anguish of this I knew it at one level to be untrue. I knew that in allowing myself to feel that excruciating pain and rage I was in fact testing myself and proving my own superiority even to that: I could survive it, I could ignore it, I could work still, consumed by fire, I would not let her destroy me. And in allowing myself to believe that I had endured the vilest kind of betrayal, I could have sympathy with myself. I could like myself.

In believing her to be the hypocrite, I was able—not to see my own infidelity in a better light (no, because in truth it never troubled me, I knew the affair itself wasn't serious enough to be bad, only its consequences were bad)—no, I didn't want to believe in her culpability in order to excuse my own. I wanted to believe in her culpability in order to show myself how much I could endure and still carry on. To prove myself invincible.

I wonder if that's the truth?

Or maybe it was simply to have an excuse never to speak to her again. To give sanction to that decision to cut all close ties, to free myself of friends and family, to act, as I thought, as His agent. Putting myself in an emotional vacuum, which enabled me to act with charitable decisiveness in the face of the war . . . Yes, even to deciding who should live and who should die. It was me who stopped the relief lorry going back to those we hadn't been able to evacuate from the hospital, when the front line reached Umuahia. We couldn't afford to lose the lorry. I instructed the driver to turn round and take his load back to the children's feeding station at G Camp, making the decision (which God alone should have had to make) that the children should survive another week or two, condemning those in the hospital even more surely than they had already been condemned by the terrors that had put them there. Oh I can see them, lying dry-mouthed and staring in their beds, waiting for relief that never came . . .

They are in the dark too. Here in the dark corners of the room, even when the lamp is on: the mangled boy soldiers, the stick infants with their balloon bellies and fly-infested eyes, the ancient-faced women with the flaps of their empty dugs dangling over their ribs. Dear God, the thousands dead, so many we didn't know how to bury them. How was that Your plan?

Please let them go. Go from me. Let them go quietly into the dark (as they did, nearly all in extraordinary dignified silence, with hardly a moan of protest). Let them go. It is God's business. I don't have to understand it.

Only my own part. Which it seems to me now, quite clearly, should have been that human one in which I failed. The responsibility of love and understanding to my wife; of kindness at the very least (since I didn't love her) to my mistress; of care and love to her child, my daughter.

Miriam never betrayed me. It wasn't in her nature. She wanted me. For which at the time I even had a sneaking contempt. Instead of conjuring forth love, the strength of her affection made me turn away. As I write each sentence, that seems to me to be the truth. Then I write another, and it changes again.

The only constant is the wrong. My own failure in love. Even with Anne—is it what I've done to her? Even as I love her blindly, fiercely, I feel the same old devils of discontent that she isn't as I would wish, that if only she were more confident, more incisive, more definite, if only she had Faith and were . . .

More like me? I don't wish that. God's love is unconditional. His love is unconditional.

The address Mrs Anene gave me was in Apapa, near the docks. Matthew insisted on accompanying me himself, saying it would be too dangerous for me to be there alone.

It took a while to find Mama Nwamaka. She was in the back room of what had been (perhaps still was) a filthy shop, windowless, the splintered plywood door open to the narrow alley, and piles of fly-infested rubbish heaped against the wall. Two crippled beggars sat propped against the wall opposite and shifted a little as we passed by, silently extending scrawny hands to us. It was insufferably hot. She sat in the shade just inside the doorway; in the gloom behind her I could make out a bed in the corner, and some heaped cardboard boxes.

I explained who I was and how I'd found her, which she took with no surprise at all, almost as if she'd been expecting me. Her eyes flickered over Matthew and back to me. She was very overweight, her breathing was laboured and came and went with a kind of low whistling sound.

'Asthma,' she told us. 'I have de asthma and fluids in me lungs. De nurse tell me I'm drownin' slowly.'

I said I was sorry and gave her my daughter's name. 'I need an address in Italy.'

She took a few breaths, then waved us into the dark stinking room and told us to sit on the bed. With effortful slowness she levered herself up onto her feet and a stick, twisted the chair round a few inches so that she was approximately facing us, and lowered herself back into it. 'De police been here already.'

'Police?'

'I no got nothing left. They been take everything now—you see?' She gestured round the hovel.

'We're nothing to do with the police. We're just trying to find this girl.'

She sat wheezing for a while, then her huge face settled into an expression of incredulity. 'For what?'

'She's my daughter.'

Next to me on the bed I felt Matthew's sudden, instantly controlled, jolt of surprise. Nothing but the truth now. I've wasted too much time.

'You go for ask de police.'

'Why can't you tell me? All I want is an address.'

There was a long silence, broken only by her wheezing breaths and the insistent buzzing of flies. I pulled the manila envelope from my pocket and extracted Lily's birth certificate. I handed it to her. She raised it to her eyes suspiciously. I could feel the sweat running down my neck. Matthew moved carefully beside me, and I nodded to him to speak.

'We don't know why the police are involved, Mrs Nwamaka. This gentleman has come all the way from England to find his daughter and it would be a great kindness if you could help him.'

'That girl a black girl,' she replied querulously.

'We know. Where did you send her?'

'Her mother ask me for send. They all ask for go.'

'I know,' I said. 'I know that. It's all right, no one blames you. Where did you send them?'

Again the concentrated wheezing, and then she raised her

shoulders in a shrug which concertinaed her double chins in a series of rich folds under her mouth. 'It too long ago. Don't you know they put my brother and his wife in de prison?'

I glanced around the room again. There was nothing that could contain any records—no books or papers; even if she knew what she was talking about, there was nowhere here she would find an address. The police perhaps would help us, if we slipped them a big enough bribe. I glanced at Matthew. But he was already asking, 'Where are they in prison?'

She threw him a look of surprised contempt. 'Bologna. Where you think?'

'Bologna, Italy?'

She rolled her eyes, yes.

'You sent the girls to your brother?'

A heavy nod. Wheezing. Then she spoke, again querulously, as if we had criticised her or her brother. 'He made dem papers, passport, meet dem at de airport, look after them good. They simple as de babe newborn.'

My head was oppressed by the smells, the sickly-sweet dirty flesh. Each time she drew a long wheezing breath I was waiting for it to come crackling out again. I couldn't make sense of what she was saying, of whatever her brother did or what his crime was. Matthew seemed to understand her; I left it to him.

'I will pray for you,' he said. 'May God forgive you.'

'I been punish,' she said angrily.

'Help us to put this right. When did your brother go to prison?'

'Two years now. Long time ago. De police finish with it, na true.'

'We want nothing to do with the police. All we want is a name and address, someone who can help us to trace this girl.' He was wriggling about, feeling in his pockets.

'You no go for find her now.'

'Please. Whatever you can tell us. What harm can it do?' Matthew suddenly half stood and leant forwards to her chair. I saw him pass something into her swollen hand, and her fat fingers *close over it like sausages. She inhaled sharply, then coughed and couldn't catch her breath. Matthew rose again from the bed, to help her, and it occurred to me that she might die there and then. But she raised a hand to indicate that she was all right, and after wheezing for a while, whispered, 'Matthew Jim Menkiti, via Saragozza 56b, Bologna. But he still in de prison.'*

'Thank you.' Matthew put his hand under my arm and helped me up. 'God bless you.' He led me out without even saying good-bye to her, led me through the filth in the alley to a quiet spot in the shade of a wall opposite, where he took a little diary and pen from his pocket and wrote something down.

'Say the name and address again,' he told me, so I did, and he checked what he had written and made a small change. He led me back, brushing through the beggars and street traders, to where his driver waited in the car.

2 A.M.

I feel unwell, a heavy slowness has come on me since we were in that woman's hovel. I feel as if I have caught her monstrous weight, her inability to draw a clean breath. What was it she said? 'I'm drowning slowly.'

Matthew and I drove away in silence, the heavy stupidity that had settled on me made me unable to comprehend her story. Back at the house I found the words to ask Matthew. 'Did she mean her brother faked their papers?'

'I think so.'

'That's why he went to prison?'

'Trafficking. Trafficking in people, yes, that's a crime.' He brought me a glass of water. 'You understand why women are trafficked, David?'

I thought for a while. 'They pay. Amoge—her mother—paid for her to go.'

'OK. That's one thing. But very often they also—they expect

the women to make money for the traffickers at the other end.'
His voice was serious and his expression so concerned I knew I had
to think of something bad. I didn't know what it was.

'Girls from here are trafficked for prostitution,' he said quietly.
'It happens quite a lot.'

Later he knelt and prayed with me. He thought of the words, I
didn't have any. He asked his boy to help me to bed and he came
to say goodnight and to make sure I was comfortable. There was
a question I wanted to ask him but I couldn't remember it while
he was there. Now I must write it down so I don't forget in the
morning. I must ask him if I can still look for her. There's no
reason why not, I think. Catch an aeroplane to Italy, go to the
police in Bologna. They may be able to help. She went there when
she was about twenty.

Stop.

And now I will read my Bible. It is always better, to have some-
thing practical to do.

ANNE TURNED THE PAGE. But the next was blank. And the next. The rest of the book was blank. As her tears started to fall she understood that this was the night he died.

She remembers now the precious relief of those tears; the simple unalloyed grief she was able at last to feel for him, knowing him to be guilty, doubting, lost. She can see him now, the Father of those last pages: sitting in Matthew's car peering out confusedly at the congested Lagos streets; kneeling on Mrs Anene's white carpet praying for forgiveness; sweating in his bed, his breaths coming quick and short, eyes searching the dark corners of his room for the mangled soldiers and starving children; sitting in Mama Nwamaka's stinking room, bracing himself with his hands on his knees to keep himself upright, understanding and not understanding her words.

He died not knowing—as useless and helpless as she was. If only she had been able to be there to comfort him, to tell him she knew what it was like. She found herself crying helplessly, like a child for something lost. She could feel the age-old bars of constricting stubbornness which had caged her off from him dissolving, leaving her weak and defenceless as a newly hatched bird. He was no different to her.

It fed, somehow, into her and Vic. Vic could be kind to her and she was glad of it. She could be comforted. She could see that things could change. She had started to imagine that she could escape the person she had been, the old hopeless Anne, that she could step out into a world of possibility.

Bitterly now she thinks, yes, she had become soft and idiotic and romantic; she had let down her defences; she had thought, somehow, that everything at last would be all right. As if she still hadn't had enough evidence to the contrary.

Present wretchedness can't quite erode it though. Perhaps she should be glad that she doesn't know how to destroy it utterly. She remembers the flavour of the time, bitter-sweet. The sense of revelations: Father, Vic, her own new self, the imagined sister—Lily. Discussing with Vic how she might try to trace her; writing to the police in Bologna, and being given a trail that led to a women's refuge, Casa delle Donne.

Lily became a figure in her thoughts and dreams. She would find Lily for Father; it was the one atonement she could make both for herself and him.

But Lily was elusive. She had gone to the Casa delle Donne after the traffickers' imprisonment. Two months later she had disappeared. Some of the other girls in the trial had returned to Nigeria. Not Lily. Maybe she had taken work as a domestic. Maybe she had a lover or a child. Maybe she was sick.

Further enquiries to the police elicited tardy unhelpful answers; Lily could have changed her name, moved abroad, died. Her papers had been faked, she was still *clandestini*. Anything could have happened, there was no way to trace her.

Anne imagined her at the side of the road, as one of the girls she had once seen in Italy a lifetime ago, with Tim. They had spent an illicit few days together while Tim was buying new stock, and driving north along the teeming motorway from Rome they saw black girls by the side of the road. Anne didn't know why they were there. There was a tall woman with a tight red top and shorts (but afterwards, when Anne called them 'hot-pants' to herself, she wondered why she hadn't realised) standing on the verge, watching the traffic and smoking. She looked like she was waiting for a lift. Then another, under trees near a parking area. She was very young and darker than the first, jet black, and she held a white parasol over her head. She stood quite still, face on to the roaring traffic, holding her parasol aloft. It was as beautiful and exotic as a glimpse of a tiger would have been.

'Look,' Anne said to Tim. 'What's she doing? It's like something in a film.'

He barely glanced. 'What d'you think she's doing? Haven't you seen the others? They're all along the road.'

The sun shone brightly, the lorries roared past; sometimes, amongst blinding clouds of dust, they pulled over onto the hard shoulder. It was eleven o'clock in the morning and the black girls stood waiting for their customers. When she thought of Lily, Anne saw that aloof patient girl waiting under her parasol.

Now the image has become insubstantial, receding further from reality with every passing month. The avenues of enquiry turned into cul-de-sacs. Anne does not know how to find Lily, she doesn't know how to try to make it better. She has not been able to change anything, or to finish Father's unfinished business. The hope has all dried up.

In the evening Vic phones her in her workroom, calling from the surgery; signalling to Anne by this action that he wants to make up but is too embarrassed or ashamed to approach her in person. 'Shall we eat out tonight?'

'Um—I don't know.'

'Well let me know when you decide. I came back for you at three, by the way. You must have left early.'

'I was in with the nurse.'

'Oh. Well, I'm going to have a shower.'

She sits motionless until she hears him go into the bathroom. He is making an attempt at friendliness. She has no right to reject it. After a moment she gets up and goes to the bathroom door. 'Vic?'

'You can come in.' He is already in the shower, steam billowing out of the top of the cubicle.

'Yes, fine, let's go for a meal.'

'OK. About half an hour?'

'Right.'

Anne goes to the bedroom to change quickly before he comes out of the bathroom. Wanting to avoid him. Before all this . . . she has to make a physical effort, like swallowing a lump, to see it as it has been. Someone else's history. He was the doctor, listening, giving her time, coaxing her forward out of darkness. She has an image of him standing, hand extended for her to take, waiting for her. So much kindness, so much patience, like a loving parent with a child.

For god's sake Anne, is that what you want? No. No. But he *saw* me, he was attuned to me. Tears of self-pity are welling in her eyes; contemptible, sentimental tears. Furious with herself, she rams her feet into a pair of precipitously heeled shoes she bought in a sale and has never worn, yanking the straps bitingly tight across her ankles. If he had gone on treating you with so much kindness you would have been smothered by it. And anyway isn't it the point—standing in front of the mirror now, brushing her hair, brushing hard and feeling some relief in the repeated bite and pull of the bristles against her skull—isn't it the point that it *did* stop? We were equal, I wasn't the sick one, the child, the flake he couldn't take his eyes off, we were partners. Again her eyes fill with tears and she beats and beats at her scalp with the sharp brush, let it hurt, let it hurt. That is the real memory. That's what you should cry for if you're going to cry. For conversations that were arguments that went up and down and in and out for hours, battling through impasses, changing direction and following each other's threads; not a parent leading a child. For sex that wasn't gentle kindness but was like those conversations; apart as well as close, urgent, alien, understanding, funny—

Again with one of those wrenching lurches of memory, changing gear without the clutch, she sees them lying on the floor convulsed with laughter, naked and literally rolling about—yes, that used to happen. She puts down the brush and wipes the back of her hand across her eyes. OK. It doesn't happen now. Staring flatly at her own blank face she allows herself to think of Tim pushing her against the wall. Watches with detached curiosity as her pale cheeks flush dark. How simple you are. How crap you are.

She turns away from the mirror with a sense of utter weariness. Yes I am bad. Yes it is hard for Vic, harder than for me. But I can't help him. I can't make it work. She listens to him come out of the bathroom and go into the spare room. He must be going to iron a shirt. Stepping lightly she goes back along the landing to the bathroom; locks herself in, wipes the condensation off the mirror, and begins to carefully apply her makeup.

They walk in silence to the restaurant, but the walk itself is like a balm. It is clear and cold and frosty and the traffic has died down, hoar frost glitters on the hedges and there is a thin elegant moon.

'Are we going to the Italian?'

'Why not?' His tone is kindly, accepting. The Italian has changed hands since their early days, become more busy and pretentious and expensive. They haven't been there for a long time now.

Once they are sitting with a bottle of wine between them he nods at her in a friendly way. 'OK. So what happens next?'

'What d'you mean?'

'Will the nurse see you again before you start the drugs? What's the time frame?'

So much for the secret. 'She's given me the stuff. I can start this month if we want.'

'Good, well, the sooner the better.' He raises his glass to hers. There is a short silence.

'Are you sulking?'

'No. I'm—it's just been quite tiring, I suppose, today.'

'You have to admit it's ludicrous. The thing about religion. Did you fill it in?'

'No. We both have to sign it.'

'What do they think, a kid's going to be born with its religion stamped through its bones like a stick of rock?'

'I suppose it's just respect for people who do believe.' How
strange after all that she ends up defending—what? Father's
position?

But Vic isn't going to argue. He simply shakes his head and
studies the menu; as they eat he asks her about the practicalities
of her exhibition, when she'll need the car, who's invited to the
opening, who might review it. He has agreed to donor sperm
and now they're discussing her work, he is calm and kind and
poised, and Anne is in a trance.

It is only when they leave the restaurant to walk home that
she suddenly snaps out of it. The sky is still clear and the temperature has plummeted, Vic begins to walk quickly and is soon
twenty yards ahead.

'Vic! I can't go fast in these shoes.'

'What?' He turns and waits for her to catch up. 'It's freezing.
Why d'you wear shoes you can't walk in?'

'I can walk in them. I just can't jog.'

'For god's sake. Shall we get a taxi?'

'It'll take as long to wait for one as to walk—'

All you need to do is give me your arm. He doesn't and she
doesn't ask. A little flash of rage about the shoes. Doesn't he see
that they are actually an attempt to dress up, to make something
of the evening, to fall in with his mood? She knows he does and
that he is angry with her for it, as if she is making too much of
it. But if I had come out in jeans and walking boots he would
have been offended. Of course. Either way, I'm in the wrong.
But she is being dishonest. The shoes—the shoes went on to
hurt—to humiliate herself. To punish herself for her anger with
him. To prove something to herself. He is entirely justified in
objecting to them. She isn't wearing them for him.

At the last corner he stops for her to catch up, and does offer
his arm. When he locks the door he asks, 'Fancy a nightcap?'

It is late by the time they go to bed; when Anne has taken off her makeup and cleaned her teeth Vic is already in bed with the light off. She undresses quickly in the dark and slips in beside him.

'Your back or mine?' His voice is friendly.

'Yours.' She fits herself against his warm body, groin against buttocks, her arm resting on his. After a moment, allows her hand to slide down his side. He is warm and silky. She inches closer, pressing her breasts against his back, hand sliding round to cup his left buttock. She feels his body tense.

'What?'

'Nothing. I just—'

'Just what?'

'I was just being friendly.'

'You've got what you want. Isn't it enough?'

She lifts herself away from him. How stupid she is. 'I don't know what you mean.'

'You think all this makes me feel like a stud?'

'I'm not—it's not about—'

'Yes it is. You're ticking the boxes. OK, we went to the clinic. OK we'll buy some sperm that works. OK we'll have a nice meal. OK we'll fuck to show everything's all right.'

'Vic, that's not fair. It was *you*—'

'Sure. It was me that took us to the clinic. Had to be, didn't it? That does actually have to be my decision. Not just 'cos I'm paying for it –'

Anne moves further away, hauls herself up, leaning against the bed head. She feels winded.

'– but because I have to agree. We both know I have to agree, before you can get pregnant with some other man's child.'

'I thought you wanted—'

'Sure. Men are well known for pining away when they can't have a baby.'

'But you said—you've said all along—'

'OK. I said all along. *I* wanted. You're perfectly right, you've never wanted anything, it's me that's dragged us through this whole sorry business because of my own inadequacies.'

'Don't say that Vic.'

'Don't say that. Right. I won't say that. Not only must I subject myself to the humiliation of paying to have another man's child, but I must also wholeheartedly want and desire it, and declare to myself and the world that I desire it as much as you, because if I don't I'm betraying you.'

'Don't do it.'

'Really?' His voice lifts. She hears him enjoying his own reasonableness. 'Let's just think about this for a moment. What actual choices do you think I have here? You're fifteen years younger than me; there's nothing wrong with your fertility; why on earth should you stay with me if I can't give you what you want?'

'I don't want—I'm not with you because I want children—'

'It's perfectly natural. As indeed is the desire for sex. I'm only sorry I can't provide service as usual.'

'That wasn't what I—'

'But I have these inconvenient feelings like failure and anger.'

'I stroked you out of friendliness.'

'Not true. It was a request for sex which due to my inadequacy as a husband I am not about to comply with.'

'Can't I show you affection?'

'No. Because it's not clean, is it.' As he speaks he swings his legs abruptly from the bed and picks up his pillow. 'I'll sleep in the spare room.'

The silence once he's gone is all-enveloping, it comes lapping into the room like the surface of water settling after a gigantic splash. It is a relief he's gone. *It's not clean.* What does that mean? Not clean because she wants something? Because it is tinged with gratitude? Because she has recognised that what he is doing must be difficult? But if she has to be punished for that recognition, where is there left for her to be?

Things are difficult for me too, she tells herself. It is symptomatic that she can hardly remember what they are, the difficult things. Everything is easy in comparison to this. She has dealt with everything: boxed it in, battened it down. I've made an orderly life, she tells herself, the only upset is him. Even Tim was— I wouldn't have done it, I wouldn't have needed it, if Vic was alright with me. Is it a kind of revenge? She endures Vic's moods but her secret revenge is to do something which would make Vic *even angrier* if he knew? Why doesn't she just leave?

Because the Vic she knows is there inside this one. And if it is only possible to distract or subdue the raging Vic, the real one will come out to her. No point in going to the spare room now. It might be better in the morning. Lying down and pulling the duvet up, she inserts the fleshy part of the back of her hand between her teeth and bites down hard.

In the library Anne has carried up and unwrapped all the boxes and positioned them on the floor in hanging order. The librarian offers to hang them but Anne prefers to do it herself. The gallery is a dark rectangular room on the third floor, with two tall windows in one wall, and a big ornate fireplace which actually resembles the one in box 12. She likes the heavy old-fashioned feel of the room. It makes the boxes more mysterious and sinister. In a clean bright modern gallery they would feel exposed; here, they can be seen to be guarding their secrets.

They are heavier than normal pictures; she will need to use two hooks for each. She paces the space between each box and the next, lays out everything ready. The librarian opens the door a crack. 'Coffee? I'm having one now.'

Anne glances at the time, eleven. 'I'm OK thanks. I've got to go out for something anyway.' She sets down the last pair of hooks, picks up her jacket and bag, runs down the library steps. Just for a coffee, she tells herself. Maybe a chocolate bar. But when she goes into the newsagent's on the corner she asks for ten cigarettes, as she already knew she would. It is cold but she needs to sit down to smoke and she hurries on to one of the benches in front of the town hall, as if she has to be there for a certain time. I'm not doing this, she tells herself drawing the smoke down into her lungs. But she knows she is. That is why she's come out of the library. That is why she needs a cigarette more than a coffee. She knows exactly what she is doing and where she is going. He won't be there, she tells herself. And anyway he'll be busy. Of course. You know he'll be busy. Well it won't take long to say. The cigarette is making her feel slightly sick, it is so long since she's had one. Why today? Why must she go there today? There is no reason for it beyond the fact that somewhere behind thought she has known, as she worked on the last couple of boxes, that when she was hanging them in the library she would go to Tim.

Yes. Go to Tim and tell him it was a mistake. Tell him she didn't want all that starting up again, explain to him that if they couldn't just be friends then it was better not to meet at all. But she hasn't seen him for weeks now, he must know she's been avoiding him. Why confuse the issue? Don't go at all. Her hands are shaking and she lights another cigarette despite the nausea. Why doesn't she just turn round, go back into the comforting warmth of the library, grab a coffee and stand sipping it, chatting with the librarian in a normal, friendly way?

If I go today to him I'll never go again, she tells herself. I promise I'll never make myself go again. She stands and takes the cigarette stubs to the nearest bin, and toils on across the expanse of Albert Square to the opposite corner. Each step feels forced and loud, as if she has not learned how to walk in her shoes. She glances at passers-by in the square but no one is taking any notice. They are all going to places, meetings, shops, the library; they are all intent and inward, picturing where they are going and what they will do when they get there. While she—nothing will happen when she gets there. She just needs to tell him it's not going to happen. She straightens her shoul-

ders and hurries to the shop, not allowing herself to hesitate at
the door, though her stomach flips and dives.

A blast of warm air and she is in. The shop is bright with
lamps and silvery things.

'Hi!' Tim's sudden brilliant smile. He is putting watches in a
display case. His eyes move to the young girl at the till, and back
to Anne. 'You want to go on upstairs? I'll be up in a minute.' He
is fiddling with the lock of the display case. Anne's cheeks are
burning. It is coming in from the cold of course; she avoids the
shop girl's eyes. Round the corner of the counter, past the little
den of packaging materials under the stairs and up to the door
at the top. She hesitates a moment then opens it. She needs the
toilet anyway; he has a bathroom up here. And of course they
can't talk in the shop, it was ridiculous to entertain the thought,
of course they must talk in private. There are open boxes of
kitchen gadgets spread over the sofa and coffee table, the room
is a mess, good, he hasn't been expecting her. As she allows the
liquefied contents of her stomach to pour into the toilet Anne
tells herself not to be so completely stupid. Of course he isn't
expecting her, how could he expect her when she never said
she was coming? How could he know the day when she would
come into town to put up her exhibition and look at her watch
at eleven and come over to his shop as if to a very particular
appointment? She flushes the toilet and opens the window, and
stands with her hands under the running hot water. I don't
have to do this. She hears him come into the flat.

'Anne?'

'I'm here.' Shutting the bathroom door behind her. 'Sorry, I
don't feel very—'

'OK?'

She nods. For a moment she can see them both. Hanging
there, as if someone above the ceiling holds their strings.
Dangling there, staring at each other, suspended. Nothing has to
happen. The mantra in her head. Nothing has to happen. Just
tell him. Then whoever is holding the strings swings them so

violently that she and Tim are hurled forward towards each other—clash together and fall tangled to the floor, gasping for each other's mouths, pulling at the clothes they are bundled in, clawing their way through to flesh.

'Tim? I can't breathe.'

'Sorry.' He shifts his weight, peeling off the condom, then presses his face into her shoulder, sniffing at her skin. 'Mmmn, sweet. You won't believe how I've missed you.'

When she doesn't reply he half raises his head to glance at her. 'Got any fags?'

'In my bag.'

He crawls across the kitchen gadgets—'Jesus, Anne, I've got to sell these'—to where her bag lies, ferrets inside and comes back with two cigarettes. 'I thought you'd forgotten me.'

'Well I was just—'

He lights both cigarettes and passes her one. 'Just?'

'Putting up stuff in the library—so I thought I'd—'

'Say hello?' He grins and she can't help laughing.

'Yup.'

'I've got to go back down in a minute; new girl, I told her I wouldn't leave her in the shop on her own.'

'It's OK, I've got to get back to the library.'

'Come back later?'

'I can't, Tim, I've got to . . .'

'What?'

'When I've finished at the library I should go home.'

'Well. Thanks for taking the time.' He grinds out his cigarette and stands up, extracting his clothes from the tangle on the floor.

'Tim? I didn't come here to—I didn't mean for that to happen.'

His eyes flicker to hers. 'Oh?'

'I can't see you any more.'

'Why?'

It is so obvious she's speechless. He is staring at her.

'What Vic doesn't know can't hurt him.' This was always his line about Fiona. Anne used to want to believe it.

'It's an internal transaction. It's no good.' She pulls on her trousers.

'That's easily dealt with.' His voice has become hard.

'What?'

'Guilt. You want it but it makes you feel bad. If someone else could tell you you were bad, you could just want it. End of conflict.'

Anne looks at him, ready to laugh. He is lighting another cigarette; he looks at her through the smoke with narrowed eyes.

'So I need a father-confessor, you think?'

Tim shrugs, unsmiling. 'Anyone. Me.'

'What?'

'I can tell you you're bad. You're treating me like shit.'

A jolt of shock.

'You're using me. Avoiding me, not answering my calls. Then turning up like this, as if nothing ever was.'

She sees it's true. 'I didn't mean—'

He clasps his fingers around her wrists, pulling her towards him. 'It's too late. You've done it. Now you should be punished.'

The moment goes on too long—Anne laughs awkwardly and ducks away from him, and he releases her wrists.

'Thanks,' she says. 'I'll bear it in mind.'

'All part of the service,' he says lightly. And stubbing out his cigarette he runs quickly down the stairs.

When Anne comes out of the library it is after five and already dark. There is a fine cold drizzle falling and she has left her umbrella in the car. She stands in the shelter on the library steps, looking at people jamming themselves into the lighted tram opposite; as it swings away from the stop it squeals sharply against the rails. She will walk through the icy rain to the car which is parked at GMex. Reverse out of her space, drive through the worm-dark underground to the ticket man and pay him, wait for the red and white barrier to lift, turn left into the throng of rush-hour traffic heading home through the drizzle. She feels in her bag for a cigarette. Not there; she's left them at Tim's.

As if that settles it she hurries down the steps and around the curved wall of the library building, away from GMex.

I'm not even going to listen to you, she tells herself, as she crosses Albert Square. I know what you're saying. I'm not going to see Tim. I'm just going to get my cigarettes. Bullshit, bullshit, bullshit. She gets to the shop just as he is locking up. The girl has already gone; Tim grins at Anne through the glass as he turns the key to admit her. When she hesitates on the threshold he pulls her gently into the shop and folds his arms around her. 'I was afraid you might not come.' His breath is warm and sweet against her face, for a moment Anne closes her eyes. Then she ducks out of his arms and moves away. He watches her.

'I shouldn't . . .'

'You shouldn't have come back. Is that it?' The warmth drains from his voice.

'Yes.'

'So what do you want? What have you come back for this time?'

'My cigarettes?'

'I don't think so. Do you?' He backs her towards the stairs.

'No.'

'No. Go on. Upstairs.' He gives her a little shove. At the top he pins her against the door while she fumbles it open. 'So what have you come back for?' His voice catches and she realises he is close to tears.

'Tim? I'm sorry.'

'And so you should be.'

'I'm—'

'Bad.' He gives her another shove. 'Say yes when you're spoken to.'

'Yes.'

'*Bad* to come back –' he pushes her again and she falls against the sofa. Then he's kneeling on top of her, pinning her arms back, his face close to hers; he is trembling. 'Bad to play these games—bad to me, bad to Vic –' holding her pinned with one hand while he yanks at her clothes with the other—'say it!'

'Yes.'

'You want me to hurt you?'

'Yes.'

'Say it louder.'

'*Yes.*'

When she gets back to the car Anne sits hunched over the wheel for a moment, resting her head against its hard wrinkly plastic. Don't sit here, they have CCTV, someone'll come and ask if you're OK. Mechanically she negotiates the way out and through the emptying streets, until she comes to the dark warren of roads behind Piccadilly. There is an empty patch of ground on the right opposite the side entrance to the station, and she pulls in here and switches off the engine. I'm alright. I'm here. I'm alone.

What will she say to Vic? If he sees—if he asks? She can feel the scratches burning on her thighs, you couldn't explain them away, scratches like that, what could you say?

He won't see. He won't notice. How long is it since he's seen you naked?

If I'm in the bath—

Lock the door. It's not difficult, just lock the door. In a day or two they'll fade away.

She has been fine but is trembling now; what can she say when she walks in? He will see it in her face, he will know. There is a sudden knocking against the side window and Anne nearly jumps out of her skin. A woman. A woman's face bending to the window, white with black rings round her eyes, she is mouthing something, she is jabbing with her fingers. Her arms and shoulders gleam whitely in the dark, where are her clothes, what does she want?

'Fuck off! Fuck off out of it!'

Anne fumbles at the ignition and the woman straightens and totters away towards the road. Swinging the car round Anne catches her for a moment in the beam of the head-lights—the boots, the tiny skirt, the sleeveless halterneck in the freezing January dark.

It's all right, she tells herself automatically. It's all right, just a mistake. Driving out of the dark streets to the orange-lit safety of the main road, to the stream of traffic, the lit bus sailing past on its way into town with stately passengers upright on its seats, she forces herself to breathe more steadily. Suddenly the memory of the Italian girl in the lay-by. Her imagining of Lily. Would she do that if Anne approached her? Scream at her to fuck off? At least she knows what she's doing, Anne tells herself, at least she knows she wants money. What the hell do I want?

The only answer she can find is hurt. She pulls off into the brightly lit forecourt of a garage, locks herself in the smelly toilet and washes her tear-streaked face. *It's not clean*, is what Vic said. In a way Tim is making it clean.

In the morning Anne puts away all her sewing materials. When her desk is clear, without allowing herself the time to stop or think, she pulls out her sketchpad and begins to draw. The container. Estelle, lying amongst the sacks and rubbish on the floor, with the gleam of light on her nose and jutting cheekbone; pervading darkness, the swell of her belly just echoed in the bulging cocoa sacks behind her. Joseph standing over her with his stub end of candle.

Her pencil races on; the squatting view upwards from her cabin window to a strip of sky, all but blocked by the container. It needs colour—the skewed top of the window frame, the looming redness, the slender strip of blue. Next the raised muzzles of the Christmas dinner party, in their bright paper hats.

The view down to the container deck from the top of the stairs, dark shapes and looming shadows, the taste of fear. Estelle's mound of belly swelling the white sheet of the opposite bed, her thin face and scrawny shoulders black against the pillow, a terrible negative. The framed slice of open sea visible between containers, fenced off by the rail as she moved towards it; that thin slice that led out and out to the infinity of sky and ocean.

These won't be boxes but paintings, paintings where every colour but blue is thick and impermeable, solid as wood. Only sky, only sea, are safety.

But they died, she remembers with surprise, in the sea. That's where they went. Estelle and her baby were drowned in that sea. Now it is clear the sea is better than the ship. The sea is freedom, the sea is calling; it sings like a siren, it beckons through barriers.

Anne lays down her pencil. While she was in the ship it never once occurred to her—did it? That it might be better to be dead. Now it seems so clearly to be the solution. To dive into that sea and spiral down to its depths. To take off and float into that bright sky. To cut the thread.

I could do that any day. Any time I wanted. The thought of it is almost blissful. It doesn't matter what happens with Vic. Or the clinic. Or Tim. There is always that blue escape. Always the sea and the sky. She doesn't have to consider what to do or how wrong she is not to have done it. Nothing has to be considered; it is simply borrowed time. She is a dead man walking. And if it is most important to paint thick bands of brown and red, with thin celestial cracks of purest blue, then that is what she will do. It is no one else's business.

It would be cutting, of course. She imagines drawing the metallic scalpel blade across her blue-veined wrist, the fine red beads forming threads then thickening to great billowing ribbons, all her painty colour gushing out, filling up the canvas of her room, red and red and red, nothing would be able to stop it.

It would be the easiest thing in the world. She thinks of it with
physical longing.

Over the next five days she paints, breaking off only once to put
in an appearance at the exhibition opening, smiling and shaking hands and leaving early with the excuse of a headache.
How clear and simple painting is, after the boxes, how easy to
fill white space. It doesn't matter about Vic, his kindness or his
rage is all one, a distraction. There's no need for her to do anything but this.

Standing listening at the top of the stairs, she waits till she
knows he is in surgery or has gone out before going down to
the kitchen for coffee or food. At night she goes to the spare
room, a part of her amazed that he is letting her do this, that he
isn't bursting in and accusing her of rejecting him, that this
simple singleness is permitted. Then she realises it's because she
isn't thinking about him; her mind is elsewhere and that creates
protection, a kind of forcefield around herself. It comes back to
her that she avoided Father in the same way in her teens, slipping between the solid tracks of his life, adjusting her own
comings and goings to his absences, able to live almost unno-
ticed in his shadow.

On the sixth day, after listening to the silence below, she
creeps down to the kitchen and is unpleasantly surprised to find
Vic sitting at the table cradling a mug of coffee. He glances up
from the paper as she enters, then goes back to his reading.
Perhaps he is as pleased to be able to ignore her as she is him.
The kettle is empty; as she runs a scant mugful into it, he suddenly speaks.

'When d'you start the Buserelin?' His tone is perfectly neutral, he could be asking if it is cold outside. It requires a reply
and she calculates dates.

'I suppose I could start it this week.'

'Then you should.' He turns from his paper to face her across
the kitchen. 'There's no point in waiting, start it this week.'

'I wasn't sure we'd really—'

'What else is there to say. Go for it.' He speaks lightly but kindly, as if all the obstacles have melted away. As if both of them know how to behave.

'I'll have to book in my injections with Dr Gray.'

'I'll do them. It's ridiculous, why should you go trailing over there?'

'But . . .'

'But?'

'Nothing. If you don't mind.'

'Why should I mind? It gives me a role.' The words are ironic but his tone still isn't, he is keeping it pleasant, he even smiles. She pours the boiled water into her mug.

'Let's just get on with it, Anne. We've beaten about the bush for long enough.'

'OK.'

'Come and give me a hug.'

She sets down her mug and crosses the wide space of the kitchen to him; still sitting, he folds his arms around her middle, pressing his face to her stomach. After a moment she clasps her arms around his head.

When he releases her she goes back for her coffee and brings it to sit at the table opposite him. He draws his chair in closer. 'Your review was good, wasn't it?'

'Review?'

'I left it on the table for you—yesterday's *Manchester Evening News*.' He pulls the pile of papers and post towards him and riffles through. 'Here.'

There is a small boxed column on the Visual Arts page.

*Recommended *** Manchester Central Library. Boxes by Anne Munro.*

Fifteen 3-dimensional boxes depict a haunting world where characters are trapped in situations like flies on sticky paper; from a hospital bed to a starchy dinner party to a doctor's waiting room. Like tiny theatre sets, furnishings and colours reflect the moods and preoccupations of the actors. The boxes are peopled by tiny hand-sewn dolls, and there are many echoes of Ibsen's Doll's House in this exquisitely crafted, thought-provoking exhibition.

'Oh.'

'Not bad, is it?'

'No.' She raises the paper to read the paragraph again.

'Have any sold yet?'

'I don't know. I should get in touch with the library.'

'You should send this review out to other papers, so they can see what they're missing.'

Anne laughs.

'I'll do it if you like. Shall I?'

'I don't think it'll make much difference.'

'It's in my interests. You need to be able to keep me in my old age, remember. Why don't you ring the library now?'

Four of the boxes have sold and people have left their names but no deposit for three others.

'How much did you ask for them?'

'£250 each.'

'That's laughable. In terms of the hours you put in.'

'But I didn't know if anyone would be interested.'

'From now on I'm your agent, right? You make and I'll market.'

So she has already earned £1,000. Ridiculous maybe in terms of her time; but in itself extraordinary, wonderful.

'What have you been working on this week?'

'Oh, just a few ideas. Nothing much.'

He checks the time and goes back into surgery; Tuesday afternoon, asthma and eczema clinic. Anne goes back upstairs. Shutting the door of her room behind her, she turns on the lights and stares at the wall of drawings. It is as different as can be from the boxes. Perhaps she should make more boxes, if people are going to like them.

That doesn't merit more than a second's thought. She paces the length of the wall; the first picture seems to be abstract. The view from the cabin window, the red square dominating the picture; above it a thin slice of distant sky-blue, and then an upper strip of brown window frame. Something enormously satisfying in that, a picture which appears abstract but is in fact entirely literal. Its actuality will only be revealed by the succeeding pictures: the window frame will be there again behind the figure of Estelle in bed; by the end of the sequence the viewer will know that room . . . its shapes, its blocks of colour, its tilting sweating claustrophobia, will know . . .

It is locked up. Pictures won't unlock it but they can—what? Bear witness? Allow a glimpse, let the viewer in to something, something he or she might not know or have seen, something that must make sense beyond the ship and the small fact of her presence on it. There is something here it is possible to paint, the certainty rises in her lungs like a sudden inrush of cold bright air.

Anne is taking her temperature. Each day the morning cross on the temperature chart plots a course which, if they were on a ship, would be leading to a destination; is leading inexorably through the passing days of the month to the one where her womb, newly and luxuriantly lined with blood-red velvet cushioning, declares itself ready for the reception of an egg. And if the actions which they have set in motion by their visit to Hargreaves are not hauled off course by one or other of them, then she will attend the clinic on that day and a stranger's sperm will be invited to make the acquaintance of her egg; to penetrate it and take up residence in the regal chamber of her womb. She will be pregnant.

And then what will happen?

It is necessary to think of this and consider what to do. It is, equally, impossible to think of it, since it is inconceivable (good word, Anne) that Vic will actually allow events to unfold in this way—and since it will be he that will stop it and only he that will know how or when he will do that, the only course open to her is unthinking, cow-like passivity.

Which isn't good enough on two counts: firstly because he *might* actually let it happen. The flicker of warmth when he showed her her review faded fast and they are back to cool grey silence, but there has been no actual conflict. Secondly because whatever happens surely Anne owes it to someone (herself?) to know what she thinks about it.

What does she think about it?

There is nothing at the end of the question but space. It is impossible to want or not want it. The most she can do is allow things to happen. *Something* must happen, there will be events, events must unfold and lead her somewhere. And if something unfolds, whatever it is, good or bad (and it is impossible to know what either of these terms might be represented by, fac-tually) then from that movement more movement might come.

Sifting aimlessly through the papers in her work-table drawer, Anne is confronted by a sudden image. A baby: an ebony-black embryo, still unformed, its eyeless face averted, its chubby stumpy arms raised in supplication. It gleams in the light: ancient, primitive, a totem. She turns the postcard: 'Barbara Hepworth, *Infant*'; and remembers, a lifetime ago, visiting St Ives with Father. Remembers the particularity of that autumn afternoon in the Hepworth garden, slanting light and the streaky green beauty of the bronzes. Father's pushy impatience with abstract forms niggling at her attentiveness. The carved child was tucked just inside the doorway. 'Here you are,' she had said. 'This isn't abstract. Isn't it beautiful?' And Father had stared at the black baby for minutes in blessed silence, before moving on slowly, heavily, his impatience replaced by silent gloom. She remembers her discomfort and irritation with him, now, in a wave of massive sadness. If only she had known. But the infant in the picture is unsullied by her wrongness. It remains inno-cent, itself. She runs her fingers lightly over the shiny surface of the card, as if it were still possible to touch those smoothly rounded limbs.

Anne has taken Vic at his word and not made arrangements with her GP, but now her injections must begin in two days; now tomorrow; now today. She shrinks from speaking to him. But at the end of morning surgery she hears his feet stamping heavily up the stairs and knows immediately that he is heading for her room. He doesn't enter, simply pokes his head around the door.

'You're due for your injection today, aren't you?'

She nods.

'OK if we do it at the beginning of afternoon surgery?'

'Yes, thank you.'

'Good.' He is gone. He hasn't yet seen or commented on any of the ship pictures. She has been evasive about what she is working on; no point in talking about it in this mood. Even so it feels strange to have him look into the room and not notice.

The day is ruined for work; she feels a pervasive sadness and restlessness. What could be more ridiculous than sitting here sketching scenes from her nightmares? The whole house is cold with unusedness, it has become a shell where two individuals move around each other with no warmth or contact. She drifts downstairs and into the kitchen. The top of the cooker is encrusted with spilt food, last night's frying pan still perches on a ring; under the sink the swing-top of the bin is stained and dirty, and fragments of onion skin litter the floor. Methodically she begins to clean. There is nothing to wash the floor with and no bread. She forces herself into her warm green coat to go out to the corner shop. The green coat feels curiously limp. When she glances in the hall mirror she is dully surprised to see how old it looks. She always thinks of it as it was when it was new— rather lovely and unusual, a fine olive-green wool, lined, with fake-fur collar which snuggles up around her face. In the mirror now her pockets sag from having her fists plunged into them as she walks; the bushiness of the collar has sunk down to a rather flat, matted appearance, and two of the buttons are loose so that the line of the front of the coat, once buttoned, is uneven. How has it got so old? With an effort she makes herself imagine shopping, going into Next or Debenhams, flicking through rails of clothes, the sudden pleasure of alighting on something. She hasn't done it for months. Do all her clothes look so bad?

As she walks through the cold bright sunshine to the corner shop, buying clothes seems a risky thing to contemplate. And in its way, as pointless as drawing. Who looks at her? What would be the point of different clothes? More displacement activity, more finding a way to fill up aimless chunks of time.

When she goes into Vic's surgery at ten to four a couple of women are already waiting to see him. She feels embarrassed to go in before them, but he opens the door and simply nods at her. She wonders if they know she is his wife.

'OK, just pull your trousers down for me.' He is fiddling with a syringe. What if he kills me, she thinks suddenly. What if he's going to inject me with air? Terror grips her and she fumbles with her zip, unable to undo it, heart pounding. Where is the nurse? Isn't the nurse supposed to be in the room when he asks women to undress? But it's Vic, you're married to him, he's seen you undress hundreds of times—

He is ready with the needle and turns, glancing into her face. 'You alright? Anne?' He reaches out to stroke her upper arm. 'You'll hardly feel it, I promise. No, no need to take your knickers off, I just need to get at your buttock.' Guiding her gently with his left hand he propels her to the couch. 'Just bend over, no need to lie down.' She feels his concentration at her back, the sudden tiny stab of the needle. 'Hold still for me—that's it. Good girl.' He drops the syringe into the bin and begins to rub at her buttock and thigh with both hands, dispersing the dull ache the needle has introduced. 'There we are. All done. It didn't hurt, did it?'

She shakes her head, pulling up her trousers.

'You'll be fine.' He smiles into her eyes. Is it a professional smile? He could smile like this at anybody, but it is warm and kindly, he hasn't smiled at her like this for days. 'Just sit in the waiting room for a couple of minutes before you go back to the house, OK?' And again he pats her shoulder; she feels the warmth of it through her shirt.

In the waiting room she sits as requested, glancing at the other patients. One woman, white-faced with huge dark rings under her eyes, stares back at her angrily. There is an old man with violently loud breathing; the air rattles and swooshes down into his lungs, where it crackles and sinks before being laboriously squeezed out again. Beside him two spotty teenage girls huddle together over a magazine.

Vic will see them all. Smile at them, pat their shoulders, honour them with the warm beam of his focused attention, offer explanations, insights, cures. He is a kind of god. Like Father. Exactly the same gesture, she realises, Father reaching out to gently pat the upper arm of parishioners at the church door, of his timid curate, of Anne herself; it will be alright, take comfort.

And here she is drawing. Filling up scraps of paper with lines and patches of colour, in a room on her own. While men like Vic touch and help people, passing on the benison of their energy. Through her despair she begins to feel a kind of rage with herself.

The clinic. It is over. Anne did not expect such a blinding sense of clarity and relief. It is over. In less than ten minutes: painlessly, almost imperceptibly. The procedure followed by a kindly nod and pat from Hargreaves (do they train them to do that? Reassure the distressed patient with a pat, like you'd calm a startled horse?), the injunction to lie flat for half an hour, a cup of tea from a smiling overalled young thing, and it is over. The last four years.

A feeling of calm, detached joy suffuses Anne's mind and

body. She is not now and never will be pregnant. She and Vic
have endured every trial; now, like characters in a fairytale they
are entitled to live happily ever after. This procedure has no
more succeeded than any of the others and it is the last one she
will have. They need never again subject themselves to
Hargreaves, clinics, drugs, other people meddling, or to each
other's distress and rage; neither of them need ever again do
things they don't want in order to try to placate or repay or get
revenge on the other. There is no blame. The child that she
might have had was Estelle's and died with Estelle. She can
smell the salt spray, feel the coolness rolling up from the water
as she leans over the rail; see, in the ceaseless slopping motion of
the little waves against the side of the ship, repeating patterns of
fractured light and reflection. She can see the light dancing in
the upper levels of the water, below which it darkens into
steady deep green, fathomless, bottomless, where the baby lies.
He has descended through playful shifting waters and flickering
light, down into steady green gloom, into peace and silence
away from the crash and tinkle of the breaking waves. He has
descended slowly into a deep and gentle darkness where he
lies—lives—away from her, safe from all the changing dangers
of the world, where he lies innocent and unscathed and benevolent, watching over her, wishing her well, gently glad of his
escape. It has been as harsh and crude of her to attempt to drag
him back into being as to awaken any others of the dead who
lie at rest, whose limbs are deliciously languorous and heavy so
that water drops through them, earth drops through them, they
sink and sink back to the bones, the bedrock, sinking blissfully
down into the earth from which they sprang. If she lets him go,
he can free her. All the past will be over.

It is nearly one o'clock. Vic will be coming for her any
minute. She finishes dressing and makes her way out to reception, where the girl smiles and says, incomprehensibly, 'Fingers
crossed!'

Seeing that the pale spring sunshine is still flaring bravely outside, Anne does up her coat (must buy a new coat) and goes out to sit on the step. In the bare narrow flowerbed alongside the clinic wall, a row of pale green spears. They will be daffodils, they will swell and form beaked buds which in their time will open yellow as chicks to the light. After spring, summer. Time will flow on, it will be all right.

When he isn't there at 1.30 she is barely disturbed, hardly ruffled by his absence. Perhaps he doesn't yet know. He will know when he sees her, that all this hatefulness is over, that there will never be a baby, that they can start to live again. Unhurriedly she sets off towards home, following the route he is likely to take in the car, looking up into the traffic to catch his eye and wave to him. She doesn't see Tim till he touches her elbow.

'You not speaking to me any more?'

It is a shock but when she looks at his indignant face she feels nothing but sympathy. Poor Tim. Of course he doesn't understand. She is the first to know that there can be peace now, because she is at the centre of it. He has been dragged into the struggle by her—she has clutched at him to save herself with no regard for his safety or his feelings. But now she can make him understand. 'I didn't see you—how are you?'

'I had the feeling I'd been trashed.'

'Trashed?'

'Forgotten. Wiped.'

It is true; she has a memory through the haze that she has watched the phone ring, listened as the answerphone clicked on, sat like a stone as his voice said her name and requested her to call. She sat unmoving and then erased the message. She can't quite remember why, now, she can't recapture the thoughts or mood of those moments, only that she was unyielding, blocking him out.

'I'm sorry, I've been working hard. I haven't seen anyone at all.'

He is staring into her face; he seems slightly appeased by her

words. 'You could have told me that. I would've understood.'
There is a smell of alcohol which strikes Anne as odd.

'I'm sorry. I didn't think. Why aren't you at work?'

'Day off. Come and have a coffee.'

She glances along the busy street. There is nowhere obvious
to have a coffee. 'Maybe another day.'

'Now. Come on.'

She is meant to be going home. She is looking for Vic. She
has something important to tell Vic, something which will show
him that everything has changed—really she should see Vic
above all.

'You haven't spoken to me for weeks. Surely you can spare
half an hour?'

Is that true? She glances at Tim. What a horrible way to
behave. 'I'm sorry Tim, I should have rung you. I really can't see
you any more.'

'That's what I meant by trashed.'

'No, I didn't mean it like that.'

'How else is it possible to mean it?'

'It's because of me. Because of my own life. I can't deal with
anyone else.'

They reach a corner and he gives a little tug on her arm,
pulling her round to the left. 'Come and tell me.'

It is a residential street. 'Where?'

'I'm staying with Steve from the shop. It's just down here.'

Anne is unpleasantly shocked. 'Why?'

'You want to know something about me? Really?' He has
been drinking, she realises; he is spiteful and sarcastic. 'I had a
bust-up with Fiona.'

'I'm sorry Tim. Won't you go back?'

'Who knows? Who cares?'

A red car going past catches her eye, but it's not Vic. She must
talk to Vic. 'Look I can't stop now, I can't.'

'You haven't got five minutes to talk to me—after all this?'

'Oh Tim . . .' But this isn't part of the plan. She should have a coffee with him, she owes him that at least—but just not now, when there is something she needs to tell Vic, something she is in danger of losing sight of, something which has been blissfully certain and must not be allowed to drift away. Tim has taken her arm and is steering her down the street. She allows herself to be led.

The door of his house is astonishingly real. Painted a deep bottle green, with a new brass Yale lock which he takes a while to open, twisting the key first one way then the other. There's a wide brass letterbox.

Suddenly it's open and they are in the atmosphere of the house, there is a pub smell of alcohol and stale cigarette smoke. He leans against the door to shut it, closing them in. Then he moves past her into the kitchen and runs water into the kettle. She stands by the hanging coats listening to the water and her own thudding heart. Go now. Go. But she follows him into the kitchen and without turning he indicates to her to take a seat. He busies himself with the coffee, spooning it into the cafetière. Then he pulls up a chair to the opposite side of the table. He lights two cigarettes and passes her one. 'So, are you all right?'

'What?'

'Is something up with you and Vic?'

Anne sucks on her cigarette. Why not tell him, flashes through her mind. Why not tell him so he actually understands and so that I am not simply treating him badly? 'We—we decided to have fertility treatment.'

He rises smoothly to pour the boiled water into the coffee. 'Vic's problem, I deduce.'

'I—yes.' He knows too much, of course.

'So where are you up to?'

'I don't know what you mean.'

'Where are you up to? Tests? Injections? Implantation?'

'Tim, you're not—'

'Has it worked?' He is watching her, as he presses the plunger down on the coffee.

'What?' She feels dazed, dizzy, it is far too hot, she will have to take off her coat.

'Are you pregnant?'

She shouldn't have come here, it was a mistake. 'Tim, I'm sorry, I've just remembered—' Rising to her feet, stubbing out the cigarette.

'You haven't drunk your coffee.'

'I'm sorry—I'll call you.' Moving towards the door. Tim moving to block it.

'*Are* you pregnant?'

Save yourself. Make it conclusive. 'Yes. Yes I am.'

'You're alright then.' He puts his hands on her arms, grasping her through her coat.

'Let me go Tim, I really am late.'

'No danger of contamination.'

'What d'you mean?'

'If you're already pregnant.'

'I don't know what you're talking about.'

'You were afraid another of mine might wriggle in.'

'It's nothing to do with you.' She jerks herself free of his grip.

'You're just going to go, like that?'

'I shouldn't have come here.'

'Kiss me goodbye then.'

'Tim . . .'

'Kiss me.'

What does it matter, what difference can it make? She moves to peck his cheek and he thrusts his weight against her, pushing her back against the coats. They give way softly behind her and she loses her balance, stumbling sideways, clutching at him to save herself. But he is falling too, and on the floor he is grabbing at her flailing arms, holding her down with his knee.

'I don't want—'

'*You* don't want. After all this—*you* don't want.' He is pushing her down, each time she struggles to get up, shoving her back to the floor.

'You're hurting me.'

'Why shouldn't I?'

As she gasps for breath Anne sees that there is no reason why he shouldn't. She has asked for this, she has walked into it with her eyes wide open. She has allowed it to happen, like every bad thing she has allowed in her life. He is going to hurt her. It is what she deserves.

When the green door slams behind Anne she moves as fast as she can down the road, looking neither to left nor right, keeping her face down and hidden by her hair. Not the main road—the other way—quieter, where it's quiet. At the end of the road is a run-down little park, hedged on one side by thick privet. She keeps herself going till she reaches a graffiti-sprayed bench; puts her hands out to the back of it and leans her weight forward, holding her back hollow so that the grazed knuckles of her spine aren't chafed by the weight of her coat. She tries to breathe more slowly. Something is dripping down her face. She wipes with her hand. Only tears. Carefully she runs her fingers over her wet face again. No blood. Maybe no one will notice. Her coat is all right—only underneath is ripped. And her back is bleeding, she can feel the T-shirt stuck to it. She must have been lying on the metal strip that holds the carpet down. If she gets home while Vic is in surgery—she pushes up her cuff and looks at her wrist. Sees the dark circle of finger marks. Nearly three o'clock. After four she can go to the bathroom and lock the door and let the water run hot and deep. A woman with a pushchair comes along the path and Anne straightens up. No one will be able to tell. Unless they catch the smell. Which envelops her like a swarm of flies around dung, the smell of him which she has to scour off herself.

She walks along the road carefully, setting her sights on visible goals; the postbox, the next lamp-post, the red parked car. A bus comes as she reaches the stop. When at last she gains the house she turns the doorknob noiselessly, pushes the door open a crack. Silence. Inside she crawls upstairs on her hands and knees. Gently she shuts the bathroom door, pushing the bolt home. Hands gripping the towel rail she hangs there, watching the room sway, blank with relief.

When she has washed herself all over she lets the water out and sits wrapped in a towel while she waits for a fresh bath to run, to rinse herself clean of the contaminated water. Moving slowly and methodically, she dresses in clean clothes, then buries her ripped T-shirt and underwear in the kitchen bin and puts her trousers in the wash. Heavy waves of exhaustion sweep up at her, making her stagger—she lowers herself sideways onto the sofa and lies staring at the blank television. What now? She lies and listens to her stupid heart pumping blood around her body, and the roar of it in her right ear which is pressed against the sofa. She thinks of listening to the sea when you put a big shell to your ear. But it happens if you put anything to your ear: your cupped hand, a jam jar, a sofa. The sea is always waiting to start roaring in your ear. It is in your blood. It pounds you and pounds you, year after year, pounds against your innards wearing them away till you are an old lady, light and fragile as a husk, an empty shell, and then throws you up on the beach, where you are finally ground to sand and dust.

Later, she notices that the house is very quiet. She hasn't heard the outside surgery door bang nor patients talking as they walk away. Is Vic even there? She heaves herself up and stands by the surgery door listening, but there is nothing; when at last she tries the handle, it is locked.

She forces herself to think back over the time since she finished at the clinic. She waited for Vic, then started to walk. For some reason she was hopeful. She was looking out for him as she walked, expecting him to drive that way. Then Tim . . . She stopped looking. But what if he had been driving to meet her and seen her walking with Tim? What if he had driven on to a place where he could turn round, and come back in her direction and found she wasn't there? What if he had driven home then and waited for her? Knowing she must be with Tim?

She picks up her feet and walks them down the hall. Opens the front door, puts it on the latch. Turns out into the street and back round the corner to the outer surgery door. Then she sees the note.

Surgery closed due to unforeseen circumstances. In case of emergency please tel. 0161 323 9876

Back in the house she sits on the edge of the big armchair staring at nothing in the darkness. When she gets pins and needles in her legs she hobbles upstairs and lies on her side on the bed.

She hadn't imagined sleeping, but must have done, because when she wakes in a sweaty panic her watch shows 7.10. It is just getting light and Vic isn't there. Every part of her body aches. Stiffly she makes her way to the spare room—empty. The hall light has been left on. Edging downstairs a step at a time she sees that the sitting room door is open. The reading lamp is on and he is lying curled on the sofa. She can smell his whisky breath from the doorway. Silently she turns and goes back upstairs.

So either he did see her and Tim, or he never came to pick her up in the first place. Of course, he wouldn't have wanted to come; she was having donor sperm. But if only he had met her on time—she could have shown him it didn't matter. And they would have been spared all this. She remembers that feeling outside the clinic. A feeling of peace and freedom. Incredible as flight.

She changes her clothes and goes straight into her work-room. The answerphone is flashing and she plays the message. Carol at the library excitedly congratulating her on the *Guardian* review—has she seen it? Anne rings BT and asks to be given a new phone number. Tim has never been to Vic's house; changing the phone should be enough. Then she mixes some browns and begins filling in dark shapes in the container picture.

She hears Vic's movements at the right times; he comes heavily upstairs and takes a shower at eight; he unlocks the surgery door at quarter to nine. There is nothing to do but work, work and keep her mind closed to any other thing. When she and Vic finally cross paths at suppertime he nods without smiling and asks how her trip to the clinic went.

'Fine, thank you.'

'Good. Sorry I couldn't meet you. A patient collapsed, I had to take her to hospital.'

'Oh.'

There is a silence. 'Is she OK?'

'No, she died. She was only forty-two.' Another little silence. He shrugs and turns to inspect his grilling bacon. 'You win some, you lose some.'

Anne nods and goes back up to her room. Either it is true or it isn't. It doesn't make any difference.

One morning there is a letter for Anne from Italy. It is in a fragile blue air-envelope, addressed in spidery painstaking handwriting. A single sheet inside.

> *Dear Miss Harrington,*
>
> *Please excuse me. I have your address from a woman in Bologna, from Casa delle Donne. Maria told me you looked for me but I am in Naples at that time. She says you have informations about my father.*
>
> *I am respectfully yours,*
> *Lily Otanga*

She has printed her address in block capitals underneath. Wordlessly Anne passes the letter to Vic. When he's finished it he glances at her.

'Think it's her?'

'Why else would she write?'

He shrugs. 'Hope of money, something like that?'

'Why wait so long?'

'It's pretty amazing if this Maria has kept your address all these years.'

'But she's not asking for anything. Only information.'

'Well write and check. Take it slowly.' He glances at his watch and drains his coffee, then lets himself into the surgery. Anne spends the morning composing her reply.

> *Dear Lily,*
>
> *Thank you for writing to me. I am the daughter of Rev. David Harrington. My father died in 1999 but he left a diary which showed he had been trying to trace a girl called Lily before he died. I think you may be his daughter, but I wonder if you could confirm for me your mother's first name, and your date and place of birth? If you are his daughter, then you and I are half-sisters, and I would very much like to meet you, and give you a small sum of money which he left for you. I am so pleased to hear from you after all this time; please reply to me, and I hope we can meet up soon.*
>
> *With all good wishes,*
> *Anne*

She takes out and then restores the reference to money. If there was no money on offer, why should Lily reply to her? Anne is dully aware that to receive the letter is extraordinary, and should be cause for celebration. But everything is so far removed—so held away from her—that the correct emotion is difficult to envisage. Mainly she feels weariness at the thought of the effort that must be made, at the organisation of a visit to Italy, at the awkwardness that will exist between Lily and herself.

Walking back from the post Anne finds herself clammy and hot and slightly nauseous. When she gets in she runs herself a bath and undresses in front of the mirror. Most of the bruising has faded; twisting to look at her spine she sees that the scabs have disappeared and new pink shiny skin stretches tight across her vertebrae. Soon all traces will be gone. The body recovers that quickly.

One evening as she is cooking, Vic comes in from evening surgery and says, 'Isn't it about time you tested?'

For a moment she can't think what he is talking about. Then she remembers. 'I'm not, Vic, I know I'm not. Leave it be.'

He walks over to the calendar and points to the dates. The certainty with which he does this shows her he has rehearsed it in his mind. 'Three weeks since you were at the clinic. No sign of bleeding?'

Dumbly she shakes her head.

'There's a tester in the bathroom cupboard. Go on. I'll finish that.'

Anne steps up the stairs one by one. He has been waiting for this. Counting the days, working it out. Whereas she had almost banished it. What now? Surely he must accept that it is over.

Pulling her jeans down she squats over the plastic bathroom jug and pees, then tears the cellophane off the neat little pregnancy-testing kit. Imperceptibly, and then with increasing definiteness, with absolute bright-blue clarity, the litmus paper colours positive. Anne holds it in front of her eyes, transfixed. Her legs are shaking. She sits down on the toilet.

Later there is a knocking at the bathroom door. 'Anne? Can I come in?' After a brief pause he comes in anyway. His eyes go to the paper. For a moment the room is quiet, as if the air has been sucked out of it. Then Vic is crouching in front of Anne, his arms around her legs, his head against her knees. His shoulders are shaking convulsively. She realises he is crying.

Alone at last in her workroom next morning, Anne rests her head on the desk and allows herself to think. If she is pregnant (you are) then it must be by Tim. Not the donor sperm, but Tim, again. All those months of trying and now the one thing—the one *child*—it is impossible for her to have. Anne mixes a dark red and puts the easel in the light by the window. The thick browns and reds she has already laid on the canvas are visceral; blood, shit, wounds. The remains they would put in the hospital incinerator. Her stomach heaves.

The sooner you get rid of it the easier it is. A morning-after pill might still shift it. Or you can have it sucked out. Vacuumed. Women do it in their lunch hour.

She moves back to her desk and lets her fingers walk over the tubes of paint. Blues, greens, greys; cobalt, aquamarine, teal. If you could paint the sea. Nobody can, of course. Turner, that's light not sea. It's sky and sunshine and cloud and mist and fire and haze and splendour and reflection and everything on earth but sea. She has a sudden vision of Lowry's sea, the curiously solid grey-green mix determinedly filling the whole canvas, its poignant, plodding emptiness. All alone on a wide wide sea. There are blue seas, romantic seas, charming curled little waves frothing at the heels of dainty galleons; there are thunderous seas with great oil-black rollers lashing over ships in peril; there are sugary-grey acrylic breakers with arch-necked stallions galloping foamily through them; there's the factual blue-grey puddle as mirror to a fleet. Hopper's blue sea at the open doorway of a room? The idea of sea, not sea itself.

And the child in the sea, who has lain at rest so peacefully rocking, Estelle's sweet sea child . . . is it him? Has he returned now to more pain, to be torn and sundered again? Must she again prevent him?

She lowers her head to the desk and cries.

That evening Anne has just got into the bath and is running more cold to make it possible to sit down, when there is an excited knocking at the door. 'Anne? Anne!' Vic.

She sits down quickly. 'Come in.'

He is already in the room. She hunches forwards, hiding her breasts against her knees. It is a long time since either has seen the other naked. 'Phone call. Carol on the surgery phone. They've got you a London gallery.'

'An exhibition?'

'Yup, a transfer. She sent them the slides and reviews and they want it!'

'Oh.'

'Well don't be pleased, will you?'

'Why did she ring you?'

'Your line's not working apparently.'

The number. She hasn't told anyone the new number.

'Smile, Anne. She says it'll be reviewed everywhere. They already want to know what you're doing next!' He kneels beside the bath and reaches into the water for the flannel. 'Can I wash you?'

'Is surgery over?'

'Yup. Cured 'em all.' He begins to soap her back. She bends further forwards. 'You're shy of me.'

'It's been a long time.'

He rinses her efficiently and sits back on his heels. Anne stands and reaches out for the towel; wraps it tight around herself and sits on the edge of the bath facing him.

'I'm sorry,' he says, lifting his shoulders and arms expansively. 'For all of it. OK?'

'Vic I have to tell you something.'

'No you don't.'

Anne turns the sentence over in her head. *No you don't.* It doesn't make sense. 'I have to tell you—'

He is shaking his head, rising to his feet, moving forward to place his fingers on her lips. 'I don't want you to tell me anything. I mean it Anne. Bad times are over.'

She stares at him. He knows. About Tim. About all of it? How can it not be spoken of?

Gently he takes the edge of the towel and wipes the drips off her neck. 'New start, OK?'

It is too hard to know what to say. Anne bows her head.

'Can I?' He is holding the edge of the towel. Anne stands and he begins to gently rub her, lifting her arms like a child's to dry underneath, kneeling to dry the toes one by one. When he has done he strokes his hand lightly across her belly. 'You're beautiful.'

Don't touch me. Don't touch me Vic, please.

He is getting to his feet. Picking up the towel. He drapes it around her shoulders and delivers the closing of it to her hand. Smiles at her and leaves the bathroom.

Vic's happiness is as pervasive as his misery has been. It fills the house like warm summer air, radiating into every corner. When surgery ends in the evening he goes into the kitchen and puts on the radio, switching back and forth between Radio 3 and Classic FM, remonstrating aloud with their choices of music and performance, humming along in his light, surprisingly tuneful voice. He begins to work his way through an unused recipe book, Madhur Jaffrey; the kitchen is full of crushed cumin and ground cardamoms, pieces of chicken lie marinating in spicy garlic-scented yoghurt. He invites his mother round to eat, setting the table properly with tablecloth and candles. She opens up and basks in the sudden warmth of his attention, like a bashful young girl.

'Don't tell her yet. Don't tell anybody, Vic, will you?'

He nods at Anne, humouring her. He seems to have no doubts. Mary ends up staying the night, as talk and wine lead on to her favourite, whist, and the three of them sit up late giggling and playing cards.

He leafs through the listings magazine and picks out films and plays for them to see; they go out two and three nights a week, 'catching up on the world' as he puts it. At the weekend he begins systematically to sort through the accumulated boxes and junk in the spare room, making journeys to the tip and charity shop; it takes Anne a while to realise why he is doing it. He asks permission to come into her workroom again, and spends a long time poring over the sketches for *Voyage* and the three paintings she is working on.

His silence unnerves her. 'What d'you think?'

'I don't know. It's strange. Because I know what it is—
because I visualised it all to myself when you first told me—it's
very strange. It's almost as if you're painting a nightmare of
mine. I can recognise it but it's subtly different.'

'Different how?'

'The colours, I guess. I hadn't imagined so much red. Maybe
I'd imagined in black and white.'

'Etchings.'

'I don't know. Didn't you say that once? But the colours are
more disturbing. They're less arty, if you know what I mean, less
restrained. But more disturbing. They disturb me.' He looks at
her and laughs. 'You've not made colours ugly before.'

'No.' She is pleased by what he says about the colours, it's
right. She wants those glimpses of ethereal blue to be the only
point of relief.

He seizes on the Christmas-dinner sketch with delight.
'These animal heads—you've nicked it from someone, haven't
you? Eighteenth century, Gillray, somebody like that?'

'Could be. I wasn't thinking cartoonist though, I was thinking more of Goya, his Caprichos . . .'

'I can almost hear the donkey braying.' Vic's glee breaks out
in a bout of quiet wheezing. She had forgotten he has such a
good laugh.

'You laugh like Muttley, you know that cartoon dog?'

He begins to clown, caricaturing himself, raising and lowering his shoulders, wheezing happily.

'Go on, get out. I have to work.'

He kisses her hand with a flourish and leaves. During surgery
he rings her at her desk. 'I've got a waiting room full of patients
with animal heads. Can I send a few up to you?' and 'Shall we
go out for lunch? It's sunny enough to sit outside.'

In bed he curls around her back and his body heat flows into
her. They are as sexless as sun-warmed stones, as hibernating
bears.

'We'll have to go back to see Hargreaves.'

'What for?'

'To tell him. Won't you have to have a scan?'

'But can't I have one at hospital like a normal person? Can't it just be treated as a normal pregnancy?' The fear of the clinic is the fear of being found out.

It is growing. Day by day, growing into a baby, whose arms and legs will move and stretch inside her, practising for freedom. Vic doesn't know. He can't know that it is Tim's—whatever he guesses, whatever bad thing he's guessed she was going to tell him, he doesn't know that. She wants to tell him. But if she told him what would he be able to say? What could he say but 'Get rid of it'?

He's happy now; happy that she is having an unknown man's child. But if she doesn't tell him, she's responsible. For his happiness; for her own; for the child's. She is admitting to herself that she is outside what could ever be condoned or forgiven, that she must keep her secret from him always and never let it harm him. In protecting him, might she at last begin to make amends?

An abortion wouldn't help Vic; it would mean everything he's sacrificed would be for nothing. And she would have killed the child twice. The child who wants to be born; who has taken root in her not because *she* wanted (because she gave up wanting long ago) but because he is ready to emerge from the shady green depths, and come onto the world's shore and play. She has no right to stop him.

The following morning she wakes early to the sound of rain hissing through the open window. A damp breeze lifts the edge of the curtain and trails across her face like a wet rag. She is filled with self-disgust. What a smug little nest of hypocrisy she's been weaving. How convenient that the best course of action involves lying to Vic, and ensuring the end result she personally most desires, whilst simultaneously allowing herself to believe she is doing it for his sake.

He is asleep, she can feel his warm breaths on her shoulder and the sense of his innocence and vulnerability is intolerable. Cautiously she slides to the edge of the bed and gets out.

She goes straight to her workroom, opening the curtains and switching on all the lights so that her work is utterly exposed. Lies. Secrets. The hidden passengers locked in silence in her memory. Father's secret child—denied—then lost. Now found? It isn't a fairy story, wrongs can't be put right, Lily can't be given back her youth or innocence, happiness can't be restored.

And Vic's naive belief that nothing could be worse than himself? That whatever she has done deserves to be glossed over and forgotten, in the light of his own behaviour? He assumes that what she has to confess to him can be dismissed unheard, holds no power to harm. Furiously she paces the length of the room. Blaming him is not the point. To blame him is ridiculous. To tell him would be destructive and indulgent.

Not to tell him would be to infantilise him; even make him at some level contemptible in her own eyes (I can lie to you. And you don't even suspect). Except that it isn't important. None of it is important beside the fact that he wants a child and he is able to be delighted by this pregnancy.

There is a bump at the door. 'Anne? Tea?' He comes in bearing two mugs. 'Couldn't you sleep?'

'I just woke up early. Thanks.' She takes the mug from him and sips at it.

'What's the trouble?' He perches on the windowledge.

'I was thinking about honesty.'

'It's overrated.'

'You don't think that.'

He shrugs. 'What do I think, then?'

'You think it's important.'

'I think what people do is important, not what they say.'

'As in?'

'How would honesty help the majority of human relations?

How would it help my mother if I told her, on the whole I'd rather you didn't call round because I find you terminally boring?'

'Most of the time she knows you think that anyway. That's why she doesn't come.'

'And on the odd occasion when I'm in the right mood and she's on good form we can have a pleasant evening, it's perfectly OK. And the awful thing hasn't been said.'

'What if I lied to you?'

'I don't know. It would depend.'

'On what?'

'On what you did. On your actions.'

There is a silence, into which the continuous pittering of the rain gradually intrudes. Vic moves to the door. 'Shall I put on some toast for you?'

'Thanks. I'll be down in a minute.'

When Vic lets himself in to the surgery after breakfast, Anne takes the car keys and her mac and goes out. She drives towards open country, pulling off the main road to park at the top of Mottram cuttings and walk up the narrow lane that curves round to the top of the hill. The drizzle is fine and steady. She hasn't put her hood up and soon her hair is plastered to her head, the rain trickling down her neck. It isn't cold, once she gets used to it; it feels almost like swimming, blinking the water from her eyes, forcing her way through the wetness. Nobody can tell her what to do. Nobody can tell her what is right. Below, empty fields stretch down to where the houses of Stalybridge begin, running on into the houses of Denton and Ashton, and on into the great conglomeration of Manchester, the towers and factories and streets, the huge secretive mass of it, wormed through with millions of lives, each lived between specific sets of walls and gates; each following its own almost imperceptibly different twisting route through. Nobody knows what is right.

There is no help.

She must decide what to do.

Pushing on towards the top, watching the view get bigger and hazier behind the rain, blurred with grey, molten almost, she sees that she has decided. To keep the child. To keep its secret. To take that responsibility.

She is at the top. All around her the rain hisses onto leaves, patters onto the surface of the lane, trickles along gulleys and ditches, with a slow persistence that seems to suggest it might never end, that one day it will wear the earth away. Wash the mountains down into the sea, which will rise up and flood the fields. She and Vic are having a child. She tries to remember if she has ever chosen anything in her life before.

ACKNOWLEDGEMENTS

Among the reference books I have used I owe a particular debt
to: Joseph Thérèse Agbasiere, *Women in Igbo Life and Thought*; Bill
Roberts, *Life and Death Among the Ibos*; Nuruddin Farah,
Yesterday, Tomorrow; Jeremy Harding, *The Uninvited (Refugees at
the Rich Man's Gate)*; Rev. W. L. Wheatley, *Sunrise in Nigeria*;
Geoffrey Johnston, *Of God and Maxim Guns—Presbyterianism in
Nigeria 1846–1966*; Karl Maier, *This House Has Fallen*;
Olusegun Obasanjo, *My Command: An Account of the Nigerian
Civil War*; Don McCullin, *Unreasonable Behaviour*; A. H. M.
Kirk-Greene, *Nigeria in Documents*.

I should also like to thank the British Council for sending
me to Nigeria, Francis Rogers, Ken Osborne of the CMS
library, Jane Maitland and Michelle Caddick of Tameside
Libraries, Louise Christian, Mary Black, Pat Kavanagh, Richard
Beswick, Georges Borchardt and Mick Harris.